Lion and Leopard

A NOVEL

NATHANIEL POPKIN

THE *Head* & THE *Hand*

—PRESS—

EST. 2012

Also by Nathaniel Popkin

*Song of the City: An Intimate History of the
American Urban Landscape*

The Possible City

For Isaak

And in memory of Regina Granne

Published by The Head & The Hand Press, 2013

Printed in the United States of America

Original cover design and interior illustrations by
Amanda Gallant

Images from *Empire Style Designs and Ornaments* by
Joseph Beunat were reproduced with permission from the Dover
Pictorial Archive Series.

ISBN: 978-0-9893125-1-6

Library of Congress Control Number: 2013949256

PUBLISHER'S NOTE
This is a work of fiction. Names, characters, places, and incidents
are either the product of the author's imagination or are used
fictitiously, and any resemblance to actual persons living or dead,
business establishments, events, or locales is entirely
coincidental.

The Head & The Hand Press
Philadelphia, Pennsylvania
www.theheadandthehand.com

10 9 8 7 6 5 4 3 2 1

CHARLES WILLSON PEALE

JOHN LEWIS KRIMMEL

REMBRANDT PEALE

WILLIAM DIXCY

VICTOR BLANC

CALEB CLOUD

RAPHAELLE PEALE

HARRIET MILLER

MRS. GREENPOINT

*We with our bodily eyes see but the fashion and Manners of
one country for one age—and then we die—*
John Keats to George Keats, Dec. 31, 1818

Mein gott—sure what a pity! To get drown'd.
George Frederick Krimmel on John Lewis Krimmel, 1821

FIRST WORDS

John Lewis Krimmel, on board the
Sumatra, *August* 11, 1818

The days in steerage go on, one and then the next, and after a while the coffee no longer tastes so bitter. We are now twelve days out of Rotterdam and not once have I accepted the captain's offer of sugar. He is tall and thick-boned, with smooth, loose skin and shiny black eyes and a mustache like a sultan's. I take great pleasure in studying that face, in noting the flat plain of the forehead, and indeed, the deep-set, shiny black eyes, the thick, silvery pink lips. These are lips, I imagine, for giving orders.

The pleasure is in my hand as I draw his features. I particularly like this silent stirring, the swelling of the air between my hands and my eyes and my eyes and the subject, and I savor it much as the captain himself lingers over a fiery red pepper, which he eats in judicious little bites right down to the stem. Is it dangerous, this feeling? If so, it only seems to prod me along. By making my intentions obvious, I force my subject to decide for himself if I should take his likeness. In the case of the captain, this is how at first I came by the bitter coffee.

I sleep lightly and my night, such as it is spent on a straw mattress on the top level of a wooden bunk, ends abruptly with the first pawing of the boys below me and the heavy pacing of a man from Ulm, who coughs miserably into his shaking hands. I dress quickly and then start the slow climb to the deck as if

I'm drawing myself out of a deep, black well. The morning sky seems ecstatic. Perhaps it is more invigorating than the captain's coffee.

During the day in the bright sea spray, I note qualities of color, I sketch the ship's shadows, I observe various aspects of motion. The ship lurches but also glides, the sails flutter but also flap, the passengers huddle in on themselves and one or two will dart away, much like a swallow.

In addition to the captain, I sketch the seamen — their long brown faces, eyes like gray pebbles, and their braided leather bracelets. Once in a while I'll finish out a decent sketch with watercolor. I count the white caps, the clouds, note the stretch of shadow. The ship is crowded with thin, severe men. Their wives, with babes in arms, have stern but unseeing eyes. I stand in the sun because there is nothing like it, at open sea. In these moments, I suddenly and clearly see myself with the others arranged around me, young and old equally, for I can be both: I see myself as infant and elderly, and I see death in all of us.

On a long journey like this, I don't know quite what I'd do without my sketchbook. I've never enjoyed reading as a way to pass the time; rather my attention is drawn outward, to all the miniature dramas before me. Why read when I can watch, or listen?

A good sketch is a faithful icebreaker, especially when there isn't a decent mirror within several thousand miles. As the very act of sketching another person tests our usual boundaries, a fragile intimacy often quietly develops, a face averted becomes in short time a face revealed, and so on, and sometimes it overwhelms the common sense.

I sketch these momentary loves; I record the brief, flaring impossibilities. This past July as I was leaving Vienna by foot on the Linz road, I encountered a hay wagon with an intricately and handsomely woven straw awning. Ideal transport, as the road to Salzburg, where I was headed, is badly rutted and exposed to the sun's intense rays. Inside was a sleeping potter with thick forearms and black, curling hair, Venetian by the look of his dress, and propped up in front of him, his wife.

Her open eyes lay across the landscape as if it were a maudlin show. I began sketching her as we approached St. Valentin on the Enns road. I was working on the knot in her scarf when our eyes met. She offered me black raspberries, and I set on her lips a wry, nearly volatile expression.

Back in Philadelphia, where science carries more influence than art, even artists tend to painstakingly render the tiniest detail. I myself follow this course. How much, then, can the artist reveal? This is a practical question for me. For example, I spent a good bit of yesterday counting white caps. Alas, they aren't truly infinite; it only seems that way. But isn't the point that they seem infinite? And isn't it the artist's job to extract the essence of his subject rather than its particularity? I wonder. The sea, bloodless as it is, seems to wash everything away.

Dinner in steerage is served from large vats passed down a long, communal table. I eat standing and come up for air as soon as possible. The captain hands me a coffee. Then I crouch and watch the sky; I strain my neck to see. I button my coat. I smell eucalyptus that I know can't be eucalyptus (I've never smelled eucalyptus), that I know can only be infinite darkness. I press against the evaporating light, I pad across the deck into the clear space of ether.

Then to be pushed down the well and into true darkness. Not true darkness, for someone has lit a lantern. The oil is rancid, but for a time until it flickers out, the burning oil drenches the usual putrid aroma. I sit at the table, which is now mostly abandoned, and a short time later climb over the two boys with spindle legs and knocking knees who share the bunk below. They giggle and belch and cry wretchedly, all in succession or all at once, it hardly matters. I close my eyes and try to imagine the ether. I listen but hear only guttural oozing. And there is sneezing too, someone sneezing who can't seem to stop.

After a while, I give up trying to sleep. I try to conjure Harriet's face. For a while I can only imagine her sister Henrietta's perfectly sculpted fingers, but then Susanna alone emerges. Just before I left for Germany, I presented her a portrait of the family, done in oil, a small canvas onto which I poured some of my most difficult feelings. Susanna is so brutally self-possessed she inhabits a space that verges on the serene. Quite naturally, as I conceived of the picture, I positioned her as the silent force around which everything revolves: a series of expressions, gazes, and hand signals. I instilled meaning in various colors, fabrics, and textures. For example, I employed the color gold to link certain people directly. I hid what was absolutely necessary and revealed what my heart would allow. It wasn't quite a masterwork. Too diminutive in proportion to its complexity, the figures themselves disproportionate, the blush of cheeks overstated. Susanna, with the unfortunate infant George in her arms, appears lost and distant instead of certain and secure. That's the way I see her now.

Steerage for certain is otherworldly. Perhaps it's best I close my eyes. Doing so, I wince, for my face is indeed filthy, my forehead sweaty, and my eyelids burn.

Charles Willson Peale, *at his farm, Belfield, in Germantown, September 3,* 1818

"It's a matter of timing," I wrote to my son Rembrandt. My pencil paused and then ran on again, and I found it scribbling things — tied up as they are with a parent's hopes and inevitable disappointments — that must have been troubling me. "Furthermore," I wrote, "if you had remained here, in this city, a little longer and come to see the artistic scene flourish, as it is now, you wouldn't have found yourself in such a haste to leave."

"Case in point," I noted, "the young German Krimmel." I swear he must be a prodigy, for his canvases appear to have come from nowhere. "Have you a chance to examine his work? Three of his precisely rendered scenes presently grace the walls of the American Academy in New York." Careful as ever in handling my son's ego, but never shying from a father's duty to correct the behavior of his children, I added, "There is much for you to teach him, for the German's pencil is as promising as anyone's. If only you were here to do so."

The response to my letter came quickly, as it often does with my second son. He made the usual pleasantries then listed the men of power and the ladies of influence who had visited his museum in Baltimore, the Rendezvous for Taste, in the week past. He penned three paragraphs on the series of portraits for which he'd been commissioned on the "Defenders of the City," as they called it, the heroic men of the recent war, blithely pilfering the idea behind my own series of portraits of the American pantheon made in the aftermath of the Revolution. Yet, as my son was perceptive to note, all but one of the "defenders," quite unlike my wide-ranging portraits, were of military men. This gave Rembrandt, a pacifist like his father, discomfort. "I must, according to contract," he wrote, "make these men appear quite beyond heroic. They are destined to be gods. I don't mind the challenge, which allows me to practice my skill at storm clouds and medallions, but I shall counter it with precise attention to the countenances of my subjects. A slightly twisted chin shall be revealed as such, as will eyebrows that hang like pelts and hair that defies all spit and oil."

I skimmed through more of Rembrandt's thoughts on this commission, for which he is being paid — overpaid, according to the present market — two hundred dollars for each portrait, before coming to his remarks on the German Krimmel, which he wrote in a manner that was to appear as an afterthought. The handwriting, I could tell, was blotted at the edges. "As for Mr. Krimmel, I'm sorry to say, the record proves you wrong on all counts. If my not being in Philadelphia is a matter of timing, as you say, then the timing was just right for me to have endured — and then rejected — the ad hoc artistic scene that lacked both training and patrons. Your Mr. Krimmel was certainly present in that fuliginous moment and at his side was the Russian scoundrel whose name needs no repeating here and who, as you well know, is at least half the reason I skipped town for Baltimore."

"Mr. Krimmel himself made a good go of it, erecting his crowded pictures that betrayed little sense of pictorial perspective or grace. He was a frequenter of taverns and marketplaces, perhaps finding a thrill in recording in his sketchbook the sordid affairs of the unlucky. I take your word on the quality of his work, but can it truly be that this amateur whose pencil was so enchanted by chimney sweeps and soup peddlers is the same artist you so admire today?"

I winced only slightly when I read this, for my son's eye has been well trained by his many trips to the Louvre and his tongue by his own high mind. But am I wrong to note in his dismissive tone a hint of his own rather notorious insecurity?

Quickly and quietly, I read on. As it turns out, the entire matter is very likely moot. Quite unbeknownst to me, more than a year ago, Krimmel was forced to leave this country to return to his native Germany. After explaining this, my son ended his letter thusly: "There were rumors about the cause of his sudden departure, suggestions of misdoings related to his sister-in-law." Krimmel, noted Rembrandt, lived with his brother and sister-in-law and their children in a house on Pine Street. "As a rule," continued my son, "rumors appall me, and so I ignored these like any others. Nevertheless, in all my direct dealings with Krimmel I was given the impression of a man cut loose. He is untrained and yet unbounded, dear Father. I think you would say he is undignified. I don't worry over him since he's retreated to his own war-cursed homeland, but have you considered what would happen to the arts of America if such a contumacious fool were let loose on our pure-born Academy?"

PART ONE

Chapter I

*T*he last time I saw John Lewis Krimmel, a smooth black pebble like a drip of ink was pressed into the flesh of his cheek and the voices of mourning doves pelted the air from somewhere beyond the trees.

Rembrandt Peale had disappeared (as I recall it), but the old man grabbed my arm as if to say, "You saw it as I saw it, Caleb Cloud."

With the earnings from my report for *Poulson's Almanac* on Bonaparte's new chateau at Point Breeze, I bought up everything left in Krimmel's estate minus the brushes and a too-large pair of shoes. This included four sketchbooks and a journal begun on board the *Sumatra*. The items occupy a small trunk in the corner of the room I inhabit on the quiet side of Shippen Street near the Passyunk Road. A Genoese sail maker with a taste for skinny boys has taken the room below.

I spent my scant earnings on Krimmel's prosaic remains. Surely, I must have been in a state of shock, filled with terrible empathy and sadness. A wrong had been committed and I, quietly, almost surreptitiously, wanted to say something about it. A writer most often chooses words if he has something to say, or thinks he does—as quite clearly, I am doing now—but not always. How could it be always? That is equally clear: nothing is ever clear or certain, two words I feel I'd better banish from my lexicon. But what was I doing? Trying to preserve his memory, or profit when one day a real art collector would deem him worthy? Perhaps. Perhaps also trying to right a wrong. One is defenseless against time, but the wrong I must have had in mind was one in which I felt myself complicit: a sketch stolen and sold away.

Now on top of the trunk is Peale's own journal and letter book, dated 1808-1826 and delivered by his long-fingered son Titian at my request. Peale had written in it of the usual things that had occupied his mind for so many years up until a week before his death—his children's incessant foibles, the harvest, his inventions, the farm hands' incompetence, attendance at the Peale Museum—but naturally, his script and the depth of his thinking had declined in the last years. I opened the book to 1821. Titian had declined to sit down next to me. I offered a bowl of dried apricots I had purchased that morning at the market. He declined that, too. "Keep the book," he said, "otherwise my brother Rembrandt will get his hands on it."

"Look. Perhaps he already has," I said, and I opened the journal to July 1821, only there were no entries.

"The pages are missing," said Titian.

For days, I let this obsess my thoughts. If Peale and Rembrandt weren't at all complicit in the death of Krimmel, then why the missing pages? Surely Krimmel's death would have warranted comment in the journal. And how had it been reported in the news? A drowning, an accident. And stunned, I had let it go. He is dead, and nothing can bring him back.

But Peale, the son of a convicted forger who as a young man had stitched the word "will" into his middle name (transforming Wilson into Willson), would go to any length to protect his reputation. That week, I hardly moved from my room, reading and rereading Peale's journal, gazing through Krimmel's sketchbooks. I read until the light disappeared and lit the lamp and kept reading. I opened the window only to hear the cry of the oysterman and the sobs of a streetwalker from a distant alley. A writer listens, he asks, he collects, I told myself. But a writer also has to decide. Is it worth it to settle on some certain kind of truth?

The first time I saw John Lewis Krimmel, he was kneeling before a tangle of plants, half stained crimson and blistered from the sun. Krimmel had in his hand an open sketchbook, its empty white page like a misprint in the cluttered landscape, and a pencil behind his ear. He was probably humming.

Krimmel said he was heading to Easton, which was exactly the place Victor, Dixcy, and I had just left—and possibly for good. Krimmel's face was thick and heavy, as if swollen, and his hair, which carried the light like clear maple resin, drifted down to his rounded shoulders. Easton, he said, without taking his eyes from the weeds and wild growth, was locked in his memory. But he said his memory was faulty. The town couldn't be the same as the Swabian village of his ancestry, where he had just visited—settling the accounts of the family pastry shop and making provisions for the care of his dead sister's children—and yet that's how he remembered it. He wanted to unlock the memory.

We three shrugged. For us, Easton was a trap, a prison. We were looking for the American Babylon. We were sure it existed, we just weren't sure where.

Krimmel finally turned away from the plants, the pencil still resting behind his ear. His brow was damp with sweat. Having just come off the ship in New York, he said he was in no hurry. Eventually he would travel to Philadelphia, where he had lived before.

But why move back to Philadelphia and not stay in New York? Victor wanted to know. Without seeming to move, Krimmel pulled another sketchbook out of a satchel that was on the ground near his feet. He deliberately unwound the clasp and then he bent to one knee, a gauzy silence about him, as he turned the pages. There: a full-page watercolor rendering of a young woman with unwieldy curls and doubtful eyes. Her dress was the color of a fading bruise.

"In Germany, there are ten available ladies for every man," said Krimmel.

"And yet—"

"And yet they are thin as rails and they can't laugh," he said, his voice flat. "They don't cry either. I had one for a few days. Her name was Hannah Beck. The insistent girl begged me to take her to America."

"And?"

"You could say she was a girl full of secrets."

"But this one?" said Victor, meaning the girl in the water-color.

"She wants to do right, everything right."

"Does she think you're right?"

Krimmel didn't answer.

Dixcy took the sketchbook in his thick, sweaty hands and leafed through it, surveying the pages with dispirited eyes and an open mouth. Suddenly, he stopped. He had paused on a double leaf filled with people—old, young, infirm, wild-eyed, serene, senseless, haughty, lazy, quiet, debauched, and drenched with rain, some diminutive on the page and yet viscerally awake and alive, ant-sized creatures hauling wood or stealing apples or crying out. Krimmel, with Victor hovering, faded back to the vegetation at the side of the road.

Silent and absorbed, Dixcy had moved on to another double leaf, this of morning glories and cornflowers and roses, buds sheathed and heavy, and every flower bathing in the invisible milk of the sun. And a few pages on: all manner of interior architectural fragments and objects, arranged on the page as if hastily gathered with two cupped hands and then allowed to drop, land, and scatter.

Krimmel had rendered his subjects with impossible precision; the flower petals and leaves, stems and thorns pierced the hot din of the afternoon. The German explained that when he first began to sketch he had been a newly arrived foreigner and therefore everything had been new, vibrant, vital, and for the first time in his life he had understood the great variety of life. He sought to observe and capture it — at first he wanted to be everywhere, seeing everything. "I didn't understand it, but somehow my pictures were going to explain it." People seemed to like them. But, he said, in reality they were terrible, and he advised us, as we were still a few years younger than he was, and certainly less experienced, to be careful not to become too confident in our work, whatever it might be.

Krimmel's brother George, a merchant, had moved to Philadelphia first, in the early part of the century. Krimmel followed under pretense of joining his brother's firm, but really because he desired to be an artist and he had heard there were opportunities. He arrived, told his brother he had no intention of joining his firm, and promptly went off sketching, taking classes at the Academy and showing his work whenever someone would give him the opportunity. The repudiation of business caused an immediate rift, but Krimmel continued to live in his brother's house with his brother's wife and children. Then the rift apparently deepened when it seemed obvious that Krimmel and his sister-in-law Susanna were falling in love — it wasn't just the death of their sister that prompted his return to Germany — and Krimmel, and not the clearly better-suited George, was sent back to settle the affairs.

"You mean people were lying to you?" said Victor.

"I mean I was lying to myself," replied Krimmel, his eyes like gates swinging open. He turned away and withdrew another sketchbook from his satchel. From this one he removed a page. Now Krimmel looked directly at Victor, who was visibly restless, and handed him the page from the sketchbook. "But then I was sent away — back to Germany. Eventually, I ended up in Vienna and that's where I learned, after some years of trying, to compose a picture."

In Vienna, Krimmel met up with a group of artists who called themselves the Nazarenes. They told him to relax. "Don't speak to your subject, let it speak to you," they said, repeating a mantra. A picture, they said, isn't a treatise — it isn't meant to convince anyone. Better if it seduces. Likewise, you have to let the landscape seduce you. Listen to it breathe and sigh and whisper. He learned to be still, and to wait. "Just when you think the bee is finished with the flower, then, just then, he gives himself to it completely, and I learned to wait for that moment, or really the very moment right before that moment, the moment of the most intense anticipation." He became convinced that a successful picture leads the viewer into the scene, rather than bringing the scene to the viewer — or even telling him what it's about.

Krimmel showed us two watercolor sketches of his native village, Ebingen. In each of them, there are figures — a farm girl carrying produce on her head and a cow and goat idling along — passing through from the left and into the lingering and partially hidden landscape. It isn't clear what will happen, only we know — because someone unseen awaits — that something will. The sketch in Victor's hand was an interior, a corner of a seemingly empty room with two latched doors and a cabinet with another three doors also closed tight. In the foreground was a rather ornate iron stove, which appeared to be lit. Or was it? Krimmel stood back as we looked at the sketch. Once or twice he put his hand through his hair. The thick air seemed to seep from the ground. "Something is about to happen," said Victor. "Someone is going to walk through one of the doors, or it's going to creak open even though it appears locked. It's silent in the room, but outside, the wind —." Krimmel stepped closer. Victor's eyes were wide. He wanted to invite Krimmel to stay with us. There wasn't any artist in America — so far as I knew from reading the magazines that arrived at the Easton library — who talked this way about making pictures. The famous painter Rembrandt Peale would look coldly at his subject in such a way that his portrait would reveal that person's flaws and imperfections — and not in a way that would suggest complexity or contradiction, but wholly in the name of exposing some ugly truth. Krimmel's intent, it seemed to me, was to fill a picture with possibility, with the unknown. I said as much to him. Victor flashed his eyes past me, as if purposely skimming my head.

Once more, the German stepped back and then closer. He had on his face not a seeking gaze, but a gaze that already seemed to know where it was landing. "When I arrive in Philadelphia," he said slowly, but with startling ease and not a hint of preoccupation, "I will teach this new idea in art."

"You mean to aspiring artists in the Pennsylvania Academy? You'll train them like the Nazarenes trained you?" I asked.

"I mean everyone I can."

"To change the direction of art in America!" said Victor.

"To give it new breath, yes," said Krimmel, dousing a bit of Victor's zeal with his even reply and looking up and then out above the grasses and meadow flowers and the summer sweet at the road's edge. "The art of America, as I experienced it, is a literal art, transcription and pedantry. There is no wonder." His eyes faded in the brightening sun. When we turned to bid him goodbye, they seemed almost entirely white.

For two days we went on walking in fits and starts. By eleven o'clock on the third day we had set out again, pressing our way along the River Road. But we weren't moving quickly, or with any obvious intent. The sun kept sneaking along a line of low clouds and every few minutes it would appear red-blue and glossy and Victor would raise his head as if he was listening for something only he could hear.

Dixcy had a dreary look, waxen and sweaty, with deep circles under his eyes. He was three or four paces ahead of Victor and me, and he walked with a lousy smirk, as if he had seen right through the trees and the asters and the clover and had come to realize it was all a dirty trick. "He only wishes to get it over with as soon as possible," whispered Victor, "whereas you and I know at least half the joy is in the journey itself." This last part he said so that Dixcy would hear.

"If that is so," responded Dixcy, "then half the joy is in

arriving. But we don't even know where we're going."

A fence appeared before us almost immediately. Dixcy put his hands on the top rail as if it was proof of our fallibility, a warning. Victor jumped the fence, leapt into the arms of a giant beech tree and wouldn't stop laughing until Dixcy inserted himself between the two bottom rails. Victor, laughing once more, relinquished his perch, clapped his hands, and said to me, "Cloud, help him up!"

We tracked fences for much of that day until at a clearing we came upon a black farmhand named Sylvester who gave us a ride to a tavern called the Fox's Ring. We ate mutton, which Victor paid for, and potatoes that tasted of embers and sat in my stomach like a pile of stones. The road lay on, the sky the color of bone, and a wind shook the tops of the locust trees, which appeared to raise their slender hands as if in some kind of ecstatic dance. For a minute I thought of my angry father, silently carting wood across Easton, his hands no more stained purple or brown or red by ground pigment but rough and splintered and cruel.

Victor put his own hand on my back and pushed me along until we came to a hamlet, or I should say a wee village, for strangely enough a small stone building with a sign that read "Library" appeared. The door was locked and we sat on the wooden step with the faint sun lost and then found, lost then found, wondering what books might be inside. Victor kept calling the village, whose name didn't seem to be posted anywhere (but which I suspected was Wrightstown), the "Font of Knowledge." We had immediately sat down as if the library was our destiny, and now we had waited for some time as if we were keeping an appointment with a person who had completely forgotten our rendezvous, leaving us alone, adrift, and yet anchored to the step. Dixcy got up, spit, walked around the side, and peered inside the window.

"Is the Goethe in German or translated?" said Victor.

"Are our thoughts and ideas really visible to us is a more appropriate question," responded Dixcy, his voice slightly strained, perhaps by his asthma. "There isn't a book in sight. Or a table or chair."

"It's empty?" shouted Victor.

"Or our vision is severely limited," said Dixcy.

"Christ, and we've been sitting here like idiots."

Dixcy tried to argue that, nonetheless, the window could be opened and we could therefore stay and sleep in the library. He made another joke about clarity in writing and even found a large rock to stand on that would allow him to reach the window so that it could be opened and we could climb in, but Victor refused to even acknowledge the possibility. His face turned red as he inhaled deeply, his nose becoming quite suddenly overstated: too strong, too powerful for the tiny building and the three friends negotiating themselves through the thrumming fields of Bucks County.

When faced with Victor's severity, Dixcy attempted to undermine his authority. He told a story I hadn't heard before. The day Dixcy had first introduced the philosopher-physician La Mettrie (a kind of patron saint of ours) to Victor's attention, they were in the yard of the Pietists's Sabbath school trying to fly a kite. Victor had said, "Of course I know him," or "I've read him before," and he even intimated that he had read La Mettrie's work in the original French. Dixcy was impressed and even excited by this because the two had just recently become acquainted (Dixcy having just moved to Easton, which was Victor's birthplace), and he hadn't yet found anyone to talk to about philosophy or even poetry. So the next time they were together, Dixcy brought his copy of *L'homme Machine* in English translation as well as the somewhat little known satire *Pénélope*, which only existed in the original French, and he began to discuss specific passages, quoting at length entire paragraphs, emphasizing the phrases he thought most notable or funny. But Victor, whose mind is well equipped for such recitations, had nothing to say in response. Dixcy sensed this immediately and pressed his new friend, who said he really only knew the text in

French and then went on to say very general things about the condition of the soul, which he called the "mind." Well, Dixcy could see plainly that Victor had lied and knew next to nothing about La Mettrie. They came to fisticuffs, a battle which Victor won by pinning Dixcy against the flaking trunk of a giant sycamore—as Victor put it, "The bark was falling like an angry and self-absorbed father's footsteps climbing the stairs"—and nearly strangling him while promising that the next time they met he would have "brushed up" on the text of the great work so that they could have a more productive discussion.

Victor, who had already begun to walk away from the library, heading out of the village, laughed and said the story had been told entirely wrong. What really happened, he said, was exactly the opposite: He only knew the text in French and hadn't ever read it in English. He didn't even know it had been translated. It was Dixcy who was unfamiliar with the original.

"But you gave me the English translation to read," I said.

"Of course. I picked it up so that I could discuss the book with Dixcy," he said. "Look, I'm just setting the record straight. Though I did beat the shit out of this nancy boy here."

I tried not to notice the change that took place just then: the sun, low and far, extinguished the clouds; behind us the bone sky became indigo and the gold of the library's sign flickered; and Victor consolidated his power. I went over to Dixcy, who looked gray-brown and sickly, and smiled stupidly. I wanted to say I believed his story just fine, but instead I said, "If we get moving now, we can make Newtown by dark, or soon after."

Moments later Victor stood in the middle of the road fifty paces ahead of us, conversing with a Quaker farmer. His hand was on the other man's shoulder. The farmer wore a customary wide-brimmed hat and long gray coat, which hung below his knees. He had a great nose and a lower lip that protruded slightly so that he carried an air of resignation or disappointment. Nevertheless, Victor was laughing when we caught up and the

Quaker farmer was smoking a long pipe and looking deeply into Victor's eyes.

"You know what he said?" said Victor after he shook the farmer's hand as we turned away. "He said I reminded him of some minister who used to preach around here, he thought I might have been his son."

"A Quaker, like himself."

"I suppose so, but I didn't ask. I told him the town has a beautiful library."

"And what did he say to that?" I asked.

"He didn't say anything at first, just looked at me a little more intently—well, you saw him—like he was trying to understand what I was saying or like he was hard of hearing. Then he took his cane and whacked my leg and asked if I liked to read. Really what he said was, 'You read a lot of books, do you?' And I didn't think about it, I just immediately replied that without books, the world would be a mighty dull place. But as soon as I opened my mouth I knew I had fallen right into the old man's trap—"

"Pitiful creature—"

"Well, I just wasn't thinking."

"No, not you, the old devil."

"Yes, he is pitiful, but I don't pity him. Thinks books are the devil's work. You know what he said? He said, 'Nothing in a book you won't find right in here.' And he tapped his heart. Cloud, you saw him tap his heart."

"Well, I saw him slip his hand under his coat like he was about to deliver a calf."

"But I got him. I said, 'Sir, that's not quite it, you have it backwards. Everything in here,' I said, and began to rub my own heart, 'every desire, every dream, every love, every bit of sadness, that's what books are for, you know. A library is like a receptacle of humankind,' I said. 'It's as if you could take all the dreams and desires and sadness of all the people who ever existed and you can try to make sense of them, try to sort through them, try to understand them, because they're all the same desires and dreams and sadness you yourself already have, you just don't know it, or won't admit, or you've been outright lying to yourself.' I could tell he wanted to say something, and each time he leaned a little bit more forward on his cane and opened his lips just a little, I went on longer. Then I stopped because, Cloud, I saw you coming. As soon as I did, you know what the old fart said? He said, 'Well, the library's closed,' and he didn't even give me a knock on the knee again, he just went on."

An hour after leaving the Quaker farmer, we stood on a tiny wooden bridge at the edge of a millrace; the sun had swollen the still pale sky and sweat was running down Dixcy's face. "Might we sit in the shade?" he wondered. I suggested we take a swim. Victor, who was flush from the heat, laughed and said it didn't matter to him but that one thing about being a three-some, we would have to always take into account each other's needs. We leaned ourselves against the stone wall of the mill-house and watched birds sweeping in and out of a little stand of plum trees. "Neither the birds nor the plums seem to mind the heat," I said.

Dixcy grunted and wiped his sallow face with a kerchief.

Victor smiled, stood up, and looked out at the plum trees. He bent down and fussed with his satchel, apparently rearranging things inside. He might have been staring into the stars, or beyond that, into his ramous imagination.

Mindlessly, I wandered away, picking up little sticks and pebbles and pieces of bark as I found them and tossing them one at a time into a crevice between two rocks. When I looked up the sweat rolled down and burned my eyes. Victor, standing at the edge of the stream, had stripped, his back to me, and then, swan-like, he grabbed hold of the current and let himself be carried away. He came to a stop, turned to the water, ducked under, and pronounced the coming of Christ. "Revelation!" he sang, his voice fast and bright, and before another minute had passed, I had stripped, careful to set my spectacles aside, and left the miserable humidity in search of temporary relief.

I swam over to Victor, who was sitting on a rock in the middle of the stream, not bent over the cool water but straight and tall as if he was reciting a sonnet, or catching flies. "Cloud," he said, "close your eyes for a minute."

"Why?"

"Don't ask questions, just go ahead, close them."

"It shouldn't matter. I can hardly see beyond you. I can't even see Dixcy on the shore. Where is he anyway?"

"Ah, Cloud, forget Dixcy for a minute. Forget all this. Picture Babylon, the walls covered in tiles of the brightest most varied colors. None of this muted haze, Caleb. In fact everything was decorated. The women were decorated—"

"But weren't they whores?"

"No, not just the whores, the mothers and the sisters too, it's just that the whores could grow rich, if they were shrewd enough. But never mind that, they planted wheat and sesame and millet and barley, just to name a few of the grains grown in immeasurable abundance—"

"Measurable, I should think."

"Yes, certainly, because they traded so much of it for spices and olives and dried fruits, which they incorporated into lavish recipes. Now close your eyes again. When you're sitting in the water it's possible to feel the breeze, even on a murderously still day. Why is that? The Babylonians made one hundred different kinds of soup, three hundred types of bread, all with ingredients procured in endless, labyrinthine markets that would make your head spin, feeling exalted and at the same time like minuscule specks on the earth because of the immensity of it all."

"Just how I felt when I was eight years old," I said, remembering the whitewashed stalls of the High Street Market, the shouts of the butchers, and the dark-skinned girls with baskets of fish on their heads. I thought to explain that I would play a little game by picturing the vendor's cries as words with each letter spelled out in the high, white ceiling of the market, but I breathed in the sweet metal of the creek and lost my train of thought.

"It's delirium," he said.

"Maybe," I said, and I felt a family of fish biting at my feet. "Can you see Dixcy? Is he coming in?"

"I thought he was, but I don't see him now."

"Yell over, he would be pretty foolish to miss this. I'm almost cold now."

Victor said it seemed like Dixcy had vanished. "But he's always vanishing, hot and cold at the same time."

"What do you mean by that?" I asked. But Victor didn't answer.

"Now listen," he said.

"Does he swim?"

"Who? Dixcy? He hasn't hit his head on a rock, if that's what you mean. Rest assured, Cloud, he isn't drowned."

"Aren't we in this together? That's what you said."

"Just wait. But let me finish telling you about Babylon. It's much more interesting. According to the Greek historians, they traded whatever they could on the open market—amongst themselves, with the Syrians and the Greeks evidently, with the nomadic herdsmen, with the Hebrews, whoever wandered by for it was the kind of place that beckoned people from great distances. A man who made things could find his place in the market. All he had to do was pay a little tax. And if he needed some money he could borrow it without even owning title to land. Even if he was a foreigner—for a stranger had the same standing in society as a native. He could conduct business, own land, sign contracts—he could even become king."

"Oh, tell us instead about the whores," said Dixcy, who had come out of the water from behind Victor and now crouched in the stream, his face streaked with wet sand and tiny pebbles.

Victor glanced at Dixcy. He cleared his throat for effect. "I will tell you that in Babylon they decorated the city with life-size murals." And then, interrupting himself: "See, Cloud?"

"See what?" said Dixcy.

"He thought you were lost at the bottom, a gash to the forehead, swarms of minnows taking infinitesimal nibbles of your enormous member—that's another thing you don't know about

William, Caleb, he's a giant among men, a mammoth among miniatures. Now what did you do, walk down the race until you found a spot you could easily cross on foot and then you came up from there. Isn't that right?"

"Tell me again about the minnows," said Dixcy.

"No, I'm trying to tell Cloud here about the Babylonians. They wrote poems, William, love stories, songs, proverbs, they wrote legal contracts and held debates. They were literate, refined people: for God's sake, they invented a civilization!"

This time Dixcy didn't interrupt, he merely started coughing, a choking, wrenching sound, as if great jaws had taken hold of his throat. Victor began to pound on his back (certainly with more than the necessary vigor) and this, magically, arrested the attack. "It works," he said, but Dixcy continued to make a whistling sound every time he took a breath.

"William," said Victor, "shall I continue?"

"I'm getting out."

"Then we'll all get out, dry in the sun," I said. "Finish your Babylonian lesson then." We splashed across the narrow stream—me then Dixcy then Victor. Lifting myself out I happened to glance back and there was Dixcy's giant penis, not shriveled from the cold water like mine was but dark and angry, like the tongue of a wild dog.

We three lay on the grass only partially clothed, Victor in the center and Dixcy and I on either side. The ground steamed us and bugs explored the foreign territory. We're all in this together. We're all in what together? I wanted to ask. Lying flat on the ground, my head was turned to Victor, who was staring straight up in the sky, smiling. His concave chest was still. "Well it goes almost without saying," he said, "that we have before us the possibility of an American Babylon. And here we've been suffocating all this time in Easton. It's not just you, William, who can't breathe."

"I shouldn't like to be whacked upon the back, thank you," I said, in a voice that was quieter than necessary. Victor's face was flush; his hair was stuck to his forehead and he was whispering, at first about an article he had read in the *Analectic* about the new plan for the city of New York, two thousand perfectly exact rectangular blocks, a chessboard unfurled into the hinterlands of Manhattan Island, a city invented for buying and selling land on the open market, as he put it, careful to align the idea of this plan with his fervid idea of Babylon, where anyone could buy and sell anything on that same open market.

"You know what else I saw in the *Analectic*?" Victor clapped his hands. "In Baltimore, Rembrandt Peale—"

"—A Democrat," said Dixcy.

"A Democrat, certainly. Well, he's hatched a plan to illuminate the entire city with gas lights."

"It wasn't in the *Analectic*. You read it in *Portico*."

"The city glimmering with magic lanterns," I said.

"Poetic, von Cloud," said Victor.

"So?"

"So the magic lanterns await us. And while we're at it, so does the hot money of New York."

"Then," I said, mostly joking, "we'll go directly to the office of the *Analectic* to demand of Washington Irving jobs for all of us."

"*Analectic* is published in Philadelphia. Says it right on the cover, number 32 Chestnut Street."

"Ah, Dixcy, don't split hairs," said Victor. "He means the *American Monthly*."

"Did you see in the *Port Folio*—"

"Oh, von Cloud, you know Dixcy. He won't read the *Port Folio*."

"Tell me, do you want to read Federalist propaganda?" said Dixcy. "But I doubt very much Peale's lamps are much more than a proposition at this point, just as the gridiron of New York is a proposition, a future, a dream. Well, the plan for New York is no less fantastic than Mr. Irving's tales."

"This seems pretty real," I said.

"What?"

"What I read in the *Port Folio*. About Joseph Bonaparte's art collection—"

"Of whatever they could pilfer on the way out the door—"

"Who cares?" said Victor. "Name something important that isn't pilfered."

"He plans to build a gallery for it not far from the Pennsylvania Academy. Until then, it said in the article, it may be possible to view the work, either in Bonaparte's apartments in Philadelphia or at his estate, Point Breeze, on a bluff overlooking the Delaware. Some of it can also be seen at the Academy on a revolving basis."

"Oh, I doubt very much it said that you can just row over to Point Breeze, knock on the door."

"Oh, you want to bet?" Now Victor was standing again. He cleared his throat; his Adam's apple floated gently, his waving hands splintered the sad and sagging afternoon air. I closed my eyes, as I now knew what was coming. Could I have stopped it? Could Dixcy?

"Well, how long could it possibly take us?"

"To do what, Victor?"

"To walk to Philadelphia, of course."

A few minutes after we began walking again, Victor stopped, walked to the edge of the road, and fussed again with his sack. I asked him what was so important. "Nothing," he said. "I thought I'd left something at the pond."

"Don't tell me we need to go back," said Dixcy. He looked at Victor with a sour expression.

"No. I saw it—" I said.

"Saw what?"

"Don't be an idiot, Victor," said Dixcy.

"Saw what?" Victor demanded, again.

"He saw you put Krimmel's sketch inside your copy of *Man a Machine*," said Dixcy.

"What do you mean—you took one of his sketches?"

"Of course he did, Caleb."

"You don't get it, do you," said Victor. "You know what that was finding him there by the side of the road—it was like finding Van Dyck at fifteen in a Flemish field sizing up the corn-flowers."

"A field isn't Flemish," said Dixcy.

"Krimmel isn't fifteen," I said, "he's older than we are — and you wouldn't steal from Van Dyck."

"And we aren't likely to see him again," said Dixcy.

"We have to go back, find him."

"You're wrong, Cloud. He handed Dixcy the sketchbooks for a reason."

Dixcy took his hands out of his pockets and drifted on, in the direction we had been going.

I demanded to see the sketch. It was the one of the girl. "You took his picture of his fiancée."

"He didn't say she was."

"There was a sketch of a stove, you might have taken that one."

"Only an idiot would walk half the way back," said Dixcy, who had stopped walking. "Half the way back, or more. Or all the way to Easton."

I figured we would catch up to Krimmel quickly because the German was stopping to observe and sketch. "He's lying in wait in the weeds," I said, "he barely moves."

"A tiger stalking his prey," said Victor.

"Oh no. More like a leopard," I replied.

"We'll get it back to him. Only not now."

I turned and began to walk north.

"Just wait, he'll come back," said Dixcy.

Victor pretended to ignore him. Silently, he brought me the sketch. "Look here, Cloud, put it inside your notebook for safe-keeping."

Dixcy mumbled something about Victor scampering along like a kitten that had a prize for its mother. "Like he's carrying a little gray bird in his mouth."

"No," he corrected himself, and shouted hollowly, "It's the other way around. The mother carries the prey for the children. But go, chase after him if you wish."

Exactly who should give chase? It wasn't clear. But then

Dixcy had already begun to walk on, which meant we were going to have to chase him.

Chapter II

I fell behind the pair of them and sat down to drink some water in front of a short tree at the edge of the road. I examined the sketch, now in my hands, and there was the hesitant smile of Harriet Miller, the watercolor mottling of her dress, the careful edge of the pencil that slid, it was apparent to me, across the outlines of his own skin—how could it not be thus?—as much as hers. Had he sketched this from a distance, with him in Germany and her in Philadelphia? I didn't know. If there was longing in the picture, was it his or hers? Only later would anyone understand the combination of Harriet's fury and reticence that had lured him, but there it must have been on the sheet of fine grade paper in my hand. And then afraid the wind might take it or a bird might dirty it, I clapped it inside my notebook, dutiful and pliable as I was, and angry at my own sad and withering weakness, I buried the notebook inside my bag.

But who had detached the leaf from Krimmel's sketchbook? I pondered this as I dozed off in the high grass and peppery weeds. Whispers of sleep came as a defense against my sour heart; there was a sound, a chipmunk or a possum or maybe a rabbit scampering in the bushes, and hearing it, I opened my eyes part way, looked down the road at the two conspirators talking, felt the sun on my face and a branch of pokeweed dangling above my head, and fell back to sleep.

Instantly, I dreamed—a half dozen lifetimes, but not in some kind of linear procession, in rational, or even irrational sequence, but as if I had plunged into a realm where all time, all feeling, all experience happens at once. Was it the pokeweed, electric with blood and heavy with black magic? And then, hearing my name called and thinking I had been asleep for some time, perhaps even an hour or two, I jumped up. My eyes flashed the ground for the sketch until I recalled my cowardice and complicity and Victor was in the same place, one hundred yards down the road, and he was waving, indicating I should return. "We're continuing south, but on the interior route," he said, "we're all in this together."

That night we slept in a two-story stone barn the color of sand. It was dark and Victor pushed the narrow door open. "Von Cloud," he said, "make sure William gets some sleep, I'm not ready to go inside." Sometime later, I woke and opened my eyes slightly. There was no more than the sound of rain knocking against the cedar roof and dripping from the rafters, nothing to see, at least but a hazy darkness, not black but brown, and I wondered if this is what it meant to be inside the earth. A moment later, I noticed the minuet of snoring, Victor then Dixcy, Victor then Dixcy, Victor then Dixcy, the rhythm utterly controlled and the passes carefully paced, as if they weren't trading snores but haunting gazes. Somewhere in here, it occurred to me, there is a pair of animals, great bulbous ants or praying mantises or ducks or foxes or rats, who are fornicating, touching, pressing against the line that separates ecstasy from evisceration. And then I fell back to sleep.

When I woke the next morning, Victor was sitting beneath a walnut tree, his long, knotty legs stretched and crossed at the ankles, his left hand fondling the curve of a languorous root, as if he were waiting for a signal from some distant star. I tried not to be wearied by his insistence that more was always possible, the day always longer, the possibility always greater than anything I myself might try to imagine. I wanted only to keep on — to keep walking — to keep an even silence, to keep Dixcy out in front. For what did I know of him? He had convinced Victor to forget Krimmel and keep going. What had he said? I took Krimmel's sketch from my notebook. Victor watched me, his hand still on the root. "He would have given it to us," said Victor. "The one of the girl with the cuttings on her head." I shrugged. The sketch in my hand — did Krimmel miss it? — had he searched across the road and in the heat and in the dim light of the fading day? I said something to Victor about how it was only an insufficient window on something I wasn't sure I understood. I wanted to say it was a picture of silence, perhaps because that morning was unusually quiet, as if all the creatures had done their work at night, but I didn't. "That's a sketch of a man at war with himself," said Victor, "you see that don't you."

I thought of my father, indeed always at war with himself. Was this Krimmel? The German seemed to hang on Victor's lips. We weren't turning back — Dixcy had somehow won out — but only months later we would find Krimmel circling the frozen pond with the deceptive calm of a magician. That cold night, the night of Peale's party, the torches were flattened by the wind and smoke rose like a signal to heaven.

Only much later, when we returned to the same pond, the same torches enduring the summer's wind, did we know anything of the madman Peale or his "pelican brood." That night, Rembrandt came to the pond, blinded by rage. Was it to teach Krimmel a lesson? We would never know. By then it was already too late for Victor — Dixcy would say for all of us.

Chapter III

On the road to Newtown, with the sun still above the trees and the air warm and calm, we three passed a short procession comprised entirely of females aged between fifteen and twenty years wearing identical brown or gray bonnets tied below the chin. They were walking in up-right pairs, as if they were carefully arranged lead soldiers with muskets over their shoulders instead of market baskets filled with apples and turnips. Thin clouds, pink on the underside, blue-gray on top and black on the edges, stretched above the yellow fields on either side of the road. The temperature must have dropped, or we hit a spot on the road that is perpetually shaded and muddy, or my own sustaining animal spirit — La Mettrie might say "life-giving juices" — fell to a silent whisper: on a long journey such energy cannot be sustained; indeed, it comes in waves and recedes of its own calling, so as I looked into the firmly erect and taut faces of the procession, I felt a bit sallow in my stomach and wished to sleep or hide. Victor must have felt something similar because he made no effort to greet them. Instead, he gazed back at Dixcy and said, "Tonight we will sleep in real beds in a warm room with a fire and quilt."

That evening I drank too much beer and found myself alone in the inn — Victor said he wanted some quiet to read and the innkeeper had been kind enough to allow him a lamp, all while Dixcy was playing a game of whist (a game that bores me) with some travelers who said they were heading west where there was land to spare, the only problem being "the savages might violate the women." This was said with red eyes and a Scottish brogue. I shrugged and drifted to the back of the room, sat down, pulled out my notebook, and wrote in pencil, "the savages might violate the women," and I thought of the sharp indifference in the face of the old Indians and of the sound of the Delaware River, steady and sad, like a constant swallowing.

A man who introduced himself as Cyrus Greenpoint asked me if I was some kind of scribe. I hadn't heard him sit down opposite me at the wooden table, but I looked up when I heard his voice, and something about the look on his face, which was wide and framed by sideburns, told me he had been there a while. Greenpoint wore a thick brown sweater vest with a wide collar, the kind usually worn beneath a topcoat, and a blue tie. He wasn't drinking anything, or if he had been, he left the glass or mug somewhere else.

I told him I was an art collector—Krimmel's watercolor sketch was, after all, buried in my notebook—making my way with a pair of colleagues to Philadelphia so that we could have a look at the Bonaparte collection. The brother of Napoleon lived there, I explained, and had managed to smuggle out some of the great works when he was exiled to America. I expected an indifferent, even disparaging response, or laughter. I felt a bit idiotic. And now, what do I feel? At least partially responsible for everything that's happened? No, not even Dixcy would hold me responsible. But didn't I know, as soon as the words left my mouth that Victor would latch on to the idea of Bonaparte? I brought up Bonaparte, I mentioned his art collection—"jewels of the Old World," I said—just as I had read in the article, words meant to entice Victor, to lead him to—.

But it was Krimmel I had to talk about then, in the whisper darkness of the tavern in Newtown, with a man I had barely just met. Never, I said, had I encountered someone so absorbed.

"Absorbed?" wondered Greenpoint.

"In his own disquiet," I offered.

"Doesn't one run from one's disquiet? One is hardly absorbed by it," said Greenpoint sharply.

I showed Greenpoint the sketch, passing it off as a kind of minor spoils of the business, and asked him what he thought.

"A pretty one," he said. He shrugged.

"You can't tell." I drew his attention to the look on Harriet's face.

"What do you mean, you can't tell what will happen? A man gets a girl like that to sit for him like that—to look at him like that—"

"It's he who is longing," I posited.

"It always is. Self-doubt turned inside-out and beaten like a rug," he said. "In my observation, self-taught people are like this, they have to be blind, or really deaf, because the minute they listen to what everyone else has to say, they're dead," he said. "So don't tell him what I said about his picture, it could kill him."

"I don't think he cares," I said, already tired of the conversation. Like a fool, I changed my tone. "The question is, does he have the talent?"

"That's not the question," said Greenpoint, foxlike. "Training and instruction are needed from the earliest possible age. Talent is only part of it." Greenpoint may have been right, but he underestimated talent. Rembrandt Peale had plenty of training and instruction, but that wasn't enough. And, like Krimmel, Rembrandt thought he could determine the direction of American art. "Krimmel is kidding himself, anyway," said Greenpoint. "They won't even give him a chance."

I could see Greenpoint wasn't quite done—he ordered another round of beers and leaned back, as if he was checking to see who might be listening. I drank down my beer. Greenpoint leaned forward and smiled. When he smiled the top half of his face seemed to lift while the bottom remained still, as if it was locked in place. Then he said that being a collector of art I must have stopped in Newtown to see the shop of Edward Hicks. "Or is he still our secret?" he asked. I sensed that he was trying to make a point. I didn't respond. Maybe I nodded or frowned, and I must have blinked, because when I opened my eyes Greenpoint's teeth were staring back at me. "Morning you'll find him in the shop. Just go down that alley there to Court Street. An art collector! By the look of you I thought you were a taxidermist or an engraver, the way you were stooped over your notebook without making a sound, or maybe a poet. Now I know better!"

He went on: "So you know, Mr. Hicks never studied at the Academy. He was never a star in Philadelphia's constellation of Peales—forgive me, as a collector you'd know all about Charles Willson's iron grip on his sons' prospects and the Academy—but Hicks doesn't aspire to greatness, or so he claims."

"Which academy? The Pennsylvania Academy? The American Academy in New York? The Royal Academy?"

"Any academy, it doesn't matter. Anyway, academies are half-steps," he said, based on the English, or perhaps French, system, the study of plaster casts and of ancient forms (although of course, being American, they don't often employ live models). Then he said he had a theory about nations. Military success isn't what ultimately establishes power. Nations are always fighting; this time one wins, the next time it's the other. What is gained is up for negotiation and therefore an invitation to further war. I noted that in this recent war with England and France, the United States had established its right to patrol its own waters and maintained its sovereignty in trade and in naval matters. Isn't that significant?

"I think you're being naïve," he said. "Respect, and therefore enduring power, will have to wait until there was such a thing as American culture. Name an empire whose power hasn't emanated from the richness and intricacy of its culture. Ottoman? Persian? Roman? What is the power of the Ottoman Empire? Is it the ferocious sultans? No! It is the quiet agony of the manuscripts, the fables of love and longing and the coloring of the illuminations. Without all that, the sultans would have no followers and without followers no mercenaries and no army!" Greenpoint took a long pull from his mug of ale.

"Name a respected nation that hasn't a well-cultivated literature or a tradition in painting," he went on. "Until there is such a thing, there will be no respect for America."

Then my mind lost its bearing and I began to think of Bridget, a wench I'd spent the night with in Point Pleasant, who told me to close my eyes as she led me downstairs, just hold my hand, we don't need a candle because I know every inch of this place, I know which steps are uneven, I know where I like to do it. And that's where we're going, I take it, I said. *Shh*, don't be afraid, she said. When we got to the bottom of the stairs, and I could hear only faint sounds, like someone was pacing in the barroom, hatching a plan while others were waiting for him to hurry up and make a decision, she placed my hand on a doorknob, which felt cold and wet, and she turned the knob with my hand under hers, opened the door and pushed me inside. It was a closet about as wide as I was, and stuffed with spools of roughly spun wool, which seemed to be stacked in uneven, precarious piles. She closed the door and then stood on the other side, asking me questions like could I smell the wool, did it smell of the field or of the barn or of the hands of the person — presumably it had been her hands — who had spun the wool, could I see anything, and if not, could I see things in my mind's eye or imagine pictures in the darkness? Then after a few minutes of this, during which I made no effort to move or respond to her questions, I realized that my breathing was growing heavy and my knees were sweating. She opened the door just slightly and came inside and carefully latched the door. I asked her why a closet should have an inside latch and she said that's just the way it had always been, when she was a girl she hid in here, the tavern was a rough place in those days, it was full of loose women who used to push her around and scare her, but here inside the closet it's like being inside the earth. An earth that's really a great mama sheep with hair so thick it doesn't move, so choked it is with mud and grass and shit, I said. Bridget put her hand to my mouth and Greenpoint was saying that magic, what he called magic, but which is just another way of saying wonder or fear, is a fake theme in literature.

"So culture is what, determination?"

"It might be," he said. He smiled again, the top of his head lifting skyward, and he grabbed my arm. "Be careful with Hicks."

"What?"

"Edward Hicks, our painter. Sometimes he has a tendency to explode."

The next morning Victor was sick. Apparently he'd spent the night vomiting. Now he was yellow and his hair was standing on end. "Dixcy told me not to get the turtle soup," said Victor.

"I don't even know if it's the right season," replied Dixcy.

"No, it's the right season," said Victor, "just the wrong inn." But he insisted he was now fine. "I may have to puke again, I don't know, I think I have gotten most of it out." We had gathered across the lane from the tavern. Dixcy was pacing along a stone wall, and I was sitting on the ground with my back to the cold stone. About one hundred paces away, according to Victor, who was sitting on top of the wall, which enclosed a farm, an old woman was sitting in a chair under a tree reading to a young boy, who was about three or four years old. The woman had noticed our presence. "She's ignoring us," he said. "But the boy keeps looking up. And each time, his grandmother, if that's who she is, grabs his chin and then pets the top of his head and goes on reading. Must be scripture."

"Of course she's reading scripture," said Dixcy.

"Cloud, tell Dixcy what you were saying about the artist who lives here. He's a painter, right? So we should pay him a visit. It will be good practice for us."

"Practice for what?"

"Caleb has an idea that we can be invited into Bonaparte's chateau if we are collectors of art."

"Well, we have the German's sketch of the girl."

"The fellow's name is Hicks, is that not right, Cloud? And Caleb has the house number."

"It's just over there."

"I'm not an art collector," muttered Dixcy.

"But would it be," said Victor, "absolutely impossible to teach a Mr. Dixcy a new profession? Ah! I do not think so!"

"Hicks is a Quaker preacher," said Dixcy, ignoring Victor. "I think he's the one responsible for a split in the doctrine. Haven't you heard of the Hicksites?"

"Well, we don't know if this is the same one. Could be his brother. And we aren't concerned with his religion. Only his art, only the depth of his imagination." Victor stood up and walked away. Dixcy looked down. For a moment I thought he was going to refuse to follow. I asked him if he was thinking of going home.

"To Easton?"

"Victor can be imperious."

"Victor is imperious, but I don't see what that has to do with it." He continued to pace along the fence. I didn't feel like moving, so I stayed where I was on the ground, with my back against the stone, straining to hear what he was saying. "You, Cloud, probably don't need me, you could go on taking your notes, bedding barmaids, I don't know...whatever else you seem to do, you seem to do it without much worry, and you would be fine, maybe even better off, without the shadow of Victor. You could go on now and arrive in Philadelphia in a few days and who knows, you might find yourself in the arms of the sister of some courtesan of Bonaparte's and before you know it you'll be standing before a Titian or a David and not even having to pretend to be anything but the charming, industrious, level-headed, and I should say sensitive fellow you are. And anyway the fair maiden won't see you for anything but—there will be no play acting with her. How it's possible, I'm not sure, but then I've been watching the way the ladies react to you. They don't notice you at first. Of course they see Victor, with his bright feathers and his little peacock dance. Only later, Caleb, one by one, they drift to you and you hardly notice, not because you are callous or even indifferent but because you believe too much in Victor and Victor believes in being the only one. That's not what he says, I know. But our Victor is really quite terrified, at night when it is just the two of us sleeping somewhere and you aren't around, he whimpers and cries. He is afraid of many things, Caleb. Now, if I have been clear enough, you can see why I am still here. I really doubt I'll ever return to Easton."

When he stopped speaking, I looked up. Dixcy was looking past me, which gave me the feeling he hadn't been speaking to me at all, I had only entered into a conversation, or a kind of speech, as it were, that he was having with or giving to himself.

"The fellow I met last night," I said, wondering if he would even hear me, "his name was Greenpoint. He said he was a broker of property, that there are people as far away as New York and Baltimore who seek fertile soil for a plantation."

"The lowest kind of merchant, the real estate man."

"He was a little drunk, but not a vulgar or even vapid sort." Dixcy helped me to my feet.

"Victor is puking again," he said and there, about fifty paces on, was our friend bent over the dusty lane and rocking slightly, like a flower pressed to the ground by the undulating wind.

It took until the afternoon for Victor to say he was well enough to pay a call on Hicks. Dixcy made him drink cup and after cup of water and said we should tell Hicks that he, Victor, was a collector and that we were merely his associates come along out of curiosity or a general interest in art. We argued about this plan and since we couldn't decide what exactly would be the role of Dixcy and me — Dixcy was doubtful Hicks would respond well to curiosity per se — we decided to say we were all art collectors interested in starting a new gallery in New York. Dixcy put on his cleanest shirt, and I clapped the dust out of my cap.

Hicks's shop was at the end of the lane. To get to it, we crossed a little wooden bridge over a small, fresh-smelling creek that, despite there being no tall trees and very few buildings, made the whole surrounding area feel like it was a shaded glen in the fold of a mountain. But the front of Hicks's shop was in the sun. Above the door was a black sign with white letters: "Coach, Sign, and Ornamental Painting of All Descriptions, in The Neatest and Handsomest of Manner." We all three shrugged.

"All I know," I said, "is that he is self-taught."

"That's a euphemism for uncontrollable," said Dixcy. "It's an insult."

"Exactly so—don't mention that, Cloud." Victor knocked and pressed his ear to the barn-style double doors. "He's in there. Or someone is," he said and knocked again. The sound from inside became clearer as we listened more intently.

"It's the sound of thinking," I said, "or of thoughts as they strain to make sense among all the other thoughts that demean them and laugh at them and undermine them—"

"'Oh, the chaos and quick succession of our ideas,'" said Victor, quoting La Mettrie.

"And here, perhaps, is the case of the artist whose imagination is kept out of balance by the sheer torrent of desires, insights, and visions."

"The miserable imbalance," said Victor. "But you don't believe that do you? Doesn't it strike you as odd that our man, who loved nothing more than a night in a brothel exercising his unkempt desires against the better judgment of the other, more stable and disciplined parts of his imagination, applied scorn, or at least ambivalence, to 'painters, poets, musicians'? That of all the passages reads to me untrue, savage..."

"He was a physician, he dealt in parts, in springs, in causes of things," said Dixcy.

"Or he detested himself," I said.

Victor knocked a third time. When no one came to the door, we wandered around the side of the building, which led to a barn and next to that a little fenced-in area with a single, sorry sheep and a pair of bruised little chickens. We stood there for a while, each of us with our hands in our coat pockets and the early autumn sun warming our faces and the gentle hillside at our backs, dark green like the fur of a creeping earth. Victor said that finally he was hungry again and wouldn't it be a good idea to try a different tavern? We crossed the little bridge back into the center of the town. As we came to State Street, I noticed a sign that I hadn't seen before. It was Greenpoint's office. The door was unlatched and so we walked in, to a small room with a fire, a single, small and uncluttered desk with a chair, and a rope-style rug in pale blue and pink and in the shape of a perfect circle. Victor stood in the exact center of the perfect circle, so tall he had to stoop slightly to fit between the beams of the ceiling. Only a moment passed before Greenpoint came through a doorway with heavy footsteps and hands outstretched to greet me.

"You were expecting me?" I said.

"I am not surprised to see you, my boy," he said, and motioned us to follow him, an act which gave the impression that the front room was show, perhaps only used for very formal meetings or meant to convey a sense of seriousness and order and modesty, none of which, at first glance, seemed to come naturally to Greenpoint. We filed in, quickly filling the next room, where we were introduced to Mr. Frances Archambault, the son of an innkeeper and property owner, who was dressed in a long, thick velvet coat, like a king, or a lion in his lair. Archambault winked at me when I shook his hand. Greenpoint quickly excused himself, saying it would be but a minute, and he opened a door to staircase and lumbered up the stairs.

The lair was crowded with account books and maps, which took up every available inch of the two desks and even the chairs up against the walls. This office had none of the austerity of the front room but felt instead like a madman's cave. In one corner a pile of account books, which mixed with little volumes of poetry and even a *Poulson's Almanac*, was about to tumble over. The only uncluttered space in the office was a little wooden shelf, which gave me the impression that Greenpoint had made it himself in a bout of excitement. On the shelf, which was about two feet long and eight or ten inches deep, were carefully arranged arrowheads and vessels, a pair of little corn husk dolls (boy and girl), a wooden mask labeled "*Meesing* — God," and several perfectly intact beaded circles of various sizes, either parts of necklaces or head pieces of some sort, which instantly called to mind the rope rug in the front room. For a while I gazed at the bead jewelry. The continuous winding circles of beads seemed to go on infinitely toward the center of each circle but then didn't, stopping instead to form another, a final central core circle of air, of nothingness, and this made me feel naked and idiotic, as if I had completely lost my bearings.

Victor, who must have noticed the little shelf at the very same moment, immediately picked up one of the dolls and turned it in his hands, looking intently at its back. For a moment he turned the doll back and forth in his hands. He put the doll down, picked up the other doll, examined it carefully, and replaced it, then an arrowhead, a piece of pottery, and was about to have a look at one of the beaded circles when Archambault, who had turned his attention away from me and back to the papers in front of him, turned slowly. "Please," he said, almost at a whisper. "The oils and dirt on your hands will deteriorate the objects."

"Then I should say you ought to place them in a glass cabinet," replied Victor.

Just then Greenpoint bounded down the stairs, pushed the little door open, and leaned out. "It is settled," he declared. "The lady reports that there is quite enough food for a proper dinner for all. Come, come. Follow me, my friends, am I not correct in assuming you are hungry? Of course, you will be my guests. Archambault, will you be joining us?"

But Archambault did not reply.

Greenpoint's apartments were nothing like either of the two rooms downstairs. Instead of being austere like the front room, they were full of color and modern furniture. A settee was upholstered in pale blue, the same color of the sky in the portrait of a woman I assumed to be Mrs. Greenpoint's mother hanging above it. And instead of being crowded and cluttered like the office, the rooms were carefully laid out. Above a black lacquer cabinet with little brass ring handles that must have come from China was a much larger version of the wooden mask on the shelf downstairs. This version had kept its original colors — red and gold—and its black eyes seemed to gaze across the room to the portrait of Mrs. Greenpoint's mother. It was as if each object had been chosen with the greatest intent and placed in a particular way to connect or contrast or simply converse with the other objects. This conversation was like a musical composition for harpsichord or pianoforte someone was playing in the corner and gave the feeling that it might gaze lovingly at the real conversation taking place or kiss it gently on the cheek: it might even take it by the hand and lead it off to another place, but it wouldn't ever overwhelm it. The Greenpoints, in other words, had good taste.

Mrs. Greenpoint came into the dining room, prompting Greenpoint to leap to his feet and introduce us as "the young art connoisseurs" he had been so delighted to meet the night before and who "have secured an appointment with the brother of Napoleon, who has a salon in Philadelphia." Each of us stood, Victor first, and bowed to the lady, whose brilliant mahogany hair gave one the sensation of tasting a smooth elixir, the head-clearing rush of it. Victor must have felt the same thing because he breathed in deeply and nearly lost his footing as he tipped his hat and ran his hand through his hair. The lady's dress was brown—not dull and sad, but full of stitching the same blood color of her scarf. It seemed certain that Greenpoint had married up. Once we had all sat down at the table and Mrs. Greenpoint's little Irish maid, whose face was blunted like the end of a stick, spooned out the soup, Greenpoint looked at me and then at Dixcy, who appeared to be suffering from a terrible headache, and then finally at Victor. Greenpoint began to eat his soup, not slowly, like most people do, but as if he were trying to empty his bowl as quickly as possible, no matter that it was piping hot, taking one spoonful after the other and then when that proved inadequate, drinking directly from the bowl. He wiped his mouth with his napkin, burping as he did so and then said, "So, you made it over to see Hicks this morning?"

Victor opened his mouth to respond, but Greenpoint held out his hand. "Tell me first about what you're looking for. History works? Landscapes? Portraits, still life, what is it exactly?"

Surprisingly, it was Dixcy who answered, speaking in a controlled and distant voice. "Well, sir," he said, "to tell you the truth, what we're looking for is *value*, the artist who is unknown, perhaps even hidden today but who tomorrow will be well regarded by the tastemakers who write for the magazines. It doesn't hurt that Caleb here is a writer, one who has some small influence over public opinion. So we're very much liberal in our taste. Victor, because of his background, is drawn to nautical works, maritime landscapes, naval battles, and the like, but that's something more like a hobby. Recently, we've been seeing quite a number of history works, but they tend to be too large and unwieldy."

"You mean the size of the canvas, is that what you're saying, or the subject, too grandiose?"

"Where are you from, then?" I asked, hoping to change the subject.

"That's a hard question to answer," said Greenpoint.

"We're from Charleston," said Mrs. Greenpoint, who frowned at her husband. Just then the Irish maid returned and each of us was served a cold leg of chicken. I looked at Victor to see how his stomach was holding up, but he wasn't paying any attention to the dish placed before him.

Greenpoint put his knife and fork down. "Now, please tell me about your meeting with Hicks. I promise not to interfere with your observations as I am curious about what you think."

"We stood outside his door for some time," I said.

"And?"

"Can I say something?" said Victor. "With all due respect, Mr. Greenpoint, and gratitude to you and your wife, you don't really believe all this, do you? Even to me, it sounds ridiculous. It's just too much. One can't live a lie."

Mrs. Greenpoint let out a burst of laughter, aimed at her husband.

"Well, that may be," said Greenpoint, trying to cover up his wife's outburst.

"Obviously you know we're not art collectors," said Victor.

Mrs. Greenpoint laughed again. This time it seemed tinged

with affection for Victor, to whom she turned. "Oh, it is almost too much!"

"I had my feelings," said Greenpoint.

"Caleb may have told you so last night," said Victor, who looked at Mrs. Greenpoint and blushed. "It was a game we were playing. I assure you it wasn't his idea. But under the circumstances, if you'll allow me a minute to explain, it was our desire to teach ourselves enough about the themes and practices of art so that we would be invited in to see the most respected collections. Perhaps foolish."

I blushed terribly. Immediately I convinced myself, for the evidence was nothing if not overwhelming, that I was a weakling who allowed others to tell him what was right, a dupe for going along, and a fool for thinking that anyone would think it the truth. Victor, on the other hand, was a king, a giant, a god, who could create and destroy without lowering his head below the horizon. Just listening to him now, there was humor and delight in his voice, there was love and kindness in his voice — and not a hint of shame (the blush, I am almost certain, was a result of the attention of Mrs. Greenpoint). Nor was he about to let Greenpoint feel shame. Mrs. Greenpoint stood and as soon as she did so, Greenpoint himself followed. And then Victor stood and looked at them both.

"Just a minute," he said, "please sit down. I want to tell you what happened at Hicks's workshop. I think you will be able to give us some insight. For we three really are in search of something. Maybe not art, but maybe artists or philosophers or inventors of things. Maybe just a chance to take part, to grab on. "We come from a small town, not much larger than this. We have walked this far and we will keep walking. Is there a better way to feel so alive? To feel that you are the ground or wind or the fields. You see, that's what's been happening to us. Caleb is taking it all down, he has his notebook, and when he writes he is building a story. But not me, I only wish to be here, to be alive. I have a feeling life is too beautiful to reflect too much."

"Go on," said Mrs. Greenpoint. "Perhaps it is we who can learn from you."

"Exactly," said Greenpoint. "In fact, you've done nothing even the slightest bit wrong!"

"So we did go to Mr. Hicks's workshop this morning," continued Victor, "just as you had suggested to Caleb, and we stood outside his door, having knocked several times, for a quarter hour."

"It was obvious he was inside," I said.

"Well it was obvious someone was inside, because we could hear that person. Maybe there was another person too, but it was hard to tell. So we waited a little longer and knocked again, but no one came to answer. But if, as I think you said, Mr. Hicks is 'original,' and we are here in this town and may never be again, we want to go back and meet him."

As we continued to eat, Dixcy began to ask questions about Hicks. He wanted to know, of course, if this Hicks had anything to do with the sect of Quakers called Hicksites. No, it was his older cousin, Elias Hicks. But Edward was close to Elias — he had been a kind of father to him — and Edward himself was a minister in the Friendly religion. He is a minister, Greenpoint explained, but don't take that to mean he is glad or loving. No, no, each day, he seems to come closer to the abyss. The abyss? Dixcy wondered, what exactly do you mean? The abyss of giving up. The abyss of not being godly enough, the abyss of completely falling apart. Dixcy said he was still confused. Greenpoint said then he would have to go back a bit further. And then he explained that he isn't the best source on the subject but that given the work he does, he talks to a lot of people all over the countryside in all the little hamlets and villages around here and also he isn't a religious man himself, which means he is privy to what really goes on in Newtown.

"Hicks is a bit of a sinner then?" said Victor, smiling without making a sound and looking around the table.

Greenpoint said it's not the word he would have chosen but he understood the joke, thank you very much. Hicks's grandfather had been a British agent. He was rich and the family lived in high style on a nice-sized plantation (which, incidentally, Greenpoint had subsequently sold not once but twice, a prac-

tice called "double-dipping," which is really the practice of getting money for free), but that was well before the American colonists realized they had grievances against the Crown. When
independence was declared, Hicks's grandfather was on the
wrong side of things. Not only that, but he was in charge in
Bucks County. He stood on the courthouse steps of Newtown
and declared that the colonists couldn't legally arm themselves
for an insurrection. The heavy-handed pronouncement wasn't
well received; American patriots, who made a majority in the
town, tried to capture Hicks, perhaps to tar and feather him.
Hicks fled to New York. His son Isaac, the father of Edward, was
also an English operative. He was accused of being a Tory and
the revolutionaries took away his property, leaving the Hicks
family destitute. This is when Edward was born. As soon as he
was born, however, he was boarded out to another family, for
his father, still considered a traitor, had trouble earning a living.

As he grew older, Edward worked in his uncle's tavern as
a lackey and a barkeep and then as an apprentice building and
painting carriages. At night with some of his friends he would
go to Philadelphia and there he would drink, visit bawdy
houses, and carouse until morning. All the while, in the workshop of his landlord he taught himself to paint, first decora-
tively and then little portraits and landscape scenes. But then
he had a bad night drinking. Perhaps he became ill or got into
a fight— having lived through the Revolution as a child of an
enemy family he had always detested violence. Under such circumstances it isn't unusual for a brooding, introspective type
to "find religion." A little blood on the nose might be the surest
beacon of God. But Hicks didn't just find religion—or morals,
however you might put it—he latched on with the intensity of
the true believer and in this case decided that no true Quaker
could accept any kind of worldly delight. To do so would be
an affront to God. Included in this affront was the making of
pictures. ("Can you believe it?" asked Greenpoint, "that basic
instinct to decorate one's nest—I mean there are birds that fill
their little nests with all kinds of brightly colored things they
find, just to attract the right mate" —or "any mate," interrupted

his wife.) So Hicks decided to abandon art. He would only paint coaches and signs and occasionally furniture, as long as it was made in a particularly simple style. This he tried for some time but the temptation was too great and he found himself making pictures.

And so?

And so he burned his brushes. A foolhardy thing to do if you're as poor as he was and so dependent on friends and relatives for support. But Hicks is a principled man. He burned his brushes and became a farmer.

"And you sold him the plantation, I take it," said Dixcy.

"No, but I sold it for him when the godly enterprise failed."

"And he went back to painting?" I asked.

"No, he went out on the road preaching with his uncle Elias. Way up into New York, shining the inner light." When he finally returned to Newtown he became more reclusive than ever. There were rumors—that he'd fathered a child with a follower, that he'd fallen off the wagon, forcing his uncle to cut short their tour—but none of them were true, according to Greenpoint. "It was as if he returned with a secret, or a jewel he'd found and didn't want anyone to know about."

"Bill," said Mrs. Greenpoint to her husband, "they ought to tell him they are writing a book about the best American artists. Caleb here is a writer."

"The only thing worse, now that I think of it, would be to say they are collectors."

"You underestimate the size of his ego."

"Exactly, and he is justly afraid," replied Greenpoint.

Victor stood. "I, for one, am sufficiently intrigued by Mr. Hicks. And, madam, I like your idea of a book. Of course, I don't know why it never occurred to me before. We've already interrogated one of them."

"This is your Krimmel," said Greenpoint. "With the intense gaze."

"He was more haunted than intense," said Dixcy, looking as uncomfortable as usual.

"The intense gaze was in the sketch Mr. Cloud shared with

me last night. Isn't that right? Mind showing it to my wife?"

"Rather elegantly self-possessed. I bet she doesn't let anything go," said Mrs. Greenpoint.

"Who, dear?"

"This girl right here, don't pretend you didn't notice."

"Well," said Victor, "for some reason there was in my house growing up a very old copy of *The Gentleman's and Connoisseur's Dictionary of Painters* and so I can easily picture this *Great American Masters*."

"It can't be a mere encyclopedia," said Mrs. Greenpoint. "That bores."

"You mean it has to say something? You are right, madam. The book should pronounce a movement—what did Krimmel say? Art of anticipation."

"Art of seduction—"

"But my husband is also right," said Mrs. Greenpoint, returning to Hicks. "You must come seeking, not knowing."

"You mean the book can't be dogmatic? Then the title should be *Searching for Babylon*."

"Oh, it can't be anything so pretentious."

"What my wife means is that you cannot appear urbane."

"You say, gentlemen, that you're writing a book of masters. Why not call it what it is?" She smiled warmly as if she had completed an unpleasant task for us. Her expression made her look like a completely different person, someone far younger and less mysterious than she had seemed at the moment of her grand entrance, with her pretty carapace of lacquered hair and fine clothing. For an instant, it was as if we had been allowed to creep through the door of a hidden chamber. The conversation halted in deference to this sudden change in her demeanor.

But where had the sketch landed? I looked quickly to my left. "Von Cloud!" called Victor. "Worrying again. I have it right inside the La Mettrie—let the philosophers debate."

Greenpoint stood up and said that he would send Archambault over to Hicks's studio immediately with a message that three friends were interested in seeing the paintings and would he accommodate them first thing the next morning.

"Archambault can be trusted," said Mrs. Greenpoint. She then offered to escort us down the lane, as she wished to visit a friend who had been suffering from dizziness. "She collapsed digging up onions last Saturday, poor thing was found with her head in the mud as if she'd tried to bury herself alive."

Chapter IV

Two hours later, Archambault came to the inn with a message: Tomorrow morning would be impossible but Hicks would see us now. We should call at the door to his house on Court Street. We did as instructed and knocked and waited again. No one answered. Dixcy and Victor stood on the marble step and I stood behind them. Dixcy was explaining to Victor that Greenpoint's survey methods were outdated, that he wasn't using a proper theodolite.

"How do you know?" wondered Victor.

"While you were examining the Indian *objêt d'arte*, I was looking around the office."

"So? Maybe there was another room where they store the equipment. Besides he brokers the sale of land, he doesn't survey it. Or is it to be assumed the same man does both?"

"It's probably because everything around here is flat," said Dixcy. "But then all the greater need for accuracy."

"Accurate is not a term I would use to describe Greenpoint."

"Exacting but not accurate."

"You mean because he knows how to live?"

"Maybe he has certain ideas, but he is sloppy."

"You see the way his hands shake," said Victor. "Do you think maybe he forgets to pay the sullen clerk?"

"Archambault?"

"Or maybe he pays him too much. There's something about Greenpoint that makes me think he's very afraid."

Just then, the door opened and out stepped a small man with a taut face and darting eyes. He shook our hands—his hand was rough and cold. A finger on the other hand was wrapped with a rag. "Excuse me," he said, "someone left a broken jar in my tool cabinet. If you need a sign made you're going to have to return later. What's it for?"

Victor explained that we'd met Greenpoint, who had suggested we pay him a visit.

"Oh, that's what that was about. I have to tell him to stop doing that."

"If you're busy, sir, we'll be on our way," said Dixcy.

"Well, you haven't said what it is it you want." All about him was a dry odor, like that of beeswax or parchment, and it seemed as if he was desiccating. He put his uninjured hand in his pocket and grunted. "I'm no artist."

"All kinds of stories are told," said Victor. "How long have you lived in Newtown, if you don't mind my asking."

"Why? Where are you from?"

"We three are from Easton," said Victor, "trying to learn something of the world."

"Sorry to waste your time," he said.

"And so we're seeking beauty," said Victor. He licked his lips. "It's all around us, actually. Autumn is coming and so shall the shadows low and drifting quiet across our faces." Victor placed his long, pale fingers on Hicks's shoulder.

"Be careful. I'm afraid the beauty you seek is merely deceit."

"How do you mean?"

"You are full of pride and pretense. And now I must find a proper bandage. I hope Greenpoint isn't the only person you have met in this town." Victor shook his hand and we two followed. Dixcy and I turned to leave, but Victor stepped back slowly as if he were parting from a lover.

And then, slowly, he turned and we crossed Court Street. Dixcy began to say that he would prefer to walk in the darkness than stay in Newtown another night, and Victor whispered — to himself or to Dixcy, it wasn't clear — "careful." Careful? Victor grabbed us each by the arm. "Let's give Mr. Hicks a minute to bandage his finger," he said. "The reality is he owes Greenpoint."

"But," I said, "who cares? I agree with Dixcy: let's find a loaf of bread and head south. The man's no artist."

Victor began to admonish me for being so impatient. Shouldn't a writer be willing to wait until that very moment when the story tumbles forth at his feet, or when the shroud disappears revealing everything?

"You sound like Krimmel," I said. "Isn't the point of this exploration to vanish entirely from the world we know?"

"Well, you can't vanish by rushing, Cloud. Vanishing is gradual, Dixcy, isn't that right?"

"Vanishing is gradual."

"So is reappearing, and I wouldn't want to rush that either," he said.

"But judgment is eternal," I said.

"What's that supposed to mean?"

"It means he knows when he's had enough," said Dixcy.

Hicks appeared several minutes later wearing a long brown coat over the brown vest he was wearing before. He stepped back inside for his hat, also brown and defiantly unfashionable with its low crown and wide brim. It seemed to swallow his severe little head. He motioned to us and turned the corner. Victor hurried up and then strode along at his side. Leaves shattered beneath our feet and maple tree pods whirled and sailed. We crossed the small bridge and into the knoll now swelling — if only for a short hour on autumnal days like this — with light. And so we entered a golden orb inside of which the falling maple seeds dangled like earthly spirits. Even the stitching on Hicks's muted coat seemed to shout and dance in the light.

Hicks looked down as he walked and seemed to mutter and

clear his throat. "You are able to listen?" he asked Victor, who responded with a bright smile and nod of his head. Hicks started talking about Greenpoint, whom he called a "strange type of animal." And then he explained that of all the "usurers" he had known, Greenpoint was the most decent. "He's a weak man, but at least he is no elitist." He reminded Victor that in his religion there are no clerics and therefore no real hierarchy. So then you are a self-taught priest, wondered Victor. Hicks said no, the idea was repugnant.

"I'm just a lost lamb," he said. Victor, who was about six inches taller than Hicks, looked down at him and smiled benevolently. Hicks unlocked the gate and Victor put his hand on his back and thanked him for being so kind to show us his work.

As the golden light was swept into the front of the barn, I felt a calm envelop me. The dust in the air glistened, the specks as if they were somehow archaic, diminutive versions of the maple pods, and I had the feeling first of going deeper, past this world and into its origins, and then of intoxication. I breathed in and perhaps I closed my eyes thinking of the strange, shuddering somnolence of the day and of Mrs. Greenpoint and her furnishings.

Then we stepped into the barn, the front of which was a cluttered mess, every inch of the floor — indeed, there was a worn wooden floor — crammed, first with stacks of wood, pieces of all different sizes and shapes laid out in overflowing piles, others stacked to the rafters (where long boards were stored). Amidst the precarious towering boards there were wooden barrels filled with metal tools, awls, bevels, files, saws, chisels, planes, a level, a small bowl of corkscrews and others with paintbrushes, which he had clearly made himself. "Intoxication" — I had to write it down lest given these new circumstances I should forget it. As I pulled my notebook out of my bag, I lost my balance and caused a chain reaction that resulted in a slow collapse of thin pieces of trim, which slid underfoot. Victor shook his head in reproach. "Not now," he whispered.

Hicks had bandaged his finger with a piece of gray cloth tied with a string and he was holding it up in the air so that he appeared to be a guide leading us through the forest. We stopped in front of a very long, partially painted board, which was leaning on a bulky easel. The board had been divided in three vertical sections or panels, with the largest in the center being made to look like a bookcase with two shelves. On the shelves were various hats drawn in pencil. In the left section was a languorous landscape scene of a fox hunt. The fox was sinuous. It had a leopard's face and aristocratic eyes. The eyes of the hunt dog were feverish. There was only the outline of an old, bald tree on the right panel and a human form, possibly sitting on a log. "We are working on this for Mr. Brown, a hatter, perhaps you know him. It will take us another two or three weeks to finish this one, but Mr. Brown has in mind another, that is, unless this talk of a panic is real. You can't trust the news out of Philadelphia. But," he said, "I know this is not why you have come to see us." Hicks moved three large pieces of wood, each about the size of the hatter's sign and placed them to the side. Hicks excused himself for a minute and returned with two candles. He handed one to Dixcy and then led us into a space the size of a small bedroom. There was a rough curtain at the opposite end. Hicks held up his candle away from his body in order to project the light. His hand was shaking. Then he moved the candlestick slowly across the space, right to left, illuminating for us, one after another, pictures of a boy standing alongside a stream or a river (in some instances it is obvious the river is the Delaware and in others it appears to be a tributary cutting through a rocky glen), with his hand affectionately around the mane of a quiescent lion. In one picture the lion looks bewildered, as if he had lost something important and had given up trying to find it; in another he looks like a dog being pulled against its will across the floor by the child; in others he looks variously frightened, dazed, or desperately weary. In one picture the boy looks like he is hiding a secret; in another like he has been touched by God. The boy is dressed as a kind of Renaissance prince, or as the Christ child, or a fancy shepherd. But in several pictures he appears like Titian's *Venus Anadyomene*, a female with her head turned, gazing inwardly to the world that might be. In every picture, the boy is grabbing hold of a grapevine. "The blood of Christ," noted Victor, and we both looked up at Hicks, illuminated just then by Dixcy's candle, his hard face twisted by sadness and shame.

Hicks jostled the candle slightly and moved around the room so we could better see. The skin of his hands, I noticed, was dry and crackled and his nails were bitten short. His footsteps creaked solemnly and Victor, as he does, cleared his throat. In every picture a cow, a kind of witness to the scene, leans over the back of the lion. Sometimes she smiles knowingly. Next to the boy lies a sleepy animal — often looking like cat or a fox, but which we learned later is a wolf — and next to it a little lamb. In one picture the lamb is the same size as the wolf, and they are lying together like tender lovers, but in most of them the lamb is like a puppy nestling in the curved maternal embrace of the wolf. Below the lion, in the foreground of each picture, is a sheepish leopard, which lies quietly with a goat. Most often the goat's back is to the picture; he appears to be watching the boy. Sometimes the leopard sleeps and other times he stares out, eyes wide, foolish and shameful for swallowing his own instinct. But he doesn't seem to be able to comprehend what has happened.

Silent still, Hicks brought his candle over to one of the paintings and drew the light slowly along the top border. "THE PEACEABLE KINGDOM OF THE BRANCH," it read in the careful hand of the sign maker, and then, in gold lettering and starting in the lower left corner (Hicks moved his candle slowly enough for a child to read): "The wolf also shall dwell with the lamb and the leopard shall lie down with the kid; and the calf and the young lion and the fatling together; and a little child shall lead them."

"The prophesy of Isaiah," said Dixcy.

Hicks nodded but still didn't speak. Victor motioned for Dixcy to be quiet. And for a moment it seemed as if we were attending church or witnessing a funeral or that Hicks was a mute. Then Hicks pointed the candle — and Dixcy followed, providing extra illumination — to a tiny group of figures at the back of the picture plane, half of them virtually unclothed and the other half in the dreary costume of the Quakers. He walked to another painting. There at the bottom, along the painted border, it read, 'When man is led and moved by sovereign grace,' and then to another painting, this along the far wall, 'When the great Penn his famous treaty made with Indian chiefs beneath the elm tree's shade.'

"He is quoting from West," said Dixcy.

"Talk, go on, talk," said Hicks impatiently.

Victor pointed to squares painted into each corner of the border. "Innocence… Meekness… Liberty… in French, Latin, and Greek."

I looked around and counted. There were twenty-two paintings. In each one of them it was late summer or early autumn, the grape harvest. "Penn arrived in early October," said Victor, "isn't that right?"

Dixcy brought his candle over to one of the pictures and then another. "Cold light here, in this one, and warm light here," he said.

"I seek not perfection," said Hicks.

"Nor beauty," said Victor. "At least that's what you say. But, sir, we are prepared to listen."

Hicks drew his candle away and placed it on a small table at the opposite end of the room. "I don't know what you want," he said to Victor. "But I think it is time you took your leave. Greenpoint is a terrible demon. But he knows not. You, my friend, you know."

"What?"

"You know how to disrupt, how to upset, and I don't wish to hear it." It was the truth, or was it? Then, in that moment, I moved closer to Victor. Perhaps I was just being instinctively loyal. Perhaps I wished to be defiant.

"Sir," said Dixcy, "we are unenlightened young men. Easton — it is filled with signs of the devil. You see?"

"Then you're traveling with the wrong person," said Hicks. The little man stared hard at Victor. "And you're looking in the wrong place. Where do you think you're headed, anyway?"

We all three answered: Philadelphia, Baltimore, New York.

"The city is but an illusion, my friends," he replied. And then, looking directly at Victor, he said: "You won't make it out alive."

"We aren't afraid of the city," I said, boldly.

"One thing leads to another," said Hicks, "the fire flickers then it catches. You don't realize it." Then: "It isn't only the innocent who get burned."

Victor, all this time, grinned ear to ear. The fire flickers then the flood. It was Victor who would design the mill, the wheels, for God's sake, the gates, and Peale who lost his mind trying to deal with Rembrandt and Raphaelle and Titian—his own creations—and Krimmel, yes perhaps the most innocent of all of us, who was then the star. Then—.

After that, it became clear that Hicks's anger had subsided. He went over to the table and retrieved his candle. "You want to know what I am doing," he said as if he was talking to himself, and walked over to each of us and, one by one, took hold of our hands. "That is, yet again, the wrong question. What I do in here has no bearing, what you do has no bearing. I know what you want to say to me, that if it—my own hand, my own will—has no bearing then why even bother doing it, or doing anything, for that matter. And I will answer that the world is cruel, men are cruel and misguided, and if you will, this is where I find the harmony between my mortal flesh and my immortal spirit, which is filled with the light of God. When this harmony is achieved, there is peace. So this is a prayer, not a painting. And that one is a prayer, and so is that one. Am I ashamed? I have been ashamed, because it looks to you like a work of art, filled with pretense and design, as if I considered myself some kind of God. That's why I went out, like you, on a journey, to see if harmony could be made to exist out there through ministry alone. I went as far as the shores of Lake Ontario, to see if harmony could be uncovered in the wilderness."

I took Dixcy's candle and walked slowly around the room, pressing the light against the pictures. A vision entered my mind, of Hicks enraged, setting fire to the workshop. And then

I corrected myself: Oh, but the fire already rages inside him and he can barely control it. It smolders in his lion, it sears the heart of the leopard, the poor beast wishes only to extend his claws and pounce…

I lifted the candle and looked over at Hicks. He was speaking directly to Victor and it sounded like he was giving a sermon. He was explaining the four humors—fire, air, water, and earth, which are present in all living creatures. He said that when one of the humors outweighs the others in the material being of a person, the result is a certain kind of personality and that personality is best understood by the behavior of certain animals. Hicks went on describing these correlations: fire, choleric as the lion; air, sanguine as the leopard; water, phlegmatic as the bear; and earth, melancholic as the wolf. These were familiar concepts, which of course the three of us disavowed as out-of-date, but no one dared interrupt or argue. Victor was smiling as he listened.

"You will note," Hicks said, looking now at Dixcy, "another correlation. This is with the very words of Isaiah, the prophet of the Lord." He explained that Isaiah singled out the peaceful animals—the lamb, the kid, the calf, and the cow—and paired them with the wolf, the leopard, the lion, and the bear. These were strategic pairings. Being docile and trusting, the lamb will force the melancholic wolf to abandon his self-obsession. Now he will have someone beside himself to think about and care for. Of course, every shepherd knows he has to separate the sheep from the goat—for the goat, though peaceful, is headstrong and will always try to dominate the sheep. So the prophet Isaiah gives the kid to the leopard. The leopard wants company, the leopard wants to drink and dance and cavort all night. He is a sensual beast. And what does the kid do? Hicks raised his eyeglasses to his forehead and slowly walked over to one of his paintings; in this one the figures are draped in cold morning light, phlegmatic light, I guessed he might say, and Penn and the Indians look like lead soldiers arranged by a child's hand, and he said, "You see, he gives him the cold shoulder," and indeed the kid is turned harshly away from the leopard. Where does that leave the leopard? With no one to play with, he can't just pounce. He has to think first, to reflect and reconsider. The leopard is a hard one to tame, perhaps not quite as hard as the lion. But the ox is heavy and slow and watchful. The lion is arrogant, and the ox just turns to him and says too bad, you'll have to eat hay with me. And the ox doesn't care if the lion strikes out. He is just as strong.

"There is no bear," I said.

"No, no," replied Hicks, "I cannot stomach the bear. He has no feeling. The cow is paired with the bear, but I cannot understand why. But the prophet Isaiah said they would live in peace." How is that possible? Look inside, he instructed. "I make it sound easy, but it isn't. I don't mean obsess over your own cursed self, seeing yourself as somehow special or somehow God-like or somehow important or somehow persecuted. I was young like you once and prone to thinking I was powerful and then consequently wasting all that power on lust and drink." Hicks leaned in closer to us. His eyes were full of torment and sadness, his lips were pursed. "You," he said, pointing to Dixcy, "you are the lone wolf. You're serious, or believe you are. And quiet, you don't say much, but you know everything. But what else, what else are you thinking? You don't wish to say, do you? Beware, friends, there is a wolf in sheep's clothing right among you. He doesn't like the sunshine, does he?"

Victor laughed and then so did I. Hicks stepped forward.

"Three times," he explained, "I have lost everything. Not once or twice, but three times is what it takes until you recognize that peace is impossible without the inner light. There are people who think it is a fine thing to fleece other people, that is a whole way of life, isn't it? Fine for some. But strip a man three times and that man will learn how to look inside. That's what I mean," he said, "about looking inside. Look inside and realize what you've told yourself is there isn't there at all."

Somehow emboldened by his talk of inner light, I asked Hicks if he had ever found the opportunity to speak with Charles Willson Peale and his sundry kin about his animal kingdom.

"Peale might as well have corks in his ears. I don't speak

to him. Difficult for a lion. Especially hard for the lion to listen. Only he'll listen to the wolf, because he intrigues the lion, because he can't quite understand him."

"So that, I suppose, makes me the lion?" Victor said, glancing at Dixcy.

"No," said Hicks.

"Perhaps the leopard then?"

"No," Hicks answered, turning away.

"You," he said to me. "A writer steals, doesn't he? He says little, but he coolly waits, he coolly observes, and he has his notebook and that's where everything ends up. His notebook is like a bucket he carries with him. He goes on his way, encountering places and people, perhaps even loved ones, and he listens to their thoughts and utterances, and he takes them, he throws them in his bucket. He appropriates. Now they belong to him. The thing is, he doesn't even want all of them. Certainly he disregards most of the things he collects. That's his power, to pick and choose, to give life and to take away."

"You mean Caleb here is a bear?" said Victor.

And all at once we three simultaneously wondered about Krimmel. A bear like me? A wolf like Dixcy? A lion like Peale?

Hicks clenched his fists. "I have said too much," he said. His eyes were wide and distant, himself like the leopard he must have imagined Krimmel to be looking out beyond us into the field. "I don't know why I invited you in here. Because you know Greenpoint and I am indebted to him. I like to talk. I wish I didn't talk so much."

That night, we ate dinner at the inn. The inn was called The Brick House and like the night before, it was crowded and noisy. A fiddler played and Victor danced with a tall woman in an orange dress. After that, I didn't see him again. Dixcy and I sat at a table near the open back door. The air was warm, but there was a stench of illness or death. Dixcy thought it was likely a horse had died and hadn't yet been taken away. He said it smelled of blood and that perhaps it meant a mare had died giving birth. It's unusual for a horse to bleed to death, usually the cause is dehydration or starvation. Sometimes a broken leg. I said that when I was young and we lived in Philadelphia, one winter it snowed for three days straight without stop, in tiny little flakes that blew in enormous drifts as tall as my father. During the storm, the city went silent, not just quiet, but muffled, as if the idea of sound had been banished forever. The morning the snow finally ended the sun glistened brilliantly, the thick blanket of snow was like an endless cloud, and the cloudless sky was the blue of the endless sea, as if the world had been turned upside down. All the city was light and for those first few hours it remained noiseless. Not even the usual banging of the knife sharpener on his rounds or the voices of the carters and the chimney sweeps. It was as if no one dared disturb the perfection. But then, slowly, people emerged from hiding. We children were first but then suddenly the street was filled with men — so many men as I'd never seen before — shoveling out the streets and sidewalks. This went on for two days until finally the first people appeared in their carriages, thinking they might go about their normal business. But one after the other their carriages would get stuck. A few fell over on their sides, dragging their horses down with them. The weather turned sharply cold and the snow, which had melted slightly in the sun, froze in treacherous mounds. Carriage wheels couldn't gain traction, horses slid into one another and by the end of the fourth day after the snow had ended, the streets of the city were flecked with dead and dying horses, sometimes two or three per square. Because it was impossible to collect them, the horses were butchered on the spot.

"The city smelled of blood?" wondered Dixcy.

But before I could answer, Greenpoint came over to our table. He sat down next to Dixcy and asked the barmaid for three mugs of ale. Then he asked about our meeting with Hicks. Dixcy said it went how he expected it would. "When you think about it, artists are dreadful human beings."

"He isn't an artist," I said.

Greenpoint smiled incredulously, once more foxlike, the top half of his head lifting to the ceiling.

"Then what is he?" said Dixcy.

"A bit of a vexed fellow."

"But he is an artist," said Dixcy, all the while Greenpoint looked back and forth at us, bemused. "And that means he is a god. What is that workshop of his, if not his own secret world?"

"The not very peaceful kingdom of the east branch of the Neshaminy Creek," laughed Greenpoint. "He didn't want to show you his paintings, you know. Perhaps that was obvious, but he doesn't want anyone to see them. To him, they are sin. But, let me tell you, it's all he can do. He tried farming, because it is Godly work, but wasn't cut out for it. It nearly killed him. If I didn't sell his property, I don't know what he would have done, tell you the truth. So he thinks he can paint simple signs for honest people—he is the best sign maker in the county— and support his family."

"But then he wanders uncontrollably to the back of the workshop," I said.

"Exactly, like a child, hoping no one will notice."

"I liked the paintings," said Dixcy, who swallowed his beer, excused himself, and went upstairs to bed.

Chapter V

*T*he next morning, all three of us were up by six and on the road a half hour later. The clouds were low and the air was humid. All the morning we walked in silence. Victor had us on a route heading east, back toward the Delaware River. In certain places he told us to walk through someone's field or open their gate and go around their barn because it would be more direct to go that way. Each time he was right and we ended up on a main road or at least on a path to a main road, which put us near to the ferry for Trenton. "Why do we have to cross the river?" wondered Dixcy. "If we cross now, we'll have to cross back to Philadelphia. We can't cover two passages."

"I want to see Trenton," said Victor, ignoring Dixcy, "it's the most beautiful city in America."

We took the three o'clock ferry and arrived in Trenton five minutes later. The approach on the ferry brought us beneath a canopy of trees, extending along the shore of the river. At the end of the trees, which had been planted in an even row to mark the edge of an estate, appeared the ovular gold dome of the capital.

"Novo Caesarea," said Dixcy.

"What the hell are you talking about?" said Victor, "Novo Caesarea, who comes up with these things?"

"That's the name," replied Dixcy, who was looking off into the distance. The bags under his eyes had darkened and his skin looked green.

"What do you mean, 'that's the name'?"

"In the original charter, that's what it's called. And it's not a good thing." Dixcy looked like he was going to be ill. He explained that Sir George Carteret was the lieutenant governor of the isle of Jersey. Sir George made himself famous—or infamous—by defending Jersey and King Charles himself, who was exiled there, from the liberating forces of Oliver Cromwell. In other words, Carteret was a flack for the Crown. "Of course," he said, "so was William Penn." As a reward, the king granted Carteret the land in the New World.

"Which tells us nothing about Caesar."

"Some people say the original name of Jersey was Caesarea and that the town of Le Pinacle was built on a Roman ruin. There may be evidence of this."

"But really, Carteret just wanted it to sound important," said Victor.

"Or Charles wanted to align himself with Caesar, who also endured civil war and capture. Charles was a giant. He stood over six feet tall and had children with a dozen different women."

"All right, lone wolf, how do you know all this? The better question is why. Maybe you should crawl out of the shadows a little more often, talk to some real people. Listen to the falls, for this time of year the river is really rushing."

We walked up a little lane behind the State House and then headed down State Street, which was lined with mansions. At Greene Street we found a covered market, still going. We negotiated for six apples, a good piece of hard cheese, and two loaves of bread. They called it water bread. In my notebook, I wrote, "The bread is salty and dry, like I imagine a clamshell must taste if it was to be lifted out of the sand and licked." The cheese was creamy, not much harder than butter. From the market, we found ourselves on Hanover Street. The houses were lined up straight. "Miniature mansions," Victor called them, "like little semblances of the great houses one block away." We walked and ate and Dixcy kept worrying that we wouldn't leave enough food for later. Victor went on calling him the lone wolf and me the bear cub. Neither of us called him the lion.

Eventually the conversation carried back to Hicks. Dixcy repeated what he had said to Greenpoint, that despite professing otherwise, Hicks had certainly invented his own world, over which he was master. "There will always be peace in his land," he said.

"But not happiness," I said.

"He isn't even master over it, I don't think," said Victor, "the opposite, in fact, these ideas—that denying one's will, for example is the way to allow in the light of God, or that the matter of man is separate from the spirit—these ideas are mastering him. He can't quite control any of it. Anyway, the animals wish to rebel. Did you see that? They're angry their will has been taken."

"It doesn't matter if he's mastering his world or if it's mastering him. The point is," I said, "he has a vision, even if it's tortured."

"How foolish," said Victor, quoting La Mettrie, "to torment ourselves so much about things which we can not know—"

"And which would not make us any happier even were we to gain knowledge about them," I said, finishing the line. "But he ought to go in *The Book of Masters*, isn't that what you thought, Dixcy?"

"Spare us the title," he said.

"We don't have to know much, all we have to do is visit the artists and listen to them and ask questions," said Victor. "Two down already."

We had turned onto Stockton Street and now we were

staring at a large, muddy creek and beyond it four of five giant mills under construction. "As far as you can see, Cloud!"

We crossed the creek and were now walking south down Broad Street. Victor wanted to continue on until we reached the edge of the city and then continue on toward Bordentown. "We'll knock at the gate of Bonaparte's manor," he said, but Dixcy, who saw this coming, said no, it was a terrible idea, that even if this were a good idea it was the wrong time. We were filthy and tired and had no idea what we were doing. Dixcy covered his face with his hands and then turned away, facing the brick wall of a building. Victor put his arms around him and said he only wanted to see the Bonaparte estate, have a sense of it, where it is and what it looks like, that ever since I had mentioned it, he hadn't been able to get it out of his mind that the brother of Napoleon, himself a former king, a man who could order armies, who could bring terror if he wished, or love if he so desired, was living so plainly among them. "Like an ordinary republican," he said. "But you're right, we're all filthy and tired."

"But look at you, you bathed last night," said Dixcy.

"I was bathed, that is true." For a minute, Victor stared at Dixcy.

"What the hell are you talking about?" I said.

"Look," said Victor, "a lady like Mrs. Greenpoint isn't ever uncertain of her needs."

That night, Victor and I lay beneath a chestnut tree on a bluff twenty feet above the river. The ground on which we lay was soft and a little wet. It was drizzling sporadically. Dixcy, who had found a spot about ten feet closer to the road under a very low-hanging branch of an old apple tree, had placed his leather sack beneath his head as a pillow. He hadn't yet forgiven Victor. Dixcy was reading La Mettrie, carefully turning the pages, and sniffling slightly. Victor was humming to himself, and I lay silently, with my eyes closed. The sky, the trees, the wind, the breathing of my compatriots, the footsteps of rodents, the city of Trenton—with its golden dome and water bread—all seemed far away, in the immense distance. For a moment, I drifted off to sleep and when I opened my eyes Victor was saying something and removing an object from his pocket. It was a little Indian doll, made of straw. "Look, Cloud," he said, holding it in front of my face, "look at the head, there is a face on both sides."

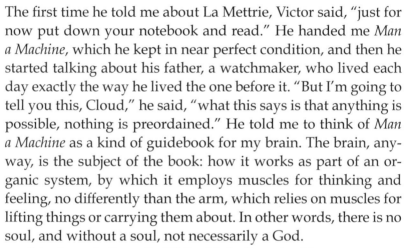

The first time he told me about La Mettrie, Victor said, "just for now put down your notebook and read." He handed me *Man a Machine*, which he kept in near perfect condition, and then he started talking about his father, a watchmaker, who lived each day exactly the way he lived the one before it. "But I'm going to tell you this, Cloud," he said, "what this says is that anything is possible, nothing is preordained." He told me to think of *Man a Machine* as a kind of guidebook for my brain. The brain, anyway, is the subject of the book: how it works as part of an organic system, by which it employs muscles for thinking and feeling, no differently than the arm, which relies on muscles for lifting things or carrying them about. In other words, there is no soul, and without a soul, not necessarily a God.

"And you believe that?" I said, feeling stupid.

"I believe you believe it, even if you don't realize it this moment," he said.

I told him then about my own father, who was a gilder when I was young. He had taught himself and then went out on his own, from church to church, offering his services. Did he believe in God? Once, he put my face onto the body of the baby Christ in a mural inside the Moravian church of York. By then we had already left Lancaster, where I had been born, and we didn't stay long at York, which, so they say, is just as well. There wasn't enough work for such a talented man as my father. We came to Philadelphia, I went on telling Victor, when I was eight and my father thought he was going to do quite well for himself as a looking glass silverer, a position he took immediately in the shop of Christian Geiss. But Geiss refused to believe that an American worker could be trained properly in an age-old craft and therefore wouldn't ever allow him to do more than prepare and arrange the tools and polish the finish product. He would finish a day's work so deeply unsatisfied that he would sit in the back of the Dogs and the Moon Tavern, with his face bent toward the brazier—which is where mother and I would find him—inventing ways to dispose of Geiss and take over the business. Soon, however, he took a position as a saddlesticher and after that a paintgrinder. For some reason in those days I always had the impression—maybe because his hands were stained purple black, sometimes blood red, sometimes the brown of shit—that he would lick his fingers, and this too must have been merely a childhood impression, because one could tell if the pigments were the right grade only by tasting them. Then one day, I said to Victor, his fingers were clean again. He had turned in his paintgrinder's primitive tools for a glassblower's apron. Glassblowing became brickmaking and then sugarboiling, and for a while he owned a tavern in Kensington. When that started to turn sour, my mother threatened to leave and my father took up with a wench whose own husband was often drunk on the floor of the tavern. So we left Philadelphia. I was twelve. My mother took me and my two brothers and my sister Ann and she talked her way onto a stage heading north. We got off at Easton. My brothers sold themselves as farmhands and I began to drift, across fields, under fences, down alleys and up to the tops of silver smooth apple trees, and eventually to the river's edge, wading in along with cattle the color of boiled sugar, hiding as I watched the Indians, especially the girls, the women, even the old women with their wide, weathered faces, their looks of indifference, indifference even to indifference, and trying to the hear the notes of their language, which is called Unami and comes to a stop like a dead bird fallen from a tree and skipping a little as it hits the ground.

It was there I had found Victor, or rather, Victor had found me. And what had I been doing? Teaching myself how to live, or so I thought, by escaping from the dumb brutality of my brothers, who it seemed had inherited only my father's magnetic attraction to failure and none of the search for perfection, for the transcendence of precision, that would eventually bring about his doom. Not that he was out of the picture, my father. No, he had caught up to us, and now wasn't he the meanest carter roaming the tiny streets of our little village. I was learning how to live, for example, by spending certain winter afternoons bathing in the light through the tall windows of Library Hall and certain spring evenings in the honey arms of an Indian girl whose breath tasted of celery, but I *didn't know how to think about it*. Victor taught me that.

Over the course of the months that followed, as the spring air became dense and warm and the flow of our rivers calmed and the Indians abandoned the river bank for their rough garden plots, the swell of carp and trout having thinned, we would find each other on the stone bridge (or beneath its arches, in the startling cool of the shade) or, if it was evening, we would crouch with the scrub oak and the dust and starry moss high above the town. On those occasions as night would fall we would marvel over the smell of darkness, competing with each other to see who could describe the greatest number and most interesting smells that together produced the feeling of evening descending, that together gave us a sense of the earth retreating into its own somnolent cave. We agreed it was a test of imagination as much as sensitivity to smell, but as the summer wore on we noticed our faculty growing so much so that we could both detect the hot breath of cattle being led across the pasture below—of course we could hear their bells striking slightly against the breeze—a sensation that led us to consider the ways each of the five senses blur into one another, touch into taste, taste into smell, smell into hearing, hearing into sight, and I felt more aware of Victor—the small pimples beneath his jaw, the strawberry blush of his high cheekbones, the confidence of the flat fingers, the deep perfume of his voice — than I had of anyone ever before. Sometimes he would bring along the slender, dark-haired Dixcy, son of the town surveyor, and on those occasions I would retreat into my notebook, silently, carefully writing, conscious of the dark shadows beneath Dixcy's eyes and of his strange hold over Victor, who would talk louder and louder while his companion would smirk and fidget. "He's brilliant," Victor whispered in my ear one July evening. We were lying on our backs facing the sky. Dixcy had climbed down the rock face to relieve himself off the ledge. "But," said Victor, "he doesn't know how to talk to people, that's why I bring him up here. Also, he's crazy."

"So?"

"So he needs us."

When Dixcy returned, Victor climbed to his feet. "Damn it!" he said. "I need to get out of here. Wait. Listen, don't answer. I mean we all need to get out of here. Nothing against Easton. That's precisely not my point. It's just simply and gloriously a village, say what you will about bucolic fields — "

"They are interesting in their own right," I said proudly.

"They are interesting in their own right, yes, and which of us thinks that telling the difference between sheep sorrel and knotweed is our best nourishment?"

"The knotweed is sour, just taste it," said Dixcy. He was now sitting with Victor and I standing over him, his eyes bloodshot and his voice shallow from asthma.

"Exactly. The knotweed flourishes here, but you, Dixcy, look at yourself, you do not. And von Cloud here is only a half a step away from being apprenticed to a canal digger."

"The canal diggers don't use apprentices, there is nothing to apprentice."

"Exactly again! And to our friend La Mettrie, what is the most untenable human attitude? False modesty, my great and willing accomplices, false modesty. Easton is giving us all false modesty. Let us go grow into what nature has provided, let us develop in ways we can't possibly do here."

"Following your logic, eventually nowhere will be acceptable. London? Paris? Babylon? No, nothing," muttered Dixcy. "I am not convinced and anyway, I'm going now. The cows need milking."

"Cloud?" said Victor.

"No," interrupted Dixcy, "don't put him on the spot. You come up with something *solid*. And you ask us again how we feel."

Victor laughed at Dixcy's pronouncement and the deep, hungry laugh hung there in the wooden air with the buzzing of the mosquitoes and the darting of chipmunks until Dixcy did raise himself and scamper away. "He's sick," said Victor. But then he turned to me and paused a moment and swallowed and put his hands on my shoulders as if to bless me or push me down into a crevice of the earth. He squeezed, he swallowed again, this time even more noticeably. "The stars will be out tonight, Caleb," he said. "I think it would be good if we both took notice of them tonight. Don't you think?" I thought to embrace him for it seemed as if tears were about to well up in his eyes, but Victor turned immediately and walked out through the tangle of scrub pines and cosseted sycamores and past the lone sour cherry tree that was our marker and that was filled top to bottom with cherries. I watched him for a while and then I lay in the ruddy, fleshy ground with my hands behind my head staring up at the vanishing sky, a color blue that made me think it must really be an endless sea.

Dixcy woke with a bad cough and so we decided we wouldn't hurry to Philadelphia. If it took two days or even three, it didn't matter. In Burlington we purchased a box of yellow plums and talked to a girl with a large nose and small eyes tending her mother's garden. The girl wore a yellow dress with gold sleeves and was singing a song about Dr. Sangrado who climbed in windows in the middle of the night to bleed people in their beds, "even if they have no fever." She came over to the fence. The hem of her skirt was stained brown from dirt. Victor asked her what time the steam boat leaves for Philadelphia. She shrugged and looked at us plaintively. Then she said a man named Varnet was upstairs with her mother. "And that is why I have these radishes to dig," she said, and smiled at Dixcy. The next afternoon we arrived in Camden, walked to the ferry dock and sat on the ground in the sun.

After a while, an attendant came over and asked if we had secured our passage. Victor stood quickly, made a conspiratorial gesture to the agent, and paid the fare. "What was that all about?" said Dixcy.

"What all about?"

"Like you're secreting us away."

"How much was the fare?" I asked. "I'm surprised we had enough."

"We had enough, and we have plenty left over to secure lodging, thank you very much."

Victor's face was flush with excitement.

"What the devil do you mean?" I stood. The sun was high and the air sheer and sharp as mountain air, the silent air of endless time.

"Where'd you get the money, Victor?" Dixcy stood now too, in the bright unceasing light and for a moment I saw us from afar and from there we appeared like foreign beasts. "She paid you — isn't that a little unbelievable?"

"What do you mean, she paid him for what?"

"Well, Victor, for what?"

"For Krimmel's sketch, seventy-five dollars."

"That's his money."

"Exactly, Cloud, that's what I mean. Krimmel won't mind if we took his sketch if we made him some money on it. It fetched a good price and she'll take good care of it."

"Then give him the money."

"Caleb, don't be so pure. We'll return the money. Victor will put half aside, and when we see Krimmel in Philadelphia, we'll give it to him first thing. He'll be happy to know it's in the collection of such a sophisticated lady."

"We're going to make him famous, are we."

"You're both of you fatally corrupted."

"Better than being corrupted fatally."

As soon as we crossed the river, Dixcy insisted that we immediately find a boarding house. "It's harder to figure these things out in the dark," he said. We came up through the market. I had my notebook out, but we were walking quickly. As we crossed Fourth Street, someone I didn't see called out, "*L'écrivain est arrivée!*"

"*Vive la révolution!*" yelled Victor, and I noticed his lips were wet as he smiled.

We found a room at the edge of the market in Mrs. Chamberlaine's boardinghouse. She was stout and hard of hearing. Her daughter Libby, who wore her black hair in a bun and smelled of musk, took us upstairs. The walls were painted burgundy. Libby wore a white, loose-fitting dress and an engraved silver ring on her finger. She had thin lips and dirty fingernails. Victor tried to draw her into conversation, but she ignored him. When she left us, she closed the door softly. The door crept back open and Dixcy went right to bed. Victor and I went out to see the city. He wanted to return to the wharf. "That's where the life is," he said.

"And you can smell the sea, I think," I responded.

We walked and talked about faces. Victor said he could guess what a person would sound like just by looking at her face. "Take Libby, the girl in the boarding house. I knew she would be curt."

"You're full of shit," I said, "and besides, you sound like Hicks. She's what—a wolf or a bear?"

"So little you know, Cloud. That one is obviously a snake."

When we returned to the room it was already dark. Dixcy was wandering around, agitated. His copy of *Man a Machine* was missing. Victor tried to calm him, tried to help him think about where it might be, but Dixcy wasn't listening. He bounced around the barely furnished room searching. He moved the same wooden chair three times. Finally, he stopped and sat down and looked up at us. He grunted and said quite dourly, "I wouldn't be surprised if this place was full of thieves."

PART TWO

Chapter VI

*Charles Willson Peale, outside the
Pennsylvania Academy of Fine Arts, the
corner of Tenth and Chestnut Streets,
Philadelphia, September 25, 1818*

Alas, Rembrandt has once more proven his power of perception. This morning, overdressed for the Indian summer and unused to the heat of the city, I had a chaise bring me to the Pennsylvania Academy to have a preview of the annual exhibition. Hardly had I made it into the vestibule when Birch greeted me in his usual affable way. Though it was only ten o' clock, I could smell a pungent ale on his breath. I ignored it, and as we walked around the hall, I listened carefully to his explanation of the work he had decided to exhibit, which included two simple pieces by my son Raphaelle, and the portrait of Emperor Napoleon on his horse by his brother Rembrandt. Just then, across the hall, workers were installing a portrait of the emperor's family by the great David. It couldn't be quite fair to my son to have placed his Napoleon, acknowledged by him to have been done in haste, in such proximity to that one by a court master.

Should I press the matter with Birch? I pondered this question as we came upon a series of animal sketches done by my younger son Titian II, a talented boy, certainly, though I doubt he will rise much above engraver. "Did Rembrandt not speak to you of his current work?" I asked, "I mean to say were you expecting something else from him? Perhaps I—."

But as I said these words, Birch with his hands clasped behind his back turned away to address a question from one of the workmen hanging the David. Left alone in mid-sentence, feeling the fool, for some reason naked despite the excess of layers, I continued alone down the long wall. There I encountered a watercolor sketch only so large, a Chestnut Street scene with the State House in the background and a scrim of people—hundreds of them like gray, mounting rats—vying for what I came to realize was influence over the vote. As the exhibition book wasn't yet ready, I couldn't check the authorship of the sketch, but I knew it to be the hand of Krimmel. Slowly, now absorbed, I looked over the work and became impressed, despite the density of the crowd, with its insight. This Krimmel had done as I had done with my famous painting of the lifting of the mastodon bones, by telling a story through the people represented in the picture—though clarity would have been achieved had he used the pictorial plane to space out the subjects. I sifted through the faces, a few of them dignified, most others quite devilish, and then looked upon the State House building, which Krimmel had rendered with precision and detail, even as it receded into the distance.

Now absorbed, I lost track of the sound of the workers' voices and the clapping of Birch's footsteps. I bent closer, for despite my near perfect eyesight, the softness of the watercolor left my mind wanting for detail. As I looked closely at the State House, where my Museum is located on the second floor, I came upon the most remarkable sight: my son Rubens, keeper of the Museum, standing on the windowsill, a slender and disproportionately long arm extended up to the roof attempting to capture his escaped sapajou Christopher Columbus. And what's more: there I was, with my head out the window, like an old fool directing him.

It took me some time to digest this deception. Nay, it should be called a thievery. Whatever Krimmel's point, whether to denigrate me or my Museum, or perhaps the practice of democracy as some foreigners are inclined to do, I realized my son had been right to warn me about the German. I made a second glance at the sketch and I had to admit there was much care and precision about it. This made me only more perplexed and angry, the German I had hoped would have much to contribute to the arts of America. Immediately, I remembered he had left for Germany some time ago. What was his picture doing in the exhibition in the first place?

A moment later, Birch reappeared at my side. Mr. Bonaparte had arrived at the Academy to supervise the hanging of a portrait done of his brother by David. Would I like to meet him? "Well, yes, of course," I responded, "but Birch, what is this all about? There's something unnatural about this picture." My voice felt distant even in my own head and the room seemed to expand, menacingly. I couldn't put to words the indignity of the monkey. "The man is no longer with us, so why the devil does his work belong in this show?"

"When John was forced to go, he left me a few works to do with as I pleased. I hung his *Cherry Woman with Children* in last year's show, as you might recall. It was you, Mr. Peale, who lauded him for the likeness of the peddler and the manner in which he told the fable of greed and justice."

"He hasn't reappeared, has he?"

"Who?"

"This Krimmel."

"I feel certain I would know it. Now, Mr. Peale, we can't keep Mr. Bonaparte waiting."

"You'll take this down."

"It's not a matter for discussion, sir." The nose of Birch was red, his eyes the downy gray of a finch.

"The *Cherry Woman* may have been worthy of this Academy, but this painting is a subversion. It's a danger."

Ignoring me, Birch took my arm. "Can't keep the emperor's brother waiting, Mr. Peale. John Krimmel is as free as any of us to speak his mind. Even from distant Germany. That's the beauty of this place, isn't it?"

I was presently marched off like a court joker. Ah, the man reeked of his ill habit, a fine way to present oneself to a king.

Joseph Bonaparte, inside the exhibition hall of the Pennsylvania Academy of Fine Arts, Tenth and Chestnut Streets, September 25, 1818

Everyone has seen that odd duck Rembrandt Peale's controversial portrait of my younger brother. A select few have even had the opportunity to enjoy the busts and portraits I put on display at the Academy. It is impossible not to see a resemblance. There should be no shame or embarrassment in confusing us. After all: I too was a king.

I have heard the rumors. Forget rumors. It is now enough to encounter such doubt on the faces I see before me.

But banish any thoughts of a conspiracy, of a grand *tromperie*, as it were, at once. Despite the striking similarity of our features and a near match in our profiles, and despite the uncanny, eerily, impossibly close pitch of our voices, and despite even the almost unbelievable story of our escape from Waterloo, which of course includes my own offer to my brother to trade identities so that he should more easily escape, I should not now be confused for him.

Instead of endlessly ruminating over mere possibilities, it is far more convincing to visit this city's petite Academy of Fine Art on Chestnut Street, between Tenth Street Delaware and Eleventh Street (clever these names!), where I can recommend a half dozen pieces I have loaned to this year's annual exhibition (these in addition to my brother's generous gift of Piranesi's engravings on behalf of the French Republic). Please, carefully look at our family portraits by Jacques-Louis David and the fine and noble bust of my brother by Antoine-Denis Chaudet. Even Rembrandt Peale's adaptation of David's *Bonaparte Crossing the Alps* at the Great St. Bernard will do. I'm afraid the original can't at this moment be removed from my salon on Ninth Street. On this subject, I should say no more.

By the way, I think the nautical painter Birch has done a splendid job making do with the Academy. What more can be expected? Perhaps, as so many Americans believe, it is a waste, all this focus on art, when there is so much a young nation must do. Or is it not even enough? Americans have a charming trait: they believe it is possible to manufacture a civilization. *Voilà!* There is your literature and your music and your art. It surely can't be possible that all one must do is name his children for Titian, Raphaello, Rubens, or Rembrandt? Can this really be? As a father myself, I understand the instinct to embolden one's offspring with a dignified name. A witty name, a family name, all this is important. But I know the fragile state of the child. To burden it! Perhaps just as I am burdened. No? Isn't that what comes to mind?

I have recently met the elder Mr. Peale, and I found him simple, a bit rough, impatient. Not a few moments into our conversation, he seized on the idea of painting my portrait. Just then workers were — gingerly! — hanging the legendary David's portrait of my family in the Academy's exhibition hall. Mr. Peale told me David had been his son Rembrandt's greatest mentor; West, he told me just the same, had been his. I sighed. I hope that doesn't betray poor breeding.

We stood together in that room a while. I was struck then by great longing for my daughters, for the slight Zenaïde, for the voluptuous Lalotte. She — the most precocious, self-possessed of all — can paint with more feeling, oh, than that poor Rembrandt Peale. I am sorry. Forgive me. I do not wish to criticize. I love this country and in many ways I find this city quite a bit more than adequate.

Eliza Hamm, the corner of Third and Spruce Streets, Philadelphia, September 26, 1818

Truth be told, the first time that little man in satin slippers came to my stand I was a little taken aback. He looked eerily familiar. Had I seen him before? A Chestnut Street dandy? Or one of Ricketts's performers, the lion tamer or the evil magician? I sold him a dozen of my best yellow peaches and a fine box of cultivated blackberries. As he bent forward to press the gold coin in my hand — "for you, madam," he insisted — I got a good whiff of lavender perfume. And — I got a dose of that pitiful accent.

I fished out the proper change from my apron and studied his peculiar olive-colored face, so waxen I might have seen my own reflection in the cheeks. When he calmly bowed his head as he turned to leave, I had to keep myself from laughing right in his face. Well then, right away I asked around. Didn't I get an earful! Of course this latest customer of mine is Napoleon himself, and not his brother Joseph, and why don't people see the obvious truth: from here, he's plotting the invasion of Mexico. Tom Birch — he's a customer of mine too, they all are these artists — called the theory a "great pile of rubbish" and explained, however, that during Napoleon's reign, this Joseph Bonaparte was, in fact, King of Spain. "I think he was quite powerless," says Mr. Birch, "and spent his time seducing his wife's chambermaid, but he was king."

Well I don't care if he was or is or someday might be a king. We don't have *kings* in this country. You come here, you work like the rest of us, and if you don't like it, well, I can point you to Mr. Cope's wharf. There's something my father liked to say. "We each go to the shitter the same," is what he always said. Excuse my French!

This "king" of ours has become a steady customer. What can I say? He delights in my apples. Each time, he presses a gold coin into my sweaty palm. I feign disinterest, even disgust. He smiles. I can't deny the feeling that one day he'll squeeze my hand and raise it to his lips. Until then, I scowl.

Chapter VII

Charles Willson Peale, Belfield,
October 3, 1818

*A*fter greeting the rather slender Mr. Bonaparte, I made it my business to interrogate Birch about Krimmel's effrontery. He called the appearance of the monkey in the picture "a harmless jibe," and in any case, "healthy for our art endeavor."

"Since when is insult healthy?" I wished to know.

"When it speaks of freedom, Mr. Peale," he said. And then added, "the practice of art is changing, sir, perhaps in retirement" — the haughty bastard, and to think who supported him in his rise in the Academy — "it isn't easy to keep up."

"Changing?"

The nautical painter ignored my question. "But doesn't your own son Raphaelle enjoy a visual pun?"

"He may be a crazy fellow — nay, he is as well trained and practiced as any artist in America." Birch wouldn't look me in the eye, but I resisted the temptation to forcefully grab his upper arm. Outside, on Tenth Street, an infant, or a cat, screeched, and Birch's attention drifted. A picture has a purpose, I noted to myself, and what is Krimmel's? To destroy me? "But what's the meaning of the monkey, Birch?"

"Consider it an advertisement for the Museum, Mr. Peale, front and center."

"Did Mr. Bonaparte comment on the art in the gallery?"

"You mean did he see the Napoleon of Rembrandt?"

"No, did he see the way we allow dissent, Birch, did you point it out to him?"

That afternoon, in my painting room, I sat near the window and reread the latest letter from my son in Baltimore. Raised as all my children were on the fruit of our American enlightenment, he is the first of the brood to make it his life's work, as it has been mine. Ever the literalist, Rembrandt has recently invented a New Method in portrait painting meant to better enlighten the subject. It was this innovation he was describing in his letter.

Following his careful drawing and instructions, I built his recommended apparatus, which employs a mirror and a magnifying glass, and set about making a picture of my neighbor, the calico stamper Tharp. This man hardly understood my interest in making his portrait but seemed sympathetic to the idea of innovation in art, and—I trust!—seemed open to granting an apprenticeship to my young wayward son Linnaeus. I sense he agreed to the portrait as a form of repayment. Last autumn a violent storm carried off his dam. We acted quickly, my boys and I, and helped him restore it, and so the burst dam did little damage to my fields and equipment. (I had been most worried about debris wrecking my little threshing mill.) Sensitive to his work schedule and not wanting to be more of nuisance than I was already, I carried the magnifying glass, the mirror, and the wooden supports up the lane, skirting the creek without getting my shoes too wet, and set up in his mill's small office.

I will admit, as long I'm already revealing so much, that I had another motivation for painting Mr. Tharp "on location." I have been toying with plans to improve my farm, and wring more value out of the land—this talk of an economic panic is unnerving—by erecting a mill seat for the manufacture of cotton. Franklin and Titian have already trained in the miller's art. Quite naturally, we have every desire to give Mr. Tharp a good deal on milled cotton, so long as we can be assured a consistent supply of water.

And why shouldn't a man fully exploit the natural resources of his property? It is a waste to do otherwise — now I had a very real need to please Mr. Tharp.

I set up Rembrandt's contraption, positioned the mirror in front of Tharp and myself next to the magnifying glass, and moving quickly began my lines. This method requires the painter to stand behind his subject. No wonder Rembrandt is so enthusiastic, because this way he can hide and avoid the small talk he says gets in the way of his honest appraisal of the subject. He is terribly high-minded. If Raphaelle refuses to take himself seriously, his younger brother Rembrandt finds it impossible to believe he isn't the most important artist in America. I've proclaimed his virtues as a skillful mechanic, a fine colorist, and at times a daring painter to presidents, to foreign attaches, to members of Congress. Through me, he knows them all.

Tharp, who appeared to lack eyelids, was silent. "Have I ever showed you my latest plow?" I said. Of course I hadn't, but so it is. "I built one and sent it to Mr. Jefferson. It's meant to be used on a terraced farm, like his at Monticello, but I use it here because the fields on my estate are narrow. Accordingly, this spring I shall plant new potatoes in the apple orchard, work I should give to a hired man, as I've developed a good case of rheumatism in the knees. The plow makes it possible, you see. And Mr. Jefferson reported back just a week ago it's already improved his yield." I went on, almost unable to control myself and certainly without his interruption, about my calves and the work of hired hands and the yield of rye and currants.

Perhaps, as I attempted to engage him in a technical discussion about the mill and the mill pond and even the dyeing technique (believing as my son Titian does that such a process might harm the fish and tadpoles creeping around), he sensed my ignorance on the subject. What could I, a gentleman farmer, want with manufacturing?

I uncomfortably stood behind and a little to the right of Tharp, with a fine view of his balding dome and an ungainly close-up in the mirror. I frankly couldn't see him. Draw the definitive outline, you uncover the soul of the man, and then maybe he'll appear before you. But not this way. Oh, the goddamn, devilish thing. You can't paint a man by magnifying every detail. No wonder Rembrandt's paintings leave people cold. Tharp, for his part, only stared ahead, into the mirror, unsure if he could move, if doing so might somehow disrupt me. I assured him he should be at ease.

It was now apparent he was losing patience. To hell with it! I took down Rembrandt's mirror, apologized again, and asked if he would still relent to the portrait. "I'll have my boy Linnaeus bring you a five gallon keg of good clear wine made from my currants, might be useful for holidays. Or do you prefer ten gallons?"

He replied quite tersely. "Don't. Don't send such a large quantity."

I walked to the far end of the room, which faced my own property, and opened the shutters and began again, this time following my usual method. "When we're through, you'll show me the new print rollers? I've heard there is nothing like it this side of the Atlantic." He said nothing. Perhaps he nodded faintly. "If you'll also allow me to inspect the cotton. My sons dream of erecting a cotton mill on my property. I should hope that when the time comes, they will meet your standard."

Alas, a portrait is an instrument. As I finally began again to paint the outlines of Mr. Tharp and the calico print man sat impassively, unremittingly solid and seemingly deaf to the silence, I considered what might ignite a positive response. Given the opportunity to see themselves as they imagine they are seen, certain men will fawn over the picture. They find it hard to stop looking. Tharp isn't such a man, not on the face of it. He wasn't paying for the portrait. If he liked it, he could keep it. Otherwise it was a neighborly act made in the name of advancing industry. And yet there was great risk to me in his not liking the portrait. All this I calibrated as I painted.

At the end of the day, with light hurriedly draining out of the room, we stood together before the yet unfinished picture. He gazed at me. Our silence was countered by rushing water. "Listen," he began again, "have the boy bring to my house a bottle of your wine so that we may sample it. My brother is to be married this Christmas and I should be glad to serve your finest. His affianced is the eldest daughter of Miller, up the Germantown Road. A fine choice he made. The girl's name is Caroline. The family is Quaker, but I imagine we can convince them a little wine won't douse the inner flame."

I left it at that. Patience (and pray, luck), I counseled myself. Once back downstream at Belfield, I took the velocipede for a stroll. I went the opposite direction, flying down my hill, following the black creek past the spring house, down past the shed, down past the cave, flying — what an invention — to my frontier. There, as I expected, was my other neighbor, Fischer. He was commanding a land surveyor, who was obviously trying to beat the coming darkness. I got up speed and cut into his field, staring straight ahead, anticipating the flame of vitriol. It's easy to get under his skin. I'm seventy-seven years old and I fly like a demon.

Christopher Columbus Peale, entrance to Peale's Museum, State House Grounds, Philadelphia, Indian Summer, 1818

I wish it to be known that I resent being used to advance any cause or anyone's career, however accidentally, and that despite the recently circulating stories that portray me as renegade or an adventurer, I am grateful for the life I have been handed. My cage, which is handsomely fashioned from rods of ash and maple, is spacious and well appointed, despite the indelible blood stains left by the tragic former occupant, whose life was ended prematurely, I have heard it said, by an idealistic bear cub in blind revolt. I pray for their souls every day and, when I am allowed, visit their bodies, which have been preserved for display in the main museum hall.

Without wallowing in self-pity, however, I can admit to a sense of despair. My cage is kept with those of two parrots and an old eagle (the bear and his sister weren't replaced), and together we inhabit the entranceway to the museum. Just outside, beyond the heavy wooden gate, is the State House garden; thus, from here, I can see the crowns of poplar and locust trees and even the black, fervid leaves of a chestnut tree and my heart aches. It is true that these diminutive species pale in comparison to those of my youth in the Brazilian rain forest. Yet, who wouldn't be affected by such a tangible, though desperately inaccessible, reminder of home, especially during the magnificently sultry days of mid-summer? Days when the city is hushed and the air is blanched and beaten and the only detectable movement is the carousing of slender leaves at the highest edges of the trees. On such days, I lose my characteristic sobriety. I do everything possible to exploit the kind heart of Rubens. Carefully holding the stair rail (to calm myself) I climb to the main gallery. I feign interest in the melancholic remains of my relatives (avoiding, however, Raphaelle's devastating display of monkey cobblers and carpenters). And twice now, thanks to an open window on the Chestnut Street side of the main gallery, I have dared to bolt.

Each time, quite to my surprise, I have forced myself to linger along the north-facing front edge of the building, in the quiet musty shadow of the cornice. Carefully, I sort through the various smells of the street (it is possible to take note of oyster brine and horse excrement in the same inhalation). This calms me. I try to ignore my own glowering instincts. I take note of a woodpecker busily at work in Washington Square. This too can't be ignored. In fact, the rat-tat-tat overwhelms reason. It is more than I can handle. I swing with surprising grace and elegance around to the rear section of the roof. I try to step across; the tulip leaves of a modest yellow poplar are just *right there*. Already, I hear the give of the branch beneath my feet, the slight rustle of the leaves…I step onto a slate tile. No, I jump back. It blisters. That's all, I can go no further. At the cornice edge I squint into the blind abyss. Having lost my nerve, I saunter dejectedly back to Rubens's outstretched arm. He affects punishment by removing the top hat from my cage.

One may think it is a great annoyance to live in such close quarters with two voluble parrots, whose favorite lines, which

I judge are best not repeated here, were taught to them by Raphaelle. But I am charmed by the parrots' sensational colors; they too remind me of home. Together, we endure a daily parade of curious humans who walk past us on the way to the ticket office. The parrots, quite to my surprise, have taught me to overcome my natural reticence and not be frightened of these hordes. Humans, it turns out, can be quite playful, especially when made to think they possess god-like powers.

In any case, I try to remain philosophic. I don my top hat and perform tricks (usually mornings), and I would be lying if I said I didn't look forward to the laughter and the smiling faces. Sometimes I even start to believe there's nothing quite so satisfying as administering to the pleasure of humans. The impression rarely lasts very long and not because I suddenly come to my senses. No, quite unfortunately, a human (perhaps one I've wound up, as it were, with my high-jinx and acrobatics) will find himself incapable of respecting the boundaries customarily maintained between performer and audience. What I mean is that he will, somewhat understandably, forget I am performing an act that's been finely calibrated for his gratification and assume I am merely a fool. No matter the intent, it is hurtful every time.

In a handful of cases, a truly frightened human engorged by a demented sense of his own place in the Kingdom of God will go about taunting me (the parrots and the eagle rarely receive this form of reproach), sometimes by imitating my own silly behavior (it comes rather naturally, I should say). But only once have I had cause to violence. The perpetrator was rather infamous in this household, a weasel-like man with tiny teeth and breath that tasted of the anus of a female *Cebus paella fatuellus* in heat. I knew his name much before our memorable introduction; in truth, the sound made by an American pronouncing the awkward Russian spelling is nearly identical to that made by the hognose snake who used to occupy the small cage to the left of the eagle. But it was always said with tone of utter disparagement. I came to connect the name with Rembrandt, whose visage, I noticed, darkened considerably the very same week.

No longer did he bound the stairs (with alacrity a horned sapajou could surely admire) in two great steps; instead he crept about and cursed and once, he sat inside the skeleton of the mammoth and buried his head in his hands.

I have to admit his sadness affected me. Thus, when the Russian with a look of perverse nonchalance dared enter through the museum gate, I sensed immediately who it was. He puffed his way up to my cage and in an abrasive, mocking tone, said, "Who is this? It must be Veronese...Hello, little Veronese, will you paint me a masterpiece?"

With my tail I reached across the cage and took my top hat down from its hook. I dropped it in front of him. "For me? You want me to wear your hat,

Veroneshka? Why don't we switch hats? Ah, isn't this great fun!" He climbed the stairs and returned with Moses, Rubens's assistant, who opened my cage so that we could exchange hats. Soon, my head had disappeared inside his; I removed it and lay it aside, flipped upside down and picked it back up with my tail. The Russian shuffled his feet as if to dance with my hat perched on his head. Moses looked on doubtfully. The Russian clapped his hands. I sat his greasy hat on the floor of the cage and climbed on top of it. "All right," he declared, "that is enough." I jumped up and down. "How dare you disobey me!" he shouted. "You oaf." He pushed Moses out of the way, ripped the cage door open, and reached in to grab his hat. That's the moment I howled as if I'd just spotted a red tailed hawk swoop down from the sky. Unconsciously, I lunged forward, and retracting my soft, serene lips, buried my teeth into the palm of his pale and slender hand.

Eliza Hamm, on the corner of Third and Spruce Streets, October 8, 1818

Believe me, I was the first to see the artist John Krimmel return from Germany. He stopped in front of my fruit stand at the corner of Third and Spruce Streets and explained to me that he took a stage as far as Frankford, stopped for a meal at the Jolly Post, and walked into the city from the north. Krimmel put down his satchels and I handed him a candle, which I had asked him to hold so that I could see his face. Then without thinking about it a second time, I slapped him hard across the cheeks with my wet palm—and then I took back the candle.

Why did I slap him? It was for retribution of course. Before leaving for Germany, the boy had done a little painting of my fruit stand, which shows me, bent over my basket of black and red cherries, in the heat of labor. In it I'm weighing out cherries for three customers, a girl and two boys. One boy has a hole in his pocket—because he can't afford the fruit, you see. The other boy mocks him. The girl, standing above the group, offers the poor boy a bunch of cherries. Now I must admit the colors catch the eye and the basket, the lamppost, and the cherries, look just as they do as you see them now. But, in my opinion, he did two things wrong. First, the picture leaves nothing to the imagination. All of us are crowded in the picture and none of us are the size we should be. Second, and this is my harsh opinion of myself, but I look like a hag. My face hovers like I'm some damned landed vulture and one of my fingers dangles at the center of the picture like the uncoiled tongue of a snake. I hear from the other artists that pass my stand that this painting had hung at the Pennsylvania Academy's 1817 annual show, the most important and widely attended exhibition of the year, they say.

After I slapped him, I had a long look at the boy. He hardly had flinched. So I peeled a ripe mandarin orange for him and the juice ran down his arm as he ate it. He pulled a note from his satchel and handed it to me with instructions. Depending on who answered the door, I was to deliver one message or the other to Krimmel's brother or his brother's wife, Susanna.

He told me further that both notes were written in German, so he wanted to be sure that I didn't confuse them. "If he is not home," he said, "you may leave it with one of his children or his wife Susanna. If he is home, please be sure he receives only this letter and not the other. Discard this second letter in that case. It is for Susanna, and Susanna alone—no children. No husband."

He pushed some coins into my hand. With that, he picked up his sack and case and walked north, toward the market. I put down my blankets and baskets and removed my apron, being careful to put his coins in my purse, and went home. My husband, the lout, must have been at the Hen and Chicks, the dim tavern just at the other end of her square. So from Second and Christian, I walked fifteen minutes to the house of George Krimmel, passing through the Headhouse Market, as I recall, just as the first autumn snowflakes began to fall. I paused to breathe in the salty aroma of pepperpot soup.

Arriving at the house, I knocked hard and then waited. My palms began to sweat, as is often my condition. At last, a young girl appeared in the doorway. She was about ten years old, with flaxen hair and a full, open face. Straight away I noticed the family resemblance. The girl had the German boy's calm intensity. As I fumbled with the notes in my bosom, the girl, whose name was Fredericka, leaned forward.

"Have you come for my father? He isn't home," said the girl, who moved only barely. "He's always working."

"Then he must be a very fine father," I complimented her. "Why don't you ask me to step inside so that you can close the door to this cold. Then you can fetch your mother. Please tell her a lady is here to deliver a letter."

The girl hesitated. "Well, I can take the letter. Is it from the ship?"

I thought for a moment about the girl's question. "No, little lady," I said, "is your mother not home?"

"No, she isn't. My mother is dead. Do you think it will snow some more?"

I checked the note again, carefully handing her the one marked for George. "Why shouldn't it snow some more?" I finally replied. The slightest layer of snow had formed on the wooden handle of the water pump on the corner. But the snowflakes had warmed the air and the wind had calmed. At Spruce Street, I replaced the other letter and headed to South Street. Perhaps the weather will keep the usual unruly hordes in check, for I was in no mood to have to navigate through a crowd.

Harriet Miller, in the garden of the Miller house, Germantown Road, Philadelphia, October 10, 1818

I remember the day John Krimmel walked into the office of my father, the lawyer Isaac Miller. Although he was a lapsed Quaker, his generous heart and penchant for social causes, like the abolitionist's society and the workhouse for young widows, forced him to maintain an open door. He himself was a widower, whose beautiful wife, my mother, a lover of fine furniture and gardens, had died seven years earlier. Of my father's three daughters, my oldest sister, the ever practically-minded, personable, and competent Caroline, lived with our aunt in Philadelphia. She had just been engaged to be married to Tharp, a Presbyterian, who with his brother owned a calico printing mill along the Wingohocking Creek in Germantown. My sister Henrietta and I remained at home, in separate bedrooms at the top of the stairs.

While my sister has spent her time mindlessly, I believe, absorbed by the plants in our greenhouse, I have spent the last several years learning the law under the tutelage of my father. Since there was no faculty for law that would take a female student, I argued, then he should agree to train me in his office. My obliging father agreed, and so began my apprenticeship. Father had books on law and commerce delivered to the house and after a few weeks of study, we began to share a chaise each morning on the way into work. Henrietta, meanwhile, spent her days in her own dream-like world of garden and orchard, humming, even clapping as she toiled joyously, oblivious to whatever other humans were doing all around her. There was a pure sensuousness to my sister, unavoidable to any close observer, including the German. Henrietta liked nothing more than to disappear into a hole or a trench she had dug and lay with the wet clay and the worms.

I began to attend meetings of the Pennsylvania Anti-Slavery Society. In the office, I wrote briefs and interviewed clients, who, for their own preconceptions, were sometimes put off by my probing questions.

But after spending enough time with the clients and their

cases, I began to see cracks in my father's liberal-minded façade. Every case was built on compromise and often, to me, what had been compromised were the very principles that had drawn me to the work in the first place. Then a colleague of my father, a certain Mr. C—, refused to sit in a meeting with me. The meeting was about a shipping line they had jointly invested in. Turns out that in order to make money, a high percentage of passengers would have to travel in steerage, sleep with rats, and eat rotten food.

I learned this myself, reading the contracts and papers when father was out at court. I also learned that it was common practice to lie on a ship's bill-of-fare in order to avoid paying local taxes. When I confronted my father, he acknowledged that in practical affairs, even the law is pliable. I couldn't understand this and walked out of the office crushed and demoralized. That night I told her father I was quitting the law. He told me I was making something out of nothing. "If the foundation is corrupted," I argued, "the house will fall," and then I left the room. Later, when he approached me again, he asked what I planned to do instead. Honestly, and with great conviction, I said that I was going to take a class in drawing, which I did, with Mr. Krimmel as my instructor.

Unlike most instructors who teach art to young ladies, who dictate each stroke of the pencil, Krimmel insisted that the eight students in the Saturday class of the diminutive Germantown Academy of Art, which also housed the finishing school of Mrs. P—, do everything themselves. Krimmel said in that assured tone of his that if the parents of the students wished to own a polished piece of art they could simply purchase one of his paintings. "It would save us all a great deal of time," he said to one overly intrusive parent.

Krimmel insisted that his students learn how to observe the world around them: "Art begins with observation." Moreover, every figure or object in the real world or in the plane of the picture has to relate to everything else. "Therefore," he said, "you will see that in a picture there is no decoration."

I must admit that I was impressed by Krimmel's serious

manner. There was something honest and forthright about him, something pure and moral, but there was also a part of him that was melancholic and sad. Sometimes he seemed lost in his own head. Other times, he bounced around the light-filled classroom, giving critique and encouragement to each student, one-by-one. Of course, it was not lost on me that he often times lingered at my work, a sketch I was completing of Henrietta sitting before a window that looked out on her garden.

But I could not take full notice. At the time I was becoming distracted by vague religious impulses I had never felt before. Did these impulses come from my innate sense of justice? I could not say. Perhaps it was my developing disillusion with my father, who had so often pilloried religious people as foolish hypocrites, blinded by dogma and power. And so one day, I stepped from my father's law office into a meetinghouse near the Germantown Road. To my surprise, I found the meetinghouse calming and the quiet — the anonymity an antidote to the pain and anger I had felt thus far toward father. Perhaps, it was a simple truth I was after, a solid foundation for living my life. A little at a time, I removed the decorative buttons and ribbons from my dresses, and began to imagine I could live without much concern for the material world and in service to God.

Seeing this, father tried to ignore the changes. "She is rebellious," he once told Caroline, "and if I push too hard one way or the other she is certain to react." And it wasn't as if I had given myself over completely to religion.

My father sensed this, and for reasons I can only suspect, invited Krimmel to supper. Around this time, Krimmel brought to class a recent painting of his, the *Quilting Frolic*. In this painting, quite possibly a fantasy, Krimmel had had the audacity — or confidence or insanity — to place me in a gold dress with ruffled collar, at the center of the picture. To my right was a quite unnecessarily voluptuous depiction of Henrietta, tossing a ribbon in the air. Between us, with Henrietta's hand on his shoulder and mine at his back, was the German himself, looking boyish and bashful, tipping his top hat to a third young lady, who was scrambling to gather various odds and ends off the floor.

I was furious and demanded an explanation. "We place our friends in our pictures, of course," he arrogantly explained. "Art is not the practice of invention, dear ladies, but of absorption. You will be like sponges too." Those "absorbed" into Krimmel's world are escorting a young man into the home of his affianced, where a quilting frolic is ending. These young ladies are gaily presenting the young man, but his presence is a surprise. Maybe he isn't expected. Maybe he shouldn't be there at all.

The sturdy young woman cleaning up the room—the affianced—is hopeful, afraid. Did she imagine herself in love? Krimmel explained to the class how the objects in the crowded room were arranged in a circle to draw the viewer's eyes to the two lovers, and into their innocent world. The two are separated only by the feeling of anticipation. There is nothing else, it seems, between them.

At the close of class, I remained in the empty room in my seat. I watched through the window all the others leave; the sky was bright and the room uncomfortably warm and suddenly, harshly, silent. It smelled of wood and crayons and of the instructor's peach, slowly decomposing on a windowsill. It took a few minutes of fiddling with some sketches before he dared come over to me.

"Mr. Krimmel," I said, "if you think you are complementing me, or my sister, by placing our images in your painting, you have made a foolish error. I am tempted to ask you to change the picture or destroy it. You have no right."

It was as if his preoccupation had caused him to temporarily go deaf, for he must not have heard me. Rather he replied, "Forget all that I just said. No, don't forget; it too is true."

"Too? What does that mean?" I challenged, feeling as if I was becoming a participant in a game.

"Listen. I will tell you," he said. "The man in this painting isn't quite so in love with his fiancée. You think he is, the look on his face is one of almost being overwhelmed by love just by the sight of her. But that isn't the case. No. He is just at that moment aware of a different feeling for a different young lady, the one in the golden dress. Do you see the way it is *this* couple who are bathed in light? The other woman, the expectant woman, is really quite in the shadow. He feels this other woman close to him, her right arm undoubtedly touching his lower back. Her hair falls in ringlets around her eyes."

"Yes?"

"He is, indeed, embarrassed. Not for himself, for the woman on the floor who thinks she is the one."

"She isn't."

"No," he said. "You know who knows?"

"Oh Mr. Krimmel," I exclaimed, having little time for this absurd conversation. "Please stop this stupid game!"

"The mother. The mother knows. Look at her venomous eyes, the way she looks at the man—and with the bread knife in her hand!"

During this entire explanation, Krimmel exuded serious-ness and self-possession, as if all that mattered was the fun-ny explanation of a picture. I would never divulge this to my sister, or my father, or to the German for that matter, but his self-possession made me ache for him, because no one should be so confident. When he was done, I had the overwhelming urge to take hold of his hand, but I could not. I decided right then I would never again wear such a gaudy dress, which made me feel better immediately, being that I had already spent too much of my life having to explain why as a Quaker I didn't dress like a Quaker, look like a Quaker, or act like a Quaker.

Just two weeks later, Krimmel came to the house for tea. Henrietta took him for a tour of her garden, and that first time, and the many times that year that followed before Krimmel sailed to Germany, apart from the most perfunctory greetings, I wouldn't have anything to do with him. (In class I merely took instruction, did the work as assigned, and left as soon as Henri-etta arrived to pick me up.) Unfortunately, Mr. Krimmel was just the sort of person father liked to have around the house. On the first visit, he had brought along a watercolor sketch he'd begun of an Election Day scene at the State House, which he intended to make into a full-size painting in oil. Father and Mr. Krimmel poured over it for an hour or two, with Mr. Krimmel listening to father's advice and insight about the various factions and political figures the artist had depicted—'tis true that Mr. Krimmel the neophyte had gotten it right much of the time—the events and confrontations that really did occur that day, the vote-buying, fist fights, drunken anger of the tradesmen, and the symbolism of the young mother and girl (purity) and the monkey that had escaped from Peale's museum (chaos).

On this last point, father, usually a man of complexity and compromise, lingered. He said that Charles Willson Peale had it coming. The narrowness of his position shocked me. I'd heard it been said that Peale's view was that control (over passions, over nature) was the basis for the functioning of the American republic. Father said Peale himself was a "wildman" who had taught himself control in order to survive. "He's going to see the presence of the monkey in the picture as a personal attack, not as a general statement—brilliant as it is—on the society." Then he advised Krimmel, "If you value your career, remove the monkey from the oil version of the picture." Did Mr. Krimmel know that there was no more powerful broker of art than Peale, and Rembrandt too, would be likely to follow his father's position?

I heard from my father that before Mr. Krimmel left for Germany, he gave the watercolor sketch to Tom Birch, the curator of the Pennsylvania Academy. Birch could hang it, if he thought it deserving, Krimmel told him, though his real intent was to paint the picture in oil. "I leave it to your judgment," said Krimmel to Birch, a fellow artist. "It can't possibly matter if the monkey raises some feathers. I'll be on the other side of the world."

It was not too long ago that Mr. Krimmel returned, utilizing that open door my poor father cannot seem to keep shut. The moment Krimmel appeared in father's office, as father recalled, Krimmel barely acknowledged the strangeness of his visit. "I went home and I did what Germans do," he explained, when my father inquired into the happenings during his absence. "I waited. And then I knew what I was waiting for and I became so good at waiting that I started to crave it." Father said if he wouldn't mind waiting a little longer then he might accompany him home, and stay there until he was situated, if he wished.

"Now I know what I need to do," said Krimmel.

Father was bemused. He didn't reply.

"And what it means to make art. In Vienna," he went on, "I learned."

"You shouldn't try too hard," replied father, probably thinking that Mr. Krimmel was trying to impress him in regard to me. "Nothing much has changed here, so you needn't worry." Father knew I would be angry if Mr. Krimmel got the wrong idea and so he finally sought to make it seem he was only thinking about the world of art and artists and not, God forbid, about his daughter's future matrimony. The Peale Museum was in decline, he said. Rembrandt is in Baltimore, perhaps successful, perhaps not, Peale himself is raising grapes and potatoes on his farm, perhaps successfully, perhaps not, and Raphaelle Peale, the more talented but unstable of the Peale brothers, is back from exile in the Tidewater, and he's making sultry still lifes. "But they're only still lifes, Mr. Krimmel."

Father said that in an instant, water noticeably rushed over Krimmel's eyes, and for a moment it was apparent he couldn't see.

"There is one change," said my father, devilishly altering his tone again. "Caroline is to be married. That leaves Harriet and Henrietta at home — well, Caroline has been living with her aunt for some time — but I suppose those two are left as my responsibility. And one of them is only interested in plants."

Chapter VIII

Charles Willson Peale, Belfield,
October 11, 1818

Patty has come by today to announce that her husband, my son Raphaelle, has returned. She was hoping to elicit from me some kind of empathy and certainly some cash to hold them over until he starts selling some pictures. I could tell by the way she stood bent over me, hands clasped at her waist, so that I might have a look at her cleavage. And the sing-songy, deferential tone of her voice. I ignored it all—the woman simply has lousy timing. Not that she isn't well proportioned. Of course she uses this to her advantage. When they moved into their house it was me—not, certainly, her husband—who insisted they install a busybody mirror. And I paid for it and had Moses install it. But I looked right into her green eyes and said, "If your husband was a man he'd come himself and not send his wife." I've begun to think that maybe he doesn't even realize the ways this woman tries to manipulate us. He loves her, but he's weak. And she runs his life.

She pretended not to be surprised by my response, but I could tell she was frustrated. She tried to make me think she had just stopped by to let us know Raphaelle was home by inviting Mrs. Peale and me to dinner. She knows her dining table is barely large enough for six—as if she has time to entertain us. Naturally, I had a thousand questions for her in mind about my son's health, his pallor, his weight, even his stool. No detail lacks importance to the empiricist. But just as I didn't steal a single peak at her bosom as it heaved before me, I didn't ask a single one of them. Control, like anything, can be practiced and learned.

Raphaelle Peale, in his house, Fifth Street near Sansom, Philadelphia, October 15, 1818

I was in my painting room, at the back of the house, where the dense, clean light is quite a bit more palatable than the rose glimmer of Tidewater, working on the white hot flesh of the inside of an orange peel, when I heard the knock. Hard to believe it wasn't my father or a bill collector or some dreck looking to rent a room. I put the brush down. Patty had gone to the market and so I eased myself down to the second floor to have a look in the busybody mirror. Three men, or boys, it was hard to tell. I didn't know them. They shuffled anxiously and seemed to be laughing a great deal. None wore top hats, but instead some kind of European tradesman's cap—and thick dark coats. The style didn't look too familiar. I assumed they wanted a room, but they carried neither trunk nor case. They knocked again.

It had been two weeks since the pain last flared and in desperation, gin drunk, I thrust my head into the one place I knew it couldn't stay buried, my wife's plethorous bosom. In retrospect, it was a sign that I wished to live. She let me drop to the floor and I swear it, I smelled her fish musk as she stepped over me. That was it. The very next night she suckled me until I felt myself disappear. As a result, the only Madera in this house is now safely stored in a glass decanter and painted on a canvas. The gout hasn't gone completely, but it is much improved, so much so I can contemplate a full day's work, but by need or habit, descending the stairs, I take one step at a time.

And so I reached the door eventually. The men in the thick dark coats were three healthy boys—but one, come to think of it, had a cough and skin like water-stained plaster. The other two were healthy as horses and full of energy, so unlike my own sharp, silent ones that I wanted to embrace them right there on the stoop. And they were polite, for as soon as I poked my head out the door, they quieted and the tallest one came forward and askod if I was tho paintor Raphaollo Poalo. To which I rosponded drearily, In the living flesh. They had come from Easton, which they noted with pride, as if it were meant to impress. Very well and what can I do for you?

Now they all three seemed to speak at once until the tallest one, with pale facial hair stiff like a frosty lawn, said simply and quietly, We'd like to have an hour with you, sir, if you don't mind. I looked them in the eyes. Whose sister had I defamed? Had I even been to Easton? Lads, I said, pressing close to them, my wife is under the impression I'm hard at work, so please, get to the point. The point, said the one with thick spectacles and the notebook, is we're going to produce the first book on the artists of America. Ha! No one has ever even thought of doing so before, said the tall one, to be succinct, it will introduce the world to the creative genius that until now has been hidden. Well, then, said I, for Wordsworth came right to mind:

> Behold her, single in the field,
> Yon solitary Highland Lass!
> Reaping and singing by herself;
> Stop here, or gently pass!

Quick as a flash, the one with the notebook responded. Sir, said he, the artists of America can no longer be passed by. I am sure you agree. I admonished him for assuming. Well don't you agree? he persisted. Are you sure I ought to? Listen boys, inside every Peruvian village there's someone—a little old man who isn't really that old, he just looks it, or a boy who just looks like a little lad but he really is older, like you—who can paint better than 85 percent of the so-called American artists. Why not sail down, have a look around?

But these lads weren't buying it. I'm sorry, sir, they said, we don't think you understand. When we thought of this idea and began to compile a list of names of artists, of course we sought advice. And your name was among those most mentioned. And that's why we're here. Aha! I said, And who was it you asked? My father? No, no, it must have been my step-mother who answered on his behalf — he doesn't manage his own correspondence anymore, you know — I don't know why but the foolish woman pities me. Or was it one of the big names, Allston, I bet, or West or the elder Mr. Birch, a fine specimen he is. Perhaps then, Napoleon Bonaparte?

The lads fumbled about, looking around as if they wished they understood me, when I exploded the developing silence — at this, I truly am an expert — I mean *Joseph* Bonaparte, of course, I said, and I winked. But I'm afraid my brush is getting dry, my dear friends, it's my brother Rembrandt who you're seeking, is it possible you've confused us, our ridiculous names have always caused problems, though it is he who has tried so hard to live up to his namesake and I just the sordid reputation, clearly, then it must be Rembrandt you're looking for, Raphaelle is a mere painter in still life, boys, and that hardly counts for a smart anthology like yours.

At which point the tall one smiled in a way that was meant to be serious, as if he had already rehearsed our conversation in his mind, and demonstrating that of the three of them he did understand what I was saying, What we would like to do, dear sir, when it is convenient for you, is talk to you about your paintings. This will take about one hour. Please, Mr. Peale, now it is you who is drawing assumptions about whose work is valuable. Ultimately, only we can decide that. Now, are you game? Oh, I liked them, their eyes like razors, the watermelon flesh of their lips. And I could see them in their little village of Easton, with its pure air, its milk, its whippoorwills, its sleepy cattle. I ought to warn them of the dangers of the city, for nothing should stain their pure hearts, although truth be told a conversation like the one they proposed should really take place in a sophisticated establishment like the Castle — with its polished floors and Shakespearian troops:

Go, gentlemen, each man unto his charge.
Let not our babbling dreams affright our souls.
Conscience is but a word that cowards use,
Devised at first to keep the strong in awe.
Our strong arms be our conscience; swords, our law.
March on, join bravely! Let us to't, pell mell —
If not to heaven, then hand in hand in hell.

I invited them in and fumbled around the kitchen for some tea while one of them—ah, these lads—prodded the stove, which had dimmed, and I excused myself to attend to my brush. For some reason I thought nothing of leaving these three strangers in my kitchen—my only worry was that my son St. George would walk in and pick a fight but, I reasoned, vigorous boys like these should be able to handle themselves, even with a street tough. So I went back to work. A while passed and they came up, one two three into my painting room, a tray of biscuits and tea.

I had no idea where they found the biscuits.

Do I assume incorrectly that you've already interviewed Sully? Vanderlyn? Trumbull I bet. Tell me, do you *like* history painting? I demanded. They sat on the window ledge, paced, leapt up, sat down, kneeled on the floor to have a look at paintings stacked there, and jammed in close to a shallow bowl of peaches (a thoroughly exhausting effort) hanging above my sketching table. Who will take some whiskey in his tea? Shh, now. This is the last stash not yet uncovered by my wife, I muttered. I apologize it isn't top quality, but an artist's life isn't easy. You can ask my wife about that. Of course, I poured my own without waiting for an answer, youth—though these were no timid creatures, how I admired their seriousness—need an example to follow.

And then the tall one, clearly the leader of the pack, burst forth, I actually do like history painting, Mr. Peale, but our views aren't important here, said he. I'll take my tea as it is, sir, thank you. What we would like very much is for you to choose one piece of art—your choice not ours—present it to us and explain it as you see it. Though, of course, every work of art is open to interpretation. Well then, I answered, your views are what's important. Your inconsistencies are admirable, I assure you. The one with the cough took two drops of whiskey and the third followed, and I stretched out my stiff legs up in the air like a circus clown. It relieves the momentary feeling of leadenness, the ache that slowly freezes my spirit. Drink up, lads, I groaned, and don't mind my gymnastics. Now, this book, what exactly do you propose?

It would be called *The Book of Masters*, one of them said. And you've found a printer? In unison, they replied—ah, so upright, so nuanced—no, no, we will wait until we have a worthy manuscript to present. The printer isn't important, I insisted. But you've already decided, then, whom to include? If you give privilege to history painting then I can guess your list. I bet there isn't a single painter of still life—and should there be? That's what you need to ask yourselves. And they said, Well, you sir. There you go again, I replied, but an illusionist is how I like to think of it. They sat forward now, the third one scribbling intently in his notebook. But aren't all paintings illusionary? they said, looking at each other. Oh! Where did I find these boys? In my excitement I leapt up on my leaden stumps and arranged a dozen small canvasses around the room. I held the first of them—the smaller of the two meat paintings—in front of me. Well, I said, breathing deeply, what do you see? You're starting us with an easy one—indeed he was right, the goat-smelling one with the notebook—mind over body. How so? The cabbage is mind—like an anatomist's drawing of the brain. And the rest, the body? I challenged them. Not for polite company, said the pallid one with the cough. In the tradition of English satire, said the tall one and tears wet my eyelids.

I held up another painting, of an ear of corn resting on a melon, some flesh revealed. Fertility, they said in unison. This one? Time. The fish? Silence. Yes, I said, something like that. This one? Touch, said one. Desire, said another. No, said the third, restraint, fear of indulgence. You may all be right, but I shall not say. And this? The fall of the bad apple. Or was I pushed, boys?

I directed them to a canvas I had been working on all year, a picture of a basket of two lemons, a sugar jar, and a decanter; in this I hoped to confront the world, which seems to me so sure at hand and yet so untenable. Everything is twisted, everything is bound, everything is at first heightened. And then soured. They got it immediately. The lemons, they aren't lemons, the carrot, the knife, the spoon…Now I was being slowly dissected. In truth, I was prostrate, allowing the procedure. We find your work very dark, very painful, sir. I don't make romantic self-portraits, I said in an off-handed way, and started to tell a lewd joke: Temptations press me close, a num'rous band, / Which find me oft too feeble to withstand.

Now I filled the teacups with whiskey and emptied the contents of my cup into my gullet. Lads, I said, your book ought not include me. Any entry on me, unless we choose to rely evermore on illusion, is a sorry view on a miserable life. And then I very nearly told them that it was the experimental mercury prescribed to me by my father for yellow fever when I was nineteen that makes me feel this way, but I didn't want to frighten them and besides that I'm not even sure it is true. I have no idea if it's true, it's just an idea, a sorry guess, which I've never even mentioned to my father. I finished the other three teacups of whiskey and asked the boys to leave.

Patty found me thus, staring at my lemons, with the teacups awry and the canvases propped up at the base of the walls. I quoted Pope: Know then thyself, presume not God to scan; / The proper study of mankind is man.

But, I said, surprising even myself, take me to church so I might be a better man. I begged her. Why, why does she acquiesce? I am nothing to be afraid of.

And so the next day we went in silence to St. Mary's. I held an umbrella for her and she looked on ahead. I glanced over at her and with my eyes traced the outline of her face and for the thousandth time tried to decide if it is a beautiful face or just the everyday beaten face of a common peasant. I resisted telling her about the boys from Easton. She wasn't smiling. Would she care that I had been chosen for such a book? Would she believe me? Long ago, I pained myself to justify my work. But she never believed an artist's income was well-earned, and it certainly wasn't ever enough. Patty, I said, as we turned on Fourth Street, yesterday I was visited by angels. I'm not a fool, Raphaelle, she replied, and she smiled sorrowfully; I had seen this smile before, the smile of pity and failure. I kneeled in pain before the Holy Spirit, but to tell the truth I didn't mind it. I watched Patty and I watched the priest and afterwards I bumped into the publisher Matthew Carey, who said he had a question for me, and would I mind taking a few minutes to consider it. I don't know what his feeling is about my father, but if I had to guess I would say he thinks him a bit of an old fool. Carey is self-important, tiresome, says Patty, but Patty sometimes misinterprets; sometimes she over-simplifies. Sometimes she forgets. I want your opinion, said Carey. Someone has put before me an interesting proposal and frankly, I'm not sure I have the ability to judge it. I haven't much of a taste for art, he said in a dry, quiet, low voice, and this is a book of pictures. For a moment I thought I had been tricked by the Easton boys. But Carey was referring to something else. Places, people I suppose, around this country. Some are of this city. But that's not all it is, he explained, it's a book of observations, and some of them quite telling, even visionary, about our country, among them things I rather agree with about politics and technology. By a Russian, no less, if you can believe that after what happened last year. What happened last year? The violation of that young girl! By the consulate general.

Sorry, I said, I don't read the papers. Well this fellow, the one who wrote me, not the filthy predator, was high up in the consul here a few years before. I don't know, maybe you ran into him, Svinin, Pavel Svinin. I can't describe him because I don't know what he looks like. Now, without prejudicing you about him, I have heard mixed things about the man. Apparently, he charmed some. Well, he got under my brother's skin, I said, refraining from describing the episode of the *Roman Daughter*. I hadn't the energy to go into it. Ah, the hell with it, I told him, I'm willing to have a look.

Charles Willson Peale, Belfield, October 15, 1818

I am presently, and to hint at the truth, rather ambivalently, looking into the eyes of a male elk. The great beast inhabits a pen I've constructed of twelve-foot-tall laths; I take no shortcuts when it comes to keeping prying eyes away from my business. I've employed the elk to power a treadmill that pumps water from the creek so that we may have consistent irrigation for the garden. The face of this elk is kind, the eyes dark and searching, his coat the brown of the oak leaf in November, and it—the coat—maintains the same satin sheen. But right now this elk of ours is looking rather ungainly. He is forced to carry such great, useless horns.

He may be the best employee I've ever had. But he isn't happy, and when I look the laconic beast in the eyes, I see my boy Raphaelle. Oh, hardly a boy, he's forty-four, my oldest son. Forty-four and the eyes of a penned-in elk. Forty-four he is, and still I support his wife and children, though the truth is, I support them all: Rembrandt's every career move, Angelica's false teeth, the production of which occupies me still, Rubens's salary, Titian's schooling, the cost of perpetual care in the Department for the Insane at the Pennsylvania Hospital for Franklin's wife Liza, the list goes on. Only the elk earns his keep.

"Raphaelle," I whisper to the elk while I clear the leaves that have collected in the herb garden, "isn't it about time to act the man?" Little good, my exhortations. That is the great disappointment of my life: nay, a parent can only do so much. As a boy, he mixed my paints, and saying little, painted as I did. He carried the palate everywhere he went, often in my own shadow. He excelled at miniatures, of me, his mother, and his coddling grandmother, his siblings, Sophonisba especially. The children in those days were in constant pursuit of each other's portrait. But Raphaelle, even then, had the most talent. He would paint all day and night.

So he would work, on the physiognotrace, making silhouettes for client after client in Philadelphia and then wherever he might travel, entertaining them with jokes and puns and silly acts all the while. I sent him to South America to collect specimens for the museum. (It is our goal at the museum to reveal every species of nature in the Americas in order to most coherently reflect on man's place in the majesty.) His brash curiosity led him as far as the jungles of Peru. He couldn't stop himself. Did we very nearly lose him to the sensational prestidigitations of a carnival man and his lily-throated daughter? Yes, though his letters were sometimes hard to decipher, there was ample evidence to make me think so. But he did return, with great wooden crates of lemurs, macaws, dozens of lizards, scorpions, brown pelicans, and a single giant brown tortoise. Then, back at the museum, using a solution of mercury and arsenic I invented, he worked day and night to carefully preserve his findings. Might I have attributed his enthusiasm, and sheer endurance, to a certain mania? Perhaps I thought it was only the presence of me, his father, inside him. If my passions run strong, however, I have taken pains to control them. I'm afraid Raphaelle hasn't ever been willing to heed my lesson. Furthermore, I cautioned him against working for too long without proper ventilation in our laboratory. But he insisted — with such terrifying concentration in his eyes — ignoring my constant admonitions. From then, his behavior has grown ever more erratic; he is driven mad by his libido, I fear, is short of will, and too rarely sober.

And so he remains a still life painter. Mrs. Peale tells me I must accept it for once and stop imagining he'll ever be anything like the leading portraitist of our time. She is soft-hearted and despite my determination to teach her about art, doesn't care to understand the difference. But the problem is thus: by stubbornly ignoring my advice, Raphaelle has laid himself a trap. His subject resists advancement. Lately he asked his brother Rubens to hang two vulgar compositions of butchered beef and vegetables in the museum. Rubens has agreed to put the degenerate paintings in our hall of mammals. Let everyone see what my boy can do.

*Charles Bird King, at the table in Sully's dining room, above
Philosophical Hall, Fifth Street near Chestnut, Philadelphia,
October 17, 1818*

But Raphaelle isn't the only one to burn deep inside. Rembrandt's
deepest desire, after all, is to invent an authentic American language of painting. A direct language, he calls it. To do this, of
course, he is forced to borrow — encaustic and mythology from
the ancients and color and form and composition from the
European masters — and to apply these elements to American
themes of virtue, self-governance, and reason. An American
painting, he says, without even a hint of doubt, must communi-
cate clearly and directly. It most certainly must not be confused
by arcane and convoluted schemes of allegory and meaning.
To separate himself from his father and from the art establishment, Rembrandt tried to leave Philadelphia every year of his
life starting at sixteen years of age, when he and Raphaelle traveled south to exhibit their own copies of their father's work.
In order for him to stay in Philadelphia, he needed his father
to leave the main stage and at the same time lend him his full
support. Rembrandt thought the conditions were met in 1811,
when he returned from Paris with those awful "live" portraits of
Napoleon in tow. Mr. Peale had just purchased his farm Belfield
in order to retire in the country; the city would be Rembrandt's.
And Rembrandt had ideas, good ones too, to overcome the
laughable American prudery with some highbrow nudity.
Chestnut Street galleries were then as now showing amateur-
ish scenes meant to titillate the desperate sailor. But Rembrandt
had another thing in mind all together: a salon for the city's best
and brightest, glibly called the Appolodorian. He placed two of
George Miller's life-sized wax nudes at the entrance and got to
work on a dreamy canvas called *Jupiter and Io*.

   Then Charles — who once for my own benefit and as I sat
at the family's dining table brought out a sketch he had made
of Dr. Franklin *engorgé*, a tramp galloping giddily on the old
man's lap — roared, publicly despairing of Rembrandt's descent
into courtesan naughtiness. The trouble was his serious son

was proving a better showman than he, the original American purveyor *du spectacle*. And so Rembrandt, quite beside himself for his father's attack, doubled down. Not only did he exhibit *Jupiter and Io*, but he conceived of something that would raise the nude to a new level, a retelling of the ancient "Roman (or Greek) Daughter," a moment in moral history when the loyal daughter, a virtuous republican if there ever was one, generously offers her milk-filled breast to her desperate father, chained to the dungeon wall.

It's at this time — will Philadelphia ever have it so good? — there was practically a portrait painter for every man woman and child. No, to answer my own question, it won't. By 1814 half of the artists had gone to other cities, namely Baltimore and New York, the brief, brilliant moment over before it even began. But there it is, spring 1812, emboldened by Rembrandt's salon and the advancement of instruction at the Pennsylvania Academy, and dare I say it, the elder Mr. Peale's retirement, a group of us ached to take over. We organized a serious minded sketch club, which met weekly in Sully's painting room.

At these sessions we would typically sit together around a large table and talk about the future of art.

These discussions would inevitably lead to Sully's complaints about the fickle art market. "But I ask," Sully would say, "does anyone know of a better way to advance the arts than for the marketplace to dictate the kind of art it desires? And for us artists to fulfill those desires? Would it be more advantageous to us and to our fragile nation to have a sovereign, or worse, a church, choose the direction? Does anyone really think so? I don't. No, sir. I don't, I don't, I don't!"

Then we'd listen as Sully or Birch read a passage from literature. One day, so unusually warm for March we had the windows open (and being March the wind blew in strange, disruptive gusts), Birch had us sketching a scene from the *Odyssey*. That day was the first time the Russian Svinin had appeared. The passage from Homer was a predictable but amenable choice: "When on the East the sheer bright star arose..." Birch read all the way to Odysseus awakening on the shore, stretching (striking his thighs, I believe), wondering, "What am I in for now?" The question crept across the table like a shadow cast by a moving cloud and seemed to take each of us, individually, by ponderous force. Slowly we dispersed around the room to commence drawing. John Clifton, from Carolina, sat on my left that day, and Svinin, was on the right. Svinin, who introduced himself as "a Russian patriot who loves your country," was working as a translator in his country's consulate. He was a strange, ingratiating fellow with bad breath and expensive but ill-fitting clothes. He spoke loudly and couldn't sit still. He said he was an academician of the Petersburg Academy and a specialist in painting religious motifs and genre scenes. Rembrandt, Svinin, the German genre artist Krimmel, and Sully remained at the table and the rest of us took our sketchbooks and chairs to other parts of the room. I sprawled on the floor beneath the open window (as Odysseus himself was sprawled across the rock) and listened to the call of the oysterman in the north portico of the State House, a voice in fact much more lissome than the wind. But a short time later, I found myself distracted, not by the oysterman or the wind, but by Svinin, whose voice kept fracturing the room.

After a while, Rembrandt good-naturedly stretched across the table to ask Svinin if he needed help. Svinin took the opportunity to efface himself. Rembrandt nipped at the bait. With Rembrandt standing beside him, right arm across the chest, left arm pivoted up to the chin, Svinin attempted to do as Rembrandt instructed. He worked with apparently calm intent, and with each change to the picture solicited Rembrandt's response. After a while, Rembrandt grew bored and retreated to his own work. Predictably, Svinin followed, making his way around the table to disguise his intent of following Rembrandt, I presume, and all the while chatting, asking inane and imperious questions of each of us. "You're interrupting everyone's work," called out Rembrandt.

"Don't bother with him, he's a bloody idiot," added Birch from the far corner.

"And furthermore," said Rembrandt, "we're not here

merely to fill the hours" — I sighed when I heard this — "but to advance the arts in America."

Svinin wasn't moved. He barely gazed up from his pad. "An American patriot should know better," he said, "than to ape for Napoleon. I daresay it is you who is the oaf!" Without taking a breath, he started working on Krimmel, who, unbeknownst to anyone, perhaps because he was so quietly absorbed, was sketching the very scene unfolding in the room. Clifton slipped out for oysters. Sully's wife brought in biscuits. Impeccable timing! Svinin made a crack about Raphaelle. Everyone knows Raphaelle drinks, and that his problems infuriate and anger Rembrandt. I should remember precisely what happened next, but that's the way with these things. The precipice comes unawares.

Days later, Rembrandt brought me into the painting room to view his *Roman Daughter* for the first time. Here, for my edification, was proof of his formula. And his father, and all of us who have doubted his utter sincerity in bringing ancient stories into the American lexicon *and* raising the taste and sophistication of the American public, could see for themselves. But I know no other way than to be direct in these sorts of matters.

I told him I admired his ambition, this instinct he has, and confidence, to try to reshape American art. "I don't have it. I wish I did, but you do, Rembrandt. I suppose you know that."

"I suppose so."

"But, I think you should stick to portraits."

He kept his gaze fixed to mine. Was this meant to demonstrate his earnestness or to cover for his despair?

"Think this through with me, Rembrandt. With a portrait, that is, a real subject, your own strength as an empiricist often enough — I am sorry but not always — comes through. On top of that, your real skill is in creating a high finish. You know that. You're a master at finish. Put them together, the result is vibrant portraiture, and clarity, as you say: the character of subject is seared into the mind of the viewer. But now you wish to tell stories, you wish to portray moral themes. I understand why. You're afraid you won't be taken seriously enough as a master unless you do. That is reasonable. Yes? Your namesake certainly wasn't content with portraits. But your desires don't match your gifts, I'm afraid."

"I should knock you to the floor, King."

"One more thing. The ideas are getting in your way. The idea of a dungeon, the idea of virtuous but buxom daughter, the idea of a prisoner held without justice. That's what you've painted here. It's mechanical. I am sorry. Look in the daughter's eyes: she is not repulsed. No! She is thinking about the idea of repulsion. Look upon her father: he isn't starving or desperate and he isn't suckling either. In your picture, we're only to think he might be. And so I can't help but feel that you've missed the point. Real people feel terror. Real people feel shame. Real people lose control."

"I see," said Rembrandt, who smiled. "I should knock you to the floor, but I'd rather not waste my energy. You sound like an idiot."

"It just doesn't play to your strength. That's all."

Ylaire Charlotte de Chevalier, Mrs. Fury's bawdy house, Fifth near Shippen, Philadelphia, October 21, 1818

I had a premonition Friday night of a man climbing through this window. I have these premonitions, or call them visions, every so often. I don't think they are real or anything. I don't even know if they ever come true. I suppose if they did, they would be genuine acts of the spirit, special powers. Like what Reverend Allen or Miss Jerena Lee have. And somehow or another that would mean I could get out of here. I could roam the countryside in a long dress saving souls, healing, bearing witness. I could tell you the Lord has spoken to me and I want to tell you what he has said. I could take your head in my hand and tell you all is forgiven. I could take your head in my hand and the book of scripture in the other and not just words but the living spirit would come loose from these lips.

It's always the same with these visions. When they come I give them a long, hard stare while I myself picture the wide, calm blue sea. Some people say it is this stare that keeps a Negress sane.

On Saturday, late into the afternoon, I got up out of this bed, fluffed the pillows, blew out the candle, put on my pink silk dress and black moon pearls, clapped some powder between my legs, and went down to the street. The salon was empty; it was dark out already, and only six o'clock. Actually no one was to be found, and it seemed a little cold, a little too quiet and dark. This time of year I'm just not used to the dark. I went back upstairs for a shawl then sauntered out the door and onto Fifth Street. My own little sister—she has just turned seventeen, three years younger than I am—works for a family on Plum Street near the Passyunk Road. The house doesn't look like much from the street, but I've been inside—the master is a ship captain with queer taste for things he finds halfway around the world. There's a whole room just for musical instruments from China. When I asked my sister Lucy if anyone plays the instruments, she scrunched her face and we laughed together. I'll stop there first to see if she's standing in the doorway or up above in a window fixing her mistress's bedding. She's usually in the doorway. Sometimes I can convince her to take a stroll with me on South Street. Her mistress doesn't know my profession (the master does), and when she finds out our walks will end. My sister may even be turned out. Well, despite her fear she gets a kick out of our walks, and I'm glad to see her shy smile. My sister is much more beautiful than me.

So for now, we stroll arm in arm, flattering ourselves with the idea that we're smart and free. Our mother often told us this is how it used to be for those of us with cinnamon skin and French in our blood. I have to slow Lucy down (she doesn't yet know how to enjoy living), so that I can look carefully into the shop windows, which I scan with the greatest deliberation. Sometimes I meet a man so thankful for my attention, my calm demeanor, my odor of jasmine oil, that he'll declare his love and a desire to decorate me. It's therefore to my advantage to know what goods are in market. I am proud to have things of taste and refinement in my dresser drawer.

That evening after I squeezed Lucy's supple, soft hands good night, I encountered a tall man with worn but well-made clothing walking along South Street. I could tell he was the reserved kind; not demented or angry, just in his own sort of space. I can respect that desire. He was in this space of his own, thinking whatever a man who looks so calm, but alive, thinks while walking down South Street. In sum, he seemed to be enjoying himself. I like nothing more than to see such a thing, especially around here, where people seem to be at each other's throats all the time. Well, maybe this character isn't from around here, I thought at the time. That's not a disadvantage. In my trade, familiarity breeds something worse than contempt. I watched him for a while as he crossed Sixth Street, gazed over in the direction of Reverend Allen's church, had a good look in a store window that glowed yellow from the light of an oil lamp and was filled with what they call genuine Indian antiquities — spear heads and headdresses and such. His hands were in his pockets. I had time, another hour or so until Miss Eleanor would send someone out to look for me, and the urge to put a silver coin or two in my pocket. So I carefully crossed South Street.

I keep my hair short and sometimes, like my own mother, in a turban the color of the flesh of cantaloupe. This makes it easy to manage. I look fine in a low-cut dress, a little loose below the bosom and tight against my hips, but I wouldn't think of wearing white gloves or carrying a parasol. No ribbons or coils of fake hair. I have other ways of drawing attention. For example, I got this fellow's attention while standing in front of the store window with the Indian flints, and wampum beads they have too. Well I gave him a long kind of easy gaze and my hand just gently nestled below my breast. I do it so well anymore I don't even have to think about it. Then I switched my gaze to the store window and said gently, and low, as low as my high-pitched voice will go, "Would you just look at what money can buy!"

He looked at me a little confused, smiled, and then turned the question back to me. "Is it shameful or wonderful? I myself

don't know," he said. I didn't know what he meant. Was he referring to the Indian artifacts? He seemed lost in his own head.
But otherwise he acted very much at ease. I let him go on a
while, carefully asking him his name and what kind of work he
did. "Charles King," he said. They call him King. He didn't ask
my name. He then crossed his arms and said he was a painter
of portraits and history scenes. He'd been thinking, he said.
"That's all. It's a question I can't answer, believe it or not." He
started to walk away.

I waited for him to go on five or six paces. "Which question
is that?" I asked. King turned around.

"Oh, it's nothing," he said. "Forget it."

I moved closer to the store window. Below each item was
a small card with a written description and the name of the
place, I gather, where it was found. For some reason the cards
were written in French. For example, "Courroie de portage, de
cuir de caribou, Riviere St. Laurent." The little labels had faded
but it was still possible to make out the words. "What do you
think this was for?" I said, referring to the courroie de portage.
As Mr. King came closer for the first time I looked into his still
downcast eyes, which were light brown. With the light from the
story window, they seemed gold. The object would be used for
carrying heavy objects, he explained.

"Like what?"

"Like a log for carving. To transport back to the village.
Could be to carry meat."

"How come you know so much?" I said. I pulled my shawl
up over my shoulders.

"This here" he said, pointing to a pair of paddles hanging
from the ceiling.

I leaned over to read the label, which had been tied on with
string. "Raquettes."

"For?"

I shrugged. "Fishing," I said. "Catching fish, like a net. Indians use nets I should think."

"Wrong," he said. "Not for catching fish."

I smiled. "Mr. Charles," I said, "to be honest, this doesn't much interest me. I have a feeling you either." He made no answer, but now, as I drew myself closer, without me saying anything more he became aware of me. It is always amusing to witness this moment. The dreary ones and the hungry ones don't even realize it. They merely grab on. The dark, drunken ones become angry, even violent. It's the sweetly sad ones, like this King here, who become uncomfortable, and attempt to cover their own desires, as if they couldn't possibly be real. There is nothing to say in this situation, but only to wait patiently and not too insistently. I think of Lucy, believe it or not, and smile sweetly.

"Mr. Charles," I said finally, "follow me." I turned around and started walking. Immediately I knew he was following. A few steps on I could feel his presence. We passed out of the city and into the familiar territory of Southwark, Charles — I think he is the dreamy sort — falling a half step behind. To fill the silence, I told him about my sister Lucy. "It isn't the religion we were born into," I said, "but she's convinced me to attend Mr. Allen's church. I didn't want to at first because to tell the truth I was afraid. To join the Negro church. That isn't exactly my nationality. And I had heard that Mr. Allen can be so stern. But I'm resigned to it now, to improving myself. I'm a holy person now."

We quickly reached the Passyunk Road, which even at this hour was busy with carts. But the funny thing about this road is that as busy and noisy as it is it suddenly ends, the stone paving turns to dirt and all that appears in the darkness are broken fences and fields that look like storm clouds thick with flies and tiny gnats. I turned right and took Mr. King the artist behind a tangle of thorny bushes and there I nestled him up against a tall tree, an oak or elm, I'm never sure of these things, and as I kneeled on the soft leaves and unbuttoned his pants and took his slender, stiffening member in my hand, I looked up at him, at the trees and at the swelling sky, and at his long face and deathlike expression, and uttered quietly, as soft and still as I could, "Shameful or wonderful, which is it now, Mr. King?"

Charles Bird King, the back table at the Castle, Tenth Street near Chestnut, Philadelphia, October 24, 1818

A week after our altercation, I encountered Rembrandt on Third Street. He was standing before a fruit peddler trying to decide what sort of grape would satisfy him most. "He's a bit indecisive. He just can't help it," I said deliberately knowing it would provoke the hag's cackle, which lurched forth across the cobblestones like the creak of the carriage wheel. "Tell him which ones his brother likes so he'll know to get the opposite."

"King, I have fixed the painting."

"Get the red grapes," I pointed out, "they look better than green—they're a bit hazy."

"I think I have it right."

But when I had a look at it hanging in its privileged spot at the Academy, forgive me, but I couldn't tell the difference. The painting, for all of Rembrandt's desires, failed. In the days that followed, it was endlessly pilloried in the halls of the Academy. Svinin, reading the crowd's reaction, took the opportunity to declare Rembrandt a fake. "I saw one just like it by Rubens," he muttered. "It's a copy of Gérard, and not a very good one," he said a little louder, for plenty of people to hear. For a moment, when Rembrandt's face thinned and his upper lip tensed, he rather closely resembled his brother Raphaelle. His eyes appeared sallow and greasy.

Sully accompanied him the next day to demand from Svinin an apology (Rembrandt's dreary newspaper defense of his originality would only come later). They were in the home of Du Ponceau, across from the State House. The Russian, Sully tells me, was coy. Rembrandt apparently stood over him, arms crossed, as a child kicking an imaginary stick. It wasn't good enough the whole affair had already increased attendance at his gallery. This fact alone would have been good enough for Peale père. But Rembrandt is too earnest. No, he wanted redemption by forcing the rascal to apologize. It was a matter of justice. Sully pressed Svinin for a retraction, but Svinin prevaricated, bowing down every so often and trying to offer drinks from Du Ponceau's cabinet. Sully wanted to pop him. Rembrandt only grew humiliated and apparently, at one point, even threatened to quit painting.

Remarkably, a few weeks later, Svinin returned to the sketch club. Though he was mostly ignored, from time to time I would find him at the Castle with some other members of the group. Once, on a warm spring evening, with the brick sidewalk covered with white blossoms blown down in the rain, he noticed our mob walking to the Phoenix, Krimmel's Conestoga rendezvous. "So where are we going?" he wondered and followed right along. Around then, he made the deal with Krimmel for a couple dozen or so watercolors, "to present to the czarina scenes of the New World."

Too bad then, that Krimmel's skill is so deeply uneven. Surely the best of the grand public scenes is the rather volatile one he did before sailing for Europe that is on display now at the Academy, *Election Day* on Chestnut Street, with Du Ponceau's house in the left foreground. The picture brings to mind a great stage show, or carnival, with hundreds of actors cast in groups of miniature dramas. But they aren't actors. Krimmel is fearless, I believe, exposing not only every two-bit magistrate and drunken pollster and corrupt Chestnut Street banker, but the entire fable of our virtuous republican system. Most defiantly, Krimmel painted a monkey that had escaped out a second floor window of the Peale Museum and had climbed onto the State House cornice, well out of reach of Rubens's outstretched hands. I don't know if this gesture was a metaphor for the disarray of the scene below, or perhaps a jab directed more precisely at the elder Mr. Peale and his sometimes absurd family, whose belief in the natural order was called into doubt by an irascible simian from Brazil.

Perhaps I can also be convinced there is promise in Krimmel's Dutch interior scenes. Regarding those, I will take credit for training him how to attain the richness of the browns. *Quilting Frolic* is a dissertation on the possibilities of that color. But I've always found him a bit inscrutable, as if he is afraid to reveal too much about himself. And yet it is often remarked how direct he is, how honest. But everyone said, to themselves, at least, when Krimmel sold his watercolors to Svinin, "He must be desperate for money. You don't sell your work to a fellow like that, he's liable to go around claiming it is his."

Chapter IX

Harriet Miller, in her room in the Miller house, October 24, 1818

For a full three weeks now, Mr. Krimmel has been a guest in our house. At first I thought this would be a strange and uncomfortable arrangement, but for the first few days he would awaken earlier than the rest of us and go out with his sketchbook into the fields and lanes of Germantown. He would return, silent as a mouse, only after father had left to go to his office. Then he would go to his room, close the door, and we wouldn't see him until it was time for dinner.

I wouldn't dare ask him what it was he was sketching or why he hadn't removed to the city.

After the midday meal he would leave again, and often we wouldn't see him at supper. On one of these instances, when father would remind us an artist's temperament is different from the rest of ours, and is prone to be forgetful and erratic, my sister Henrietta looked up solemnly from her plate. "It isn't an excuse for being rude," she said.

"I doubt he means to be rude," said father. "He just made a long journey and he has a lot on his mind. Harriet, don't you agree? It's our role to be welcoming to our guest and accepting of his character."

I didn't answer. Did father mean for me to feel sorry for Mr. Krimmel?

"But where do you think he goes?" asked Henrietta, with uncharacteristic care.

"I shouldn't think it's our business," I said, finally.

"You are too severe," she said.

"Did you not just call him rude?" I answered. My sister has no firm grasp on reason.

To distract me, and no doubt in some convoluted attempt to draw me back into the practice of the law, father tried to talk about a case in his office of a slave who had become a refugee in the house of a family assigned to her by the Pennsylvania Anti-Slavery Society and whose permanent freedom my father was hoping to secure. One day the slave, a woman about the age of my sister—"but with a hard, unremitting expression I had tried to ignore when I met with her," he said—was gone. Not only that, but she slit the throat of the lady of the house, left her to bleed to death on the floor of her bedroom, and ran off with the young son of the lady's maidservant. And now the two of them have vanished."

"Why are you so certain it was the slave who did it?" I asked. "Because of a hard expression?"

My sister, across the table, was silent, eyes lost in the ether. I put on a hard expression.

"Because, counselor, there was a witness," said father.

"Enslavement, perhaps, produces ill-effects."

"Justice can be hard to decipher."

"You mean to say, Father, more than one person was harmed."

"I mean the law is complicated."

"And now you wish I should return to it?"

Just then, Mr. Krimmel, who had entered the house quietly through the back door, slid into the dining room. There was a kind of boundless expression on his face, as if he had just made the most spectacular discovery. It was an expression I must admit I distrusted, and yet I found myself drawn to it—to him, rather—searching for the essential truthfulness of his square lion's face and his amber hair illuminated by the wall sconce behind him. Father instructed Henrietta to go to the kitchen to tell Ruby to bring Mr. Krimmel a plate, but he politely declined, saying he had no desire to eat.

"I want to ask a favor," he said. Father's chair creaked as he bent to look up at Mr. Krimmel still standing.

"Sit down, at least."

He bent over the table, his hands in a ball. Mr. Krimmel excused himself to father, who, he said, already had heard some of what he was about to say and then he began to explain about the Nazarenes and a new approach to making pictures. "I have wanted to, but I haven't brought out the sketchbooks I filled during my time away," he said, his voice like pooling liquid, "but in them you would see me struggling to find the essence of this approach. That is what has been occupying me these weeks."

"We were just commenting on your solitude," said father.

"I have been focused."

"Solitude isn't it," said my sister.

"Never mind," said father, "Mr. Krimmel, what is it you wish to tell us?"

"I had written to Mr. Birch at the Academy requesting to instruct a course on this new mode of art, for the Nazarenes taught me that making a picture starts with the eyes and not with the pencil. And he has accepted. I received the letter today. But, I am unprepared to lead others on this journey."

"Of course you are well qualified," said father.

"The Alps of the Nazarenes are intoxicating," said Mr. Krimmel, "you can't judge from experience there. I want to put their methods into execution here, to hear the words spoken in plain Philadelphia air to make sure they retain their magic. I ask your permission to spend a few weeks teaching Harriet and Henrietta. As a test."

"It isn't my permission you need."

"I am certain I understand that," said Mr. Krimmel, his eyes beseeching me and then darting away.

"I have apples to pick," said Henrietta.

I looked and saw her eyes fixed on Mr. Krimmel, and the heat drifted like a cloud and colored my face.

"It isn't possible," I said. My voice was stubbornly tentative. "It isn't possible for me to go back to drawing. There are days I must spend at the almshouse. The place is full of young ladies, through no fault of their own quite different from my sisters and I—"

"I shall pick the apples at dawn and then take the lessons on drawing," said Henrietta.

"They will be lessons on seeing," said Mr. Krimmel, with certainty on his lips.

"I can spare but a week," I apparently said, just before my father rose from his chair and Mr. Krimmel put his hand to his heart.

John Lewis Krimmel, a wide open field in Germantown, late in the day, October 25, 1818

On the wide field below Morgan's Lane, I have placed a table and three chairs, and in a small sack a small bundle of paper, a few pencils, a jug of water, three of Henrietta's apples, a wedge of white cheese I procured myself from the village store on the Germantown Road, and a hunk of bread spared to me by Ruby, the servant of the Miller house, who has a wicked sense of humor and an ass fat as a plum. The autumnal wind, if I am lucky, will consider my situation and remain, as it has been these last few days, calm and delicately quiet. I am a man of few needs.

It takes us only ten minutes to walk to my preselected position. From here, the earth goes off in all directions. Or rather, I might say, it converges on this point with the hunger and ferocity of vultures crashing upon some sweet meat. It isn't clear that my charges would appreciate the metaphor! Nevertheless, I have them place their hands on the ground. This isn't earth, I tell them, but the skin of living animal, warm with pulse and life-giving juices. Henrietta hears this and I think she understands, but she creates a picture in her mind of worms and roots and moist brown humus. This is her living earth. Mine is the sleeping leopard that could spring at any moment. Harriet, in a gray dress so plain it only reveals more sensationally her slender coiling flesh beneath it, flashes her sharp eyes at her sister, and tells me the ground is wet and cold, "more like a corpse, Mr. Krimmel," she says, "than any breathing thing." Her voice has almost perfect clarity in its pitch.

The sleeping leopard, I ask them, as we slowly circle the table and chairs ourselves like animals of prey, or pietists about to conduct to a ceremony, how do you see it? As an object at rest, calm, quiet, sincere as a slumbering child?

"Every creature must rest," whispers Henrietta.

"What? I can't hear."

"Every creature in the bosom of its mother."

"Is just as likely to be a killer," says Harriet. She is looking at me now. Is it a look of corroboration or approbation?

"He'll stand up and eat you!" says Henrietta, following her sister's lead. She raises her hands like mock claws of a beast and bears her teeth.

Ah, I say, we have gotten ahead of ourselves. "We can't imagine the potential" — I pronounce this word carefully — "without seeing the present state." They look at me with heavy eyes. "The leopard might just as easily continue his slumber."

"Mr. Krimmel, you're confusing us."

"John. Harriet, please use my Christian name."

"I am not sure — "

"I mean to say, ladies, that in the living force of the earth, there are contradictions, facts that tell us opposite things." I stop. There is silence, though, I notice, some twenty or fifty paces away, the wing flap of a hawk or a vulture. "There is both death and life together," I say, finally. "The first thing we are going to do is sit at this table and stop our minds from wandering away; this wandering is a terrible trait of mine even as I am focused on the matter at hand, or think I am. Let our eyes become used to what's around us, let our minds and our eyes be drawn to it, so that eventually, today, tomorrow, the day after, we begin to see the things we cannot see now."

"We aren't to draw?" asks Henrietta.

"No, sister, don't you see his point? In order to be able to incorporate this potential, we have to study what is here. What might be is found inside what is, perhaps that's a better way of understanding it."

"I shall keep the sheets of paper and the pencils in the sack," I remind them. You never know when a wind will come and blow everything away."

Harriet Miller, at the back of the Miller house, October 25, 1818

The table was terribly rough and stained by the rain and sun. I wondered where he had found it — of course, it occurred to me that he, John — for God's sake, Mr. Krimmel — may have pilfered the table and the chairs from someone's farm field. With plans to return them, no doubt, at the end of our exercise, as if nothing had ever happened.

For a long while we sat at the table in silence. I faced to the south and the light streamed past my eyes and I felt Mr. Krimmel watching me from behind. My sister, with her chair in front of the table, faced the opposite way. She folded her knees to her chest and breathed heavily. I attempted to follow Mr. Krimmel's directions, to look deeply into the world before me, to erase frames and boundaries. "Categorize things in your mind only if it helps you to recognize how many elements contribute to the landscape," he said, though truth be told I wasn't sure I understood. Did I wish to?

A white-tailed rabbit scurried beneath the dried stalks of aster. I followed that rabbit as far as I could see with my naked eyes; I pressed and pressed my eyes into that field until I had the sensation that I was pressing too much, pressing into blindness and as soon as I relaxed my eyes, there, a short way off, was another rabbit, this one the gray of the wooden table, and another — three more to the immediate left and a lone moth the color of candle wax and suddenly as if in mid-dream my mind left the rabbits and the field and the moth and all the things Mr. Krimmel wanted me to see. I felt my body warming, my upper lip and my neck and my thighs most particularly. To my surprise, I imagined Mr. Krimmel watching me alone in the field, sketching me as I—naked and plain with nothing even covering my skimpy breasts—bent to observe the plants and insects at my feet. He too in my corrupted imagination was without clothes, and smiling softly, not hungrily as I had once figured on, but with a certainty and calm that was most unassuming.

My eyes had indeed been shut and when I opened them I turned swiftly and suddenly, as one wakes from a dream, to find my sister gone from her chair, wandering up into the fields back toward the Germantown Road. I looked over to Mr. Krimmel, who saw that I was surprised and perhaps a bit unnerved and guessing that it was because I disapproved of Henrietta not following the rules he had laid out, said, "It isn't anything to worry about"—he put his hands to his face as if he were a myopic reading a book—"your sister sees the world up close."

"She has no sense of the larger picture."

"Perhaps there are larger pictures in tiny scenes, whole worlds, some so small you would need a magnifying glass to see."

This I understood. Who is to say one world matters more than another?

"For that reason," Mr. Krimmel went on, "the scale of the scenes we create on paper doesn't matter. What matters is that we are drawn into the scene because for some reason or other we can't turn away from it. This is an act of seduction."

I said nothing.

"What do you see out there, Ms. Miller?"

Rabbits, I thought to say, one rabbit then others, a small earth of desire and hunger. But those words froze inside me. "I see a barn and the line of the Ridge Road and the smoke from the chimney of a tavern."

"Do you also see the chimney?" Mr. Krimmel put his hand on my shoulder. I held my breath, or rather in that instant I had none, only the confusing instinct to tear myself away.

John Lewis Krimmel, in his room in the Miller house, October 28, 1818

It is an imperfect experiment. I see that almost immediately. It is one thing to teach a person to see the world as an artist might and it is quite another to translate the visions into pictures. Would Harriet and Henrietta's pictures they began to draw, finally, on the fourth day of our abbreviated course, have been much different had I focused instead on drawing instruction?

I have no certain answer. As they work in silence, I tell them only that if a picture captures what is latent in a scene, it can grow in the imagination of the viewer. If a picture shows only an object as it is without even hinting at all that might be, it is dead to the imagination.

"In any case, you may throw away my pictures," says Harriet. She is ruthless in her repression.

That afternoon we return to the Miller house. I have carried this experiment far enough, I say to myself. Birch has approved the class, so you must go ahead and teach it. But if I do so, I answer, it shall never be offered again. That is nonsense, I conclude, and just then I am moved beyond fate and certainly reason to have a moment in private with Harriet. Her lips are fuller and softer than her slender being, I tell myself, they are the doorway to her heart.

For hours I wander the streets and lanes of Germantown, I even consider walking to the city. It has been more than three weeks since my return and I haven't seen Susanna or my brother; I could return there and at once give up the game. George would, I believe it, take me into his business—

But I could never—no I must never—. It begins to rain slightly as I climb the Germantown Road back toward the Miller house. Be glad your experiment is over, I remind myself, my hands sweating, my eyes heavy, and I slip on the slick brick pavement, turning my ankle and nearly winding up on the ground. The art of America is bound by dogma, watched over by a zealous gatekeeper. "But you are through the gate," I whisper to myself, and now I step gingerly on the turned ankle. The elder Peale, said Birch in his letter, was generous in his praise of the *Cherry Woman*. I can't fill sketchbooks quickly enough.

Harriet is bound to be alone in the house. It is likely she is sitting in her small chair reading and I imagine my hand taking her candle fire away. In Ebingen, I searched for her face in the darkness of the Tavern Die Kanne, in the back of that grease-smelling place near the brazier where the town's young ladies huddled and the wall was black with ember. The drawn spooks I would spy and often sketch in the limber light were desperate and strangely proud and sometimes charming, but among them there was not a single one who would wake up in the middle of the night and declare to the world she would do it justice. That is an American trait, I remind myself. And is that why I love her? Can I admit, with truth on my lips, it is that and not —? Is it not that she exists in a separate, very nearly distinct and unreachable sphere, the skin and breasts and bones of her very nearly locked away? That isn't how it always was, I recall sourly in the pit of my stomach. At the time of the painting of the *Quilting Frolic*, her dress was playful and though reticent, she was always sure of herself. Is that why I now desire her so?

Harriet isn't sitting in the small chair reading with the aid of a candle when I arrive wet and heavy, head sunk and mind knotted. She is standing at the edge of the porch intent on the song of the rain. She is smiling, her curls defying countless hairpins in the damp. "Mr. Krimmel!" She very nearly laughs. I must be careful, I think, I must assume nothing.

"You are pleased it is over," I guess. "The experiment."

"I have much to do," she begins. No, nothing has changed, now I realize, the harshness, the distance, perhaps I missed it, transfixed too by the song of the rain.

"Yes," I say, and now I am for the first time back from Europe, foreign and strange.

"Mr. Krimmel, you need to dry."

Am I pleased she notices? If so, something happens because I resent it and I resent my own reaction. The rain thickens noticeably. She is getting ticked by the drops as they hit the brick floor and bounce up to her legs, even her cheeks. "You too are wet now," I say, and in one motion take her in my hands and try to press my lips on hers. Immediately, I am aware of my mistake.

A force propels me backwards. She has already vanished inside when I hear her voice in my ears. "Have you now forgotten, Mr. Krimmel, your endless remonstrance on the act of seduction?"

Harriet Miller, in the parlor of the Miller house, November 5, 1818

My older sister Caroline came to the house last week, dry as a bone on a day of blowing rain that came in great soaking gusts. For the last year she's been living with our Aunt Elizabeth Hodges in her house in the city. She'll live there until she gets married this Christmas, and that suits Caroline, who loves to be at the center of things, just fine. "And when I get married, Harriet," she said, "you ought to take my place in Aunt Elizabeth's house. It's no good for you to be trapped here. It's fine for Henrietta but, my girl, not for you."

I appreciated the concern, I told her, but I couldn't see how it would be possible. Father and Henrietta both need me and soon I will be made a minister at the meetinghouse. I have my commitments to keep. "Well they have meetinghouses in the city, sister," she replied. "And our aunt needs someone. Henrietta can learn to take care of Father, and don't forget I'll be living out here. I can look in on him. And besides, you're going to return to his law office. At least he wishes it, Harriet."

I ignored this and Caroline told me about the plans for her wedding, which would be in the Presbyterian church on Pine Street in the city. "I've been to that church so many times now it feels like home to me," she said, "and I am glad because the minister has a frightening reputation, but to me he is so kind and understanding. Well, he is stern, but he acts so differently in my presence." The whole thing is going to be a grand to-do, with everyone involved getting into gaily decorated chaises and riding out to the house of her new husband's family, which is next to the Wingohocking Creek. They have a mill and a factory for printing on fabric. "Oh Harriet, won't it be a scene if it's snowing on my wedding day? And there is going to be steak for everyone and exotic fruits and wine and little cakes with double refined white sugar and brandy. Oh, and you will indulge yourself just this once, just for me." She smiled as if that were it: she understood enough about the world, quite enough for her to get on with such remarkable faculty. Then, offhandedly, she handed me a book, *Poems*, by John Keats. She didn't have the patience for it, she said, but I knew there was something about it that frightened her.

Later, I put the book on Henrietta's pillow, but it was I who dreamed so vividly, as a poet might, I suppose, of my sister's wedding. The carriage wheels were stuck in the snow. I had willfully gotten down in order to push the chaise. Knee-deep in the snow was I and for some reason I could see the breath of the horse, whose head should have been out of sight. But there it was, teeth and hairs and pearly steam. The coachman himself — it was Mr. Krimmel, I think — stood over me as I pushed against the prickly iron of the wheel and against the sharp wind and I burrowed myself, as it were, in the job at hand, I remember nothing else but the pushing, and then after what seemed like hours I realized no one else was left but me. Caroline — this I knew without thinking it — had decided it would be easier to walk. And I swore I heard her gleeful yelps, delighting in the snow on the day of her wedding to a man of substance. This was the outburst that stiffened me awake.

The rain only deepened my anxiety. The day Caroline showed up it came down in angry bursts, but now it seemed as if Germantown was simply and permanently wet, the water seeming to come from above and below, equally. The half-bare branches exuded heavy grapes of water that wouldn't burst and plummet to their end; no, indeed, they were simply absorbed in the bitter stream. And so I postponed what would be my second visit to the almshouse. Henrietta, cut off from the pleasure of the garden — on the day of Caroline's visit she had stuck her ladder inside one of the last plum trees still to bear fruit and got knocked to the ground, only to appear at tea time painted with mud and grass—had burrowed herself in the house like a terrified possum taken to his hole. She hoarded no provisions, no nuts or berries, but the book of Mr. Keats's poetry given to us by our sister. This book—such slender sustenance—Henrietta in her bestial way devoured silently over the several days of rain. Our father made a faint attempt to inquire about the text, only to find himself rebuffed. He had, he said, inquired of his literary friends if they knew of an English poet named Keats, but not one had. Henrietta merely groaned and lurched away.

I let her be. The rain continued into its fifth day; admittedly I was bored and far more than my sister, trapped. For I had work to do in this stupidly unjust world. The light inside me burned against the assaultive gray, the gray that dimmed even the lightless afternoon, sodden, chilled, imperturbable: the gray, indeed, that does not matter. What meaning could the random affections of nature have for our spiritual inquiry? The light comes from within and not—certainly, for there is none!—without. But in this case I took the weather at its word and turned inward, momentarily away from the world, and directed my attention to my sister. It was a sign. Dear Henrietta, softest of souls, wouldn't you like to share? I will not judge this poetry of yours, but why has it absorbed you so?

Chapter X

Rembrandt Peale, sitting at the desk at the back of the Rendezvous for Taste, Holliday Street, Baltimore, November 9, 1818

I often think about composing replies to my father's steel-tipped missives from within the tested walls of Fort McHenry. I wonder if he truly understands that unlike most artists I run a business, really two businesses. Three, if you count my Baltimore Gas Works. This is just the way things are. This isn't Paris, this isn't even London, and God knows it can't be anything like Rome, though I must be honest, my feet haven't yet alighted on the Italian shore. No, this is a country of peddlers. That's what liberty hath wrought, neither grace nor beauty but deals and commodities.

But I'm no Federalist, effete, Europhile snob. I'm no John Lewis Krimmel, albatross on the American psyche. I'm not even Charles Bird King, patron saint of humility, and while I'm at it: I'm not Charles Willson Peale, though people assume I must be just like him.

And, quite contradictorily, they also assume I prefer to be called the "American Rembrandt" or just "Rembrandt," and, so confused, they greet me with "Hello, Mr. Rembrandt," as if that makes a bit of sense. None of this bothers me, I won't let it. This has been the case all my life. Raphaelle was a terror before he became a crazy inebriate and I, being his next younger brother, was his constant target of beatings and practical jokes, all of course under the watchful eye of our father, who has written completely earnest treatises on domestic harmony. I would do my best to ignore Raphaelle's constant need to push me down the well, as it were, only once in a while, and I regret never ridding myself of this habit—I do lash out—leaping onto him fist first from our sleeping loft or hurriedly, with shaking hands, painting over in meanest black one of his primitive portraits.

Don't define me—oh, but everyone wishes to. It's practically sport. Dad: "If you settled down here and found the right price for your portraits, you would never lack for fortune as the leading portraitist"; West: "The time for portraiture is over, you must learn to be a history painter"; Latrobe: "The history painting, my dear man, is a play on the public's liberality—stick to making honest portraits"; King: "I'm sorry, but you only have talent for portrait, *The Roman Daughter* doesn't play to your strength, it just doesn't ring true"; Birch, Bonaparte, Dunlap, Svinin, Neal, never Sully, but my father, over and over again, accusing me of being too concerned with ideas and not with my commercial prospects, too much a chemist, a showman, a mercenary, a fraud (my gentle brother-in-law Robinson), an egomaniac, too impure, too fragile, too focused on Baltimore ("Tell me again, Rembrandt, why Baltimore?"), a capitalist, a religious man, too loyal to my family, and never, never loyal enough.

When King, with the nerve of a New Englander, sat me down at the awful thespian tavern the Castle, as if he were a messenger from God to hand deliver the truth, I nearly did smash my frosted mug in his face. And he didn't even know what he was talking about, going on about "the idea of suffering," "the idea of justice," my painting was about the precise moment of moral decision; the fuliginous act hadn't even yet occurred. If you wish to pull me down, it might be best to know what you're talking about. But I handled the situation with grace and order, holding onto his eyes with mine in order to take control of the situation, and then recognizing that the critique meant more to him than me, even giving him additional room to add further comment. When I saw him a few weeks later I pretended to have attempted—though surely, never well enough—to improve the canvas according to his guidelines. Now let me say just as a matter of justice that King has had neither the experience nor desire nor vision required to compose a picture from history. He makes — stiff, yet also obtuse — portraits without great benefit of genius.

There has been no lack of discussion over the role of art in America. This is an ancient conversation begun by my father, who also — and please know, he would be the first to admit it — lacks the creative imagination of a master (Raphaelle named his first son for Dad, but not because the name is lauded at the Academy). Yet he desired to be an influential artist and West gave him a good start. But lacking immensity of creative purpose, what was Dad to do? Well he smartly set about to signify the dignity of individual character through portraiture, which he could do quickly and cheaply and thus quite immediately made artwork a commodity — not quite as prosaic as molasses or beer — with a price that would fluctuate according to the relative supply and demand. Dad being Dad — he is a reformed revolutionary, but his heart has always remained in the right place politically — he desired his work should also serve a greater purpose, that of developing the civic institutions of this great new nation. So he made portraits of the heroes across the political spectrum — from Tom Paine to Gouverneur Morris — and put them in a gallery as the American Pantheon, which eventually became our family's first museum. This is the original imprint of art in America: as commodity and as institution, like the treasury, in service of the nation.

My critics blame me for holding American art to this same imprint. But why is it only up to me? I am just one man. Because as in everything people want it both ways. They want me to apply the full force of my creative vision to raise American art and finally propel it from its infancy, but at the same time they wish to place on my back an easy label: Peale, showman, sycophant. Furthermore, I am a mercenary, a marketer, a stage director; the art itself always secondary. And what am I doing just this very instant? Drawing up entry coupons to my museum and gallery, the Rendezvous for Taste. Admit two for the price of one. Tonight, a special show emblazoned by gas light. Art

lit for dramatic effect does so much to heighten a clever painter's intentions. Let us imagine: a man's character, already en-
nobled by the use of chiaroscuro, now it shall virtually speak.
It is a commanding performance. And just wait, because even
that isn't enough to excite the public about art, I've invented
a scheme not just to light the inside of the gallery but also this
entire square of Holliday Street and all the streets around it,
lanterns not merely glowing but all together capable of making
night as bright and comfortable as day. When all the gas pipes
are laid they will carry a constant and controllable supply of gas
to the lamps. This is at least the hopeful intent of my Baltimore
Gas Works. The engineers tell me we will break ground this
spring.

Well clearly then, I am guilty as charged. Rembrandt, they
say, sometimes directly but sometimes they don't have to, I see
it in their eyes, don't you believe in making art for the sake
and love of art? You, who have studied the great masters, who
have spent countless hours standing on the hard floor of the
Louvre as if floating in among clouds of Titian and Van Dyke
and Raphael, you recognize, don't you, the Godlike surge of
creation, the tingling of the fingertips, the feeling? A painting
isn't a book, Rembrandt, they say, you can't sit down to write
it beginning to end. It must—there is only one way!—a great
work will only come in a fit of inspiration, like a fury.

And I say, because I desire nothing more than to advance
the prospects of this discourse, you don't know what you're
talking about. Did God conceive the world in a single fit? But
let us anyway consider the point of this endeavor, that is to de-
vise, from our own experience and certainly from the tradition
passed to us, an art not only suitable for this nation but one that
elevates its purpose of self-government. How is that for inspiration? We don't paint for arbitrary gods! No, indeed, we paint
to make us better citizens.

Perhaps this seems obvious. That's another thing they say, I
repeat myself more than is absolutely necessary. To some, nevertheless, it isn't obvious—nor is it even desired. Now then, an
example. I refer to the German genre painter Krimmel, sure-

ly one of those walk-on artists who owes his "success" to my father. In fact, I have a letter from him in which he calls the German "a prodigy," in a glowing review of the picture of the fruit peddler. Mind you my father might as well be the father of all American artists. And they still come to him, even in exile at Belfield, where he spends far too much time arguing with Fischer, his neighbor, over water rights to the Wingohocking Creek. They come to him as if on pilgrimage, and he obliges each and every one with a tour of his obelisk, his Chinese summer house, his spring, his "pedestal of memorable events," his cave, and even the musky elk. His word opens doors, it clears paths, and to the young artist, his is often the sole voice of encouragement. All this must have been granted Krimmel.

So how to explain his now infamous *Election Day* scene, a kind of Dark Ages riot of backhanded politicking and drunken vote-selling in front of Dad's museum at the State House. Here is art that is neither uplifting nor, hardly, illuminating to the cause of our republican system. Visually, I should say, it is a cluttered mess. Yet sinister. Two stories above the conflagration on the street, and contraposed to the actual facts of the day, Krimmel depicted Christopher Columbus, the wild Brazilian sapajou monkey brought here by my half-brother Linnaeus for use in the natural history galleries of the museum, escaping from a window in the main room. Poor Rubens, dear good heart, is half fallen out the window in vain pursuit.

So what can explain Krimmel's insolence? He is either by nature ungrateful or, under the cover of "genre painting," wishes to expose the terrible blemishes of his adopted country. I presume the escape of the sapajou is meant to emphasize the disorder on the street below, but I am certain it is also intended to deride our family's lifelong project, to illuminate the natural world as a system carefully ordered by God. And furthermore, does he really wish to deny man's true dominion over nature? If he is, by chance, a member of the Academy (even in absentia), he ought to be removed and kept from participating in future exhibitions.

Perhaps it is easiest to say that Krimmel is only representative of Philadelphia's decline. How many of us dedicated artists have left — with the same words on our lips, "if only…" Certainly I don't have time to be driven to the depths of frustration by lip service to art, by half-promises, by insults. I can leave that to the likes of Krimmel. I frankly don't know how my father puts up with it.

Charles Willson Peale, Belfield, in the last light of the summer house, November 9, 1818

Autumn has in fact deepened. Birds are falling from the trees like the pendulous first rain drops of a summer storm and I will admit to being susceptible to the gloom. The birds are mostly starlings, and one red-breasted nuthatch, and — found amidst a soft pile of poplar and elm leaves — a juvenile eagle. Titian is to identify the eagle properly when he returns to Philadelphia, but for now Rubens has taken it to the museum to be preserved.

About a week ago, when I noticed a kind of haze developing in the right eye of my elk, I found the first fallen bird. It isn't hard to guess my immediate thought. Yes, I imagined a painting done by my eldest son. *A Still Death*, that's the proper name for it. About two years ago I had all but given up, that's how sick Raphaelle seemed, and he did pull himself up and start painting again. I was so pleased by this development and my faith in a father's guiding hand restored that I immediately began planning to paint his portrait. In my picture, my oldest son would be a man of grace and talent in command of his art; a painting not to trick the eye, but alas (reason having long ago lost its influence over his behavior), to appeal to the most hopeful elements of his soul. Immediately, I sent him a letter requesting he visit the farm for a sitting. Secretly, I also sent a note to Patty, asking for her assistance in promoting my project. I am still waiting for a reply.

At times like this I myself walk a great deal, the length and breadth of my own land, with the wind brilliantly clapping against my forehead, and down past Mr. Fisher's into Germantown. I walk unheeded. It is not wasted time. I am alert as ever to the winds of change. I can find myself standing below the stone wall of the Chew estate in an hour's walk from the farm and breathing in the odor of the apples they carelessly let lie to rot on the ground. The odor is for me the exact pitch of my mind's heavy feeling: repulsively sweet and lazy. I walk ferociously on, not bothering to pay much notice to the sky so hot and heavy and black above the field of late purple asters, whose last blossoms will shrink with each passing day.

Lately, since the plow I designed for Mr. Jefferson's terraces proved inadequate for the broader spaces of my farm, my interest in farming has begun to wane. If I am honest, I may observe a connection. Perhaps I am simply out of seed. And so might I sell the farm? But in this economy, and still without a proper millseat, I would go bust. Now when I look upon my great obelisk, inscribed with my own sacred duties to myself and others, I no longer feel certain what destiny has in store. My plan has long been that I should be interred below the obelisk, but now I'm not sure I can acquiesce. Screw it, I should say. I don't have any plans to die.

Raphaelle Peale, at the small dining table of his house, November 9, 1818

You should have seen the look on his face, Raphaelle, said Patty. I was studying the dull patch of freckles on her high forehead, a clump that might be mistaken for a bit of filth. We were in the gloomy dark at the pitted end of the dining table and my head ached. But to tell the truth, I preferred the darkness. I had wrapped my feet in a blanket to keep off the draft. My fingers fumbled lazily with the wax drips from the one burning candle and Patty put her two hands on my one in order to calm the fumbling.

The poor old bird, she said, referring to my father, staring the whole time at my bosom as if it's the bust of George Washington. At least I know where you get your dirty mind. Jefferson, I reminded her, he doesn't give a wit about Washington: That he is mad, 'tis true; 'tis true 'tis pity, / And pity 'tis 'tis true — a foolish figure.

She gave me a wicked, terrifying look. Oh, he's so full of himself. But, he'll send for you in a luxury carriage so that you can recline all the way to Germantown.

I don't remember when my father first suggested he take my portrait. Perhaps it was even before he moved to the farm. Now he was on it again. I'm still supposed to be a respectable gentleman painter. I had nothing to say. You're not listening, said my wife. I winced and muttered, Luxury chaise for the invalid? Swaddle me in butcher's paper — my head is aching enough I promise you, but I won't dare touch a thing, I promise you that also. Don't promise, Raphaelle. Then just lay me on the velvet couch. I'll sleep all the way to Belfield. So that my very own father can resurrect me. Well, that's what he wants. He even said so, to me. 'If he presents himself to the world as someone serious...' He'll take himself seriously, I said, finishing the sentence, and you press your alluring bosom in his face. To feed my children, my love. Then came another beguiling stare.

It is absurd to try to conceal anything from Patty. For a minute I considered telling her everything. But what would everything be? Instead — and why not? — I grimaced at the ache in my legs. Would you put some water to boil? I'd like to soak my legs. So you better go out there and let him paint you, she said, ignoring my request. For once, just do as he asks. Let him resurrect you, if that's what he wants. It is better than sitting here pitying yourself. 'Tis true, 'tis true, 'tis pity. 'Tis pity you won't stay sober. But you're not even halfway decent, Raphaelle Peale. She said this with a softening voice. Did I note even a slight contentment and affection in her eyes? Ah, my wife, her raven hair now dulled, the flame doused, damn it, even the hot firelight down below.

No, no, you don't, Raphaelle, she said, and left to fetch a water basin. I had to bury myself. She was hard and rough as sand and still the dulcet eyes shamed me to the point of arousal. It was no wonder my father paid the note on this house. Was

I conscious all the years of intentionally wearing away her goodness and trust? Back then I couldn't quite predict what I might say or do, my madness was all but uncontrollable, but right now my legs ached too much to sneak off. So I sat there half-dead like a sea lion perched above the purple frigid water. I tried, from memory, to inhale the waxy aroma of her bosom. Take it out of your mind, she said when she returned. And I don't know when, so don't ask. You'll make this much easier if you don't ask. Remember, when I even so much as gaze at you I am forced to imagine the sweaty flesh of some creature from the tidewater or a common Southwark hussy in your embrace. Is she at least a poor Irishwoman? No, Raphaelle, I much prefer to pretend the filthy room where you find yourself, when by stunning miracle you are well enough to walk the streets of this city, is occupied by a Negress, black and foul as the privy. What I mean to say is that it turns out I don't pity you. Her face was ruddy and smooth above the candlelight and her hands, which rested now on the tabletop, appeared stubby, red at the fingertips, and worn. I wanted to take those fingers in mine and devour them.

Angry at herself, or so it seemed to me, she stared right through me. I sighed miserably. Don't try to tell me you are half-decent. In recompense, I replied:

> *We have offended, Oh! my countrymen!*
> *We have offended very grievously,*
> *And been most tyrannous. From east to west*
> *A groan of accusation pierces Heaven!*

At last the water had reached a boil. She set my feet in the basin and descended I to frothy hell—I couldn't feel a thing—and turned away. She lit the lamp as if by doing so she was to defy even death. She wanted to know what Carey had said. His teeth are black, did you notice? You sucked right up to him. Look at me, Raphaelle. Explaining all this was going to be a bother. She would have questions I probably couldn't answer and she would decide immediately that I was being exploited, especially if I revealed what he intended to publish about my family. I even thought she might advise me to have nothing to do with the man. I had sensed that controversy surrounded him. He has asked me to advise him on a book and I agreed to go to his office. He received me, my dear angel, with surprising enthusiasm. The book is an illustrated history of this country by a Russian diplomat. Mr. Carey asked me to judge if the pictures were worthy. You mean the Russian who insulted your brother? So he wants to print a book by him? Doesn't he look a little like a possum? Maybe you heard Rembrandt say so. I've never seen him. Carey says the last Russian attaché violated a child. So this would help mend relations. What's the real reason he asked you? Did you give him an answer? I told him in my opinion the watercolor sketches were a mixed lot and that I had a hard time imagining they were all done by the same hand. There are landscape views, which are generally uninteresting, and street scenes, Philadelphia scenes. These are sophisticated pictures. Could they have been done by the same hand that did the landscape scenes? Anything is possible, I told him. He asked me did I think there were too many Negroes in the pictures—and there are chimney sweeps, sawyers, a great mass of cavorting bodies right over here, outside of Reverend Allen's church—and I said these were well-drawn scenes of high merit. I said in my opinion the street scenes were original. Whoever made them has a pencil capable of recognizing the tiniest detail. These aren't like Papa Birch's engravings where everyone flutters around like a careless butterfly. No, they are real. I might even say they are unsettling. So you really advised him to publish a book by the Russian who humiliated your brother? Is that a problem, you can't even stand to even be in the same room with him. He is pretentious and you have more talent, she repeated for the thousandth time. He is treated like a king and you don't say anything! He's a terrible fawner, a fake, an imp, and he preys on your father's kindness. He would step right over you if he saw you lying in the street.

The missives gave me heartburn. But, Raphaelle, are there going to be ugly things about your father in this book? You're hiding things from me. Why don't you let me worry about my father? When it's me who has to deal with him to feed this family? You're deranged! The Russian is right, so why shouldn't the truth come out? It isn't just my brother whose talent is over-stated. It's only overstated in his own swollen mind, Raphaelle. And it's you who will have to face your father.

Anyway, there's going to be a second book. So you don't have to worry, in that one all the legendary Peales will be lion-ized. A second book? What do you mean, a second book? *The Book of Masters.* And you're in it? I don't believe it! I tried to tell them they had made a mistake, those gentle boys. Listen, don't you go bragging around the neighborhood. There's no certainty about a book until it arrives on the bookseller's shelf. Now the water had turned cold and my ankles began to stiffen. What a shame I am such a lousy husband, Patty, because your scent, it calls me and still, I wish to answer.

Rembrandt Peale, from his house near the Rendezvous for Taste, Baltimore, November 17, 1818

As soon as Dad and his stone-faced wife arrived here in Baltimore he asked for a tour of my gas light district. I had expected this. In his most recent letters he'd stopped ruminating on his usual topics: Angelica's teeth, Jefferson's farm imple-ments, my brother's menacing behavior. No discussion on the future of painting. I've yet to hear if he's even tried my New Method. Of the usual litany, hardly more than a regurgitation of plans for a cotton mill at Belfield. Now, however, he was using the cotton mill—truth be told, a dangerous and expensive fan-tasy of his—as a comparison to the gas works. Two business plans side-by-side. And here's why the mill is a careful, rational idea based on known technology and the gas works is a fateful stab in the dark.

Almost as soon as we stepped out of the house a needlelike rain turned the air into a mineral steam. The questions he asked as we walked had a similar quality of water pelting—no, seeping—until finally my mind was soaked and listless. Will each lamp have its own valve? Or is the flow of gas controlled by one central valve? Have you considered just how bright you wish to make the street? Is it quite possible that gas-lit lamps will alter our very useful concepts of day and night? Night is for sleeping, he reminded me, if one is to hope to be healthy and productive. Why five lamps for each side of each standard square when if the locations were staggered only four would be needed? Can existing oil lamps be retrofitted for gas? That would make this more cost effective, he reminded me, and he offered to design a standardized pipe and coupling so that the lamps could simply be converted instead of replaced. And this I remember word for word: "At no cost to you and your investors."

His face—his eyes—peered out through the iron air with the usual startling clarity. Would he invest knowing that in doing so he would enable me to surpass his own achievements with lighting? I am just old enough to remember the debacle of the triumphal arch—the monument with its one thousand oil lights and rocketry catching fire and exploding outside the High Street market on the eve of the celebration of the end of the Revolution—blowing him off the scaffold and nearly killing him. Dad was pilloried as a fool and we children weren't allowed to mention it or ask questions. When people came to the door, we were strictly prohibited from acknowledging that Dad was ill or in bed. Nay, we were told to say he had already recovered and was on a planned excursion to the eastern shore of Virginia, where he was taking sitters. The truth was that the accident had laid him low, lower than I've ever seen him before or since; week after week he was as if in a stupor, with death in his eyes, and nightly I climbed into my sleeping loft imagining he wouldn't ever get up.

But that was his war. The explosion of the triumphal arch must have sent him back to the fields near Trenton, to the battlefield, where he saw the enemy inside himself and for the first time in his life he flinched. Doubt kept him in the bed so long, the doubt that we children were instructed to ignore. After forty-five days, a week of which he spent saying he no longer knew who or where he was, my father rose from his bed, and that is when he started on the drawings for the shadow light show.

Now more than ever I understand the desire to start, as he did, from nothing, and, as he stepped over himself lying there recovering with salves on his burn wounds, to leap ahead. Always forward. Would I do differently? No, of course not. I would want it just the same. To rise from the bottom, that is the trick, to make oneself from the stark machinery of one's will. That he did soon enough, rebuilding the arch himself, and at his own expense. "A great and new Order of Ages commences," he inscribed, thirty feet in the air in brilliant gold. From then on outfitting his museum with the latest inventions in illumination—the gallery lights, even the motion picture shadow show. The show lasted just two weeks—surely patrons were afraid the museum would catch fire—before Dad took it down, reusing the wooden planks for the monkey's cage. This act seemed to finally and fully revive him and he had me paint the cage yellow, red, and blue.

When, back at our house, he asked to see the investor's prospectus for the Gas Light Company, I admit to becoming animated. Months ago, I mentioned the need for investors. So I pulled out our prospectus and explained in the clearest layman's language the cost of the project, the minimum investment, the schedule of dividends, etc. But as soon as I began to explain, I realized he didn't quite understand the mechanisms of modern finance. He just doesn't get it. There's a price to pay for ready capital. "Who is paying?" he kept asking. "Paying for what?" I replied. "Paying for the gas," he said, and then, "Son, don't get burned." Or maybe I don't have it quite right, "You're liable to get burned."

Why, he wondered, did I feel so compelled to pay dividends right away to investors? I tried to explain that a grand project— we shall light this entire city eventually—requires ready capital. "Do you know how much your Waterworks cost the city councils?" I said.

"The damn thing exploded, you know—the boiler."

"It still cost tens of thousands."

"And still it blew."

He told me that I would end up making my investors rich. "These men who are conditioned to cheat will fleece you. You'll end up owing *them*, you who have made *them* rich, and you'll have nothing to show for it, least of all the time and where-withal to become an even greater painter." Then he went on about what Ben Latrobe told him this summer. "America will be no different from England," Latrobe apparently said, "a land of vast dehumanizing factories run by nervous, unmanly pinheads who have conditioned themselves to grow fat off of the rest of us."

As we supped later that evening, Dad announced he'd like to attend service at our church, the First Unitarian of Baltimore (the architect Maximilian Godefroy, a close friend of mine, designed our dazzling new church building, which opened a few months ago). I purposely responded in a cool manner. Such a declaration is usually meant to coax an argument. Organized religion is one of those signposts in Dad's mind of a threat to rea-son and self-reliance. He is an old fashioned deist, who believes God is in everything but really nowhere. All laws are natural laws. We were taught that from six months, that and how to draw a straight line. Prayer, in the doctrine of the Peale family, was something for the weak. I tried to change the subject—this was one of those frustrating times I hoped in vain to elicit *some-thing* from Hannah. But I knew better. He was curious about Godefroy's building, he said. I stayed silent. He had heard it was a revolutionary design. Yes, I had told him myself. And the service, it must differ from that of other denominations. This went on: the hunt and my denial until Eleanor cleared the table.

After supper, he insisted on a game of whist, "to settle the mind before repose." My father's eyes were fixed to mine. Eleanor kept shifting her glance; she rose to fill our water glass-es. The other woman looked out, fearfully. While we played, I kept thinking: my father is a stick in the mud; with all his liberal principles he is too close-minded to change with the times. This vision was somehow sharpened by the mostly absent wom-an by his side. Does he not see that the country is changing?

Religion isn't, as he sees it, a threat. Religion is our hope for a just society. And religion, not as theology but as the visceral reality, must therefore be reflected in art. This is the artist's burden. I am sorry, but laws can't act alone. But that's what I saw: a man made slight by retreat into his own solidifying beliefs, nay, his own myth. It sent shivers up my spine.

Chapter XI

Charles Bird King, in the market, High Street, Philadelphia, November 18, 1818

One thing you can say about Philadelphians, no matter the brightly colored parasols or the gilded vis-à-vis or the handfuls of private little societies (in Dr. Franklin's Philadelphia it was said there was a club for every seven citizens and a separate religious denomination for every two): they like to talk, preferably in the middle of the street, and certainly in high voice (and sometimes with fists). And I don't mean the *bruyante cris* of the street peddlers, but the penchant — in the Quaker City, no less — for revealing what's on one's mind. Oh, this tedious place! Everyone has an opinion.

Of course there are the discreet Third Street nobles who keep their mouths and their fortunes behind their high brick walls, and Quakers, who only seem to shout at each other but silently leer upon you as you stroll by. But aside from his youth amidst the gentry of Maryland and aside from the affiliation of his current wife, Charles Willson Peale hasn't much aspired to be either an aristocrat or a Quaker. Why he married a Quaker spinster so late in life is a subject of speculation. Rembrandt says that he thought the woman, who is twenty years his junior, would care for him when he got old. "Dad," he says in his customary way without the possessive "my," as if to indicate the old man is somehow equivalent to God, and therefore everyone's father, "has the old fashioned idea that it's productive for a woman to work, and being young she would share in the household responsibilities. But this woman actually does nothing. That's the tragedy of Dad's retirement." Pity Rembrandt feels the need to overstate because he is probably right. Similarly, I've heard it said the woman was so reserved, so shy and fearful, he thought he would easily order her around. There is another theory that says good old Dad married a Quaker to atone for terrorizing the Friendly people during the heady days of the revolution. Apparently he was a member of the band that went from house to house arresting the wealthiest among them thought to be loyalists and sending them into ignominious exile in Virginia. Yet because he was never a true believer — indeed after the war repudiating the principles of terror — he wished by marrying a Quaker to atone for his sin. Could this be? I'd say it's doubtful. Charles handily deploys guilt, but not on himself. Actually, the man just charges ahead, eyes forward, *nose* forward, and that's exactly how I found him on Chestnut Street as I was hurrying back to Sully's place to gather my things before catching a steamship to Baltimore.

To be exact, I had stopped in front of the university, the mansion the perennially overeager Philadelphians had built to be the house of the president and which both Washington and Adams, fearing a conspiracy to forever condemn the capital to Philadelphia and a populist Democratic backlash against such apparent luxury, foreswore. A strange sight indeed, three Negroes each in a butcher's brilliant white coat, which glowed in the low yellow light, and the faces of the men like embers, and their hands like rusted hooks caught hold of shrouded bodies. One-by-one they carried these bodies as one toddles a colicky babe, over the shoulder, from a wagon and into the university.

At first I had thought they were the carcasses of animals to be used in the teaching of medicine — it is said that the internal mechanisms of a pig is close to our own — and yet here and there was a shock of hair, a toe dangling like a Christmas bell. Did I wish these were, in fact, merely pigs? But what then to think of the Negroes caressing them so? Just then Peale pounced upon me, and so caught up in the disquieting scene before me, I was easy prey.

He took hold of my shoulder with a rough, hard hand and I turned, surprised to see it was him, looking hale as ever, a drop of condensation at the tip of his nose. Eyes gleaming. As usual, he wasted no time with pretense or niceties (a trait I can sometimes admire). But he spoke softly, almost gratuitously. The conversation went like this: "King! You ought to pay us a visit out at the farm. I bet you like clean country air and we grow all kinds of roots, I don't suppose you know how good they are for your digestion."

I smiled and nodded.

"I saw where Birch put your *Carroll*." I'm sure you're aggrieved, but that's how things go at that place, and I can only do what I can do. Well, you're cheating your Philadelphia audience."

Still, I smiled.

"By only sending one painting, you're not doing yourself any favors. What with the market turned soft, there are young artists piling into old sail lofts. You ought to be here to teach them something. They need it. Right? Don't you think so? I thought your *Carroll* stood well along Raphaelle's still lives. I'd never thought myself to put the two of you together. Ah, but he has it hard with that demanding woman."

He grabbed my shoulder.

"And you? You're still cavorting with my son in Baltimore, I hear. Mrs. Peale and I just returned from a journey there. And tell me, are you as impressed with the gas light project as I am?"

"I know he was anxious for you to see it, sir," I said.

"I mean—you have a feel for things down there better than I do, and *you know my son so well*—" I was caught in the teeth of the raptor, but I refused to acknowledge the presence of my own blood. No, it wasn't my blood at all, and I knew this, just as I knew Peale would bite harder the closer I came to the answer he sought. Of course, I didn't know what that answer was. The man doesn't ever reveal his doubts about his sons, and yet it is obvious he has them, and yes, I am a trusted friend. Had he promised to invest and now was having doubts? Or was he initially doubtful but now, after visiting, euphoric? I was caught and I had a steamship to catch. "King, if you don't mind telling me, have you invested anything in the gas light project? You know why I ask. I have certain expertise in this field, useful experience."

"Which I should think he will welcome."

"He will," Peale answered, and I felt the grip ease. His eyes, nevertheless, bore upon me and nestled me closer. "Now I see you're looking a bit cold. You ought to dress better. The key is to layer your outer garments so that your body can respire. Do you supplement your diet with medicinal herbs? At this time of year, especially, you ought to. Learn from the Indians, my boy."

I nodded and looked off toward the wharves.

"Now, what's your perspective? The portrait market still strong for gifted painters like you and Rembrandt? I mean, it seems difficult to gauge things nowadays. Every few days you hear some other speculation about the state of the economy."

"Really, I have a steamboat to catch." Peale was closely shaved; tiny blood vessels like blind fetal worms were visible just below his cheeks. He was right: I was chilled (I had been walking at a rapid pace) and started to shake slightly from the cold. I silently ran through the steamboat schedule; there was time, I counseled myself. From Sully's, where I was staying, it was only a ten minute walk to the landing. Still, I had yet to secure my passage.

"Well, now, King, am I happy to have run into you. But, King? Why be there when everything he needs is here? Mrs. Peale is waiting, just waiting, for a gaggle of grandchildren to take care of. I've no doubt Eleanor could use a break."

Then the wind must have shifted. The Negroes returned, one-by-one, to the wagon, and thus again each cradled and then hoisted over his shoulder a shrouded corpse, the last of which seemed so small it might have been a cat. And, finally, brutality being strong enough to discharge the truth, I spoke. "The problem, if you want to know it as I see it," I said in a quiet and steady voice, "is that Rembrandt has been lied to all his life."

"What the devil do you mean?" he said, and I stared indiscreetly at his bewilderment. "You are opposed to the gas light plan?"

"I think you know," I said, but before I could say more, he turned and walked away, and though I was heading in the same direction, to very nearly the same spot (his museum and Sully's apartments are just around the corner from one another), I allowed him to race ahead. I watched Peale cross Eighth Street, a hawk preparing to take flight. Then I went on, slowly. Had I wounded his pride? The city—perhaps it was the low clouds and cold wet air—seemed hushed, almost silent. If a carter pushed by then, I may not have realized. If a chimney collapsed I wouldn't have heard. I wasn't sorry to be leaving. Being in Philadelphia is like the sun just now, smothered by the hot breath of everyone's anticipation. How withering. Now I was passing through the cloud, walking with haste down Chestnut Street. The black hussy in the pink dress is in this cloud somewhere. She smelled of jasmine and wanted to talk about colors of paint. I told her brown, of all colors, has the most extraordinary range, which I explained to her, I had for many years been carefully manipulating. She laughed and laughed.

Ylaire Charlotte de Chevalier, in the Almshouse, Spruce near Tenth Street, Philadelphia, November 20, 1818

I was shivering in the doorway of a rundown Negro house on Fourth Street with my hand over my mouth trying not to breathe in the odor of the privy and burnt embers and rot that came from through the cellar door, and I was trying to hold myself together. The wind had apparently nothing better to do than harass me, but I put it into my mind to focus on the orange flame of light hitting the corner opposite, imagining the Lord would strike, and light me a fire. Since Miss Eleanor kicked me out I stayed a few nights at the almshouse, but they didn't like my praying, I was whooping it up something else. And all I did was turn a single trick, but I don't think that was it, it was the praying and singing, and marching from ward to ward. If only Lucy could have snuck me into her house because after that I was forced to take a few nights in the China Factory where I got pushed down by a tub of a man with shaking hands and a howling cough. Usually, to protect myself I cover my eyes or look the other way, but that's not the least bit possible at the China Factory. That house is all trouble, and I know it. And don't believe the rumors that it's filled with exotic Chinese girls, either. It's just yellow eyes and Portuguese sailors. The next day I snuck out and met Lucy at the corner of Fifth and Lombard and we walked to Reverend Allen's church together. Lucy wouldn't look at me. Did I look that bad? Did I smell that bad? I tried to make up for it by jumping and writhing and praising and shouting more than usual, but the service only exhausted me and after a while Lucy walked away and sat down at another bench. I haven't seen her since.

The light on Fourth Street began to blacken and there passed Mr. King the painter. He stepped right off the curbstone and very nearly into an oncoming carriage. I let him recover himself — he was lost again in his own head — and then continue on a few paces until he had nearly gotten to Sassafras Street and then I called out, "Mr. Charles King, you had better watch where you're going!"

He didn't hear at first and again I waited. They always turn, Lord knows they turn. Mr. King had on a look of panic. Quickly, however, he crossed Fourth Street. He was carrying a case. "I don't expect to see you in Helltown," I said, "but nice of you to drop by."

He tried to explain he was catching a steamship and was late. "Go on," I urged him and I looked away. "And will I see your mindful countenance again?" But then he didn't answer and I got it in my mind to keep him for a while. "Come with me down Moravian alley. A souvenir of Philadelphia."

"Oh, I hate this city!" he said.

"Take the light of God with you back to Baltimore."

"My steamship leaves from the Mulberry wharf at a half past five."

"Then you've gone too far, Mr. King."

Then, instead of turning back, he moved a little closer. I put my hand on his chest and he looked away. For a long while it seemed I leaned against the brick, which was cold and damp, and I could hear the voices of young boys playing in the courtyard at St. George's. "I notice you haven't got your turban," he said. "I should think it would keep your head warm."

"It's for the sun, believe it or not, Mr. Charles, not the cold. But I don't have my pearls, either. Listen now, I'm going to walk this way down Cherry to Moravian alley. You had better hurry."

I waited a moment, closed my eyes, and I set the flame of God inside me. Oh, and then my eyes, my cheeks, my lips were aflame, they glowed so bright they burned and when I lifted my eyelids, bright and warm and decent against the coming night, I expected once more to be alone. But Mr. King stood next to me, with his back against the wall of the building, in his usual pensive pose, and now watching me open my eyes he walked away, in the direction of Mulberry Street, where he would turn to the wharf. "Good-bye, Mr. Charles," I said, and watched him, so lithe and slender—smaller in girth than I—so quiet he was against the world.

You are not filthy, I said to myself, and one day you will enter the almshouse and—oh, pity that poor frightened Quaker woman, no she wasn't frightened, just unnerved, just confused, there was something steely about her—singing the praises of God, march them off free, no, no I don't hate this life, Lord, I don't hate this life. And then I did what comes easiest to a woman of my design; I made myself invisible and pushed along, down, indeed, into the silvery darkness of Cherry Street.

When, a few minutes later I encountered Mr. Charles King standing beneath the tobacconist's sign at the corner of Cherry and Moravian, he was nervous as a cat, short-stepping this way and that. Be still, Mr. Charles, be still. "You are a little prince," I said to him and led him through a carriageway and into an empty workshop, which smelled of feathers and bones. He said nothing but stroked his own hair and stared to the ceiling as I knelt and pulled out his member. "You shouldn't leave Philadelphia so unsatisfied, Mr. King," I said and gazed up as I began to perform for him. He was still pensive. "No, no, my friend, that would be a shame." He wasn't watching, but what was he thinking? It wasn't possible to tell. So many of them become shameful and angry when I show them the path to God, and I see the fear in their eyes, because yes, I do gently extract from them command over their will. To find God, you let all earthly control go, isn't that right? And there are some who react against this, and in doing so they command me and spit on me and assault me with dark and dreary words and I want to tell them to let my big black lips have their way, I won't bite, my friend, I won't bite. And there are others who yell "hurry up, damn filthy Negress, hurry up," and they squirm and scamper and stamp their feet. I have found there is a type of man who stands still as an ass covered in flies, and so seemingly untouched by the presence of God, and he only draws to a conclusion with a short little burst, like a sun shower that only lasts so long and brings no relief from the drought. But Mr. King is no such hard, unfeeling man. I might even suggest, based on the look of despair on his face, that he feels too much, so much more than he can bear.

And quite to my surprise, before he had even made any sign of reaching the point of fulfillment, he put his hand on my shoulder and asked me stop. When I, so focused as I was on the task at hand, at first refused, he persisted and in a gentle voice said that this sort of intercourse was fine and pleasurable but wouldn't ever truly satisfy, and couldn't we find ourselves a proper room? "But you have a steamship to catch, if it's not too late," I said, yet to rise to my feet and still with his member in my hand. To this he gave no answer and so, to help him relax I cautiously engaged him in conversation. "Look at me," I said, "what color am I?"

"What color are you? What do you mean what color are you?"

"I am not black as night, am I?"

"No, let me see. Be still. Just be still. No, you are umber mostly, with some of the pigment of carbon black, and, I think, red ocher. No, not red ocher. Vermilion, but not too much of it."

"What was that queer brown? Why am I not that?"

"Brown isn't ever queer. Purple is queer. Lemon is queer. You mean Van Dyke, I suppose, though I should hardly know why that kept in your head. But Van Dyke? No, you are not Van Dyke. It has no substance to it, no discernible thickness; and furthermore it has a translucent quality, like a memory, and you are full and thick, rather like the indecipherable future, Charlotte."

I went on about my business. God reveals itself unexpectedly. And how well I—descendent of a proud, free Creole family from Le Cap, with all of our saints and all of our oils, brought to the height of ecstasy in the African Methodist Church, of all places—know this is so! Doubt not, I told myself, lead and he will follow. Follow on, little lamb!

My friend Mr. King began again to relax. Very soon after, I stopped to confirm our way forward, but I found him so very near to the heights of heaven, I lost myself in a dream of Mr. King and I stepping out of the meager Helltown darkness and through the smart, bright, decent city, mindful of the tall trees and the smell in the air of pepper pot soup, and to the stoop of Miss Eleanor's house, and there with such a respectable man by my side, that shrewd woman would forgive me and take me back into her custody. And just at that moment, as the door opened and we were greeted by the tanned voice of Pervis, the doorman—oh, Mr. King you'll wait until tomorrow to leave, now won't you, I know it is so—he came to his emphatic conclusion, which I must say went on and on and on.

Chapter XII

*Joseph Bonaparte, in the window of his
second floor study, Ninth Street near
Locust, Philadelphia, November 21, 1818*

There is a certain refreshing earnestness to this city, which can feel rather like walking through a child's nursery. Nothing and no one is hidden and each one has his own job. Over there is the grinder, with his cart, his grindstone and wheel. All day long, captivated by his own industriousness, he sings the same song. From around the corner, approaches a young lady with the clearest skin and eyes blue as the Mediterranean of my youth, who carries a basket full of radishes on her head. Her cry—it too is repeated without end and without fatigue—is so plaintive as to break my heart each time I hear it. I must do her the favor and purchase some radishes. I dare say it is inevitable that as usual I will be charmed by her seriousness and self-possession. Sometimes it is enough to remind me of my Lalotte. I am told the radish girl cares for the other little ones at home (she hasn't ever spoken to me of her mother). The father is a sailmaker at Forten's. When I asked in my most halting English who takes care of her, our radish girl replied, Uncle James. Mr. Forten, indeed. A black man who sports far more exquisite suits than this one I am wearing, who notably prefers to mix the races in his shop. My friend Ingersoll says he is dangerous, but his reasoning isn't sound on the question.

It is lovely enough today for a ride on the skiff — such a grand gift from M. Girard! — to my estate at Point Breeze. Ah, to amble along one of my garden paths or through my spacious house, to sit and study the busts of my brother Napoleon, to luxuriate about that most sumptuous of sculptures, Canova's masterpiece of my sister Pauline. Oh, but I am daydreaming. How I miss my family!

I must not forget to purchase apples. A half a bushel of bright yellow apples with dashes of red and green pigment as if splattered with paint. Wondrous! I have been fortunate enough to find a woman, a great swarthy, rubescent, rather pleasingly ungraceful woman (so like the black-eyed widows of Corsica), who at this time of year sells these most curious apples. She occupies a bench near the corner of Spruce Street and Third. She despises me. How wonderful it is to observe her. So I tip her freely.

Is this cruel?

Imagine my astonishment upon seeing this peddler that I realized she was the subject of a picture hung at last year's show of the Pennsylvania Academy. The painter, a German called Krimmel, who makes the tiniest, most precise little strokes with his brush, has transformed this quiet spot into a moral inquiry! And there at the center of it, is the cherry woman (as he calls her), a queen on her throne. Truthfully, the picture is horrendous, but I was so delighted by its innocence and pretension that immediately I began asking where I could find the artist. He's returned to his native Germany, I was told. I assumed the cause of his returning was the defeat of my brother, for his nation was unnecessarily ravaged during our last occupation. No doubt the boy was called home to help rebuild.

But then I thought to ask the cherry woman herself. She stared at me a moment and then ignored my question. She returned to her cries and pretended to straighten her selection of golden French pears.

"Don't worry," I said, "it isn't important." I turned away. I walked three steps toward the river.

"Wait, King."

"What is it, my sweet?"

"John Krimmel has returned," she said, as if revealing a state secret.

"And you know where I might find him?"

She gazed back at me with a twisted expression. "Last I inquired of Tom Birch, he didn't know. That was two weeks ago."

"He has disappeared?"

"No one I've asked has seen him."

"But you think Birch would know?"

"If you find him, King—"

"You wish to have the picture? I'll acquire it for you as a gift."

The dear lady straightened up and gathered herself together. "If you find him, send him here."

Within two days of contacting Birch, I found myself in the neighboring village of Germantown—it is a quaint place of high walls and wide brim hats. After an hour of searching, my man Maillard hit his jackpot and he returned to the chaise with this artist—not at all so high minded as I had imagined—thoroughly charming, in fact, with a handsome face and deep-set eyes.

Right away, because why beat around the bush, I told him I was going to present him with payment for the painting of the peddler, and to make arrangements at the Academy to have it delivered to my city home.

His response was exceptional. "It is no good," he said, with such confidence and poise that it made me like him still more.

"Au contraire," I replied, merely to see his reaction.

He stopped me, indeed, his eyes quickened, taking note of the glimmer of sunlight across the red ribbons of my coat and then the fine white skin of my cheeks, and I readied myself for words of protest against my brother's occupation of his nation, I heard in my head declarations of sorrow and anger. For just a moment I imagined the man was capable of violence, and a slight fear rose across my upper lip. I searched his face for the recriminations that would surely follow, I gazed at his puffed hands and back again at his eyes, I thought to call out to Maillard only a few feet away polishing the door of the carriage.

"It isn't for sale," he said.

"But," I said, fibbing only slightly, "I have already given Mr. Birch a deposit."

"I am sorry, then. Birch will have to return it."

Ah, the pleasure of negotiation. "Maillard, give Mr. Krimmel the payment for his painting and set aside a slight administrative fee for the Academy," I commanded, never removing my gaze from the German, "and retrieve back from Birch our deposit."

The German smiled sadly.

"Mr. Maillard is preparing the gold coins now."

"That picture," he began, slowly, "is a poor representation of my talent."

"Let others decide."

"No, the artist should decide." Then the charming young man set out to explain the manifesto of a group he had joined called the Nazarenes, young men apparently unscathed by the meager existence brought about by my brother's occupation of their land, and he described to me his resulting theory on painting. "The power a picture has to create a feeling is a latent power, emanating not from what is in the scene, but what might be."

His gaze had grown heavier, as if he were carrying a burden. He isn't sure his approach will be accepted here, and he is right to doubt it.

Maillard brought the payment.

"Why not teach your method at the Academy?"

"Birch has already acquiesced to it."

"Then consider this a supplement to the meager salary."

His face returned to its calm, inward appearance. The ladies must find him hard to resist.

"Have you visited the Academy recently?" he asked.

Of course, I replied, describing the works from my own collection recently installed.

"Can you tell me if you noticed a different work of mine? I wasn't sure if Birch had hung it."

I had to admit I hadn't noticed. "Mr. Peale was clamoring for my attention."

"It was made before I returned to Europe and consequently before I met the Nazarenes. Yet, in the approach to the scene I've inadvertently followed their rules."

I can anticipate the world, my brother often claimed.

"If Birch has hung it, I recommend you have a look."

Discreetly, I motioned to Maillard to put away the coins.

"And if I find it capable of creating a 'feeling of what might be,' Mr. Krimmel?"

"I will have to return to the city at the start of the year. I begin instruction in January."

I acquiesced then and returned his intent gaze. Maillard helped me to my tufted chair and we continued our tour of the village.

How surprised my Julie-bird would be if she saw me walking the streets, conversing so freely. But this is America! Every man is happily engaged in his own pursuit. I was once a King, but here in this city I am a man like any other. I walk where I like. If my presence amongst the peasantry creates a bit of confusion, that may be because Americans aren't too well versed in world affairs. And faces are easily confused. No one has ever spit at me, and just a few have bowed, turned flush, and called me emperor. So be it. The truth is my extraordinary younger brother, driven wild by ambition, is rotting away in a British prison. I miss him desperately and am all alone. I am ill for the lack of a woman to cherish. My dear sad little Julie-bird has become an obdurate martyr. I fear she too is rotting away and will never join me here.

Madame de Staël entered my dream the other night; she kept directing my hand to unravel her grand turban. A most unnatural woman! But no, it isn't that. My brother has always been disappointed in me for lacking ambition and strength of will. He has always driven me mad with aggression, which perhaps I do not have. But why then, when I offered my life for his with utter seriousness and clarity of mind, did he shoo me away to be rescued and brought to America? Was his will already broken? Was it fated this way? Now I learn that he is ill in prison; he has no freedom to move around and is kept in a rain-sodden barn. And I, a free American, am trapped by my own insidious guilt. Isn't it quite all right to be content with what one has?

Charles Willson Peale, Belfield, November 24, 1818

I woke at half past four, drank two glasses of water, and with the wind in my eyes, walked past the sleeping elk's pen and into the barn. There, I milked the two cows, remarking to myself on the double economy of doing one's chores oneself. It is apparent that many a gentlemen farmer, if that is how I am to be labeled, pays good money for his own idleness and sloth. It is like purchasing one's hastened demise. The body in motion stays in motion, says Mr. Newton, the body at rest stays at rest. I don't need to be convinced of the better alternative.

I set down the bucket of milk, took a spade and a basket, and so I trudged, suppressing worry of danger, through the fetid late autumn field, which felt thick and even overgrown (and not winter raw or empty), into this splendid darkness. The sky was the black of wet ink, blotted in places where clouds showed through the darkness. One stares into the darkness as if it is made of substance, as if it can be touched or felt or even inhabited. Nothing in darkness is greater than darkness. In day, the experience is opposite. The air has no form, no mass. It has no structure. The air signifies nothing more than the state of the weather. It is cold, it is humid, or it is crisp and still it is nothing.

In painting, the blue sky is not only an object of its own merit, but it carries with it various symbolic meanings. Likewise, clouds, the rays of the sun—mostly invisible to us—become the life force of the landscape picture. Naturally, Birch's nautical scenes, mere paeans to war and national feeling if not for the otherworldly clouds, come directly to mind. And so it is, yet again, the opposite when chiaroscuro is employed by the painter. Darkness thus becomes, exquisitely, invisible. Only the subject comes forth; only the person matters.

I stepped through the little apple orchard, taking care not to trip in a fox hole. Mrs. Peale says she will withhold sympathy for me if walking in the dark I fall into a hole and break a bone in my leg or wrench my back. I don't tell her that at times like this I feel myself a hawk. (The savages who once roamed this land knew something, I believe, of the power of this feeling.) The hawk never sees the little mouse clambering through the leaves made papery by the hoarfrost; he doesn't have to because he senses the vibrating earth. And thus I become the hawk and just the feeling of it increases the acuity of my senses. So on I went, beyond the third row of trees and there, finding my prey, I planted myself, now no longer the hungry raptor but as a small child alone amidst God's creation. This is, after all, my own earth. As I hunched over to begin my work, the clinging heat of mold and decay rose to warm my face.

When Raphaelle arrived last Wednesday to sit for his portrait, he was armed with a thousand diversions. He walks slowly and now with a cane but insisted I take him for a tour of the late autumn garden. "You aren't bundled well enough," I said, but since I think it best in these cases to push on, as the will only grows in proportion to its obstacles through practice, I gladly acquiesced. Mrs. Peale came to the door with a heavy blanket made of horsehair. My son draped this over his shoulders, holding it closed across his chest with one hand while grasping the cane in the other, in such a way that only heightened his appearance of derangement (the blanket trailed behind him). We made our way along the stone path now covered with a skin of leaves, past the greenhouses and, pausing briefly, I started to explain my deep appreciation for the place. "You will note," I began to say, "once we rise to the bluff of the summer house, how gratifying it is to sit still and ponder nothing but the glories of nature," but as I did so, I worried that such a statement might sound to my son as an endorsement of excessive repose and so I quickly amended the statement to include a phrase on the way "such careful study of nature has improved my ability as a colorist." We climbed, slowly enough, up the stone staircase I had built myself, to the Pedestal of Memorable Events. Each of the eighty events is denoted with a little engraved star, but I drew his attention to a single star without descriptor, a space left for an example of the positive progression of the American philosophy yet still to come, with the intention, while looking him over, of suggesting that the place be reserved for a notable advancement of his own. But this too I amended on second thought. Instead, I said, and not without truth, the space has been reserved for the glory of industrial invention, perhaps the steam engine, perhaps the prosaic, nay ingenious, mill.

While eating our small, simple dinner of boiled potatoes and cabbage — Raphaelle spent a great bit of time making jokes about the austerity of our meal (at my expense), which Mrs. Peale unflinchingly and quite calmly deflected — I asked him to tell me how he thought he ought to appear in a portrait.

"I think you had better ask that question of the man with the pencil," he responded.

"But don't you care how you are presented to the world?" I looked across the table. Alas, the boy looked tired. His ears were blotched red, his skin waxy. Upon his arrival at Belfield, I had looked him over carefully. He was clean-shaven and wore a high collar and a cloak. He carried no odor of alcohol, but seemed to mutter to himself rather frequently.

"Well, then," he said, looking around the room, "why beat around the bush. Paint me for what I am."

"That's what I do intend," I said.

"No. Paint me as flesh. A good cut:

> *Now where's the difference?*
> *to th' impartial eye*
> *A leg of mutton and a human thigh*
> *Are just the same — for surely all must own*
> *Flesh is but flesh and bone is only bone.*

"That line of argument has already been taken." What a faculty he had for remembering snippets of writing, and still...

"That may be the point. Surely you can improve it. I should think a porterhouse cut with some curls of onion." He brushed his hair with his hand. Did I imagine this, a hand rheumatic, claw-like? I guided him into the painting room. The fire in the hearth barely glowed and I took some time to stoke it. I then arranged him in front of an easel and canvas of his own and put a palette in his left hand, a brush in the right.

"Then why not paint me as Raffaello?" he said a bit imperiously, pausing for effect. "You don't get me, do you? Paint me in the style of Raffaello Sanzio. Shouldn't there be a drop of guilt in my eyes? No insipid despair, what I want is guilt. It's more pleasing." He paused and I allowed him to go on nonsensically. "Anyway, I have always desired that—as a joke, you see, what you might call a gesture."

"You don't need to act a fool anymore, dear boy. Suppose I just paint the person I see before me."

"And isn't that the quite real Raffaello?"

For some reason he felt the need to press the point. I tried not to resent the constant go around. I was already growing tired of the crazy fellow. I wished to make his portrait as a sign of defiance and if he hadn't that capacity then I would have to provide it for him. The portrait would resurrect him. "I will paint you as Raffaello Sanzio, one of the cleverest members of the papish religion and, my dear boy, a master of the portrait."

"Then I shall die in the arms of a voluptuous whore. There will be glory, at last."

In that moment I never felt more certain that I would outlast Raphaelle—not only Raphaelle, but every last one of them. My day that begins at half past four ends punctually at a quarter past ten. That's nearly eighteen hours awake, a full fifteen of which is spent in the act of work: six on farm chores, care and feeding of the animals, mending and rebuilding farm utensils and farm buildings, and working in the garden, six in the act of painting—I am determined that the portrait of Raphaelle will reestablish my own reputation as a portraitist—and three in the planning of my cotton mill. Glory, I am certain, will come in the spinning of the waterwheels, even without the aid of my recalcitrant sons.

The rest is spent eating (one hour fifteen minutes spread over three light meals) and writing to my children. And who of my children, or even my wife, twenty years my junior, comes close to this example of vigor? Rembrandt? He requires too much sleep. Rubens? He very competently manages my museum but lives in the delicate mold of a Roman bureaucrat. During his long supper break, he strolls aimlessly around the city or idles about the State House gardens. The second Titian, I imagine, works hard on his naturalist exhibitions but is easily distracted. The rest I need not mention. Mrs. Peale tells me I am a wretched father for expecting so much of my children. "Let them be!" she says. I tell her I don't get her point. "But they must live their own lives! One way isn't better than the other." I can only look on impassively but with secret joy in my ice blue eyes. One's children are, indeed, like one's piece of earth. They must be cultivated, pruned, clipped, fertilized, and arranged to one's liking.

With the wind beating down on my unprotected neck, now crouched on the ground beneath the apple trees, I began to dig. A single, last leaf of the apple tree twirled around and around, making a scattered, intermittent sound, the very quality of the noise of children playing upstairs. After digging through the raised beds beneath the apple trees, I came to realize I had estimated wrong—this patch of orchard had been harvested already. I advanced to the last row of trees—and here was the mother lode of potatoes. So be it, there were enough to deliver with the sample bottle of wine to Tharp, a chore which Linnaeus hadn't ever completed. He'll only work, he says, if he is to be paid explicitly for his services. Room, board, and the infinite patience of his mother aren't quite enough. Since he was a boy, Linnaeus has driven me, with efficiency and predictability, to anger. I won't stand the obfuscation or the undercurrent of deceit. But I've always studiously avoided taking pity on the boy. And so he left for some time and joined the navy, despite my admonitions against war, only to return with a monkey on his back, a sword in his belt, and a sad, shit-eating grin on his face. His sisters fall for it every time.

But now where were the corks? It had been my intention to reach Tharp before he became busy at the mill; I lost nearly a full hour cutting down a cork from an old bottle of whiskey I found in the barn, only to have it crumble into tiny pieces and fall into the wine. I kept my temper in check during this fitful exchange, which also resulted in hitting my head on the pediment to the kitchen door. Luckily, the slight welt that rose above my right temple was mostly invisible to the unknowing eye. At last, I employed a decanter, whose glass top would have to suffice. Now instead of laying the bottle down on top of the potatoes, I would have to secure it standing up for fear of spilling. I did so, resting the basket every few paces and sweating profusely despite the chill and the wind.

There was now enough vulgar light to see clearly and for this, and just for a moment, I felt a usual pang of sadness, for never do I feel as defiantly alive as in these earliest hours, when the world expects a man of my age and standing to be auditioning for the hereafter. Should I be spotted doing my farm chores at the early hour by some perspicacious neighbor who thinks he's witnessed the installation of madness, it would only be so much more of a pleasure.

Rembrandt Peale, in bed at home in Baltimore, November 25, 1818

It is doubtless true that many a son has arrived at a moment in his life when he is in a position to observe that his relationship to his father is reversing. Is this what is happening? For so long we have parried as equals. He has relied on me for ideas and in-spiration and I him for gusts of wisdom. But the father, so long embedded in a position of authority toward the son, slips with age. The son rises. He takes pity on the father, whose hand be-gins to shake. He begins to sound old, his ideas and arguments outdated, his letters repetitive. Time exerts its influence. The roles finally reverse.

Does he surpass the father?

Years ago in Paris I saw and carefully studied the products of the European masters. My point in spending twelve hours a day upon my feet in exhaustive study in the great halls of the

Louvre was to select from their beauties, discard their defects, and methodize their systems of painting. Eventually, I formed a union of these masterpieces in the picture of my brain. It has always been my intent to improve on that picture.

It took some time to recognize the defects, for even I was seduced by Titian's *Judith* and Van Dyke's *Delilah*. And yet these paintings have no hold on the American mind. This was the greatest defect and my most striking epiphany. The republican has no time for obscure allegory, for hidden meanings. No matter the skill, the finish. No matter the "poetry." Unless it is useful, unless it can instruct, a painting is wasted on the American. To do thus, as I have determined from careful observation, a picture must be accessible, simpler and more direct than even the admonitions of the bible. And so I shall produce a painting of moral instruction to define the potential of allegorical art in America: this my father hasn't ever done.

And this, now, shall be my calling. To double the moral imperative, the figures in the painting will feel real because they will be fully life size. The message delivered will easily carry the weight of ten preachers. Michael Angelo, my oldest son, is this morning to help me erect a scaffold in the auditorium of my museum.

But Michael Angelo is lazy and with this weather—gray, chilled, and damp as it has been for nearly a week—I cannot expect his help until noon. I must anyway reply to my father's latest letter. King was here a week ago, grinning from ear to ear and looking at me as if searching for an answer, to what I don't know; Christ, I wanted to tell him to get out, to get his own painting room, even giving him a list of empty buildings. I thought for sure he was going to start asking questions about the sign in my museum window, "CLOSED UNTIL FURTHER NOTICE DUE TO BAD ECONOMY." But he didn't mention it. Then he surprised me with a pair of news items. No doubt these emerged from his lips in the "spontaneous moment," but strictly speaking I do all I can to not be taken off guard. And there it was: he was leaving Baltimore to move to the District of Columbia, his grandmother's inheritance had finally come through. Good for him. Maybe he could pay me back some rent? No, he merely purred and stretched around the room like the stealth little cat he is. "I shall stake my tiny claim to the nation's capital." Good for you, my dear New Englander friend. You can't help but succeed, since there isn't any competition in the wasteland. Don't forget to collect your brushes on the way out the door. But then: "I ran into your father as I was leaving Philadelphia, Rembrandt. I understand he's going to invest? That's great news."

"Invest in what?" I said in reply. I am not in the habit of letting all the world in on my business.

"The gas light project, what else. Don't be coy."

An apt word to come out of his mouth, but sure enough the next day brought the news in the officially declining penmanship of my father. "I've come to agree on the merits of your visionary plan and wish to place some capital in your venture," he wrote. "Perhaps with the gains I will be able to lend more active support to all your brothers and sisters." Now then, proceeds from the Gas Works are to support my sister, whose husband, Mr. Robinson, is the project's most vocal opponent? Or is it merely to keep my brother in rum and hussies?

Once — as I recall it this was before Dad brought live animals into his museum — a raccoon took up residence in our cupboard. He immediately declared we would trap the animal, to preserve and study him, but the first Titian Ramsay said no, and as my father was partial to the boy, the raccoon was left to be. We rarely saw the masked beast, though Rubens, who took his art history quite as seriously as I, gave him the name Pietro Longhi, for the Venetian genre painter who filled his canvases with scenes of masked revelers during Carnevale. This Pietro was indeed quite mysterious to us, as he seemed to appear and disappear without reason. It turned out that Raphaelle, who stuffed food in his pockets and therefore occasionally spread our dinner scraps around the house, was to blame for his erratic presence. A spotting was nevertheless often a cause for much commotion. We came to think of him as a family mascot. Sometime that winter Dad mentioned he noticed an odor, which he described as "burning but without fire," but which he said he couldn't trace to its origins. He was confounded. Once, he grabbed my arm and pulled me to the exact spot where he had detected the odor. We stood there bending ourselves in hope of catching a waft. I couldn't smell it. Then, a few days later, standing across the room and secretly observing our matronly housekeeper and wondering if Eleanor, her petite daughter, honest and sweet as a plum — who had no idea the effect her presence had on me — would age into such an unlovely creature, the putrid odor came to me. As quickly as I seemed to grasp it, however, it was gone, a pattern repeated in our house for days. No one could quite put a finger on it.

Nor could I, now, put a finger precisely on the miserable sense of discomfort and even doom that I was feeling as I sat to write a reply to my father. A rumor, probably started by Robinson, had spread that gas-powered lighting would cause explosions and fires. A public outcry would delay us even further.

Michael Angelo came into my painting room just as I had commenced with the letter to Dad. He was still in his bedclothes and I, unnerved and feeling unsteady, lashed out at him. I have never found it easy to be a gentle father. Nonetheless, a few minutes later he returned, clothed and alert. (I had warned him against recalcitrance.) Very quickly we got to work, arranging the heavy pieces of hardwood and lathe into a suitable scaffold, fully twenty-five feet long and ten feet high so that I could work on the mammoth painting all at once and wouldn't have to move the scaffold from place to place. I observed my son working; every few minutes he stopped and looked around with apprehension, probably wondering why I hadn't hired someone else. The boy never has been drawn to work. I willed him on knowing that his fragility has often given his mother and me trepidation and reminded us of his oldest uncle, my brother, a drunk and wastrel without an ounce of moral fiber. One makes choices in life. My new painting will be called the *Court of Death*. Implicit is this idea: we are each of us the most profound judge of our own behavior.

Raphaelle Peale, at the back of the Man Full of Trouble Tavern, Philadelphia, November 30, 1818

Returning from the inquisition at Belfield, I climbed those damn winding stairs, one at a time with rest in between; these ought to be servant's stairs, but they're all we have. I sat for a minute in the lone chair in the room and tried to stretch my knees; my ankles throbbed. The floor was worn and knotted, the gray walls bare with only Patty's strange, unsettling crucifix over the bed. Above my head was a sketch my father did of me and my tragic little brother Titian Ramsay so many years ago for his famous staircase painting. I tried to banish thoughts of winter coming and the coming year—1819, my forty-sixth—and to banish the incessant pain.

It was useless, all useless. My legs were like axe handles as I descended the stairs; I took my coat from the hook and unclasped the door. The wind swirled at my feet and sent drying leaves sliding, now unhinged, across the sidewalk. I turned toward the river and hunched my shoulders and stepped down into Fifth Street. Without thinking I was heading to Helltown. After a while, I began to walk a little faster. For the first time that night, I moved without seizing up, and without stopping. I let the oysterman pass. I inhaled and stole a peak at his oily broth. I looked into his white eyes and moved on through the crowd milling below Walnut. I let my fingers drag along a brick wall near Third.

The crowd thickened around the market. There was awful shouting coming from behind the line of carriages. I assumed it was just the usual insipid politicking. Perhaps some important election was impending, and a bunch of partisans had gotten themselves a little too steamed up. I didn't care enough to avoid it, so I walked on behind the carriages toward Chestnut. Doing thus, I brushed up against a short man in a top hat. He turned to me, his pocked face with its horse nose and double chin illuminated by a sorry candlestick he held in his shaking hand. With the other he grabbed my upper arm, and made the effort to give it a vicious squeeze. I didn't have the strength to pull away and so received a primer on the Catholic conspiracy. The filthy, backwards Irish were coming, shouldn't I like to know, the almshouses were already overrun with them and soon it would be our neighborhoods and schoolhouses subject to papal dominion. Now look who's found Philadelphia a friendly town? Walks around like he owns the place? The papist Bonaparte, wants to take over the world. They're behind the Second Bank, too, I was alerted. Girard, you see, the greedy little Frog, and from whom do you think he takes his orders?

As I ducked out of the way my right leg seized; I turned, let the pain flare as long and slowly as it might—it is equivalent to Patty's wretched nagging—and then absently reversed course to cross the city the other way. South Street with its hot little groups of people collected at street corners came to my lurid relief. I passed the same oysterman, now leaning against a tree outside of Mrs. Fury's bawdy house. A fiddler was playing somewhere; I walked slowly, hesitatingly on. As the scream of the fiddle grew louder I ducked through a door and passed into the dim light and flicker of the Man Full of Trouble Tavern, calling out to all assembled: What is a butterfly? At best / 'tis but a caterpillar dress'd!

Unanswered, I grabbed a seat at a large table near the fireplace and far enough away from the fiddler, who sat in a chair by the door and laughed while he played. Laughed and shuffled his feet. I sat next to Jimmy Cox, the printer, who breathed thickly through his mouth and whispered dirty jokes as he looked over a hand of cards. On his face a half-serious, half-mocking expression, a passive mouth and greedy eyes, eyes that seemed to draw me, yes, from my wretched chrysalis. It took only a short glass of rum and predictably I was leaning over to answer his jokes with the worst worn couplets from my father's day, or even before:

> *Scarce had five Months expired since Ralph did wed,*
> *When lo! his fruitful Wife has brought him to Bed.*
> *How, now, quoth Ralph—this is too soon, my Kate,*
> *No, Ralph, quoth she, —you marry'd me too late.*

And:
Wisdom it is Clear
Doesn't come from Beer.

And:
He'll have a sep'rate Bed; — 'Tis her Desire;
Sheets warm'd, Bed made, the smiling pair retire;
The Cause tho' hidden, yet the same their Want;
He sends for Miss, and she for her Gallant.

Now then, Cox had me going. To please him further, I did my best imitation of Hamilton, the overstuffed tobacconist, who sat across the table. I pinched my eyebrows and unbuttoned my shirt collar and while leaning back, pounded my middle finger on the table. This produced the intended effect. Now present the man a cigar, ordered Cox, but Hamilton, true to his character, ignored him. My own supper arrived just then: fried trout, six fried oysters, and a leg of pheasant. I devoured the oysters and the pheasant and quite instinctively and incapable of stopping myself — and yet, who can argue with the pleasing laughter? — I offered my trout to Cox. But it wasn't me offering the fish, it was the trout itself, crispy golden brown and salted, doing the talking; I merely, and yes, artfully, and with practiced skill, moved the dainty jaw in time with the words, Eat me, Jimmy! Eat me, Jimmy! Hamilton reached across the table with his short pink fingers to stick the tip of a long corn pipe in the poor trout's mouth. Cox, in side-glance, looked me over and, measuring the depth of my sickness, raised his forehead in a look of bewilderment and meager sympathy. He needed barely move a muscle to turn away.

Chapter XIII

John Lewis Krimmel, in the silence of the Miller house, November 30, 1818

I don't begrudge Harriet her silence or her confusion. I see the way she escapes what she thinks she is seeing in the hearts of her sisters. I see the way she avoids my eyes, which come for her even when I don't bid them to, when I tell them to stay away, to give her the space she requires. The almshouse is becoming her salvation; she goes there to prove to herself—as if the minutes and hours there will amount to something she can touch and feel and know, like a theorem—that she isn't Henrietta, she isn't Caroline or Mr. Isaac Miller.

She won't be mine, either, she tells herself, if she is hot on the tail of justice.

This is her proof.

It's all right, I want to tell her, the words quietly unleashing in my mind and on my tongue until they build and become heavy on me, and I can't figure out where to put them. I remember my first days in this country, in this harsh city, with its oyster brine and chatter, and my surprise at seeing my brother George so easily accustomed. The greatness of America, he would say to me, is that everything has a price, there isn't an inch of land that can't be transacted, there isn't an hour of time that hasn't been given a clear value. For a time, I believed him.

I found the logic of it refreshing and I felt I was living in a new way, without superstition or confusion.

So I followed him into business and I saw that the price of something became more real than the something itself. That is when I turned back to making pictures, but then I found that I was thinking first of the price the picture would be given before thinking of the picture itself and I began to hate the coldness and resent my brother's capitulation.

And so I came to rely on Susanna, with her forthrightness and straight back, who had refused to shed the graciousness that she had come with. She drew me into the circle of her being and she allowed me to breathe. Intoxicated, I forgot the prices of things, and I began again to make pictures. I filled my first American sketchbooks and I brought them to her with the ex-pectation of a child. At night, in my own bed I longed to be with her. I let myself hate my brother, who so excelled at business he rarely came home.

Then one night in the unbearable silence I went swiftly to her and just as swiftly and surely she rejected me and she took me and my bitter shame in her own shame and held me to her bosom and nestled me like a child. I tried not to look at her; I didn't need to look at her, I couldn't look at her, she was on the other side of a wall she didn't need to explain; the wall was her inexplicable, enduring love for George. Susanna brought me to her bosom in order to reject me, and I knew then I would forever reject the false simplicity of a price or a clear, certain principal of moral judgment and if I was going to make pictures they would have to deny the falsehood of certainty. I want to say all this to Harriet as if to comfort her in her shame and confusion. I shamed her but only because I love her and she loves me, but her love is tangled and knotted so that it hasn't room to breathe.

Harriet Miller, in the parlor of the Miller house, November 30, 1818

All this bad weather has driven Henrietta to the summer house, where she sat on the cold brick floor surrounded by piles of sticks and leaves and other garden refuse; standing above her as I was, she appeared no differently than she does while weeding or pruning or digging away, that is to say mortised to the fecund earth. She was making decorations for our sister's wedding. "I am being useful," she said to me with such sweet — oh, unnerving — insouciance, and went about the nimble twisting of a stick to form a wreath. This possibility, of the entire family indulging in Caroline's nuptial, as if she were marrying some kind of aristocracy — these are hard souls after all, striving, decent Presbyterians — hadn't readily occurred to me. Of course it had been apparent all along. Even our father, usually dismissive of the aspiring type, has been gleaming. The talk at supper has been about her future husband's business, evidently a most successful indigo printing mill. Father was given a tour by Mr. Tharp's brother, who is responsible for the mill operation, and he came home boasting and promising new dresses for all of us with lovely colorful prints. Of course as he went on I grew indignant and angry. And father was oblivious to my discomfort. Finally, I said, far more harshly than I intended, "Such a mill is a foolish waste."

"You wouldn't say that if you saw it, Harriet," he said. "You can't believe how powerful these water wheels are."

Henrietta said little, as usual. But all the while she was inventing wreaths of bittersweet, a bridal crown of jasmine and honeysuckle ("Smell it," she said to me, holding out a bunch of desiccated sticks, "still fragrant"), and a garland of pine and hydrangea. By the second day, I had enough of the rustic festooning; I wanted something real while everyone else played around.

So I went, as I often did, to the almshouse to offer myself to the sad, loveless victims there. There I stood below the warden of the almshouse straight as possible, hands clasped, and asserted my desire to meet privately with one of his inmates, the African streetwalker Charlotte, who had been brought in, I had been told, for selling herself on the streets of Helltown. She needed legal commandeering, certainly, and someone to talk to, I was sure.

"You are sure she is here?" he said.

"Is she not then?"

"You will have to wait."

"So, she is here."

"You will have to have a seat," he said, and so I sat and so he stood, head bobbing slowly, shoulders drawn, doing nothing. And for some time he did nothing. Several others appeared at various times at his warden's station; with them he conversed in whispers, in bobs of the head, in the light of the sharp winter sun. I refused to drift in the unwitting silence.

An hour passed before I stood. "I can find her myself," I said.

"Just a minute," he said, unleashing a volley of inactivity and resistance. "Let me give you some advice. Forget their names. While you're at it, forget their faces."

I ignored him and wandered off down the long passage that bifurcates the first floor. I walked quickly, thinking all the time of what I would say to the street woman, how I would talk and how she would listen. I was tempted by my imagination: to bring her home, to give her work, surely my father would understand the weight of the cause at hand. A mere wedding could not compare. And so, left alone to my own resources, I searched the corridors, rooms, corners, doorways. I returned to the chamber where we had met before but found only a group of wenches huddled closely on a bed looking at a book of pictures laughing coarsely and clutching each other shamelessly. I pitched my voice above the terrible, shameless din to demand the whereabouts of Charlotte. I did so two or three times until one of them, whose voice was sweet and mellow and surprisingly hopeful, said, "Shh, there is a lady in the room." And, again, I inquired about Charlotte's whereabouts, but only one of them knew her, "a washerwoman at Mrs. Fury's place," she said, "and that Negress can talk her way out of everything."

"I suppose not," I said. Had I known that once again I was only fodder to a game, that I was to be fooled with and made a fool of, would I then have withdrawn? No, I whisper to myself now, and for a moment I feel like I'm being offered a glimpse through the thick skin of Mr. Krimmel to the shame he's swallowed, if in fact he has.

They only act this way because they themselves are frightened, I must remember, and I tell myself not to despair.

In my own fear, I looked upon them as a pack of wild dogs, dogs in heat.

"Was she a servant of yours, miss?"

"She's no washerwoman. And anyway, lady, what are you? From the Magdalen Society?"

"Oh, I never seen her, and they made me stay there a year, until I turned seventeen," said another.

"And then?"

"I waited until the day before and then I escaped. They were sending me to a poor God-fearing family in the sticks, it was my last chance."

I turned the corner into a hallway reserved for the victims of the steam engine explosion at the waterworks. At the end of that passage I would find the staircase to the lying-in ward—where, indeed, those ill with venereal disease are also kept—and continued my search for Charlotte. Was I foolish to think I would find her? Did it even matter?

I wasn't five paces down that corridor of misfortune when I heard the strumpet's gallop coming from behind. She was small, taut, steely, and possessed an upturned nose. "We have her," she said.

"What is it?"

"The Negress Charlotte, she's come in our chamber right now. You want to see her, don't you, lady?"

"That is evident," I said and I thanked her for finding me.

Her name, she revealed without reticence, was Mary Ann Walsh, and she was abandoned to an aunt in Southwark when she was six and then indentured—"and it wasn't just the washing the master expected me to do" — when she was twelve. "So I don't know much about a home life," she said, "but if a man came along who could make me comfortable, I wouldn't turn my back. What about you, lady, you got a husband?"

"Tell me, why should you care so much about a man? You seem to me perfectly capable of handling yourself in the world."

"Isn't that a little obvious. Anyway, the men seem to like me." We had arrived back at the room. She opened the door and for some reason guided me in, as if I wasn't sure of where I was going. I looked around the room: five white harlots, no Charlotte. "Charlotte—"

"But she's right here, lady, don't you see?" Now I was pulled to the bed, enveloped like a new bitch in their heat and hunger and the book was thrust in my face; it was an old book and I remember first the smell of it, heavy and musty and stained with brown like the grain of wood. And then the picture — "See the Negress hussy!" — in gaudy watercolor, an African with a preposterous anatomy placed, as was soon revealed by the turning of the pages of the book, in no less preposterously grotesque positions, one after the other of sexual depravity in the greatest possible detail. The laughing was no less savage. And was it possible that I could make myself heard, that they would understand *me*?

And then one of them said, "I think she likes it!" For I could not take my eyes from the images, despite my face burning with shame. Was it me or Charlotte they wished to defile? Eventually, I stood and pushed them away. I tried not to shout; my stupid bonnet cinched my forehead, and like a careless child, I tore it off and threw it to the floor.

Charles Willson Peale, in his bedroom, Belfield, December 1, 1818

It being the end of the week, Mrs. Peale bid me beneath the covers last night. She is a sturdy woman with sharp, calcified breasts that remind me of the giant conch shells I used to find as a young boy wandering along the Eastern Shore. It is my habit to caress them while she scratches my balding head. Then she sits upon me and I amuse her. This has been our regimen since the earliest days of our marriage, when at fifty she discovered that a man could make her blood boil. When she is ready, she signals me and I turn her around, climb on, and fuck her from behind. This has remained one of the most reliable rituals of our union.

I have noticed recently, however, a creeping fear. As we near the summit of pleasure, I have begun worrying: Is this the last? The fear is mutinous. It mercilessly scorches my good sense and all the good feeling that should follow such sacred marital intimacy. Then I find myself becoming angry and unpleasant, like a fitful child, without the strength of reason to bind his passion. And last night the fear came to fruition. I climbed upon her but I couldn't get it up. Just then Mrs. Peale was in full heat and tried to force the matter, but I was unable. She turned over, grabbed a hold of my member, and yet it shrunk away even further. What's more, her hands were cold as ice; they were the hands, it seemed to me, of death himself.

PART THREE

Chapter XIV

*D*ixcy said he'd rather not go, his head ached. "Anyway, I hate to be a stranger in someone's house at Christmas," he said.

"It isn't about Christmas, William, it's about us, our project," said Victor. "Anyway, you don't turn down an invitation from someone like Charles Willson Peale." The ceiling of our room at the top floor of Mrs. Chamberlaine's boardinghouse tilted above us like a limb half fallen and propped against a neighboring tree, and Victor, who looked even taller since we had arrived in Philadelphia, seemed to defy it. His Adam's apple floated somewhere in the foliage. At least that's how I saw it. I was sitting on my bed. Dixcy was sitting on his. The wind rattled the half-sized window.

"You don't need me," said Dixcy, whose eyes were gray-yellow and stunted.

"He's waiting for us to leave, Cloud, just in case Libby knocks and says Christmastime is a little lonely with just her and her mother. Then he won't have any worry about being in a stranger's house at Christmas."

Victor reminded us to stick to our mission: to acquire from Peale a promise for letters of introduction to as many of the masters on our list as he was willing to write. And, if Rembrandt

Peale were present, as his father said he would be, to arrange a time for a formal interview. "I like the painting he did of his wife. It's full of feeling."

"Victor," Dixcy said to me, "is a bona fide Romantic."

We found a Germantown stage near the market. Victor got the driver to knock off seventy-five cents from the price and we arrived at Peale's gate just after four. At least, in the fading light, we thought it was a gate. Really, it was the side wall of a shed, on which was elaborately painted in trompe l'oeil a garden path leading to a gate, upon which was affixed in bas relief various representations of American themes, like temperance and industry. The best was a depiction of the Roman Mars fallen down. I said Peale must have been a pacifist.

"He loves to deceive, it seems to me," said Victor. "And he does it well. Do you see all the detail, so that it looks like you're looking right through?"

"It's doubly deceptive," I said. "Once you realize it's faked, you become even more interested, for example in this depiction of America—"

"She has such wide eyes, Cloud."

"For seeking the truth, no doubt. And you go on chatting even in the growing darkness of a December night."

"Look here at this depiction of the water wheel, the wheel is turning backwards."

"Might be," I said, "and, Victor, you don't even realize the real gate is right here, and it's unlocked."

The trees were black silhouetted against the sky, rose-stained by the vanishing sun. We drifted up into Peale's field. There was the slight sound of wind and of children's voices, which mingled in the air. To the left, the ground rose to Peale's obelisk, where he wished to be interred. Victor trampled over to see it. His footsteps crackled the leaves and his breath below that and still the wind and the children. "Never return an injury," he called out. "Cloud, listen, it's written here, 'It is a noble triumph to overcome evil by good.'"

I told him I had no idea what he was talking about. For a minute Victor disappeared and then the sky was silvery black above the trees and pink below. He seemed to take forever to examine the obelisk and then suddenly he grabbed my shoulders from behind and said it was going to be an interesting night. I asked him what he meant by interesting and he said it seemed like Peale lived in a dream. "Still his French is god-awful," he said.

"What do you mean, his French?"

Victor explained that on each of the four sides of the base of the obelisk was an aphorism. "Or really a dictum. Neglect no duty, be content work hard and live in peace, etc." Some of them were written in French.

"Doesn't seem that unusual."

"Yes, but who is he speaking to here in his own garden?" Victor had a finger to his mouth and then he motioned toward a barn. Under the eave there were two figures shyly embracing. "Kissing cousins," he whispered, "have a look." I shrugged. "She keeps saying, 'kiss me,' but I don't think he has a clue." As soon as we moved toward the house the girl took off right past us, away from the house. The boy, a little dazed, wandered our way. He was eleven or twelve years old, with a fine black mustache and shifty eyes. Victor introduced himself and shook the boy's hand. "This is my friend Caleb, you can call him Cloud if you like. And who are you?"

"I'm Michael Angelo," the boy said. His voice cracked miserably and then he led us inside.

"We need no introduction," said Peale, his eyes the eternal blue of a mannerist heaven. So taken was I by his eyes, so effortlessly and deeply blue, that I nearly missed Victor's deferential gaze on the old man. Victor called Peale heroic; he mentioned Washington, Jefferson, he described our impressions of Philadelphia, he talked about the bounty of the High Street Market. And I looked away. Did I know? Did Hicks stand over me whispering in my ear? The lion will only listen to the wolf, isn't that right? And the wolf, my friends, he is always hungry.

Michael Angelo ducked under his grandfather's arm and got lost in the crowd. Peale instructed us that supper would be served at eight promptly. By then, he said, we would have met all the charming members of his family. "Well, you're already acquainted with the devil Michael Angelo." He took Victor by the arm and led us down a hall, past the kitchen, and past another room where two men who looked about Krimmel's age—one of whom, I later learned, was Dr. John Godman, who would become the husband of Rembrandt's daughter, and the other, Peale's grandson Coleman Sellers—were standing before a piece of drawing paper, designing some kind of apparatus for dissecting human remains, and then into his painting room, newly completed.

There was an unfinished portrait of Raphaelle most calmly gazing back at us, brush in hand. Peale, who had stopped at the entrance to the room, now strode across the floor like an academician on the cusp of the proof of God. "I presume you know this great man," he said, "for years I have been haranguing him to come sit for his father. Well, I don't know what changed his mind and this time he came." Peale assured us it was one of his best portraits. "And why? Because I discovered something about my son that he doesn't even know about himself; it came to me as I was placing the first pigments on the canvas and then again as I set his chin and as he gazed back at me, he spoke to me, he said, 'I don't paint portraits because I am afraid of disappointing the sitter, with apples I have no such worry'— and that's why I placed those apples in the picture, you can see them outlined there on the wall behind him—and I said back to him then I will show you what's really inside you, a man of great empathy and understanding. Do you not see that in his eyes, the same as his mother Rachel, from whom he inherited this reticence, because if he sees for himself what's inside him, what is hidden to all the world, including himself, that is, his empathy, he will come to know that he is just the man to be painting portraits."

Peale again gripped Victor's arm and he looked at him intently. "He just has to have trust in himself," he said, and as he did so his eyes watered slightly, almost imperceptibly, and he started to think and say something more, also imperceptibly, and then fell silent.

Victor tried to fill the silence by describing our interview with Raphaelle. Peale asked a few questions, mostly about the state of Raphaelle's house and if it seemed that he had been sober, but after a few of these questions, to which Victor provided vague answers, Peale lost interest. He wanted to know, instead, if we were restricting our book to living masters.

"That goes without saying," replied Victor, "if they aren't living we can't interview them."

"Then the book would become no more than an encyclopedia," I said, "and that would be the death of it." But then Victor looked at Peale and asked him why he had asked. Peale didn't respond to this. Instead, Victor looked at me and said by his count, there weren't fifty masters in America, maybe twenty-five or thirty at the most, and he started to name some, ticking them off on his fingers. Then Peale turned to me and said that he could use a decent writer, as he was in the midst of petitioning the governments of both the city and state to make his museum a public entity and therefore give it permanent status in the State House.

"This city doesn't know what sort of treasure it has in its midst," he went on, his gaze tightening, "and so I need to do some convincing. This city doesn't see what's right under its nose."

Peale smiled as Victor turned to me and said, "I think you've just been offered a job, Cloud."

Peale had about him a slight, sweet scent of rot one often detects amongst the elderly. The odor didn't hang in the air; rather it projected forth in thin little excretions, like the shameful droppings of an incontinent old dog. I am sure Victor didn't notice.

A little later, Victor managed to claim the attention of Rembrandt by parroting our friend Mr. Greenpoint's line about a nation needing to have culture before it is respected in the world, which I had told him and which was the subject of a long conversation on the Camden ferry dock during which Dixcy argued that a lack of a commonly understood high culture was exactly the strength of America, as long as it doesn't devolve into no culture, or the culture of profit, which leaves everything else bereft. In fact, he said, having no apparent high culture scares the living shit out of our rivals in the Old World; they can't know what to make of us that way. Now Victor was talking to Linnaeus — of the Peale children in attendance, Titian, Franklin, and Linnaeus were closest to our age, and so we had been naturally drawn to them.

"We've been hearing that same line our whole lives," broke in Linnaeus, "but when war came, what really mattered?"

Rembrandt, overheard his brother (or half-brother, really), and, not all that differently from his father, he strode quickly across the room like a preacher tricked again into believing there was a soul to save. Linnaeus made a fist and in a friendly manner knocked me on the shoulder. "Victor laughed, I'm not sure why, but everyone else became silent, and his laugh lingered," I wrote in my notebook. "He doesn't mind being so exposed." Linnaeus noticed Victor's laugh, and he noticed that I had noticed too.

Before Rembrandt could say something — for it was clear he had come over to challenge what Linnaeus had said — Linnaeus laughed and said, "I know what you're going to say, you don't even have to bother saying it."

But Victor stepped in before Rembrandt could respond and introduced himself and me to the painter. As we shook his hand, Rembrandt's gaze was fixed on the doorway at the other end of the room. His eyes were startled and yet calm and his mouth was pressed straight and aloof. It was as if he had tried out so many demeanors he wasn't sure which one he should assume. Perhaps none of them suited him or perhaps he wasn't sure if duty or desire was more important. He might have lashed out or he might have stood idly still, dreaming of bed.

The bed in his father's house could hardly have been comfortable.

Linnaeus glanced at me, as if to say, regarding Victor, are you responsible for this odd fellow? Because I'm not really sure what to make of him. Victor interrupted the meted silence by moving closer to Rembrandt. He wanted to tell him about our book of masters. Rembrandt said he hadn't heard about it.

"Have you talked this over with Dad?" he asked, his voice simultaneously piercing and distracted.

"He knows about it, he supports it," said Victor, "that's why he asked us here." Rembrandt looked back across the room. His eyes landed here and there and his feet shuffled slightly, as if to say he was bored. Other people's ideas made him weary. But it was also evident in the parsed air that he was feeling threatened.

Victor, for his part, was waiting for Rembrandt to ask him questions about the book, and so he refrained, as long as possible, from revealing details.

"It's doubtful, but I can try to find time if you wish to speak to me about it. But you may have to come to Baltimore," said Rembrandt. "Did you wish me to suggest the names of other artists?"

"We have a list," said Victor, offhandedly.

"Did you wish to reveal it?" replied Rembrandt. Mixed into his rather high-pitched voice was a small measure of pure hatred.

Victor strung some names, the obvious ones, across the chill air and an ember crackled in the hearth. At the end of the string he placed Krimmel. "The German sketch artist," Victor called him.

Now Rembrandt made no attempt to disguise his disdain. "Sir, you must be joking."

"I think we know —"

"You think you know? You don't know a thing. A 'book of masters,'" he said, his voice shaking slightly, "how about a 'book of fakers'?" A bitter tirade rose from his narrow throat. The tirade was confusing for the words seemed tangled, one idea caught up and knotted with another, shame astride fear and looped over righteousness, and at the end, a blotted period: "Krimmel, this master of yours, he's a fraud. A man without real training can never be a master."

Fraud? What really did he mean? A master can teach himself; perhaps all he must do then is teach others — but no, he must be a true master of his craft. And was Krimmel? Rembrandt's voice played on. And yet why so insistent? Why so angry?

Rembrandt turned and stepped back. His father was crossing the room in the direction of our group, and Rembrandt inserted himself between his brothers Linnaeus and Franklin. Peale seemed to come from nowhere and affectionately put his arms around his three sons. Rembrandt straightened up.

"Our father will talk about this night for months," said Linnaeus. "Won't you?"

Peale looked at Victor. "Has Rembrandt told you about his giant canvas? Life-size figures, with which he means to grab the imagination. And a speaking picture, no less."

"What Dad means is that for the first time a painting will be in direct communication with every man," said Rembrandt. "No hidden meaning."

"Straight to the mind," said Victor.

"But without bypassing the heart, I hope," said Peale.

Rembrandt's behemoth painting, as described to me by Titian Peale (who says he wants to be the first artist to accompany a group of explorers on an expedition to the northern tundra) is "a warning."

"A moral declaration, you mean," I said, "like a sermon."

"No," said Titian, "a warning to our father, who he thinks won't dare try painting something so grand anymore. In other words, what Rembrandt means: get out of my way."

After dinner, I found Titian alone at the far end of Peale's painting room, sketching. He was quieter, more still than any of his brothers. His fingers were long and pensive, his eyes hazel, his cheeks slight, his hairline already receding. Somewhere else in the house a clock struck one, two, three…I began to count in my head, my eyes tracing the lines of Titian's fingers.

"The smaller they are, the more fascinated I am," he said.

"What?"

"The animals." Titian explained that he liked to draw rodents, birds, insects, flowers, and he had gone with his sketchbook on one or two exploratory expeditions to the west. My gaze and my mind wandered and then I refocused. I told him there was much to admire in this philosophy. Then he said that he had asked his father if he would give him a salary to work in the museum as Rubens's assistant. "The museum is feeling tired," he said, "it needs new ideas." But Peale wouldn't go for it. "He wants me to work in the cotton mill with Franklin and Linnaeus. But if you know my brothers then you know working with Linnaeus means doing twice the work. The mill is a foolish dream, anyway."

I told him he should go on another expedition, forget about the museum and the mill.

"The old man owes me, that's how I feel about it."

"Maybe he'll come around," I said, "your father must be aware of your desires."

Then Titian looked at me. I wondered how often he ate. "Like all of us," he said abruptly, "I am caught in his web. It is a brilliant web, isn't it? He is a master spinner. Sometimes I think my father isn't given his due. He wants it, doesn't he, wants to be called the 'Father of American Art,' and if that were to happen, it wouldn't matter if the city or the state or even the president of the United States took over the museum, people would respect him. Some do anyway, or I suppose they fear him. But he wants you to think he's built the web with a plan."

"Perhaps he wishes to believe it himself."

"And the rest of us are imperfect, of course. Well, my aim isn't to hang there in the web doing whatever he says, struck immobile."

"Dangling."

"I suppose I'm the one who is dependent. Do you read Washington Irving?"

I affirmed, and mentioned Dixcy and Victor and our scheme to walk into his office in New York.

"He puts down a character, paints his whole life in a paragraph, and in the next that character is dead, and his relatives are selling his books, his candelabras, his house is a ruin."

"Well, Irving is interested in ghosts," I said.

"Could be, but there is always madness, even the housewives are mad, the gentle student is mad. That's what I like. We wish to be mad, don't we?"

"Not your father," I said, smiling.

"No, not my father. Indeed, not. But, he is mad, you know. As mad as Ichabod Crane."

"We all have our demons," I said.

"Our own heads torment us."

"But we can't cut them off."

"You know what my father always said to us? Whenever one of us became angry or frustrated. He would say, 'Keep your head.'"

"Sage advice."

"Unless the head is the source of the madness."

"Worse to cut it off, don't you think?"

Victor, meanwhile, was nowhere to be found. Nor was Peale, for that matter. And indeed they were together, measuring the length of an invisible millrace, calculating the width of the gates and wheelhouse. They had been gone what must have been an hour, or two. If this were madness, now it was ours. "He is a genius, von Cloud," said Victor, his cheeks red, eyes alight. They had come in for dessert.

"And so you too have a job?"

"We're going to build the mill! By my calculations this creek can support a dozen looms, or maybe more, enough cotton to keep Tharp's presses moving."

"Tharp?"

"The neighbor, Cloud, he runs an indigo dye mill just upstream. Anyway, we're going there right now, or soon, Linnaeus and Titian will take us—they're skating on the millpond."

"You don't know how to build a mill."

"Just a temporary obstacle. But don't you get it?"

"You mean to ingratiate yourself. And aren't Linnaeus and Titian and Franklin supposed to run the mill?"

"I'm not going to run it, Cloud. I'm going to help him design it. We're going to think together. Look, these are fine fellows, but none of them want to get to work. This is Babylon, right here, or have you already forgotten?"

"You've stopped making sense," I said.

We followed Titian and Linnaeus up the path to Tharp's mill pond to go ice skating. As soon as we turned the corner from Peale's house, we could hear the sounds of shouting and laughter and after a few paces we could see the glow of the torches that had been placed at the edge of the pond, flashing and sweeping with the wind.

I asked who would be there and Titian explained that the Tharps were industrious people; it was their mill. "Tharp's not buying," muttered Linnaeus. "But tonight, a skating rink, in the summer, a swimming hole."

Victor said not a word as we walked on.

"Ichabod Crane's tree," I said to Titian as we passed a giant elm, with branches like the arms of God.

"It's a bad dream," said Linnaeus.

"What?" I said.

"The mill—none of us care much about making cotton—well, maybe Franklin would if he didn't have to do much of the work," said Linnaeus.

"He wants to set us up in business so he can stop supporting us," said Titian.

"More for our brother that way."

"It's the future, the way I see it," said Victor. "If you don't do it, somebody else will."

"Sounds like a threat," I said idly.

"The Tharps are decent people," said Linnaeus. "Dull, but decent."

"Apparently, you don't have to be much more than dull to get a girl like Caroline Miller. You just need a little money."

"The younger brother, James," Linnaeus explained to us, "just got hitched to the very lovely Ms. Miller."

"She's going to run his life," said Titian.

"You wouldn't mind it if she ran your life, dear brother. And anyway, since she's sure to be there and it is the holiday time of year I would be very surprised if her sisters weren't there too. The sisters, my friends, are a different story. The next one is Harriet, tall, smart as hell. She'd be impossible to be married to."

"I'd put up with her!" said Titian.

"That's how we're different, then. I can't stand a woman judging everything I do, but you're right, she'd be good for you, Titian, because she could match your wit."

"She's got a mind?" said Victor.

"She's not a scold, but she's not too playful either, and I think she reads a lot. But, gentlemen, she has her eyes on Krimmel, the painter, or Krimmel has eyes for her."

Victor gazed back to me. Why did Rembrandt say "fraud?" he asked me without speaking. Why did he use that term specifically?

"And then there's Henrietta," said Linnaeus. "She is more like a cat than a human being."

"She won't look you in the eye."

"She is there but she's not there. She's not slow, it's just that she doesn't pay much attention to anything, so she appears slow, more like a blind girl than a mute, if you know what I mean."

We came to a clearing and the sky was silver and the moon was low behind the trees. There were a handful of figures on the ice. Only one of them was moving with a strange swiftness, like a long steady wind, back and forth across the pond. He wasn't wearing a hat. "I can't tell who that is," said Linnaeus.

"You know who I think it is?" said Titian.

Victor and I looked at each other. Neither of us spoke.

"I think it's Krimmel. Is that strange fellow back?"

"Nobody else has looks quite like that," said Linnaeus.

"I can't imagine anybody skates like that either," said Victor. "Whoever it is, he's chewing on something."

Linnaeus found us skates and introduced us around. James Tharp was building a bonfire "to keep the ladies warm." Henrietta Miller was on the ice. She wasn't skating fast, but she wasn't skating slowly either. Harriet was standing on the side of the pond, watching. Victor asked her if perhaps she didn't like to skate. She didn't answer. Caroline came out of the house with a basket of little tea cakes. Everyone who wasn't on the ice took one but Harriet. Krimmel, I noticed, kept looking over at Harriet. I think he was somehow paralyzed by her complete self-control. It was the first time we had seen him since finding him sketching by the side of the road. As long as I could, for he was on skates and I stood at the edge of the pond, I fixed my eyes on Krimmel.

"Not now," said Victor, apparently watchful.

We strapped on skates and went out on the ice.

Krimmel had an airy sort of look to him, perhaps from being out of breath, perhaps because his curly hair was flapping freely in the wind and yet perhaps to counter this he skated faster and faster, in tighter and tighter circles. When he finally stopped he was out of breath; his chest rose and fell and mist formed at his teeth. I had the uncontrollable desire to tell him about his sketch, hanging as it must have been among the other perfectly arranged objects in the salon of Mrs. Greenpoint. Or was it perhaps affixed to the wall of their bed chamber? But Krimmel acted as if he had never met us before.

Then he skated off before I could remind him of our conversation at the side of the road, the ideas of the Nazarenes, the sketch of the brazier in the empty room, before I could tell him how meeting him, and yes, swiping his picture, had forced a seed to germinate inside us. We met Hicks, we walked, and we fabricated ourselves. Victor signaled "not now" again, and I wanted to tell Krimmel about our book, our interview with Raphaelle and the others, and the conversation I had just had with Rembrandt. "He gave me the feeling he would do anything to stop you," I wanted to say.

Krimmel's look softened. His face in fact, I had only then realized, betrayed no famine, war, family dispute, or whatever had gone on between him and his brother and his brother's wife Susanna. It was as if he had made a life out of ducking. White breath slipped out from between his fleshy lips; white wind ran along the pond's edge. A little later Victor and I made short circles on the ice. Krimmel, skating backwards, gave me the feeling of someone trying to remember his lines.

Linnaeus and James Tharp shared a flask, which eventually was passed around to all of us. Krimmel waved off the flask and kept skating. Caroline explained somewhat dourly that he had been staying at her father's house for the past few weeks and had yet to visit his own family. He hadn't even ventured into the city. Everyone, she said, thought it was about time. "He doesn't get along with his brother," said Caroline, "but it is Christmas and everyone should get along."

"You mean he should sweep things under the rug," said Harriet, who seemed to be staring off into the far distance, which is hard to do in the dark of night, and which gave me the feeling she was deeply unsatisfied with everything around her. But then, all of a sudden, she put on her skates and leapt rather gracefully onto the ice; a single, high-pitched laugh burst out, and she flew off to find Henrietta.

"He won't go unless he has to, I don't think," said Caroline.

"It's not really your business," said her husband.

"But, everyone agrees he should go. He has to go at some point and why not now? He stays here to be near my sister, but she's not going to respect a man who is so smug he won't even pay a visit to his family, his only family in America."

"Shall I insist you have another swig from the flask, my dear? Or never again allow it?"

"Oh, I like John," she said to Victor, ignoring Tharp, her voice running like an underground spring, her nose red from the cold, "I don't know if I like him for my sister, a poor artist is going to live a difficult life and she needs someone to take care of her so she can go off and fix things, but I think he is a good person and I like having him around. He's not always very aware of the impact he has on others. His demeanor is so honest, in a way — in a way I suppose he is not at all — that he thinks everyone responds rather clearly to things. But there effects on others, for example, of appearing out of the blue on our father's doorstep and asking to stay."

With her gaze still on Victor, she took Victor's arm and said, "Why don't you two take him with you back to town in the morning? Stay the night with us and the three of you can catch an early coach."

We spent the rest of the night skating with Linnaeus, Titian, and Krimmel. Tharp never came out on the ice; Henrietta and Harriet skated arm in arm in semi-circles at the edge of the pond. Linnaeus challenged Victor to a race, which ended up being best of five, then best of seven, then best of eleven, and which ended with Victor red-faced and Linnaeus offering to take Victor the next time he sails to South America as a merchant marine. Titian managed to take the arm of Henrietta, who followed along with a hand over her eyes as if the sun was straight overhead. This left Krimmel to coax Harriet to take his arm, which she did eventually. But their skate was short lived. Krimmel wanted to go inside and get his sketchbook. "Stay on the ice!" he shouted. As he stepped up on the rock, shifting all the weight to the foot that remained on the ice, the ice wailed. A crack ran back toward the center of the pond. Henrietta screeched. I heard Krimmel laugh—his foot hadn't fallen through—but Harriet demanded everyone abandon the ice. "Once it's compromised, you never know," she said.

Caroline had beds made up for us and for Krimmel, who accompanied Harriet and Henrietta back to their house, promising to return so that we could all leave in the morning together. Victor said he wanted to wait up for Krimmel, and anyway, he wasn't tired. Just the opposite, in fact, the skating had awakened him and now he felt full of energy and focus for the first time in days. "I forgot what we were doing," he said obliquely. Then, almost absently, he began to talk about the way an artist lives in the world.

"Just because they are inherently observers and thus tend to separate themselves, in some ways they are the most alive."

"Well, sure," I said, "I think that's obvious, and anyway, what makes them artists or writers, is that sense of awareness."

Victor began to talk about his father, the watchmaker, who works in his tiny workshop doing the same thing over and over, day after day, year after year. Does he once look up and out the window and wonder about this abstract idea of a clock and what it means to set up such a rigid accounting of the world?

"Maybe," Victor continued, "he gets a feeling in the pit of his stomach that his work is inadequate in the eyes of God, but it goes no further than that. This is the difference between the artist and the craftsman."

"My father thinks only about little gears," Victor went on. "Ah, Cloud, he is a supreme craftsman, don't let me mislead you. When you make something that is your own, even if it is only one thing among thousands just like it, you have to make it the right way, or it's not worth doing at all."

"You're thinking about the mill."
"You think it's foolish."
"Not so...I simply don't understand it."

Chapter XV

*A*n the morning, we walked with Krimmel to Market Square, a longer walk than I had foreseen, and ended up taking a nine o'clock coach. Krimmel spent much of the ride sketching Victor, who slept from the moment we turned onto the Ridge Road. His eyes were moving the whole time. We got off at the market. The sidewalk was jammed with hucksters and porters from the various inns looking for clients and for a minute I thought we had lost Krimmel—that he had slipped away through the crowd without saying good-bye.

"He's found a place in the sun," said Victor, and indeed, there was Krimmel squinting and blowing into his hands to keep them warm. We stood there silently for a minute. Victor was saying something, but with the din of the sidewalk I couldn't understand him. Was he explaining the stolen sketch? The sale to Mrs. Greenpoint? It was impossible to hear. Then Krimmel suggested we join him at his brother's, it's likely dinner would be served in a while. "My brother is prosperous enough," he said, "and he likes Christmas, and despite being a thorough American he insists on a real Württemberg Christmas," and then he explained that their father was a *conditor*, a very specialized kind of baker who makes only fine pastries, not rolls or cakes, and that his wife Susanna would have made some of the old recipes. I said there is a conditor in Easton named Bravermann, but no doubt these recipes are better. Krimmel didn't reply. I got the feeling that Susanna didn't enjoy making these traditional pastries, or that making them only made her homesick. "He insists she follow them exactly," said Krimmel. "In some ways my brother is detached from the world of the home, but this isn't one of them."

We walked through the State House garden and then into Washington Square. Krimmel said everything had changed. "The potter's field," said Krimmel, "now, it's a pleasure garden. Where do you suppose they put the bodies?"

"Oh, I think they're still under there!" said Victor and we exited the square onto Seventh Street, a block from Krimmel's brother's house.

But the house was empty. Krimmel knocked on the door and looked in the front windows. It seemed obvious no one lived there. He carefully climbed over a wall in the alley behind the house to try the back door, which he said was usually open. For ten minutes he carried out a meticulous search, not with the urgency of someone desperate to find the lost, but with the regard of a scientist conducting an experiment. In the end the experiment failed, and he sat down on the stoop, his eyes focused somewhere in the distance. Victor, meanwhile, knocked on the neighbor's door. No one answered. But two houses down, a very old woman with a thin nose and yellowing blue eyes came to the door. She wore a matching brown apron and bonnet made of thick fabric in a simple, sturdy style. She laid her hand on Victor's hand and stole his gaze in the same deceptively quiet manner. Then she squeezed his hand and said we must be the men to dispose of the property. Victor explained that we weren't property men, but friends of the family that used to live two doors down. "We were a little surprised to see the house empty," he said.

"Well, I feel sorry for whoever moves in," she said after some thought. "But really, a house is a house. One is the same as the other." She paused again. Victor shuffled his feet—he was stooped over for the woman's benefit—but her grip held. "When the little girl died we didn't think much of it, but that's the way consumption works, it travels with the family. It doesn't stay in the house."

"Which little girl do you mean, if you don't mind my asking?" inquired Victor.

"I didn't mean an infant child, my boy. A sturdy thing, but strangely quiet. *Silent.* You wouldn't ever know if she was there. One day, there was a wail, she finally made a sound—we could even hear it, my own daughter said it chilled her to the bones—a horrible wail and that was all."

"She died," confirmed Victor.

"You should come inside, it's much too cold. My granddaughter is just home from the market. She'll bring you tea."

"I'll go find Krimmel," I said.

Before I could turn away, the woman let go of Victor's hand—and his gaze—and for a moment she looked as if she had forgotten everything or had suddenly remembered something that had happened decades before, perhaps when she was a little girl or a young lady, something unsettling that at the time had made her say to herself, "I'll never forget this," but of course she had, and now remembering it she felt even more unsettled, or disillusioned. Or just downright sad. But she recovered quickly and breathed hard up through her little nose in a birdlike manner (though I had the feeling more of a vulture than a starling or a finch). "Krimmel is exactly who I am speaking about," she said. "Who do you mean, 'Krimmel'?" Victor told her it was John, who had returned from Germany. "He is here? Then tell him to come here now, I have news for him."

I went across the street and up the square to the west, almost to Eighth Street, to try to find him. I looked in the tavern on the corner only to get a whiff of stale ale. But no Krimmel. Then I walked all the way around the square, crossed Seventh Street and found him crouched down on the curbstone making a sketch. "I left my camera obscura in Germantown," he said. "I was stupidly in a rush. Please move out of the way." I was surprised then to see that the sketch was of his brother's house, but not from where Krimmel was sitting across the street. Instead this was a view from the sidewalk in front, as one would see it if he were leaning up against the wall of the neighboring house and looking across the front stoop to the street beyond. It was an insider's view, or quite possibly a memory. On the right side of the sketch was the front of the house. A section of bricks was already rendered in detail, as were the trees and the street lamps in the background. The stoop was articulated in such a way that it revealed the geometry of each of the four slabs of marble that formed the whole, and I suppose Krimmel's point—or is it just the artist's habit?—is that the stoop is just the sort of thing we see regularly but don't really see at all. We perceive a single object, the stoop, but rarely imagine it is really three or four separate objects joined together. It's as if our power to perceive objects is still undeveloped (La Mettrie says this is the state of being "dumb"). Or maybe we're just lazy or so burdened with our existence we haven't the time or energy to think of a stoop as really being four pieces of marble that someone has mined, cut, polished, and lifted into place.

But then here was another thing that Krimmel saw differently than seemingly the rest of us do: his stoop seemed to hover, or more accurately float, in the foreground of the picture, as if it had no weight at all. As if it were a cloud. A woman stepped across the cloud. Krimmel had only drawn the outlines of her dress. She seemed to hold her right arm across her stomach. Her eyes were distant but somehow they glistened, as if she were staring off into the sun. Was she leaving the house? It was hard to discern. So roughly sketched she might well have been a ghost.

I told Krimmel about the old woman, but he only nodded and kept sketching. "She became very animated," I said. "Not excited exactly, but actually a little frightened."

"Then let's let her calm, no?" His demeanor had assumed that of a sailor willing to put up with any aberration of nature.

Eventually Krimmel put away his sketchbook and we went to the woman's house. The granddaughter answered the door. She took Krimmel's hands in hers and instantly began to weep. From inside the old woman yelled, "Bring him here!" The granddaughter led us into a small room that smelled of cooked pork and potatoes. Victor sat with the old woman at a table covered by a stained white tablecloth. She didn't stand when Krimmel entered the room, only went on rubbing the tablecloth with the tips of her fingers. She did this mindlessly, but also fiercely, as if she kept finding new wrinkles in the tablecloth or fallen crumbs. Krimmel went to her and bowed politely, and immediately she became the mourner and he the man of solace. She ordered him to sit and told him the extent of the news. In November, the ten-year-old Catherine had died of consumption. The illness didn't last long, she said, the child just simply disappeared—until one night she screeched and that was it. The granddaughter said she ran over to the Krimmel house as soon as they heard the screech, but that it was already too late.

"But I noticed something else that frightened me," she said to Krimmel, "Susanna wasn't there by the girl's side. I asked your brother where she was, but he was too distracted to answer. So I left the girl's room, real quiet, I was trying not to disturb anyone, and finally I found her, John." The granddaughter began to cry again. She looked up and tried to wipe her tears, but couldn't become composed. Victor cleared his throat and gave the granddaughter a handkerchief.

"She found her, John," said the old woman, who spoke in the same unadorned tone as she had when she received us at the door. "Bent over a basin spitting blood. John, I am sorry, but she died the first of August. Your brother has moved the rest of the family to the Northern Liberties."

Victor's idea was to bring Krimmel back with us to Mrs. Chamberlaine's boarding house. Victor said then we would "admit the mistake" and promise to get the sketch back. Before I could respond, he changed the subject.

"Dixcy's either given up on us or he's forgotten all about us," said Victor.

"You mean because he's found a more obliging roommate," I said.

"I mean because even Dixcy wouldn't turn down a desperate girl at Christmas. He may be surly but he isn't unkind." Then, after a meal, we would accompany Krimmel to find his grieving brother in the Northern Liberties. "If he so desires."

The old woman stood up and made Krimmel promise that we would all return. The granddaughter said she had asked the eight-year-old Fredericka, the younger sister of Catherine, to write to her about their new house and neighborhood, but she hadn't yet received anything. "I know she's going to write me, but it must be hard for her to find the time."

"That's right," said Krimmel, who seemed to reengage with the group, if only for a moment, "she'll have to run the house now."

We heard Dixcy's voice as soon as we entered Mrs. Chamberlaine's house. He was sitting at the table with a chicken leg and a bowl of soup. Libby was sitting across from him buttering a piece of bread. She had a tankard of beer. Mrs. Chamberlaine came out of the kitchen and shook Krimmel's hand, and then I took Krimmel up to our room. Without saying a word, he sat on my bed. Then he stretched out. I closed the curtains and he fell asleep.

Downstairs, Victor waited until I sat down before telling us what the old woman had told him. "The old bird just started talking, Cloud, when you were finding Krimmel. Her granddaughter kept trying to quiet her, but she didn't care, she talked right over her. I don't know why she wanted me to know."

"It's your baby face," said Libby, "she trusts you."

"That doesn't seem likely. Really, I would say she was worried about Krimmel," replied Victor. "I think she's got something against the brother. Well, I am sure of that."

"Then she's a busybody," said Libby, who looked at Dixcy and smiled.

"I wouldn't say that," I said, "more like what Victor said: a tough old bird, swoop down and grab you away."

"Listen, she said that the Krimmel family wasn't exactly picture perfect. She said 'picture perfect' because Krimmel did a family portrait, which hangs, or rather hung, on the wall of the parlor. But she said she always wondered why he painted himself and not his brother as the man of the house — "

"Shhh," I said, "let's keep our voices down."

"Oh, Cloud, didn't you say he was fast asleep? Then he can't hear us. Now look, apparently Krimmel was the wife's lover, that's why he painted the picture that way. She said it took her a while to figure it out, and then Krimmel went to Germany. Actually, he was sent away, she said. The brother George is always working, she said he's determined to restore the family's fortune, which apparently had been lost under Napoleon's rule. She also hinted that the brother-in-law in the village had run the pastry shop into the ground. Someone had to go straighten it out."

"So he just learned his mistress is dead," I said.

"Not only that," replied Victor, "the mother of his child."

"Child?"

"Or children. The old bird was only sure of one. An infant boy who died in 1812."

Later that afternoon we sat in our room. Krimmel was eating toast and slices of orange brought to him by Libby. It wasn't clear he was paying any attention to us. Victor paced the length of the room. When that proved to be an insufficient preoccupation, he began to recount for us a story by Washington Irving he had been reading in the *Analectic*. The story was about a young German student in Paris, around the time of the French Revolution. The guillotine, which stood menacingly over the large square in front of the Hôtel de Ville, was in full use, day after day. Well, each night the student, who was alone and lonely, foreign and friendless—"a stranger in a strange land" is how Irving puts it—but who no doubt possessed a lustful imagination, dreamt of a single, radiant beauty, a Passy maiden he had ofttimes seen standing on the Pont Neuf staring into the Seine. Sometime later, the German was walking home through the old district of the Marais—and why he was in that part of the city when the lecture halls were in the old Latin Quarter wasn't clear—

"Quite probably he had just visited a brothel in the blacksmith's district behind the Bastille," said Dixcy, interrupting.

"Though," replied Victor, "it is just as likely he had been browsing the latest titles in a German bookshop"—rain was coming in torrents as he crossed the Place de Grève half in somnolence, or a state of shock, just to protect himself from the furious storm—"No, no!" said Victor, interrupting himself. "I'm sorry, but I can't continue. I won't."

Krimmel looked up quietly, as if he had just awakened. He told Victor to continue the story. "Don't hold back on my account," he said.

"No, I can't."

Victor had his eyes on Dixcy. He began again.

Crossing the square, the German came into sight of the same maiden from his dreams. There she was in the open rain, in some state well beyond despair. Quite literally beside himself, the student convinced the sorry mademoiselle to accompany him to his apartment near the Sorbonne. He told her of his dreams and she admitted that she felt a similar inexplicable attraction to him. Nevertheless, for they were both strict rationalists, they stared back at Fate and decided not to get married in the old-fashioned, traditional sense but to form a contractual union. They didn't need God, or any ancient traditions, to signify their love. In the morning, the student went out to find a larger apartment. When he returned, he found her still in bed, but in an odd position that drew him to the bedside. He came over, turned her over, and found her pale as a corpse, which of course she was.

"I'm sorry, Krimmel," said Victor, but he didn't answer.

"He should have stuck with the whores near the Bastille," muttered Dixcy.

Victor ignored him and went on. Very calmly, the German went out to the street to seek help from a policeman, who accompanied him back to the apartment. The German must have imagined that, in his absence, someone had broken into the apartment and killed the defenseless girl. But the policeman took one look at her, laughed —

"He laughed?" I asked, admittedly incredulous, and Victor said, "Well, at the very least he laughed inside, to himself" — and said to the now distraught student, I know this one well enough, she was guillotined yesterday, and perhaps, he seemed to imply, for good reasons. The German couldn't believe it of course, but when he went over to caress his bride, the officer pulled off the silken collar she wore around her neck and down tumbled her head onto the floor.

Victor stopped and for a long time there was a pitched silence. Krimmel, who had been lying on the bed facing the wall while Victor told the story turned to face us. "It wasn't like that," he said, but at once a dreadful sense of loss came over him, and he said he wished to leave.

But he didn't leave just then. Instead, he took out his sketch-book and began again to draw. I wasn't sure if he had started a new sketch or if he was still working on the one of his brother's house. Dixcy seemed to be half asleep. I looked at Victor. His eyes flicked away the coming darkness. "You understand we didn't mean to make off with the sketch of Harriet Miller. It just happened is all."

Krimmel was silent and for a while no one spoke.

The light retreated, leaving the air chalky and loose, like the mud beneath the earliest melting snow. "But we're going to re-possess it and then return it to you," said Victor. He made no mention of the money. His voice seemed to condemn the truth as some trifle. "And we promise, of course, that you will be featured in our book."

"Mr. Krimmel is the heart of it, is he not?" I said.

After a while, Krimmel put down his pencil. He wondered if sometime soon we wouldn't mind making him an introduction to Raphaelle Peale. "A while ago I did him a wrong," he said. "I need to make my amends."

Chapter XVI

rimmel left Mrs. Chamberlaine's house the next morning and weeks went by before we saw him again. Victor was still fixated on gaining an audience with Joseph Bonaparte in order to see the art collection at Point Breeze. So he took a job as the morning barkeep at the Castle. Tom Birch was the key to Bonaparte, Victor said. "It's strange, Birch is an Englishman, his nose is red and eyes are sallow, his accent as thick as I don't know, the Scottish heath, and yet he has Bonaparte's confidence. And he comes into the Castle every morning at ten."

"He has the ear of Peale and Bonaparte."

"That's not all, Cloud."

"What do you mean, 'that's not all'?"

"I mean the barkeep at the Castle is the job you should be doing if you wish to be the writer of Philadelphia—"

"Who said I wished—"

"The place is a rumor mill."

"And what of the real mill?" I said sharply, interrupting. We three were crossing Market Street at Sixth, just above the market.

"When it is done, I'll invite you both to weave some cotton."

"A load of shit," said Dixcy. "The creek is frozen and you're just awaiting the flood."

"Wrong!" replied Victor. "Mr. Peale never lets nature stand in his way."

We sat down in the back of a crowded coffee shop.

Victor told us that he found Tom Birch more than affable. "Even Krimmel has some pretension," he said, "I mean the way he's almost always sketching, it's his way of pushing everyone else off, but Birch has none of that. He could be a drayman or a clerk in a counting house. Get up in the morning, go to work, stop at the tavern on his way home, sleep well at night." Birch told Victor that getting us into Point Breeze might take a while. It had taken him almost a year. "But more important is the king's idea for a palace of art right in the center of Philadelphia, not less grand than anything in Paris. Cloud, it's your story to break."

"You're full of shit," I said. "And pretentious too."

"A Louvre, von Cloud! I'm telling you, nobody knows."

I had recently submitted an article to *Poulson's* on the closing of three notable art galleries on Chestnut Street, including Washington's wax museum, with its life-size model of the execution of Louis XVI. The closings were the result of the economic panic. Also the river had been frozen since Christmas, and so the port was all but closed and as the galleries depended on sailors who would pay twenty-five cents to see pictures of nudes, or in the case of the wax museum, various scenes of debauchery, which Victor had discovered on our second day in Philadelphia. Ticket sales had dried up.

"But, look, I've heard something," he said. A barmaid rang the bell.

"In the rumor mill?"

"No, this is real." Victor's jaw seemed to sag slightly. He sat forward. "One day at the Continental, right at ten o'clock, Birch came in, as usual. A few minutes later, in walked Krimmel."

"How did he seem?"

"Normal. Well...for Krimmel."

"Normal? After—"

"He carried a sketchbook, of course. Birch tried to order him a beer, but he declined. He made no notice of me."

"Hard to believe," said Dixcy.

It was Birch, Victor could see, who was out of sorts. He kept looking up from Krimmel to the door. They were meeting in regard to a course Krimmel was to teach at the Academy.

"A course on the methods of the Nazarenes," said Dixcy.

"Yes, how did you know?" But Victor didn't wait for Dixcy to answer. Krimmel, said Victor, had come to the meeting to discuss the details of the course and to find out who had enrolled. The first thing Krimmel said was "If it is more than fifteen, then I will teach a second section." Birch didn't reply. "I would teach it every day, if there was the demand. You know the symbol of the Nazarenes? A man with his back turned, about to walk into the unknown. That's what this is, Birch, the art of the unknown."

Birch gazed out the window. A beautiful woman in an emerald dress went by. The men smiled at each other. Victor said it was obvious they were friends, but something wasn't right. Though he never left his chair, "Birch gave me the impression of someone continuously tripping."

"One doesn't 'continuously trip,'" said Dixcy, "one just trips and falls."

"Finally," said Victor, ignoring Dixcy, "he gripped the table and told Krimmel the news." The course was being canceled.

"Now it's Krimmel who must have fallen to the floor," I said.

"Hardly. Krimmel didn't move. He said, with complete calm, 'this is a mistake' or 'you've made a terrible mistake,' and he began to argue the decision, point by point. Birch looked at him sympathetically. But not with his usual warmth. There was something hard and distant in his response to Krimmel, and his eyes were dry and cold."

Krimmel pursued his argument, asking again how many had enrolled.

"He's going to find them and teach the course on his own," I said.

"Wouldn't you?" said Dixcy.

"Birch said that quite a few had enrolled, but that wasn't the problem," Victor went on. "Then he interrupted himself and said, 'I am very truly sorry.'"

"But none of this makes sense, did he not explain why?"

"Oh, von Cloud, it's obvious why, you heard Rembrandt Peale—"

"But what does Rembrandt know, or really care?"

"Apparently, quite a lot."

"What do you mean by that?"

"I mean they didn't just take away his course on German painting, they've removed him from the Academy."

Mr. Poulson asked me to cover the inaugural ride of a hot-air balloon, which would take off from the Vauxhall gardens at Broad and Walnut, in three weeks, on the first of March. When I went there to interview the owner of the garden, a portly man with tiny spectacles and tufts of hair growing from his ears, I found Linnaeus Peale sitting at a table inside the glass-enclosed winter garden drinking an Italian-style coffee and reading the paper from Rio. Rio, he said, was paradise on earth, and he described for me the spectacle of Carnival. "You wear a robe for five days like a lion king in his jungle lair, and I mean that literally. Your friend Victor will come with me and if we don't catch the yellow fever or the scurvy, I promise we'll send for you first thing." But how had a paper printed on the eighth of January arrived in his hands on the fifth of February when the port of Philadelphia had been closed because of ice? Linnaeus didn't feel like answering. He told me to sit down and offered a coffee. "Listen," he said, "my advice to you and your friends is steer clear of my family. It's rotten from the inside. Or maybe you, being an outsider, will be treated with respect. It comes down to this: my father refuses to employ me in the museum, but instead of receiving an answer to my request, which was merely for a temporary position until I find a ship to my liking, I receive a vinegar-drenched letter from my brother in Baltimore."

"Rembrandt."

"The very one."

"What does he have to do with it?"

"He has to tell me that I have no more right to assistance from our father than anyone else. And furthermore, the nest is out of worms: ticket sales at the museum are down thirty-five percent—he cites this precisely, as if I care. But apparently he's the one counting the money. So then I write him back and say in that case why don't you employ me in *your* museum?"

"And what did he say?"

"He told me to go fuck myself. No, he never wrote back. I thought about sending him a ledger sheet accounting of the assistance given to each of us by our father, but I don't have the energy for that sort of thing. And I don't really care. Anyway, the ice will melt. This paper says three Brazilian ships are due into Philadelphia before the end of the month, so what do I have to worry about?"

Then, when I finished my coffee, which had been flavored with brandy, he said, "Tell Victor to get ready."

To go to Brazil or to go to work on the mill, I wasn't sure.

After weeks sending letters asking for an interview for our "book of masters," we received a summons from Peale, who asked us to meet him at his museum. The day of the meeting was unseasonably warm; Dixcy nevertheless wore his topcoat and hat. "Christopher Columbus eats shit!" said the parrot in the entry foyer. He repeated this three more times before we made it up the stairs.

Peale was standing in the office, staring impatiently at a bookshelf. "I don't know where the hell Rubens puts things," he said. "I don't know where anything is. Now what do you boys think? The city just raised our rent again." He looked at us as a money lender looks at a customer, expectant and aggrieved.

Victor shuffled above me. Nothing had happened beyond some initial designs for Peale's mill. "I'll go there," Victor told me, "and he'll have me pose, as a subject for a picture, and he will 'draw his outlines,' and I will begin talking about the optimal depth of the forebay, and von Cloud, he isn't interested. Oh, when I am finished posing we'll pull out the plans and lay them out on the table or we'll walk along the stream and he'll describe to me an idea he's come up with for selling the cotton, but we won't ever sit down to refine the plans. When we do sit down at the table it's to talk about his recalcitrant children, and I am never sure if I am supposed to agree with his cutting analysis — for if I agree I am insulting him — or if I am supposed to take their side and give him some insight on the cares and motivations of the younger generation. So I do neither, I just shut up and play games with his eyes, which betray a hunger he isn't all that desperate to control."

"I told them attendance is down," Peale continued, now looking at me directly, "this ought to be printed far and wide. If the people would read that my museum provides a service to our developing nation it would follow logically they would support it, and the city would be well motivated to provide us the necessary funds to continue our mission. Don't you see, the city should be paying *us* for the service we provide, not the other way around." Without taking a breath, he enumerated the museum's operations, explaining that he could no longer afford $1,200 monthly rent he had agreed to last year, never mind the $300 more the city was now demanding.

And then he wiped his brow with a handkerchief and looked at each of us, one at a time, and began a long monologue about how despite everything he has done for his country he is treated as a second-class citizen in his city and how every time he tries to remind people of this he feels like his words are landing on deaf ears. "I refuse to be one of those old men who live only in the past. Nay, I shall not be one of them. But, tell me then, how do I state my case? Rubens won't do it, that is not his way, and his good name seems to have no value, the seed won't take in the barren soil, my friends, and so it is left to me. I must create the seed and fertilize the soil both; I apologize for the crude metaphor, but it is the reality, and it is only my fault for imagining it should be any other way. I have offered to the city to make my museum a part of our patrimony, just as they do in the great states of Europe, with the difference being that this museum isn't for the purpose of aggrandizing a particular despotic regime, but to educate our citizens about their own history, both natural and man-made—a much surer way to elevate the soul."

Dixcy whispered something in Victor's ear. Victor shushed him, his eyes intent on Peale, and I could tell he wanted to interject because his Adam's apple kept shifting, like an exposed worm seeking the countenance of the soil but finding only air, and finally diving back down to its native darkness. He put his right hand through hair and I saw his ears were red.

"Now don't sit down," continued Peale, "because I want to show you something, a new acquisition." He took my hand and led me across the gallery. "I have a theory," he said to me in a low voice, "or maybe it's a vision, a theory married to a vision, let's call it, that cities need outsiders to propel them forward; native-born citizens lose their fervor, or get lost thinking that everything that is has always been that way and will remain as such in the future. Strangers, and I use that word with intent, they perceive a strangeness, that is the city strikes them as new and different, and it excites them. And I do mean excite in the most divine sense of it, it titillates, does it not? You know what I mean."

I nodded.

"Then you agree? The native born are bored, or complacent, but they can be influenced by the nervous energy of the stranger and that's what gives the city life. But there are too many people who forget this city's greatest moment came when it was filled with strangers. To be more precise, it was when the proportion of natives to strangers was about three to one."

"You mean a city needs new blood," I said.

"I came to this theory after observing my own children, none of whom have felt the same satisfaction in this, their native city, as I have — and that is because I remain an outsider and I always see it anew."

"Which explains your difficulties with the city councils, perhaps," I said.

"Part of being a stranger is trying to figure out how to change the city while pleasing the native. It's a game I once excelled at. But where are the other strangers?" Peale paused. We were standing at the end of the long wall of cases of the various preserved birds and waterfowl of the Americas. Peale turned, with his back to the display. Victor said something about the silence of the birds. He placed his hands over his ears for effect. Peale pushed his spectacles up onto his forehead. His dry skin was covered with a slight film, like a wash of curdled milk. Krimmel isn't pleasing the natives, at least not the right ones — but does he care?

"The stranger becomes the native, isn't that true?" I said. "The tables turn."

"It's a worthy observation," said Peale, "it may be true."

"Is it not possible to be both stranger and native, depending?" said Victor.

I kept my eyes affixed to Peale's. Krimmel hasn't tried to please you isn't that what you wish to say? "But isn't it likely a stranger will have his own views, they may be quite different — "

Victor interrupted. "Our concern, Mr. Peale, if you don't mind my saying, is Krimmel."

"It should be your concern, my fellows." Peale replaced his spectacles. His tie was half askew. "You see the cost of disruption," he said, his eyes boring into mine, the claw feet at the edge of them peering out from behind the arm of his spectacles like great wings for beating. "Take it as a warning."

We crossed the room back to the other end and around the corner. This was the section Peale reserved for "curious art," mostly his own work or that of his children. On the wall to the right were six drawings by Titian: a "scissor-tailed flycatcher," a bird (unidentified), butterflies, three cicadas, two herons, and a beaver. On the left was Peale's famous staircase painting and off to the side some silhouettes and miniature portraits by various members of the family. Next to them was a small still life by Raphaelle. "This is what I want to show you, boys, this new picture by Raphaelle." It was of a bowl of strawberries, some flowering strawberry vines, and a pitcher of cream on a wooden shelf. Peale explained that Raphaelle had started the painting in Virginia, but had come home to Philadelphia to finish it. "He came home more inspired than ever."

"Oh, yes," said Dixcy. We had seen the painting partially completed in Raphaelle's painting room.

"But do you see what he has done with still life?"

"You mean because time isn't still," said Victor, referring to the tiny reflections of the painting room's windows on the glass pitcher.

"And the vine grows, extending into infinite darkness," I said.

"And you see the way the flowers look like stars in the night sky. Is this not a veritable work of genius? I can tell you that both Rembrandt and I have tried to master the use of chiaroscuro. For a time when he was younger, Rembrandt was obsessed with the idea of it. But only Raphaelle, who everyone has forgotten, has achieved perfection. I can only speculate why this is so."

"I can tell you," said Victor. "It's because he isn't afraid of the darkness."

"His talent is not always obvious. He is constantly being overlooked," Peale complained, with the strained look of a man who keeps getting robbed. Peale rubbed his hands together and explained that he had imagined his two eldest sons on successive pages of our book, Raphaelle facing Rembrandt and Rembrandt facing Raphaelle. "Once, long ago, they would have wanted it this way." And then, to Dixcy, he said, "You understand they must have equal treatment."

We three faced Peale in silence. "I don't think that's possible, sir," said Victor. Peale bent forward. He picked an invisible piece of lint from Dixcy's lapel. "It's not because, as you assume, of Raphaelle."

"Well, if the boys don't wish to be on facing pages — that was only a suggestion."

"It isn't that. We haven't even thought that far ahead. It's because of Rembrandt's feelings toward Krimmel."

"He won't be in a book with Krimmel," I said.

"And Krimmel must be in your book? The man was removed from the Academy, what standing — " The look of a very old man passed across Peale's face — it was the look of muteness. Only in this case it was cold — frozen — a menacing cold.

"He will be, yes."

"You think my son is heartless, unfeeling." His voice hung in the air before us. "He wears a high collar and stands aloof. He hides. His words are withering."

Peale stepped down a corridor and we three followed as if punished. But what had we done? Hadn't Peale agreed? Hadn't he himself had to chafe over Rembrandt's predilection for ideas and not feelings in his work? Hadn't he whispered, rather hopefully, that the *Court of Death* might reach the heart as well as the mind? We came to a room no larger than a pantry stacked with frames and canvases, wood boxes, and crates. From the depth of the vault — my God, wasn't this the vault of American culture, weren't these the national jewels? — Peale pulled a medium-sized painting, Rembrandt's portrait of Rubens —

"It's a good as anything hanging here."

"And you can see it's full of 'feeling,' as you put it," said Peale.

"Better than that, it's full of understanding and compassion."

"It's strangely quiet, almost calm," I said.

Peale now made us sit. No longer old, no longer menacing, no longer melancholic, he bent toward us and pressed his fingertips to the top of the table. Keep your Krimmel, he seemed to say. His voice lowered, his teeth clacked. "I am torn on him. Nay, I once helped him when he needed it, praised his skill, found him commissions, and I too noticed his confidence and aspiration. No one with a steadier pencil, no one so attune to detail—and no one, in this city, who loves to draw and sketch and paint as he does. But I won't disguise my disgust with his naked attempt to renounce the art of reason—to renounce reason and order itself. Should we let this man loose inside the Academy I might as well accept my own premature demise—the demise of my brood, the demise of all of this." He stood up, flashed his eyes at us, and smiled.

"Fine, but now!" Peale cleared his throat with malice, as if he would never again hear of Krimmel or his son's aggravating stubbornness. Fine, he appeared to be thinking, these boys are energetic but they're tiresome and they're nowhere near as rough as I am. "Save the museum, I'll save your book."

"The way to save the museum," interrupted Victor, "is to finally build the mill. The thaw is coming, Mr. Peale."

"I will decide that," muttered Peale, old again and toothless, and then a moment later once more in control. He spoke in a whisper. Victor and Dixcy would go to Baltimore and interview Rembrandt—"and provide him whatever other help he'll need. Interview Mr. Bird King if he's there and possibly Mr. Trumbull, who is often in the capital. And Caleb will write on this situation with the museum and the government."

"And?"

"And should it be necessary, I shall write the preface to this first book of masters, my boys. Now, you can see I have tickets to sell."

Chapter XVII

A few days after Victor and Dixcy left for Baltimore, on a day of bright sunshine and high wind, I decided to take a walk. The city was noticeably busier now that the weather had begun to warm, and the port had opened again for business. There were children and hucksters everywhere; one after the other, dark-skinned girls carrying fish baskets on their heads rose from the riverbank, eyes distant, detached, as if to say, These aren't our fish or our baskets or our city, or for that matter our bodies, which are clearly separate from our souls. Our souls are in the bosom of a real god, one who doesn't spend half his time inventing suffering and the other half weeping for it, or they are on the rough shore of Africa, hiding in the dark shadows of the Portuguese ramparts, laughing at the dark shadows under Portuguese eyes. La Mettrie wasn't thinking about the strange existence of these girls when he said soul and body are one mechanism, or it could be his calculation of the power of soul (or "imagination" as he calls it) was limited; in his view the soul and body are intertwined, but the soul follows the body's lead. He didn't believe it could be the other way around.

I walked fast and yet with a sense of wonder; the high wind seemed to lift me and after all, my compatriots were

gone and I felt free. There were a few swollen buds at the ends
of high branches, hot coals waving impassively at the indigo
sky, the buds and the sky desperate for each other, like secret
lovers forced to sublimate all feeling until dark. And I couldn't
withhold my gaze. I turned down Chestnut Street hoping to
glimpse tender beauty of the female human sort. What color
parasol would be in fashion this spring? The answer, if I am not
mistaken, was crimson red. Near Fifth Street, in the clear light,
the palms of a sawyer's hands seemed to glow, as if illuminated
from within. I stopped for a moment in front of the Carey and
Lea publishing house and bookstore, reading the titles in the
window, mostly dry political commentary and minor treatises
(at least in my view). Nothing on art or literature. Carey had
been mentioned to us as a potential publisher, but in light of the
offerings in the window, this seemed far-fetched. In any case,
Victor refused to talk to a publisher until we had written at least
half of the entries.

I decided to go looking for other publishing houses and
bookstores. Remarkably, it hadn't yet occurred to us to do any
reconnaissance. Were there other books on American artists already in print? And who carried books on art? I began to worry
and almost instantly a feeling of hopelessness washed over me.
In the bright, hectic city I felt completely detached. If I simply
disappeared from this corner this very instant not a soul would
notice. I ran through the various scenarios: Mr. Poulson saying he knew all along I was worthless and he would have to
write the piece on the hot air balloon himself, Victor and Dixcy
rushing around the city for a fortnight or so and then Victor
coming to the stark conclusion that it was up to me, if I wished
I would turn up, and Dixcy muttering, "It will be simpler this
way." This is the same thing as freedom, I tried to convince myself, the fewer people who know you, or care, the freer you are.
And then: You're still walking through the gates of Babylon,
and not even the whores seem to pay you much attention.

The rest of the day I went in and out of bookstores: Rufus
Little's dark shop across from Old Swede's Church on Swanson
Street, George Giles's place on Federal Street, where a pregnant

lady who looked like she was forty-five or fifty years old was sitting in the doorway, Picard's on Second back towards the city. Picard's skin was tight, smooth, almost luminescent. He stood in the doorway of his shop, which is inside the courtyard of one of those buildings you think at first is merely a squat two and a half stories and shallow at that, but which has been incrementally added onto. I suppose he feels claustrophobic inside the store, or he had noticed the nice day and wanted to feel the sun on his face and on the tops of his shoes (though truthfully the sun wasn't really that strong, it only seemed that way so early in spring), because he never came inside the store while I browsed his shelves. He just stood with his arms crossed, squinting into the sun with his thin lips closed. On the shelves: a treasure trove of French medical books, including François J.V. Broussais on chronic inflammations, Bichat's famous *Traité des Membranes*, a complete set of Voltaire, and a lovely addition of Robert Burns's collection of Scottish folk songs. When I had finished browsing, I went to ask him if he ever carried books on art or artists. "Hmm?" he said, pretending not to hear me. I looked more closely at him — he was older and slighter of stature than I had thought originally — and tried to restate my question. Then he spoke, in a whisper, "You wish to know what customers want? What they want! They want me to tell them what they want. Good day."

At McCarty and Davis, who call themselves printers first and booksellers second, I found a book of recreated maps of cities as they looked when William Penn visited them. The point was to pinpoint the influences on Penn's plan for Philadelphia, but the most interesting thing in the book was an entire section on the great fire of London, with color plates and a map showing how the layout of the city changed after the fire. After McCarty and Davis, I went to Hector McGravy's shop on Ann Street, and then I knocked on the door of Thomas Wardle's, but no one answered. I sat on his step for a while eating a roll and listening to a conversation between two ladies, perhaps sisters. The one lady, who sounded like she worked for a silk dyer, cutting the silk or mending it, seemed to be telling the other one that if she wanted her to steal a silk kerchief or bow, she would have to wait. One of the other dyers had recently been caught. "He was one of those cocky types," she said, "with one hand in your pocket and one on your tit." Just then a man, I assumed it was Wardle, the owner of the bookshop, came up to the door. He looked at me, put a key in the latch, muttered "Just a minute," and then closed the door behind him. I stood and looked up at the sky and breathed the sour, brittle air. On Wardle's sign was a carved color portrait of Shakespeare inside a coat of arms, which was decorated across the top with a roll of parchment, a stone castle, and a torch. The name "Wardle" was engraved in such a way that it appeared to extend from the ruffles in the Bard's sleeve. Inside, the place had none of the pretensions of the sign. It was merely a clean, almost empty-feeling shop and all was painted buttercream. A wooden table held neat little stacks of books and a few more were kept in a glass case behind the proprietor's desk. The man sat at the desk; already his face was buried in a book. "This is all you have?" I asked. And then, "You are Wardle?"

There was a drawn silence, the sound of cord before it catches fire. Then, said the man at the desk, without looking up from his book, "Wrong on both counts."

"You don't carry books on art or artists?"

"What makes you say that?"

"I don't see any."

"You jump to conclusions rather easily." He looked up. He was bald; there was an unlit pipe and a sack of tobacco on the desk. "On that table over there is the complete pantheon of English letters, Milton to Lord Byron."

"Lord Byron?"

"Yes, we even have that fellow Keats."

"But no art?"

"Why not say what you're looking for?"

"I'm only curious if you think a book on American artists would find favor in the market."

"American artists?"

"American masters."

"How old are you, sir?"

"Twenty-two."

"And thus so quick to jump to conclusions. I recommend you go see Mr. Chapman in his shop at Tenth and Filbert. He's blind, but he knows a thing or two about art."

The Chapmans began publishing art books in Liverpool in the 1780s. They came here because of Birch. Also, I subsequently learned, English industries are far more advanced, and thus more competitive, than ours. Old man Chapman, blind though he is, wanted to continue the old traditions, and so he came to the New World.

There were no other customers inside the store when I entered. It was dark and cold inside. I shivered. The brazier wasn't lit; the only sound was the manic wing-flapping of a bird in a cage. Chapman's specialty was books to commemorate exhibits. These contained mostly engravings, but a few had etchings or block prints. I had started flipping through the catalogue of the 1812 Pennsylvania Academy annual show. The first etching I came to, fittingly I suppose, was of Raphaelle's famous deception piece that once hung in the Peale Museum. I've never seen the painting, and the etching in the catalogue wasn't very good, but the story that's told is that it once tricked the president of the United States. The picture is of the Peale Museum catalogue, the pages worn from being thumbed through, hanging from the wall. Raphaelle painted it to either prove he could fool anyone with perfectly executed trompe l'oeil or that people were stupid enough and blind enough to fall for the trick. I wonder what Peale said to the president when he grabbed for the catalogue only to discover it was mere semblance? Funny, I had in my hand a semblance of the semblance in a book very much similar to the real thing.

The old man came up to me, silent as a cat despite the cane, and asked me if I'd like to have a seat while I looked at books. I duly sat in a chair he brought over for me. When I tried to help with the chair, he ignored me and asked what I was looking at. Then he asked if I was an artist. "Maybe you're one of the artists in the show? No, you're much too young, probably too young to be spending your afternoons lingering in bookshops." I said I was a writer. "Well then," he said, "we're after the same thing." And he looked at me as if I was the one who couldn't see.

Chapman's entire presence, I now realized, had a feline quality — nervous and implacable at the same time. After a few minutes of conversation, during which he correctly guessed my age, political affiliation, neighborhood of residence, and father's occupation — former occupation, that is — the bell on the door jingled and he rose to his feet instantly and grabbed his cane. He opened up and Krimmel and Raphaelle were sucked through the doorway. "I was in the necessary room when you rang," said Chapman. "Now tell me who we have here," he said to no one in particular, "I recognize the footfall."

"Mr. Peale, Mr. Raphaelle Peale," I said, "and Mr. Krimmel, the painter."

"What's left of him," said Raphaelle, who was walking with a cane, and meanwhile Krimmel reminded him who I was. "We're on the hunt for a particular German picture which John — I mean Johann — has in mind."

"Something of Graff? I have landscapes by Koch, a book of Runge's portraits."

"That's not it. Johann, whom did you say you wanted to show me? It's been enough German for one morning, but re-mind me your name again — that's right, Caleb Cloud, Sir Cloud from Easton, and how are your compatriots? I'll never forget that day, by the way, when you boys stormed my door and I thought 'peddlers,' only no, glimmering angels. Now, hold on just a minute, I have a line for you. Johann, tell Mr. Chapman here the name of the artist, a friend of Johann's, equally up and coming from the way it sounds, a real ball of fire."

"Begas, Carl Joseph Begas."

"Trained in Paris, if that means anything, does to some people." His voice trailed off sleepily.

"I'm searching for the portrait he did of his own family. I

need to show it to Raphaelle. My description is useless."

"And Johann would be delighted to purchase the book in which it resides so long as someone would recognize his own brilliance and let him back in the Academy. The *Election Day* picture, in my opinion, in case you confuse my name with the independence of my mind, is a masterpiece of subtlety and nuance."

"Begas," said Chapman.

"Could be in with the French," said Krimmel. "Or with the Flemish."

"There is a serious young lady holding a guitar?" said the blind bookseller. Krimmel answered in the affirmative. "Then I know it. It's at the end of a book put out by the press of Dresden, an anti-Romantic treatise I had shipped here because I thought some of the academicians would appreciate it."

"Did they?" I interrupted.

"They often fail to appreciate what's in their best interests. One day they will."

"This man is a treasure of Philadelphia, Caleb Cloud, you see what I mean?" said Raphaelle. His hands shook slightly as he pointed to Chapman with his cane. Meanwhile the old man asked me to help him retrieve the book. A stool was secured, and after several unsuccessful attempts at pulling a book down, showing it to Krimmel, replacing it, and trying the next one, I finally came upon the little volume, which Krimmel translated as "Retreating Forward." "It's a play on something Goethe said about the Nazarenes, though he probably didn't know what he was talking about. In any case, I don't much like it, but I like this painting."

"Listen," said Raphaelle, once I had climbed down. He came in close, breathing heavily. For a minute I thought he was about to collapse on the floor in front of me. "I have a good one for you, it's not what you would call optimistic, tell me if I have it, Johann."

"It is exactly that: optimistic," said Krimmel.

"You can decide that, Caleb. Now, listen:

What dropped us all into abyssmal woe,
Pulls us forward with sweet yearning now.
In everlasting life death found its goal,
for thou art Death who at last makes us whole.

"I got it, didn't I?" insisted Raphaelle, but Krimmel wasn't
listening. He was paging through the little book while Chapman crept around as if he was going to pull another, yet somehow better volume out of the floor board and hand it to the
painter. Raphaelle came still closer and started telling me about
his "German morning," how Krimmel had come to his house
with a serious look on his face, a look he couldn't quite interpret,
and insisted they go up to Raphaelle's painting room, where
they might be left to talk "man to man" without interruptions
(which Raphaelle clearly had no argument against). As soon as
they sat down in the painting room — Krimmel seemed to have
no interest in the paintings — the German started apologizing.
Raphaelle thought at first the apology was for dragging him
into the mess with his father and brother when Krimmel started
talking about another painting, *Interior of an American Inn*. In
this painting, Krimmel had used Raphaelle as the model for the
drunk, red-faced tradesman being admonished by his young
wife and little girl. Raphaelle said he hadn't seen the painting.
It wouldn't be the last time someone had the idea to use him
as such a model and Krimmel, apparently, said he had passed
through a phase in which he imagined art could be used to ame-
liorate the public morality, a foolish phase that he put an end to
precisely by adding that monkey to the *Election Day* scene.

To this, Raphaelle leaned back in his chair, feeling in that moment he was older and clearer-headed than his guest and guessing that he had come with more on his mind than an apology
for something that hadn't bothered him in the least (he hadn't
even realized he had been insulted). Then, just in that moment,
Raphaelle realized that he too had something to reveal. Once,
he said, he traveled around South America. In Peru he met a
wide-eyed carnival man with hairy ears, who offered Raphaelle
his daughter. This was a favorable arrangement. Raphaelle

admired the strange father, a poor, simple man who desired more than anything to feel in his chest the rising whisper of the crowd's applause much more than even the plunk of coins as they landed in the girl's bonnet. But one day, while standing in the white sun of the Andes, it came to him that the man wasn't traveling across the continent (as even his daughter insisted): he was going from hamlet to hamlet in progressively shrinking circles. At the end, in the center of the circle, he realized, would be nothing. "Despite the sun, which is brighter and more diffuse than any sun I have ever seen, I saw only a dark hole, as dark and frigid and, mind you, as alone as I could imagine. I had this same clarity of mind in my painting room with Krimmel sitting there. I was drowsy and then I saw him staring intently at the fly on the peach. Of course: the paintings, which were not Svinin's but which the Russian had claimed were his own, were done by Johann here." When Krimmel confirmed that he was the author of the Svinin watercolors, Raphaelle thought that he would express anger, that he might even blame him for promulgating the lie. But just as Raphaelle wasn't concerned about the painting of the drunk man in the tavern, Krimmel didn't seem to care that his work had been pilfered. Actually, he said he had sold the pictures to Svinin thinking that one day they would make it into a book on America. (He called Svinin harmless, to be taken with a grain of salt.) Krimmel started looking around the painting room and just then something seemed to occur to *him*: Raphaelle was the master of deception. He kept staring intently at the fly on the peach. "I am waiting for it to move," said Krimmel.

"For a while," continued Raphaelle, now standing near the front window of the bookstore, "there was no sound. My head felt enormous, and soft, slightly dented like a grapefruit is, not exactly round, and Johann began to speak. He told me about his sister-in-law, the *frau von meinem bruder* is what he called her, about her dying." I interrupted Raphaelle to say I had been there when he learned she was dead and he replied, "Well, he told me everything. Everything, Caleb." Krimmel, said Raphaelle, then started talking about a strange young poet who had given himself the one-word name Novalis. The poet, whose real name was von Hardenberg, had died young. He wasn't even thirty, but had been a student of natural philosophy, metallurgy, literature, art, and particularly religion. He developed a kind of theology of light and darkness, life and death, in which they are intertwined, "two sides of the same coin, equally beautiful and seductive." Seductive, Raphaelle hinted, was Krimmel's exact word. The pinnacle of Novalis's career was the publication of a six-part poem called "Hymns to the Night," from which the lines he had recited had come. Krimmel had himself recited his favorite parts of the poem, which is part verse and part prose.

But Krimmel hadn't brought up Novalis without purpose, for he was struggling to come to terms with the death of Susanna and her child. She lives in me, he told Raphaelle. He explained that until Susanna's death he hadn't fully understood Novalis, who had invented a way of understanding death as the silent force of life. The existence of death, said the poet, is why our hearts sometimes swell, why the winds excite us, why a voice can haunt us. And in the end it is death that makes life whole, death — or sleep or darkness or night — "who hauntest the bosom of the tender maiden, and makest a heaven of her lap." Krimmel had moved away from the painting of the peaches and the fly. Now he stood in front of Raphaelle. "The floorboards in my shabbily built house were whining. It might have been the voices of the dead, Caleb Cloud, and Johann Krimmel had this intense look. I wanted to give him just a spot of whiskey to calm him down, but my legs ached — the pain today is terrible — and so I didn't move. And that's when he stopped himself short and started talking about this artist Begas. Johann knows him. Anyway, this fellow has painted a picture of his family, the living and the dead in equal measure."

"Done frequently enough," I said, interrupting.

"Maybe so, but he has something else in mind. Let me see if I have this right," answered Raphaelle. He looked over at Krimmel, whose mouth was open and who was now leaning over the little book like a hunter stalking prey. "Here you go," said Raphaelle, lowering his voice in exaggerated fashion.

"This is beloved death he is talking about, by the way, though I think you understand that; 'never suspect it is thou, opening the doors to Heaven, that steppest to meet them out of ancient stories, bearing the key to the dwellings of the blessed, silent messenger of secrets infinite.'"

"He wants to bare some secrets."

"The dead will do the talking. Krimmel just wants Novalis and Begas—and, now, Caleb, he wants me—to help him."

From Chapman's bookstore we walked over to the Castle. Though he had been gone only a few days, everyone wanted to know when Victor was coming back. Had he returned from Baltimore? He didn't get into trouble, did he? We need him here, said the barkeep. I bet he's found a lass, Nothing there he couldn't get his hands on here, He's got adventure in his belly, Don't think so at first, he looks so young, Ah, who but the young, look at these fellas here, I don't know, I don't think they make them like they used to, When I was their age...When you were their age there weren't so many damn preachers, Baltimore wasn't much more than a hole in the coast line, Oh, what kind of hole? This went on for ten minutes, with the conclusion being that the young ladies of Baltimore, though easy, are but a poor semblance of their Philadelphia counterparts. "The wealth of frozen beauties," said Raphaelle.

Mr. Tom Sully, with his hands in his pockets, walked in and put a coin on the counter and then came over to our table. He tipped his hat to Raphaelle and he and Krimmel embraced, Krimmel breathing deeply, with evident satisfaction, and I thought for a minute he would weep. Sully pretended he hadn't known of Krimmel's ousting from the Academy. "I am out of it," he said. "I spend all my time in the studio. Either that or with the young ones."

"You haven't put them to work?"

"I refuse it," said Sully, "no offense to you, Mr. Peale."

"No offense taken, I assure you," he replied.

"We like to pretend we are a merry band," said Sully, "there is a skit at every supper and sometimes I'm the lead." Raphaelle kept sniffing his glass of whiskey. Soon, the conversation turned to the market for paintings. The price of a traditionally sized, three-quarters view with hands had dropped, in some instances, below fifty dollars. Raphaelle shrugged and Krimmel pulled out his sketchbook. He wanted to show Sully a drawing. Sully asked me how our book was going. Raphaelle interrupted before I could reply to ask Sully what he thought of Svinin.

Sully clapped his hands. "A fool."

"A dangerous fool?" I wondered.

"Depends who you ask."

"Well?"

"Let me tell you a story. One day, sometime after Svinin left, a few of us were talking. Just like now, we were trying to figure him out. Well I'll admit to going easy on him. Despite every-thing, I thought he was harmless. Never gave it much thought until the to-do with Rembrandt. Then King, who is a cheap bastard, or frugal anyway — "

"Only he was waiting for his inheritance, but never mind that, there isn't a bad bone in his body." Sully's eyes flashed like bunting at the front edge of a storm. "King quietly admits he had loaned Svinin seventy-five dollars. 'Did he pay you back?' I asked him. Nosirree. Then I laughed and told him he was prey. But immediately, both Birch and Bass Otis admitted they had done the same. Otis, I don't know where he got it, $150. Birch said he did it to shut up the Russian, but I think he was covering up."

"He didn't ask you for money?" said Raphaelle. "Hell, he didn't ask me. I might — "

"I don't know what would have happened. He never asked. I guess I got lucky."

"What if he returned to Philadelphia?" said Krimmel.

"Would my brother forgive and forget?" said Raphaelle.

"Better you to answer that, Mr. Peale."

Sully said he had no choice, now that the panic had settled in, but to join the crowd and produce a grand history painting for public exhibition. The idea, he explained, is that you can sell five thousand or ten thousand tickets for twenty-five cents and make $1,250 or $2,500 easier than you can sell the painting for $500. "You can sell tickets, put on a show."

"My brother will make a show of his death court," muttered Raphaelle.

"Trumbull has built an exhibit stage for his *Declaration of Independence.*"

"And he'll use colored lights and fireworks, should he have to."

"But I'm not so sure of myself."

"Ah," said Raphaelle. "We are not all Rembrandts."

"It's not that, Raphaelle. I'm in favor of the market. We artists are part of it, plain and simple. But I've never been a history painter before. Of course you see. It isn't the same as making a portrait or painting a still life or, Mr. Krimmel, painting a genre scene."

"And so?"

"It will be Washington crossing the Delaware."

Raphaelle rolled his eyes.

"Forget I said so. I mean to treat the president as a man about to enter the unknown."

"The pitch black waters of the Mighty Delaware."

"Quite frozen then, in late December," I said.

"Well then you cannot expect crowds. The hero must be no less than heroic," said Raphaelle. "The message of the painting must be clear, the painter's intent in the open for everyone to see. I only hope Rembrandt has enough courage to ask me to pose as the drunk or the suicide."

"Krimmel, too, is working on something new," I said, fearful of silence.

"More alive than the *Court of Death*?"

"My heart is broken, Sully," Krimmel said, "and I have no

recourse with my brother." Krimmel looked pale.

"And, Mr. Thomas Sully," said Raphaelle, "poor Johann has angered my brother."

"And threatened all the Enlightenment," said I.

"I too am resigning from the Academy, in silent protest," said Raphaelle.

"In my painting," said Krimmel, "the dead and the living are equal. I doubt my brother will want it—he is what you might call a true American. He prefers not to look back."

"Then where will it hang?"

"We will start a new society," said Raphaelle, "Caleb Cloud, you are the first to hear it, the revolution has begun, boys, down with tyranny. Johann will hang his masterpiece there."

Krimmel bent to his case to find a pencil and sitting up his feather eyes sought Sully's. "A salvo has been fired."

Chapter XVIII

 few days later, a note arrived from Victor in Baltimore. In it, he instructed me to take his and Dixcy's things and move into a room with a single bed. "Rembrandt," he wrote, "may be a bit more complicated than we imagined. He is anyway motivated by anger. His work has impressed William, who has come around on him, and I will agree with his assessment that he is no genius (but may be a master), or his genius is in his desire and persistence, much more than in his vision. He despises the elite (that's why he left Philadelphia, he told us), but he is one himself. He desperately wishes to connect with Mr. Everyday, Cloud, the sailmaker or the countinghouse clerk, and he thinks that though he can't adequately speak their language he can reach their conscience with art. William, surprisingly, is in favor of the approach, but I wonder if he can't speak one language, how is he going to speak another? But Cloud, there is something else. William thinks he is suffering from consumption. His eyes are more drawn than ever. Sometimes he is florid and sometimes pale. I asked him if he has spit blood but he wouldn't give me a straight answer. Rembrandt's wife Eleanor has been looking after him. (What he really needs is a visit from Ms. Chamberlaine, do you suspect she knows yet his secret?)"

As a postscript, Victor said Dixcy would remain in Baltimore for the time being, but that he was going to take a steamship to Trenton and then ride a coach to Newtown. "As I promised," he wrote and then, quixotically, "I am anyway needed."

At the boardinghouse, I had decided to tell Libby about Dixcy's condition, but then when I saw her the next morning briskly attending to her chores I couldn't do it. She isn't a beautiful thing—her eyes are too close together, for one—but she is both solid and sprightly, giving the impression that she possesses infinite desire. Perhaps she is merely nervous. I told her that Dixcy and Victor had been detained a while and so I wanted to switch rooms for the time being. She feigned disinterest and went about her business of cleaning up the kitchen. For a while, I watched her singing sweetly, and low, and scraping the blackened spoons. I thought of a story for *Poulson's* on the improvements being made to the Waterworks. "Libby," I said, "Ms. Chamberlaine, I think you should know something." I told her what Victor had written in the letter.

She squinted, nodded, and said, "Men aren't very observant."

"You knew this?"

"As soon as you three walked through the door."

"And still."

"And still, what? Half this city is diseased." Her arms, I noticed, were thick and muscular and she smelled of tallow and lard. On her face, below her right eye, was a black smear, a mark of immunity, perhaps, or the ash of a thunderbolt.

All the while I was slowly collecting information on the issue of Peale's museum and the increased rent he was being charged by the city councils. Naïve as I was in those days—and torn over Peale and Krimmel—the issue at first seemed clear: the old man was being gouged unfairly. Either the city didn't want the museum in the State House or it wanted to put it out of business. But why? "They are blind and on top of that foolish,"

said Peale. "Our sole mission is education and improvement and yet I have to beg them to see the value."

"Would you like to see the record of the account?" said the clerk of the councils. "Anyone can see it." The clerk was a lump of a man with an empty face. Face, eyes, voice, each detached from the other. He didn't look at me when he spoke. "The record begins with 1790, naturally."

"Naturally?"

"1790 until 1799, when the state abandoned the building, no rent paid. I can't speculate further on the nature of the agreement between Mr. Peale and the Pennsylvania assembly. 1800 until 1810, rent charged $3,600 for the year, or $300 per month."

"And rent paid?"

"Zero. Rent charged, 1811 up to and including last year, 1818, $600 per month or $7,200 per year, eight years, $57,600 total."

"And rent paid, zero?"

"Rent paid in full years '11, '14, '15, '16. Rent paid in '17, $4,250. Rent paid in

'18—"

"Zero?"

"Zero."

One afternoon in early June, while I was eating the dinner prepared for me by Libby, Victor—who had apparently returned to Baltimore from Newtown—and Dixcy walked through the door. They sat down as if they hadn't been away for two and a half months, as if there were nothing more wrong with Dixcy than a common cold. He appeared about the same: hair matted, seaweed hands, blunting eyes. "Keep eating," said Victor, and then he stood and went into the kitchen to find Libby, who silently brought out two bowls of soup and then a plate of duck and potatoes.

"She knows," said Victor to Dixcy. Dixcy said he couldn't care less. "William," said Victor to me, "has some news for us." The news was that beginning in July, Dixcy was to begin working with Rembrandt Peale as a special assistant on his traveling exhibition of the *Court of Death*.

"Cloud, William is to handle all the arrangements, the permits needed from each town, the transportation for the painting and for Rembrandt, the lighting, the construction of the little building—Rembrandt calls it a 'temple'—that will house the painting, everything behind the scenes. It was Mrs. Rembrandt Peale's suggestion."

"And you?" I wondered. "How did you find Mrs. Greenpoint? Were you able to obtain the sketch?"

"The sketch, I can assure you, will be back in Krimmel's hand soon."

"What does that mean?"

"It means what it means."

"It means you're still a thief and I'm a liar," I said. "They're asking for you at the Castle. Returning there or back to the mill?"

"He needs you," said Dixcy. Was that it? Three words that slid by and now the gate was open.

The next day, Victor went to Germantown. At Belfield, he said, he was to negotiate a contract with Tharp. With the contract, they would proceed with designing the mill. I said I thought it had already been designed. He said they completed a preliminary design, but then Peale had had second thoughts. He had, unbeknownst to his family, put the farm on the market. "He's desperate," said Victor, "an unjust fate for a Founding Father."

"If you can call him that," said Dixcy.

"I just call him full of shit," said I, as the words fell fallow to the floor.

Apparently, Rembrandt was an abysmal man of business. The Rendezvous for Taste, his gallery and museum, had run out of money and was closed. Rembrandt was trying to convince his brother Rubens to move to Baltimore to take it over. The rumor inside the Peale family was that Peale would then sell his farm, come out of retirement, and resume management of the Philadelphia museum. (I said nothing, at this point in the conversation, about the information I had on Peale's museum.) Rembrandt had lost all his investment in the gaslight project. "The trenches had been dug," said Victor. "They remain like still open wounds."

"He is stronger than we think," said Dixcy.

A week later, in Raphaelle's painting room, Krimmel was pacing around. He kept pushing his yellow locks out of his eyes. His face was pink and he wore a poorly tailored pale blue suit and an open collar. His painting was propped against the wall. "A masterpiece," said Raphaelle, "better than Begas, just stand in front of it Caleb, stand there with it a while as if you're in the room too, the dead are alive and the living are plunged into madness. Is this not the most exasperating madness, this picture? You don't have to walk into the room, Caleb, Krimmel's family is going to leap off the canvas and walk in here, and then you'll never tell who is dead and who is alive."

"This man is the master of deception," said Krimmel, grimacing.

"No, no, *Johann* is one who has done it, with his infinite, infinitesimal brush strokes. By the way, have you seen his brushes? I only wish I had brushes this tiny when I was doing miniatures myself, have a look for just a minute at the creases in Susanna's dress, the grain in the wood of the floor! Do you see the little fella's resplendent manhood? But look at him, Caleb, look at Johann. Do you see how finishing the painting has put him at ease?" Krimmel was pacing still, his footfalls oddly soundless.

"I have to give it to George," said Krimmel. He said he had begun to feel like a prisoner, and looking at himself in the picture was making him feel suffocated all the more.

"He can do with it what he wants," whispered Raphaelle.

"What would you do?" I said.

"'In such strange passion, if I may once more / Review the past, I warred against myself—'"

Then he explained that Johann needs everything out in the open. "Unlike the rest of us, he can't bear to lie."

In the painting, Susanna, wearing a red dress and with her legs crossed, sits in a chair in front of a window. Outside the window is a continental landscape, which is heaven, or eternity. George stands behind her, his face red with sorrow, two fingers split apart to represent the rending of fate. Three daughters are linked to the dead mother. The one in the green dress is the silent Catharine, the girl who screamed but once and that was it. Krimmel himself stands to the right of Susanna; he leans against a drawing table and he is sketching. There is utter, futile despair in his countenance, as if someone—not a friend or a lover, but all human existence, or God himself—has taken his heart in hand and is squeezing hard. His left hand is slipped inside his coat, resting on his heart, but not in a theatrical way that draws unnecessary attention to his despair. He is more like the lion in Hicks's kingdom than, say, Rembrandt's dryly lactating Roman daughter: Krimmel is dying inside. At his feet are the remaining living members of the family. On Susanna's lap is a baby boy, with a look of clarity, or quite possibly dementia. He looks both abundantly healthy and also badly wounded. He stares straight ahead. The boy's bare right arm is stretched out toward Krimmel and he points to the artist.

"As if to say you're his real father?" I asked, with trepidation.

"Oh, no," said Krimmel. "In my carelessness I dropped the boy and he died."

Then Krimmel sat down near the right window, in the chair Victor had occupied when we first made our visit to Raphaelle. The room wasn't hot, but it was stuffy, and for some reason Raphaelle had left the windows closed. For a few minutes the three of us sat in silence. Raphaelle had closed his eyes. Briefly I thought he had fallen asleep. He finally grimaced and stood with some difficulty, somehow prompting Krimmel to start talking about his brother George and Susanna and the family in the house at Seventh and Pine. George worked most of his waking hours. In America, he had started off as a merchant, then a clerk in the custom house, then an adjuster for a firm that insured ship cargo. He kept trying to go out on his own, so he would quit and try to make it himself or with a partner, usually another clerk, until that failed and then he would seek employment with someone else. This meant that he was rarely home, especially in the phases of self-employment, when he would sometimes sleep in his office. "He hardly sleeps, anyway," said Krimmel. George never understood why he wanted to be an artist, but because Krimmel didn't have a conventional trade, he could help manage the affairs of the house and the family. This was how George understood the trade: Krimmel's time as surrogate father in exchange for room and board. This was why, in an earlier portrait of the family, Krimmel put himself in the role of the family man. In the picture, Susanna and the children are gathered around as Krimmel enters the house (with a newspaper in his hand); George is present only in a portrait, which hangs on the wall behind the children.

"Naturally, with another man in the house," said Raphaelle. "Nothing a man can do, really."

"Yes, I suppose I am something my brother is not."

"'That father lost, lost his; and the survivor bound / In filial obligation for some term / To do obsequious sorrow: but to persever —'"

"My brother was very much alive! An obligation, yes, but that is always insufficient. It was Susanna herself, you have to understand she was a woman of intense feeling, and my brother—"

"A man of trade."

"She could not disguise her feeling."

"That's why you left?" I asked.

"Yes, I had to."

"Caleb, did you hear the Russian is coming?" said Raphaelle, interrupting. He had begun to treat a new canvas. "We're going to set him straight."

"And what about the book? Carey still wants to publish it?"

"If Svinin wants it published, he's going to have to face up to our friend here. Carey says he won't publish unless the Russian tells the truth."

July 4, in the afternoon, I convinced Victor to go over to Centre Square to see the celebration. Since returning from Baltimore, he had seemed more and more restless. "We should go to New York, Cloud, spend some time with Vanderlyn and the other artists there, meet some new people. We never intended to settle here, did we?" Then he started talking about Babylon and the notion of "pure freedom," which, he said, was based on unfettered exchange. "In New York, this is easily understood. It's the way things are. It's the grid plan," he reminded me, "and it has no value outside of exchange. Here, things have value, or rather, people place arbitrary value on them. Arbitrary and irrational, Cloud," he said.

"You've never liked July 4," I said. "You told me that before."

We walked past the Second Bank of the United States under construction. A lone man with a horse face and a wooden crutch stood outside the gate with a placard that read, with improper spelling, "CORUPT." He stood perfectly still as we passed by. A military parade started at Fifth Street in front of the State House; Victor purchased a jug of cider for the rest of the walk. He looked only straight ahead as he walked, as if afraid to learn or see too much and I did most of the talking. "Victor dismisses as quickly as he accepts and absorbs," I wrote in my notebook. "He is afraid of Dixcy dying, or rather afraid of witnessing the decline. Now I understand why he was so supportive of Dixcy going to work for Rembrandt: so that he won't have to be faced with it himself."

The crowds began around Eleventh Street and extended up Chestnut to Centre Square. There were vendors selling lemonade, cider, beer, peaches, and a woman campaigning for temperance was passing out broadsides. There were oystermen lined up with their wheelbarrows from the entrance just past Thirteenth Street all the way to Rush's fountain and there were drunken soldiers and flags of every surviving regiment from the Revolutionary War. Three boys played with a toy canon. A fourth tried to ride a little dog, a collie or a mixed hound of some kind, and he accidentally stepped on its paw, causing a terrible howl. "A cathartic bellow," said Victor. "Think about it. How many times a day does this dog get his feet stepped on? A little dog like that wandering around a crowded city and half the people are pulling carts. What do you think? Three, four times? And yet each time I bet he lets out the same mournful cry, as if he is forced to reconsider his own existence."

"Which is pathetically short."

"In which any wound, no matter how small, can be a mortal wound." Then, a few minutes later, he said, "Aren't you glad human beings aren't like that? It would be insufferable if every time I was jostled or mistreated I howled to the end of the earth, or to the core of my being."

"You just grin and bear it?"

"Or take the pain out on someone else. Bury it in cruelty, Cloud, that's the way."

A little while later, the sunlight now scraping the ground, leaving patches of fire across the square, we spotted Krimmel setting up his camera obscura. As he worked, he was chatting with the cherry woman. She seemed to be trying to tell him something she thought was important, but he was ignoring her, shaking his head and going right on adjusting his apparatus.

No one else was paying him any attention. Victor purchased a small sack of cherries from the woman, who said something about being excited by the cannon fire in the distance.

Krimmel had been there for hours already, sketching "little, insignificant vignettes." Now he was measuring the spaces with the camera obscura so that the final picture would have accurate depth and scale. "It is the barest semblance," he said, "but sometimes that's all we need to recreate the scene."

"Plato," said Victor, "says semblances don't reveal the real truth of things."

"But he is wrong, I think. I'll show you my sketches from today and you can tell me whether the artist isn't capable of revealing what our regular eyes can't, call it truth if you want."

When Krimmel finished putting away his equipment, the cherry woman called him over. She stood slowly, like someone awakening from a terrible nightmare, and with a look of pain on her face, and she pulled him close to her and whispered in his ear.

"What was that?" asked Victor.

"Oh, nothing. That woman will never let me forget something I once did. But she is strange and unpredictable. She just called me a 'vile dog.'"

"That's funny," I said, "because it looked like she wanted to embrace you."

Krimmel said we should walk with him back to Germantown. There was going to be a gathering at the Miller house. If we wanted, we could sleep there and return to the city in the morning. Victor acquired another jug of beer and we stopped for a while at Bush Hill so that Krimmel could sketch the scene. The sun had set and everything was pale and quiet. We sat at a wooden table on the lawn near the woodpile. A hawk flew overhead and for a minute I got a terrible chill, as if the raptor had cast a permanent shadow. I looked up and it was gone past the trees in the yard and beyond the old house itself, which looked rather like a ruin. I lost myself in thoughts of a black servant girl, Lucy, first her eyes, eyes which truly shined, then her lips, which were full but also straight, in a way that made her seem dignified and careful (but not uncertain). Her flesh was thick, emollient, glossy, and also restrained, and yes, respectful, her breasts enormous but not grotesque, her pubis silent as the dawn, her great ass as I turned her over in my mind trembling like the preacher's hands as he holds beneath them all creation, an ass more moon than sea, more launch than dive, more light than darkness, and meanwhile Victor was talking about the Miller sisters, trying to remember which one was which, and in the distance Krimmel could be heard, like a squirrel clamoring about the underbrush and weeds.

When he returned, I told him Victor had arranged for the return of the sketch of Harriet.

"We hope it isn't too late," said Victor.

"It's better to have the real thing," said Krimmel, as if waking from a dream and without really answering the question. "Though I can't be sure that's true."

And so we walked from Bush Hill to Germantown, the light disappearing behind us, and for much of the way in silence. For a while, as we found our way back to the Wissahickon Road, Victor was talking about a girl he met in Baltimore. She ran a coffeehouse there for her father, who had been put in jail for stealing bricks from a brickyard. "Hirsute," he said, "like climbing through a jungle." Krimmel took a long swig of beer and I asked him if he had decided what to do with his family portrait.

"I finally went to the house in Northern Liberties," he said. "My niece answered the door and I went in. She was unusually shy, but after a few minutes she started talking about her mother. 'I talk to her every day,' she said, 'and she told me she is worried about Papa and Uncle John and that I am to make sure they are all right.'" After a while I took the paper off the painting, I didn't think about it beforehand, and as soon as she saw it she turned away, her back to the painting, and said, 'No one remembers baby George, but I do.' My brother walked in then. I hadn't seen him for three years. He looked at me and then at the painting and said, 'I see you've improved at your drawing.'"

"He didn't say that," said Victor.

"Then he said, 'Am I right, I suppose you bring this as an of-fering,' his English has almost no accent. 'Yes,' I answered him, 'I could not come sooner, I had to finish this first, I am sorry.' He pulled out his pipe, stuffed in the tobacco, and lit it. He really had a cunning look on his face."

"Not in the painting," I said.

"No, but he is measuring, always measuring. After a minute, he said, 'You understand, this holds no value to me. The value is yours, not mine.' After that, if you can believe it, he offered me a room in his house."

"So you could help raise the children."

"Anyway, it doesn't matter now. It's been purchased by a collector."

"Not just any collector, is it?"

Said Krimmel, with his hair matted by sweat, "There's noth-ing to hide."

"Then it is Bonaparte?" said Victor, very nearly over-whelmed with delight.

That evening, with gray light in the distance, we arrived into a forest of torches and flags. Henrietta Miller, with her fecund air and strong arms, had decorated the house and garden for the celebration of Independence. Krimmel went over to Harriet, leaning against a wooden post; Victor bowed obsequiously, and Harriet, trying to shuffle out of the way of Victor, nearly landed in my arms. For a moment, I entertained the fantasy that I could charm her-who-could-never-be-charmed and who never would acquiesce, so it seemed, to the determined assault of a man like Victor or Krimmel. My mind wandered and my eyes held their ground and for a moment Harriet's, but the fantasy ended with the discharge of someone's musket somewhere and Harriet turning away with disdain.

Krimmel led us inside to the room he had once inhabited.

He stored away his camera obscura and put down his sketch-book. For a moment, he gazed at his sketchbook and pencils as if he might bring them downstairs to the party. He searched around for a smaller pad and stuck it in his pocket. Then he removed the pad, flipped through it quickly as if he was try-ing to find a certain sketch, and put it down. Then he looked up at Victor and me and said, in a tone of curiosity more than whimsy, "I wonder what will happen tonight."

The party seemed to be divided into two sections. Isaac Miller's friends were sitting at tables on the porch facing Henrietta's orchard. Caroline and Harriet and Henrietta's friends were prancing about the lawn to the right and some were dancing in pairs. Caroline's husband Tharp was fixing a torch that had almost fallen. Every few moments, while he worked, he would stop and take a swig from his flask. Victor had already insert-ed himself into a group standing around telling stories. From the porch, where I was standing, Victor's voice, above all oth-ers, could be distinguished. He was asking if anyone else had ever seen any of Hicks's *Peaceable Kingdom* paintings and when everyone around him said no, they had in fact barely heard of Hicks, only that he must be related to Elias Hicks, Victor started to describe Newtown, and Hicks's shop, and even Greenpoint, each pause in the story eliciting a short burst of laughter.

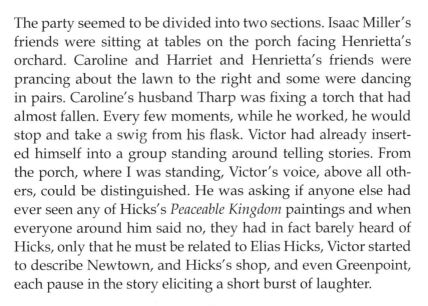

A little later, Victor introduced me to a girl of medium height with a secretive face and silver hoop earrings. Who was she? Her name was Mary Bench, a classmate of Harriet's. They sat next to each other during Krimmel's drawing instruction.

"Apparently, every one of them was in love with him," said Victor.

Mary smiled, as if to say everything in the world is absurd. Was there Irish in her voice? There was fog and sea, perhaps, or stone and heath, or smoke, or its opposite, damp. She has witnessed someone dying of consumption. But who hasn't? She has raised her own brothers and sisters, scrubbed their underwear and their faces, let them run wild in the yard. We talked about catfish and waffles, the mud that collects on the Germantown Road, and the flower of foxglove (like an infinite, vertical perspective). Then she walked away and I didn't see her for a half hour, or more.

"You are a master," said Victor.

I ignored him, thinking that what I would like was a taste from Tharp's flask; Harriet drifted into view and I drifted beyond the clot of bodies to the edge of the lawn. Mary Bench was pretty, perhaps even stunning, but I wanted more of the dirt and haze in her voice, more of the thick (not chubby, fattened, sweaty, lazy), almost masculine hands she held at her side. I couldn't chase after her, I knew that. No, Mary Bench would decide what she wanted, and when, and she would make these decisions with the certainty of a woman used to having to figure everything out herself.

It was just then, as I turned my back away from Victor, fireworks flashed in the short distance, beyond the roof of the house. Everyone, of course, turned to see what would come next. Then there was a red flare and a white and a long thump and something mean about it, something unforgiving, something even in the honeysuckle air of Germantown, with its quiet industriousness and potent simplicity, with its insistent reserve and moral clarity, with its cool and quiet shadows: a defensive brutality I had felt all day. The flares and thumps and crackles and the laughter and the clapping and the yelps (Victor yelping too, unmistakably) went on in short waves of sound and motion. Was this the rhythm of war? Fire, cry out, reload, fire again. My thoughts drifted to Hicks, maddened by the celebration of Independence, standing in his workshop, fingers white with fear. Small fingers, tight face, spry figure wound like a musket ball, ready to flare at any time. No, no, afraid of this power, which must be willfully denied. No one is listening, the thumping continues, and Hicks winds tighter, angrier still.

If we don't destroy the brutality within us it will destroy us, the dream of America dissolved in the bare anger of becoming America. I drifted further still, beyond the arbor, beyond the vegetable garden, and down a brick path lined with flowers. Realizing the air in this part of Henrietta's creation was cooler and more lithesome, I stopped. I breathed. I told myself to wait until Mary Bench had made her decisions. I was helpless, anyway. I turned and came to a row of apple trees. Had I come around to the orchard without realizing it? Drawn instinctively to the trees, with their broad mass and low, horizontal limbs, I reached out. The air smelled of night and minerals. I had the sensation that my eyes were closed. But were they? When I opened them, or thought I opened them, there were two figures before me, together, apart, together again. Secretive as children, magnetized as children to one another. The sound of Krimmel's deliberate voice. The silence of the other, plundering darkness, her own darkness, her own territory, her own domestic dream: it was Henrietta, who lived like a bed of leaves in the eternal forest. The figures flashed and disappeared in the shadows. I stood there dumbly, staring. What in God's name was I doing? I stood there until I was sure of what was happening and then I walked quickly back to the party, sick and excited all at once.

In October, I took Mary Bench to the opening of the annual show at the Academy. It was our first appearance together in public. All night she had a look on her face of bemusement. In her mind, art, or as she put it, drawing, was another form of expressing oneself, not all that much different from talking. She had taken Krimmel's class because even as a child she had found herself doodling, sometimes making little pictures of stars or suns or trees. Sometimes, if someone would ask her a question she would respond with a picture. Krimmel, she had thought, made pictures for this reason. In fact, she said, he was known as the "silent sketcher." Thus she took the class as one might be inclined to learn French or Greek. It was a matter of developing a faculty of expression. Her mother, who hadn't any notion of being refined or educated, couldn't understand why she would bother with a class when her pictures were just little scribbles, but Mary insisted and in the end her oldest brother, who worked for the inventor Oliver Evans, paid the tuition.

Mary only looked at me blankly when I explained why Krimmel's painting of his family wasn't in this year's show. She must have thought it ridiculous that anyone would take the time to decide such a thing. "Who decides what's important?" she said.

My short lesson on the aspiration of American art truly sounded ridiculous.

She laughed. "Do the rest of these people pay these theories any mind?" Her hands were on her hips.

"Actually, they fear dissent."

"Mr. Krimmel is irreverent. Ask Harriet Miller that." Or, perhaps, Henrietta?

"In any case, we won't see his work here." The painting of Susanna and the children was hanging in an empty Chestnut Street gallery along with leftover wax figures and a preserved hellion cat brought back from India. Raphaelle had insisted he put his painting up for the same period as the Academy show.

"It's as if the Renaissance never happened," she said.

"What?"

"Well, what if I like a certain picture and you don't? Everyone has a different opinion. Even in our class, Mr. Krimmel said everyone's drawing is important. All that matters is the making of the picture. If you want to get better at it, you just practice. But he never said, 'Now, class, let's decide who has made the most important drawing!'"

"This is about the fate of the country."

"Men are fools."

Desire clinched my chest, let loose my fingers.

"Let's get out of here, it's too crowded. Take me to see his painting."

The word in the crowded hall was that Krimmel could not have done the painting anyway, so it was on justifiable grounds he had been excised from the Academy. But who among the crowd had seen the painting? That didn't stop the speculating. Had he ever done a picture quite like it? No, there are the market scenes and the grand scale parades (though in truth these are done on rather small-sized canvases) and the street vignettes he sold to the Russian. Speaking of which, there is a rumor the Russian con artist Svinin is headed back to Philadelphia. Is he here tonight? I heard he was spotted in New York. If he were here you would know. Why, you mean there would be commotion, I don't believe Rembrandt Peale is here. No, I'm referring to the terrible odor that emanates from his mouth, maybe you should have a handkerchief ready to cover your nose. And, I have heard, a hand over your wallet. I am trying to imagine those scenes Krimmel is famous for, like the family returning from market and the country frolic, do they have the style and control this master work is said to have? Perhaps, but they are lighthearted. They are fancy, certainly, but not lighthearted. Well, there is none of this direct and yet also complex despair. How do you know? Have you seen the painting hanging in that forlorn gallery? They've given it some pretentious name. Yes, I heard that, the Society of American Artists. A society of two? Another fraud perpetrated by that crazy fellow Raphaelle Peale. Why, he ought to be removed from the Academy too. These men seem hell-bent on denigrating the art of America. Birch, if you want my opinion, is the real perpetrator. He put Krimmel's subversive painting in last year's show. It was only a watercolor sketch. Its point was nevertheless made. Peale is going to put an end to the whole thing, if you ask me he is well justified in protecting his pantheon. The taste of America can't be manipulated by a wild-eyed foreigner. At least he isn't forcing the nude on us. You mean like Rembrandt Peale? You never know where the enemies lie, that's the thing. They could be hiding in your own closet. The true reason they rejected Krimmel? Have you heard? It angered Peale. I read it in *Poulson's*. Fine, but that's not it, the painting isn't anything like Krimmel's other work. You're saying it's someone else's? I've never known Krimmel to use such a rich palette. I hear it's like the work of Rembrandt Peale when he returned from Paris the first time, the red lips, the red crinoline, the infinite brilliance of the blacks. Actually, it wasn't Rembrandt Peale I was thinking of. No? Tell me, who in this city is the master of deception? A different Peale, you mean? Once made the president of the United States scratch his head in disbelief.

"But you know it is his picture," said Mary Bench, after overhearing. We were working our way through the crowded hall.

"Well, I think I know."

"What do you mean, you think you know? Mr. Krimmel doesn't lie, I know that for a fact."

"He sought the help of Raphaelle Peale. He painted it in Raphaelle's painting room."

"So?"

"Exactly."

"What?"

"Never mind."

A moment later, Charles Willson Peale came up to us from behind. He shook Mary's hand and told her I was the prize of Easton—"Mr. Cloud here and his little band of brothers, this city will never be the same!" Mary looked at him doubtfully. Peale didn't disguise his lechery. Did Mary herself enjoy it? Her lips were parted and then she smiled while looking the old man over. I asked him what he thought was the best work in the show, but he talked right over me. The room was crowded and quite loud, perhaps he hadn't heard the question. Rembrandt, he said, had discovered a way to get around the Academy show. "Who needs all this nonsense if you can just as easily take your pictures directly to the people?"

"You're talking about the *Court of Death*."

"And that's why he doesn't need to be here tonight, forced to compete for the attention—"

"You don't mean to say museums are to be obsolete."

"I mean to say, my dear boy, that art for the sake of fashion is a dead end. That's why it's so stuffy in here tonight. There is too much talk and not enough—"

"Silence," said Mary Bench, interrupting. Peale looked at her curiously, as if a family of sparrows had leapt, one at a time, from her hair, which was piled (quite fashionably) on top of her head. "Hardly anyone is even looking at the pictures. I agree with Mr. Peale. What's the point?"

"It's opening night," I said, "so it's normal to have a crowd. On any other day the room is empty and you can meditate as long as you like on your favorite picture. I rather thought you would enjoy the spectacle."

Peale reminded me that I had promised to help publicize his campaign for the city to support his museum. Why hadn't I written yet on the subject? Why hadn't I come back in to the museum to talk to Rubens? I thought about what the State House clerk had told me and I closed my eyes for a moment. Before I could answer—for a moment I thought of Krimmel skating on Tharp's mill pond and I remembered, too, Peale in his prime had been an avid skater, on the Delaware no less, a river, when it is frozen, choked by ruts and knots in the ice, and I wondered still, why is there something so insistent about Krimmel?—the old man came closer and he whispered in my ear, "I am sending Rubens down to Baltimore to try to save Rembrandt's museum. With this economy it may be altogether too late, but I have been faced with worse. That means I may have to install myself back at the helm of the Peale Museum. One hates to go backwards, but on the other hand, one goes with the punches, my boy, if he is to survive. To tell you the truth, one has to do more than that, one has to come out punching." Peale leveled his gaze onto mine.

"You perhaps know why I haven't written that article," I said.

"You are brave, my boy," he said, eyebrows fair, once red, tussled wildly, "and smart enough to see things clearly — and you're independent."

The floor had vanished, Mary's hand in mine. I undid it.

"You know the truth of Krimmel's so-called masterwork. Who is going to let him get away with it? But not at my boy's expense. A Peale isn't a ghostwriter, Mr. Cloud."

"Raphaelle told me himself —"

"Raphaelle is a frightened drunk, a joker. He's playing a joke on himself — his favorite subject. That painting is going to the collection of Bonaparte. It has the wrong name on it."

"Krimmel has talent enough."

"You know the truth of it," he repeated. His face was calm now and he gazed again at Mary. "Mr. Poulson's readers like to be informed."

"How would it be proved?" I wanted to say, "I have witnessed Krimmel's misery, I have seen the anguish and the seriousness in his face —." But Peale had returned his hard gaze and he leaned forward, as if to disrupt my own thoughts. Now he grabbed hold of them.

"That painting, Mr. Cloud, is the work of a master," said Peale. "You don't dare sit on a lie."

As we exited the hall into the courtyard, Mary noticed a silver earring on the brick pavement. She reached down to pick it up. Was I afraid of the truth? For a moment, I felt unsteady, but then the cool air and the faint smell of a chimney put me at ease. Mary removed her left earring and pressed this new one through the hole.

"Now you don't match."

"Does that disturb you?"

I thought of the salt smell of the Indian girl beneath the poplar tree at the edge of the Delaware. "Hardly." I looked at Mary and relished seeing her break our gaze first, hands back on hips, smiling.

The rogue gallery—formerly Mrs. Martha Washington's Wax Museum—was more crowded than I had imagined it would be. Krimmel's painting was hung, alone, on a long wall and it was illuminated by gaslight. At the entrance was Raphaelle Peale wearing an emerald green coat and a feather hat. He was handing out a pamphlet. "Tired of hypocrisy?" it read, "Join an artists' society that values the teaching and advancement of the arts, not the making of egos."

"It's a crusade, Caleb Cloud," said Raphaelle. His eyes were yellow in the lamplight.

"All the Academy is talking about this painting."

Mary Bench slipped inside.

"'Rome and her rats are at the point of battle.'"

"*Julius Caesar?*"

"*The Tragedy of Coriolanus*, comrade. You should spend as much time reading as you do writing, Cloud."

"Whose idea was this Society of American Artists?"

"For this," said Raphaelle, "I will take credit. Johann is only silently complicit. I have counted 127 people through this door tonight, but that was as of an hour ago, and now I've lost count. Our friend is inside. He refuses even a wee taste from my flask. Caleb from Easton, your lady has a preponderance of—"

"Of beauty."

"Of beauty. Life is to be suckled from, isn't it my lad!"

Already, she had found Krimmel in the deep corner of the room. He looked bashful as ever, his coat of black plush a bit too small so that it clenched at his shoulders only making his lion's head seem heavy and brave and everlasting.

"Mr. Krimmel says he has lost his chance with Harriet Miller," said Mary, "but I have told him it is Harriet who suffers for him!"

"This is quite a success," I interjected, "and inside the Academy—"

"I already told him there are three hundred souls quivering like little birds over the specter of a German named Krimmel."

"But not swarming like vultures, I hope," said Krimmel.

"Only one."

"The venerable Mr. Peale. Raphaelle is hell-bent on a war."

"It's not bound to impress the sensitive Ms. Miller, but, Mr. Krimmel, I am certain you know that already."

A few days later, we received word that Dixcy was too sick to continue working for Rembrandt and was once again under the care of Eleanor, the painter's wife. "He is dying," said Victor, who would return to Baltimore immediately.

"And what then of our book? It too is dying."

"You are callous today," said Victor.

"And the mill? Is that, too, another figment of the Peale imagination?"

Victor was wide-eyed, an unbearable countenance. I looked away. The room was gold with autumn light. I closed my eyes. I waited to feel his long, slender fingers brush my shoulder and then I listened to his footsteps, certain as ever—how can one live without hesitation?—as they—ah, I am sorry—consumed the floor and then the stairs and then the endless worn brick that leads beyond the corner of Sixth and Arch and out into the world.

That day I ended up at the gallery in front of Krimmel's painting. There was Krimmel's shame, his face collapsing on itself, a shadow across his heart. Susanna, willing to face anything. George's fingers split in two—and the children, each portrayed as only Krimmel could have remembered them, or as he had sketched them, before he returned to Germany. No, if this was the work of Raphaelle—.

If this was the work of Raphaelle, how could it contain the pulse of the living?

Certainly, Krimmel was there in Raphaelle's painting room.

Krimmel with his sketchbooks and Krimmel standing back toward the wall and Krimmel springing forward to say no, it must be this way. Raphaelle giving way—No! No, then it couldn't be, Raphaelle would always give way.

Raphaelle would always give way.

I walked up Chestnut, past the City Hall and the State House, past the slender limbs of the plane trees, my feet slurring in the mud, past the university to the Academy. Birch was in his office at the top of the stairs. There was paint on his fingers and a speck of blue, a muted blue—like the shell of finch's egg—on his spectacles. The curtains were drawn. "I am confused," I said, explaining the situation. "Krimmel is a friend, but everyone knows his ambition."

"Same ambition as all of us," said Birch.

"Peale is sure," I said. "Raphaelle has a career of deception."

"But it isn't his style," he said.

"Well, sure. But does that matter? I'm not saying Krimmel wasn't involved."

"Do you know the picture quotes from me—quite directly, in fact." Birch looked down at the papers on his table. "The view through the window," he said, "it is a direct interpretation of the view I did of the Delaware from Bonaparte's estate."

"An interpretation."

"Can I truly say more?"

"And you aren't angry?"

"None of us are so foolish, Mr. Cloud, to think that we don't learn from each other."

I went to Belfield prepared to present Peale with the facts as I understood them. He greeted me at the gate. As we walked through the gardens, decorated with the last flowers of the season, he guided my attention to the diversity of the plantings, "representative of the best of nature," and Mrs. Peale brought over tea, which we drank in a Chinese house built just for this purpose. "We'll skip the ceremony," he said dryly. Mrs. Peale, a matronly woman with dark inward eyes and cheeks that had turned red, carried the tray of tea across the garden. After tea, Peale leapt up and took me out across his orchard to the edge of the Wingohocking Creek. "Always, my dear boy and you must listen to this old man, you may not hear me now, but some day you will, always, the best course is the one of adaptation. Steady your nerves. The world changes. There are two keys: stay ahead of the times and know your strengths. You know what I'm referring to. Manufacturing is our future. You should see all the information your friend Victor has collected. It's convinced me, we don't need Tharp. Nay, we'll put the stream to use without him." He grabbed my sleeve and walked another ten paces on. "Here will be the millhouse, the wheelpit, the headrace, and here," he said, waving his arm emphatically, "all according to Victor's design. He doesn't let on, but his ideas are the most precise I've ever seen." He went on, a wildman in his dream hunting. "This will be the dam, the water will rush through here, and pool up in our mill pond, we've done the drawings already of all the shafting, gears, throstles, spindles, and bobbins. It is a great act of engineering, I observed, just to calm the wind, to harness the creek in such a way, it hardly seems possible." Indeed, was it? The creek wasn't running terribly fast, nor was it terribly wide in this section. "To situate a mill in the proper way, you have to have all the elements. In other words, it is a balance of speed, pitch, and depth, and there has to be room enough for the millhouse." Construction would begin in the spring. When the creek is running fast? Wasn't it best to wait until the late summer?

"What about the museum, Mr. Peale?"

"Ah, my boy, that is what I meant by being aware of one's assets."

"I understand. The creek—and others have already harnessed its power."

"I had the idea for a mill long before Tharp came along and built his. I am fortunate to have waited, of course; the technologies change quickly. And your friend, he pushed me, very gently he has pushed me along. But you asked about the Museum."

He held up his hands. I had a desire to sit in the grass, to close my eyes. "This time next year, the machinery will be in operation, the creek will be put to use, and yes, I will be in the city. It is time to rethink the Museum. The public tires quickly. Don't you agree? The public and its representatives in the City Councils. As soon as you become stale — ah, the metaphor is a good one — they have no use for you. You can't feed them breadcrumbs!"

An entire hour passed and then I said, "The article I submitted to Mr. Poulson, Mr. Peale, it isn't the one you had expected."

Poulson printed my story on November 20. "Changes coming to the Peale Museum," I wrote, "but will it remain in the State House? And furthermore, I wondered, how much should the city spend to support a private museum? Especially with a significant backlog in unpaid rent. Mr. Peale argues with merit that the Museum is for the public good. "In fact," I wrote, "he has offered to the city councils and to the assembly to make it publicly owned, so long as it is given a permanent place in the State House, and at a nominal rent." In that case, who would manage it? But, by consistently failing to pay his rent hasn't he already taken liberties with the public trust? Moreover, if the board entrusted to steward the Museum decided it no longer wished for Mr. Peale or his son Rubens, the present manager, to continue in such a capacity, what might happen? "The Museum is, in essence, yet another of Mr. Peale's illustrious children, perhaps the most illustrious." It is doubtful, I surmised, that such a change could ever be truly amenable to the Peales. As long as Mr. Peale remains, he will, rightfully perhaps, desire to assert control.

"Have you heard of the French funambulists?" asked Victor, who had returned from Baltimore.

There was no response from Peale.

The week my article on the Peale Museum appeared, Svinin did as well. He checked into an inn on Mulberry Street with his manservant and an assumed name. I took it upon myself to talk to the innkeeper, who was a friend of Raphaelle. Svinin had been there three nights already and had failed to pay when he started complaining the room was no good. He ordered his dinner, and when the owner of the inn refused to bring his meal to his room unless he paid the bill, he sent his manservant down to beg. When that only produced a chicken leg and some broth, he started insulting the waiter and demanded to see the mayor. This went on for half a day until some exiled French royal, an enemy apparently of Napoleon, who had known the Russian from years past, happened by the inn and loaned him enough money to satisfy the innkeeper. That very day, Krimmel and Raphaelle paid the Russian a visit at his inn.

At first, when they arrived, the Russian refused to see them. He had the manservant send them away. On the subject of his book, he demanded to speak to Mr. Carey and said that Carey had promised him an audience at the publishing house. But when he arrived there he was told Carey had gone away on business. "That's not possible," said the Russian, "I was given this exact time for a visit, and if I'm not accommodated I will take my work elsewhere." But, in fact, Carey had left the city for business in New Jersey.

Svinin left Krimmel and Raphaelle waiting. Naturally, they spent the time in the tavern, Krimmel sketching happily and Raphaelle throwing his voice and telling dirty stories. Krimmel had expected the Russian's obfuscation and he had told Raphaelle they would wait. "He changes his mind, he always does," he said. Eventually, the manservant returned but this time with a demand: that the two artists promise to loan the Russian an advance against the sales of the book. Of course, they laughed in his face and sent the manservant away.

The sun was already down and the barkeep was lighting the lamps when the servant returned. Krimmel and Raphaelle were welcome to come up to the room, but might they order a meal or two and bring it with them? Knowing that hunger would only make the Russian more savage and extreme in his demands, Krimmel agreed (Raphaelle made a joke about having himself carried into the room on a platter).

Right away, Svinin did most of the talking. He told them about the New York Academy of Art, which had recently expanded, and about the harbor, where he counted almost two hundred ships, frigates, naval vessels, fishing boats, and steamers, and he mentioned a meeting with Governor Clinton, during which he was shown maps of the proposed and completed sections of the Erie Canal. Svinin, dressed as a Russian naval officer, with ribbons, begged Krimmel's forgiveness for taking the German's pictures as his own, revealing to Krimmel and Raphaelle that all he had ever wanted was to be a famous artist, "lauded and loved the world over." He could think of nothing else even though he possessed no talent. Then he began to weep. Krimmel reminded the Russian that he had paid for the pictures. It was therefore up to him what to do with them. But not steal them, wailed the Russian, who got down on his knees and begged forgiveness.

Krimmel stood up. He sensed that the whole thing was a show. Raphaelle sat in the corner, his legs in pain from the gout. By now he had been drinking all day. Krimmel accused the Russian of making up the information in the text. "For example," he said, "it is evident you didn't actually attend the worship of the Africans at Mr. Allen's church." Then Krimmel mentioned two or three other things he had gotten wrong. Svinin pretended to look in his case, as if he were searching for his notes to double check, as if it were an issue of transcription, and that's when Raphaelle, still sitting, decided to quote Lady Macbeth.

Then Svinin looked at Raphaelle very seriously. It was Raphaelle he looked at and not Krimmel. He began apologizing to Raphaelle for what he wrote in the manuscript about the Peale family. Raphaelle had memorized the passage and seamlessly he began to recite it: "'If it were enough to bear the name of a celebrity in order to acquire his merits, the Peale family would be a collection of geniuses. The five brothers are named for the most famous masters: the eldest is called Rembrandt'" — which is wrong of course, just like Svinin to get such a thing wrong—"'the next one Raphaelle, the third Titian, and so on. One daughter is called Angelica, another Sappho. They are all painters and very wretched ones.'" Naturally, Svinin pretended he didn't mean anything by it, it was written in error after the awful incident with Rembrandt. He genuflected all the way back to the floor and he begged forgiveness again.

"He writhed on the floor like a bitch in heat," said Raphaelle.

Then, everything seemed to have changed. Svinin started lashing out at both of them, but his face was colorless, like paste—"instead of hot, he went ice cold," said Krimmel—his eyes moving slowly around the room. Moments later, again, he focused singularly on Raphaelle, as if Svinin were trying to get him to take his side against Krimmel. He reversed his position on the watercolor sketches, now claiming that it was Krimmel who had stolen them from him, and that it was Krimmel who owed him money. "You tried to humiliate me," he said, "and you're a traitor."

"Seemed more or less accurate to me," said Raphaelle. Krimmel said he wasn't sure if Raphaelle was referring to the Russian's description of his family or his claim of being humiliated.

Chapter XIX

About this time Dixcy returned seemingly in better health, and the three of us went together to Bonaparte's New Year's soirée. The party, it was suggested to Krimmel, would last three or four or even five days, and it wouldn't just be attended by the elite of Philadelphia. Bonaparte liked to prove that he was a true republican and so he made a point of inviting his Bordentown neighbors, some of whom, like Mr. Hopkinson, were landowners and gentry, but still others were farmers and merchants and even laborers. There would be artists from New York, Krimmel said, industrial men from Trenton, the entire French consular delegation (despite the return to monarchy), and, he assured us, the house would be well supplied with ladies.

Dixcy had returned two days after Christmas. "William was too acerbic for the disease," said Victor, "he looks better than ever. The consumption came, got one tongue lashing, and slithered out the door."

Nevertheless, Dixcy refused to present himself to Libby. "She is waiting for you, William. Von Cloud, don't you agree?"

"And now it's Christmas again and she is still lonely," I said. Dixcy muttered something unintelligible.

"The great serpent hasn't permanently recoiled?" teased

Victor, but Dixcy had opened a book. He was reading a tattered copy of Rousseau's *Creed of a Priest of Savoy*. "Happiness
descends from justice," he read.

"I don't know if I love this or I hate it, if these are the most
brilliantly unassailable observations or they are the work of a
feeble mind."

"Feeble?"

"Lazy, I mean, and therefore of no consequence."

That night, about an hour after we had all gone to bed, Dixcy
crept quietly to the door. He didn't return until the morning.
Victor snored as if he were a feral animal on the hunt. Or was he
the prey? After a while, the snoring became a symphony of the
absurd, a sound of desperate intensity and extreme detachment;
there were three animals then four then for a moment only one,
the victor, I presumed. I laughed and then quite ridiculously I
wept. The cold tears that stained my pillow were the last thing
I remembered before morning.

Krimmel had offered us a ride on Bonaparte's skiff, but we forgot and so we took a steam packet to Bordentown instead and
walked the mile upstream to the manor house. It was already
late in the afternoon, the sun vanishing through the trees before us. The sky was perfectly clear and delicately blue fading
into quiet, into porcelain or ivory. The trees were bare and our
shoes crunched against the thick mat of leaves. Dixcy didn't
look better than ever, that was the gold flaring in Victor's eyes
or Victor's need to animate everything and everyone around
him. Dixcy stopped twice on our short walk and both times it
appeared that he would begin to cough and spit blood. Both
times he stood alone, back turned to us, and for some reason I
remembered they had fought in the courtyard of some church
in Easton, Victor claiming he had read La Mettrie in the original
French and Dixcy knowing better. Who had won that fight?

Dixcy didn't cough up any blood and we went on in
silence. We were greeted at the gate by a man in a beaver hat

and inside—the most sumptuous and decadent interior any of us had ever entered—we were shown to our rooms. "The wicked man makes himself the center of everything," said Dixcy, quoting Rousseau and laughing contemptuously.

"Soak it up," said Victor, "one man's self-interest is another man's pleasure."

"You finally got here," I said. "It took only a year."

"Hush, both of you, this may be Babylon. In any case," said Victor, with the same satisfied expression and the same words he used at Greenpoint's, "you won't find this in Easton." And hadn't we this time really made it?

I smiled thinking about the bank of the stream where we lay talking about Babylon and the grid of New York. "We have made it, then. Isn't this the slightest bit real?"

"He calls himself a republican," said Dixcy, referring to Bonaparte.

"He also calls himself a count, but not a king; he loves his despotic brother but also his fellow common man; he burns with magnificence, but, I am told, contents himself arranging flowers; and you, a democrat, refuse to listen to what half the people have to say."

"Whatever you're trying to say is getting lost in the music of your voice," noted Dixcy.

"I am trying to say, William, that only a fool who lives in a boardinghouse, when invited to the Castle for a never-ending party in celebration of the new year, cries injustice. You sound like an unrepentant Jacobin."

I suppose, at that point, Victor thought he had some control over the matter. But a knock soon came and we were ushered into Bonaparte's salon. Two glasses of champagne and Dixcy appeared to smile. He spent a great deal of time looking into the eyes of a nude by Natoire. "You agree she is a dream," said Bonaparte, when he came over to us (we had thought to come to him, but were told to wait, the count prefers the liberty of making his rounds). "Let your imagination go, no?"

"He is like a phantasm!" Victor whispered in my ear.

Like vapor or fire, or was it ice?

Now Krimmel entered, an expression of reticence and confidence all at once.

And a moment later: Mrs. Greenpoint, dressed in a white, slender cut dress with an oyster-colored brocade, lapis velvet coat with fur lining, and Indian feathers. Her head was wrapped in a Moorish turban with pink fringes and black stripes. She looked at Victor with an air of disappointment tinged with pity, for she knew immediately he hadn't told us she was coming. "This is the king's lair," she said, to no one in particular. And then to me and Krimmel, who stood nearby, "Well, it is so. My husband keeled over while filing a deed of sale with the magistrate. His signature went unfinished and so did our marriage, it turns out. Victor has been kind enough to offer me a respite from grief." She handed Krimmel his sketch of Harriet. "Worse yet, I'm told I must part with this."

"We—all of us—must apologize," I said.

"Mr. Krimmel is the real prince here," said Mrs. Greenpoint.

Krimmel glanced quickly at the sketch, as if he were afraid of what he might see. He held the page at his side and he seemed to breathe as if he were underwater, as if he weren't breathing at all.

"You appear to have reversed the years," said Dixcy to Mrs. Greenpoint, who had come over from the opposite end of the room, breaking the silence. His black hair was rather carefully combed. She replied to his comment with a smile and steered him away from the group, remarking as she did: "The horn of plenty motif is a trifle overdone, wouldn't you say?"

A night and a day and it was 1820. "The wind howled—you can hear it all through the house," I wrote in my notebook, "and all night Bonaparte apologized. We are led to believe that each night the party will grow until, on the third, it will reach the height of decadence. There will be a performance and 'illuminations.'" Tom Birch said the lights would be white. "The count disapproves of the use of color because it reminds him of war."

Krimmel's family portrait hung in the library. Bonaparte had eight thousand volumes— more, I was told, than the Library of Congress. Dixcy sat at a marble table all that next morning studying an illuminated manuscript, the story of Leila and Majnun. I had never seen him so calm. "You wouldn't think I would like these pictures," he said, "but I do. These people, look at them, they live in a world of pure desire. That is decadence." I looked around the room we were in, the mantle, carved Italian marble, and at the twin candelabras with Bacchanalian nymphs. "No, Caleb," he said and went on with his study. The pages were hung with text, like stockings on a line, slanted as the earth. He turned the pages with almost ridiculous reverence. "This is decadence. Why? Because they are aware of death—look at the eyes, the wind blows but they can't feel it." He showed me lovers at the moment before embrace. I told him that Victor hadn't yet been seen that morning.

"Just before embrace," he said. "The moment you touch her, she becomes only stone."

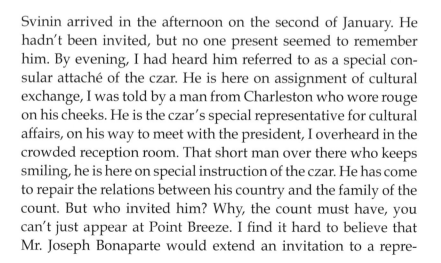

Svinin arrived in the afternoon on the second of January. He hadn't been invited, but no one present seemed to remember him. By evening, I had heard him referred to as a special consular attaché of the czar. He is here on assignment of cultural exchange, I was told by a man from Charleston who wore rouge on his cheeks. He is the czar's special representative for cultural affairs, on his way to meet with the president, I overheard in the crowded reception room. That short man over there who keeps smiling, he is here on special instruction of the czar. He has come to repair the relations between his country and the family of the count. But who invited him? Why, the count must have, you can't just appear at Point Breeze. I find it hard to believe that Mr. Joseph Bonaparte would extend an invitation to a representative of the czar. Is it the same czar who handed Napoleon defeat? I don't know, one can't keep track of the changes in every foreign government, perhaps we are witnessing a moment of détente.

Victor had won ten straight games of billiards (and five the previous evening before retiring to Mrs. Greenpoint's room). Svinin came into the room with the man with rouge on his cheeks, who also wore a coat of black velvet and a top hat with a ring of fur. Svinin had removed his hat as soon as he entered the house. The man in the velvet coat and the top hat insisted that Svinin challenge Victor. Svinin claimed he had never played, but the other man went on about how we must all learn the customs and traditions of each other's nation. Perhaps later you will teach us a Russian game, or even a dance, he said. "Shall we put a wager on it?" Svinin protested at this, saying no one should place a bet on his behalf, but that he would play, if only as an act of friendship.

"I hate to make a fool of myself," he said.

At first, he held the stick like a squirrel gathering nuts. And then, naturally, one lucky shot followed the other. When it was over, and Svinin had won, he claimed that he was due a portion of the wager. "That is the Russian tradition," he said. Victor's face was as red as the curtain.

"Perhaps a bit of music to soothe the red beast?" Svinin moved to a bag he'd left on a yellow chaise. "I suppose it's my turn to continue the cultural exchange. Shall I play something by one of the great Russian composers, or would someone be willing to take up the bow as I was willing to take up the stick?"

Victor took two steps after him before Dixcy intervened and extended a hand toward Svinin, prepared to take up whatever instrument would emerge from the case. A gleaming violin.

"What shall it be, Mrs. Greenpoint?" Dixcy began to tune while Svinin stepped back, greedily expectant, it seemed, to witness another humiliation.

"Play 'Hail, Columbia,' Dixcy. Victor has lost his purse, but he has not lost his fighting spirit."

We then watched, astonished, as Dixcy played the song

with ease, filling the rooms of Point Breeze with the first notes of the new year.

The next day, Bonaparte arranged a morning of riding on his estate. "A garden should retain its beauty even in winter," he announced. "Of course, you will tell me if you think I have achieved this ambition." He winked and went back inside. Dixcy stayed behind, with the 8,000 books. Mrs. Greenpoint, Victor said, had slept poorly, and she was laying in bed with *Endymion* by the poet Keats. Svinin made a point of riding with us, but halfway through Victor dismounted.

"I need to take some notes on the garden plan and probably Svinin should go ahead so as not to get too cold." Svinin protested. "But," Victor said, referring to me, "Cloud is slow with his pencil, and this could take an hour. At least Krimmel isn't with us, between the two of them, Cloud taking notes and Krimmel sketching everything he sees, one might freeze to death."

Finally, we got rid of him. We walked our horses to a point, the river silver, the sky glass, the air brittle. Victor was smiling, his teeth like souvenirs of ivory, the color of the clouds tinted by the far reach of the winter sun—that is to say they seemed to evoke all eternity, all wealth, all glimmering gold, all species that walk the earth. "Naturally," said Victor, "the gardens of Babylon weren't beautiful merely because of the shade of the fig trees or the scent of the almond trees but because of their juxtaposition to one another and to the pathways and the views and the colors used on the high walls and because the architect of the garden was aware of the quality of the light at every point in the day at every point in the landscape."

"Man in control of nature."

"No, man understanding how to arrange a prayer. It's like putting the words in proper order not merely to make sense."

"No, of course not," I said, "but so that the person reading—or perhaps writing—the poetry would have the sense of digging into the earth and flying up into the sky all at once."

"Swollen with desire," said my friend, with his face to the river, to the sky, his teeth now transformed back into tools for chewing, "but also full, and satisfied. Standing in a garden you should feel finished, von Cloud, that's what I'm trying to say."

When we returned from the ride, Rembrandt Peale was sitting — tall and straight and yet with a prepossessing calm — in the reception room with Joseph Bonaparte. Dixcy had gone back to bed. Rembrandt had stopped by only for the afternoon — what was it that motivated the visit? He was to cross the river after dinner and make his way to Belfield. He must have seen the Russian — and did he know Krimmel was there as well?

Yes, said Victor. Rembrandt is playing it cool. "Remember what Dixcy told us: the *Court of Death* has been a smashing success everywhere it has gone so far, Baltimore, Washington, Charleston. He's vindicated, Cloud, he makes Krimmel look like an art student. In fact, he will greet the German cordially, he will congratulate *him*. What is it with the Russian, anyway?"

"He is nervous."

"He is like a shit stain you can't get rid of."

That night, saying Mrs. Greenpoint was tired, Victor disappeared at an early hour. Svinin, I was told, went for a moonlit walk (I was also told he had gone to inquire about ice fishing on a nearby pond). The billiard room was empty. Dixcy was reading. "The lamps are always lit," he said, surprised. Krimmel was playing cards and sketching the other players. His family portrait had held up over several days' viewing. Was it his alone or his after Begas or his with Raphaelle's help? Or Raphaelle's with Krimmel standing behind him? Did it matter?

Svinin appeared next to me. He was disheveled. "I must apologize, but I have to leave first thing in the morning," he said. "I will not see you." He bowed. "Yes, I'm leaving. But I could be back the next day. I have business to attend to in New Jersey. I may have to go to New York." I told him the party was ending tonight, everyone would be gone by tomorrow afternoon. "But there is always a party at the count's, no?"

"I wouldn't know," I said.

"I like you, Mr. Cloud, always honest. Maybe, my friend, you should get up early too, see me to my chaise. Or come with me on my travels."

Of course, I politely declined.

Svinin didn't appear at supper. Victor brought a tray of food to Mrs. Greenpoint's bed. I was awakened by the smell of smoke around eight o' clock in the morning. I had been dreaming of Mary Bench. We were swimming and the water was hot, like soup. I found Dixcy in the hallway, coughing. He said he was on his way to wake me, but he had pounded on Mrs. Greenpoint's door and no one answered. We both yelled and I started to kick the door, but the smoke in the hallway was thickening. Dixcy told me to go, he would keep knocking, but I grabbed him and carried him away. Once we get outside, I'll break the window, Victor and Mrs. Greenpoint can jump. Was Bonaparte in the salon? Where was Krimmel? Did I run from room to room? I remember crackling and water dripping from my nose. I told Dixcy to grab whatever paintings he could. I took Krimmel's from the library. Outside, the ground was frozen, strange, I remember thinking, and fierce and frightening, impermeable, impenetrable. Krimmel was still inside, someone said, he is rescuing, he knows what to do, he is calm in these situations.

Krimmel did emerge.

But where was Victor's room? Which window? Which side of the building? Which wing? Then the roof collapsed. Here was Bonaparte. I remember his eyebrows like spider legs and Dixcy at my feet shriveled and sobbing.

PART FOUR

Chapter XX

*Harriet Miller, in the Miller house,
November 16, 1820*

Pardon me if I seem terse. One doesn't encounter true evil until she crosses the Mason-Dixon Line with the express purpose of finding an African—in this case a female twice removed by way of ancestry from the shores of Africa and born an American—who has been taken by a slaver. One must fix in her mind—and don't waver, don't delude!—that even in the nation's capital the African is some-thing less than dog. A dog is rewarded for its loyalty while a slave is kicked in the gut, a slave is despised because she can't even run on all fours and duck under the fence. I well know the white Christians of the South don't have a monopoly on cruelty when it pertains to African people. The very powerful apparently need to crush and humiliate as a means of moral elevation or survival. But having now witnessed their behavior, I can definitively report that the North is Jerusalem, correctable in the eyes of God, and the South a bright burning hell.

In this case, the African is also a harlot with a proclivity for trouble, naïve or restless or fearless enough to think that as the legally indentured servant of a man of standing in Washington, DC, she could freely attend to his marketing without fear of capture. Or did she do something to invite attention? To this day, I can't answer that question.

And yet that same woman is today a free person somewhere in New Jersey. Where, I can't exactly tell, what she
does from day to day, I am not certain. I delivered her to the
Reverend Richard Allen, as she so chose, and Mr. Allen, who
was far more gruff and even dismissive than I had anticipated he might be (I remain a naïf from the Germantown Road),
interrogated her on the spot. Charlotte, to her credit, responded
with the deepest humility, quoting scripture, and she defended
her employer, the artist Mr. King. "It is not his fault this has
happened to me," she said without any weariness in her eyes,
"he is as innocent as a babe. He took me in, he cared for me, he
gave me clean clothes and food, but none of this was his idea."

"None of what was his idea? The decision to walk the
streets, to spread your legs, to give up your God-given freedom?" Reverend Allen was, quite frankly, as angry as a double-crossed slaver. There was sudden violence in his face and
at the same time a sadness in his eyes, which were like pools of
mud without bottom. He took Charlotte's transgressions as a
personal affront, an affront against his life of work, against her
own dignity, against the entire race of African people. No doubt
he had seen too much, he had been let down by too many, but
I also had the feeling he had given up on his dream — all our
dreams — of true equality for the African people. Now he was
going to take his anger or disappointment out on Charlotte. He
spared me. He didn't acknowledge me. She was an easier target,
I suppose.

But perhaps I have changed. When I finally decided that
it was no good to profess my religion and yet to do nothing to
change the world and that it was my duty, if I truly believed everything I said I did, to go back and practice the law, I also decided to be even more still and humble. In the face of antagonism
I wouldn't waver or shake as I had. Nor would I become shrill
and self-righteous. Good lawyers, I have learned, are always
well-prepared. They study all sides of the issue at hand. They
learn the relevant law backwards and forwards, to the point of
having memorized every line and principle, every constitution-
al decree and every case thereunder. They ask questions before

making demands. And they pursue their goals with a relentless precision.

What was my goal here? Was it to release this person of clearly questionable moral standing from the slaver's clutch or was it to reform her behavior and therefore her soul?

One would have to precede the other, I told myself, and clutched my own spirit, which was full of boundless hope and desire. But a lawyer is most of all a sober character. I must not betray the expectation!

Dear Father was of course overjoyed when I told him I was going to return to the law. "I knew it," he said. "This will be my greatest joy." I said I wished to work exclusively on cases pertaining to manumission. I had heard about Charlotte's fate from Mr. Krimmel, who had heard it from some friends of his. He wasn't aware of my previous, though rather brief, connection to Charlotte and he only mentioned it, he said, because whenever he sees an African he thinks of my desire for justice and equality. Mr. Krimmel has such strange notions about the world. For example, he is opposed to slavery, and even, I believe, subjugation of the African people, but he would never consider participating in the work of our Society. He will happily make sketches of the public life of this city, it's one of his favorite themes, but I don't think it would occur to him to cast a ballot. It is a circus, I have heard him say, in reference to our American electoral tradition. Is this the perspective of an immigrant, who considers himself still an outsider, or an observer, who is happiest with a sketchbook in hand?

Mr. Krimmel moved out of our house shortly after the New Year, 1819. When he returned once, sometime after our Fourth of July celebration, which he had attended, he made to me a formal proposal of marriage. I told him flat out no. "We would make a terrible pair," I said, "and I don't think you really know why you want me to be your wife."

"When I look at you, I know," he said.

I told him that wasn't an answer. (And that was precisely the moment I decided I must return to my work as a lawyer.) "You can't look at me and know anything."

"I do not beg," he replied, "but I do not give up easily." He came to our door some weeks later with the purpose of inviting me to see a picture of his in a gallery exhibition, but I was in South Carolina, hunting for Charlotte. My sister Henrietta was called inside to speak with him. She said he was strangely formal and acted as if he hadn't lived in our house all those months. He might have invited her—what a relief if he had!—but instead thanked her for receiving him, asked to be remembered to father, and left. She said he spent barely ten minutes in the house.

In Charleston, I met in secret with members of the meeting-house, who set up an underground chain of communication to the house where Charlotte had been taken. The exact location was a matter of some confusion as the man who had purchased her at a discount from the bounty hunter—just to compose these words makes my blood curdle—owned both a plantation and a city house, and we weren't sure where she had been taken. Our best guess was that she was being kept as a domestic in the plantation house, away from the plantation owner's wife, who lives in the city. This, apparently, is common practice. It is also apparently easier to erect a chain of communication into a plantation house. There are runners in the country who pass word among the slave quarters and even into the masters' houses. (For reasons that need no explanation, Charlotte was kept in the master's house.) I met her on a wicked October night, the tops of the palm fronds whipping savagely, and the sea, it felt to me, swelling with the intent of divine providence. A gig driven by an itinerant peddler—who earned seventy-five dollars, paid by the Pennsylvania Anti-Slavery Society—picked us up and drove us in bristling darkness to a barn on the outskirts of Georgetown. There we slept, Charlotte gripping my arm, until a giant black man appeared, fed us each, and packed us with luggage headed for Baltimore.

She tried to run, the poor devil.

I found her preaching on a street corner. Actually she was shouting into the air, blind Jesus come to me. She told me Reverend Allen would send her out into the country to preach the

Gospel. Back in Philadelphia, as we neared the corner of Sixth and Lombard, she tried to run again. Reverend Allen spoke of fire, of all the earth, and especially, he said, the oceans, in a blaze of endless fire. "Fire is the only thing that purifies," he said, and his eyes awakened from their melancholy. "And do you know what a fire does? Do you know what a fire does to wood, to canvas, to rope? Do you see a ship before you? And you know what fire does? And what fire does to stone and brick, and what fire does to iron and what fire does to wheat and what fire does to cotton and flesh, to teeth and bones? Does it purify? Young lady! Or does it blister and burn?"

Charles Bird King, in the study of his house on Fourteenth Street, Washington, District of Columbia, November 20, 1820

It wasn't the same, dare I say, as it had been on the streets of Philadelphia. The first weeks were transcendent; I tasted power, I had the feeling of participating in a ritual, of being anointed a knight, of having the command of a tribe, of squatting like a nomad under a tent. There were genuflections, there were schedules so deeply ingrained and mutually understood so as to appear to be the work of God, there were poems, oils, carefully placed words in French. There was order. I worked as much as ever; I commanded the brush like never before, I had visions in the night of paintings and in the morning I painted them. And then I sent the whole set to Newport, to boost the cultural offerings in my hometown.

In short, I was king of my house and don't let anyone tell you power carefully controlled doesn't produce ecstasy. The most sublime is anticipation.

Better yet: I kept my own melancholy at bay. Or to be more precise, I deployed it to its highest potential. The Negress was keen to play along. It gave her pleasure to enjoy such profound security — I say that word now with the deepest contempt — to be thinking and acting, to be taking footsteps as if carefully scripted, as if predestined. I had never before felt this pleasure.

But I couldn't keep her. She wandered, "out to find my people, Mr. King, I feel a calling, Mr. King, and I'll take care of the marketing, don't worry, Charlotte understands how to handle herself." This happened several times, and each time, because I had rid myself of other household servants, our arrangement was to be entirely wicked, and what does one man really need, each time she returned empty handed. I did the marketing. I never said a word and she stepped back into rhythm. Days more this would last and she would slide away again. I considered following her, I considered warning her, I considered sending her north, and each time, taking me for a fool or anticipating my anger, she would only increase my pleasure. Until one day, she didn't return. Three days passed, the sun was high and bright and the clouds like fine etchings, and I walked, much as I did as a boy, without stop, without constraint, from the top of the Capitol Hill to the place they call Murder Bay.

Let me say the Negress is fearless. She says all blacks are invisible and therefore the world is hers, she can go anywhere. "But it is dangerous," I protested, "and anyway, you are hardly invisible." She smiled the shy smile, convinced a white man walks the earth without knowledge of the true laws of nature. I walked, I inquired, I lingered in alleyways and behind buildings, I spent a night drifting from one brothel to the next, I considered begging favors of my friends in the White House. And what would they have said? Grab yourself a replacement, they breed like mosquitoes.

I persisted with my inquiry. She is dead, I heard back, or sold into slavery. She is fearless, I responded. It was my doing, I reasoned. I removed her from her life as a free woman of color in a city without slavery, in a city that for all its blemishes furnishes hope to African people, and brought her to a place crawling with bounty hunters and saboteurs. A more interesting place, believe me, a less haughty place certainly, but nevertheless a place full of traps, even if you're invisible.

Charlotte, I learned later, turned a trick with the wrong man. The dirty slut found herself in South Carolina before she could find feeling in her bound hands.

Chapter XXI

Eliza Hamm, at the corner of Third and Spruce Streets, November 20, 1820

Change is in the air, I can feel it. It feels like hurt. I don't mean hurt feelings, misunderstandings, disappointments, or even sadness or anger. I mean the pain in my lower back, the result of years of lifting heavy boxes, of sitting on this bench in this bent position, like some guppy gasping for air. Now when I breathe in, my lungs have begun to hurt. They burn like fire, a fire that burns inside out. And my wrists, excuse the litany, are swollen twice the normal size. I can barely pick up a pineapple.

The hammering doesn't stop either, I can hear it clear from Chestnut Street, like a flock of frightened birds pecking away at each other. They say the Second Bank will be completed this spring. "Biddle's mausoleum," is what they call it. I say it doesn't look like it belongs in Philadelphia. Right now it's giving me a headache.

Well, that's what I mean by hurt, the kind of hurt you can't ignore, as hard as you try. And when I say change, what I really mean is hurt. Maybe I mean death. Two people died when King Joseph's house burned. The funny thing is that the King didn't seem to care, I mean about the fire and the works of art that were lost—though not, apparently, John Krimmel's picture—and the last time I saw him, which was only a few weeks ago, he was beaming. Plans for the new manor are already complete, he said, and I pretended not to listen. Then he started talking about the gardens, which were to be enlarged, and his eyes batted feverishly. He would supply me with fruits, but as he was well aware of my acumen in selecting the best varieties (why carry the same things as everyone else?), these would be the best European varieties.

I laughed and I looked away. What do I care about a royal garden?

I walked the length of my stand. I can be patient. The King was fussing with a batch of strawberries. He was setting aside the ones with blemishes. I let him play while I struggled to straighten my back. "Let me pack up your things for you," I said.

"I desire to be a citizen like everyone else."

"Oh? I'm certain you are more than that."

"No, my dear lady. I don't wish to be more. To be less, perhaps."

"How did those people die in the fire?" I didn't smile.

"They couldn't get out."

"No one tried. Is that true?"

"I want to be like everyone else, but not everyone understands that. My name —"

"What does that have to do with it?"

"I am a target, perhaps too easy of a target. Did you know the Russian scoundrel? He lived here, not far from this corner, I understand."

"I might recognize him," I said and shrugged. One of my pineapples was rotted.

"A foul-mouthed liar. He's double-crossed everyone. A typical diplomat."

"How would I know?"

"Duplicitous cretin, he makes a fool of half the people of this city. He won't ever be found and punished."

"Punished for what?"

"For setting the fire, dear lady!" He turned his face away as if exasperated. He thought I didn't understand.

"The poor souls," I said, "what a terrible way to die."

John Lewis Krimmel, inside his room near the corner of Seventh and Chestnut Streets, Philadelphia, past five o'clock in the morning, November 27, 1820

I stretch the canvas, carefully wedging the wooden supports, and dress it properly. I take as long as I want with the dressing. I don't force it. I have already made countless sketches. Countless times I have closed my eyes in order to imagine the scene of my inspiration, the pitch of the light, the arrangement of figures, the direction of movement, the velocity of the winds, even the quality of the odors. The sketches themselves have changed, one from the other, so that it is possible to read them as a kind of journal of my approach to making the picture. In my sketches I allow myself the greatest possible freedom of composition and form. I even play with the figures, experimenting with facial figures and expressions. Thus, my sketch-journal may or may not be a linear progression. Perhaps it will be confusing to read.

Eventually it becomes time to put the pencil to the canvas. By definition, what am I about to do? Compose a picture, surely, and that must mean asserting a necessary order. But does the world I seek to record desire to be so ordered? Or does it will me otherwise, to restrict the power of my own hand in order for the inherent condition of nature to reveal itself?

To make the picture, I must resolve the conflict.

To step outside the door this morning, I must resolve the conflict. Yes? Yes, it is true.

I have told myself to wait. I have told myself that in order to achieve the best outcome, one thing must follow the other. I make practice sketches of objects, of figures, of gazes, of pieces of things, and then I make a rough sketch of a scene, which might be quite inscrutable, and I make sketch after sketch until the picture in my mind's eye matches the picture on the page. Then I color. Then, only then, do I proceed to the canvas. Why should it be any different in life? One thing by necessity must follow the other. But one thing hasn't always followed the other. Or the progression hasn't always seemed so clear. As a child I liked to write. I wrote stories that were much like the stories my grandfather would read to us, stories about dragons and giants and knights. Today I don't even read. At the very end of the day, I would sit in the window right above the bakery. It faced west, so I had enough light until the very last moment, and I would invent stories about knights riding into Ebingen. The giant of Ebingen lived in an unusually small hole at the bottom of the goat's pulpit, far from town, but he could hear the vibrations of the knight's horse, and this would awaken him. However, more than writing these stories, or even listening to the stories told by my grandfather, I liked to work in the bakery, measuring and mixing flour, eggs, buttercream, sugar. George was never interested in it and my sister was small and so it was always assumed that like my father I would become a conditor. It was a very special thing to be a conditor.

Then I was sent to school and for a while I forgot about mixing flour, eggs, buttercream, sugar, and this is when I started to draw. I drew tiny portraits of my classmates. Then Napoleon came, and this was something like a knight entering our village, only the giant seemed powerless, and I was removed from school, and as my grandfather was failing, assigned to work with my father in the bakery. Famine followed war and George went to America. For three months I was given instruction in drawing. I don't know how that came about. The bakery couldn't survive during the famine. There was no wheat, milk was scarce. And since then I've taught myself. I said, "I'm not going to learn to draw in a classroom," which is funny since in America I have taught drawing in a classroom, and I will teach my students everything I have taught myself in the courses we are inventing for our new Society of American Artists, courses that will remove dogma from our art and replace it with genuine exploration—and we will explore ourselves most of all. When I was young and hadn't yet stepped foot in America, I said to myself, I'm going to learn in the world itself, because it is the world that is so interesting. I thought I would progress faster this way. Only in Philadelphia did I seek instruction, but that was to augment my own intensive practice. I never thought of marriage, but I wouldn't marry anyway until I had reached a point first of mastery and second of recognition and success. This is what I mean: one thing must follow the other. And I wouldn't show my pictures until I had mastered the art.

Could it be that in America the order of things is scrambled?

Or perhaps, there is no expected order?

Nature is to be our guide, they are fond of saying, but do they really mean it?

It is clear, anyway, that I was very quickly seduced. I could make pictures and show them in the very finest exhibition space in America. Certainly, this is success. Already, I have made it. Which isn't to say I didn't work hard, constantly improving. Indeed, one of the last pictures I made before returning to Germany, *Election Day*, was one of my best. And then I saw my pictures in comparison to the court painters in Württemburg. And then I met the Nazarenes. It was the Nazarenes who taught me to restrain my brush and look more closely at nature. Nature will teach and if you listen closely you will learn.

Then Raphaelle Peale taught me to elongate my brush strokes. And he told stories all the while I painted my family portrait. He told me that the important thing about a picture is that each person will see it differently. He learned this, he said, when he and Rembrandt traveled together as itinerant artists. They were very young and knew nothing about the world. For a while, the two brothers got along well and they played a game to pass the time. They would take turns taking portraits; the one who wasn't taking the portrait would have to guess the reaction of the sitter when the picture was finished. Well, after a while they became adept at manipulating the response. They could make the person laugh or curse or cry, it wasn't really that hard. That's what they thought until they started to notice that if two or three or four people were shown a single portrait, each person would have a slightly different reaction. It got to the point that they couldn't quite anticipate the response. Then they began to notice patterns, for example, the color red, if used on a dress or a drapery, was received better than the color green. Though sometimes red would provoke a terrifying anger. They learned later that having been raised by a Deist father they were somewhat ignorant of the religious meanings of colors. They noticed, too, that if they presented a sitter with an open mouth it made him appear less serious, perhaps even less morally upright, than he had wished to be portrayed. Even worse was a smile, Raphaelle said, because a smile, particularly if it is more than a slight grin, makes the sitter look foolish. "We talk with our mouths, we express with our eyes," he said, and if it appears the subject is trying to say too much, the viewer of the picture, unable to form his own thoughts in response, will walk away. It was that advice, given to me as I composed the portrait of my family, which gave me the chance of mastery.

Without much thought, soon after the portrait was complete, I proposed marriage to Harriet Miller. Her reaction might have been anticipated. She is testing me, I concluded, and quietly I withdrew. A few weeks later I returned to their house. This time I wouldn't assume anything. Henrietta, alone in the house, answered the door. Harriet had gone to rescue Bird King's Negress streetwalker I had told her about, the one who had been stolen and sold into slavery. I asked when she was expected to return. Henrietta said there had been no word yet from her sister. At first, the girl wouldn't look at me, then all of a sudden her eyes were begging, and I sensed her rising, slowly, almost imperceptibly, like a cat. Quietly, I asked her about the garden. "It's dying," she replied.

"Dying?" I said.

"Winter is coming."

I began to take my leave and she turned away, as if confused or wounded.

"John Krimmel," she said, "have you read the poems of John Keats? His initials are the same as yours: J.K. Don't you think that's interesting?"

"I'm not sure why it should be."

"Both of you have the same initials."

"Many people do. You and Harriet, for example."

"When I read them, I pretend it is your voice I hear."

"Why should you do that?"

"Come, just for a minute, I will show you." She pulled me up the servant stairs and into her room, her footsteps heavy but also quiet. She entered the room first. The shutters were closed, the air was dank. It smelled of drying flowers, perhaps herbs, perhaps dirt and roots. I walked across the room to open the shutters. Oblige her, I counseled myself, but I knew it was nonsense. Oblige her what? No, said Henrietta, taking hold of my arm. "I have them memorized, every last word, my John, we don't need any light."

"I am going to marry Harriet," I said.

"Tell me what year were you born?" 1786, I said. "It says Mr. Keats was born in 1795. It doesn't matter."

"What doesn't matter?"

She began to recite something from Keats. Her voice was rushed. And then it stopped. "July 4 you loved me." She laughed. Nothing more than a kiss, I explained. "Then you can kiss me now." She lurched at me and of course I saw she was a child. She will always be a child. I tried to push her away, but she was sturdy, rooted. Instead, she grabbed my arm. I broke the hold with some force, my eyes bearing down on her. I had forgotten that unlike her sister, Henrietta is slow and secretive. "Why do you betray me?" she said quietly, in a voice that wasn't hers. Without pause, she began to recite a poem of Keats, but now her voice was muffled.

I'm gone already, I tried to tell her, and anyway, I refused to hear.

Raphaelle Peale, inside his painting room near Fifth and Sansom Streets, past two o'clock in the morning, December 3, 1820

Can you believe it, Patty says this morning while she's lifting my feet into the boiling water, it's almost been a year since the fire at Bonaparte's. Why should I have an opinion on the fire?

I wasn't there. I wasn't even invited. I haven't even spoken about it to Johann, who was there, and whose painting, thanks be to Fate, had survived. Of course the Russian is a madman and a liar; the question is did he mean the fire for Bonaparte or for Krimmel? The fruit peddler said that Bonaparte, who is a regular customer of hers, seemed unfazed by it. He was already talking of rebuilding and, she said, of planting a thousand trees. A thousand trees? The man thinks he is some kind of god. The Russian set the fire, she said, why else did he leave all of a sudden? But no one saw him, I responded. Was this true? The only details I had were from my father, who had, of course, written about it in a letter. He said Rembrandt had been there, but since he has no taste for these kinds of affairs or the people who attend them, he declined the invitation to stay over (the lucky bastard). The Russian, according to my father, avoided all contact with Rembrandt. He slithered away like the snake that he is. Worst of all, since the Russian's book will never be published now, word got around to my brother and my father that it was to contain a condemnation of our family. Perhaps my father assumed it was Matthew Carey who had allowed it. Nothing in his letter was a direct condemnation, but then I am used to veiled messages and oblique attacks.

Eliza Hamm, *in the darkness of her house on Christian Street near Second, Southwark, ten minutes before midnight, December 5, 1820*

Raphaelle appeared yesterday, trying to stand up straight and limping horribly. The poor thing was squinting against the morning sun and his face was clouded in the steam that came from his open mouth. Alas, he was breathing heavily and he had only walked a few squares. He was in search of grapefruit, but I hadn't any. I showed him lemons, the apples that were still being pulled from the cellar and still firm and crisp as the day they were picked, grapes from Corsica, just like my King. He spent a long moment staring at the lemons. He asked if he might smell them and he took two in his hand and brought them to his nose. I inquired if they were to be the subject of a picture. If so, should it matter how they smell? He made no reply.

Then Raphaelle recited a line from a poem. How he remembers all these lines, I don't know, but this one mentioned dancing daffodils, which seemed to me so strange and unlikely a thing for him to say. He must have realized my confusion. "Lemons," he said, so quietly and slowly I had to place my hand on his shoulder and lean in closely in order to hear. "The color of daffodils. And aren't we anticipating the arrival of spring?"

Flustered by this, which seemed even stranger still, I'd just assume to hear these birds strike up a conversation about the scourge of measles or the price of bread than to hear Raphaelle Peale, with his limp and his tattered coat, speak of the coming spring I said stupidly, "Your brother is no fool."

"Has someone accused him thusly?"

I smiled.

"It is a great deal more difficult, madam, to render something smaller than it really is than to enlarge it or affect its actual size." Then he went on for some time about the "brilliant boy" who died in Bonaparte's fire. Surely, I knew him, tall with the nose of a nobleman, eyes like the festive balls Germans hang from little trees at Christmas. "I have heard that the boy died swept away in the embrace of a widow, glory for him no doubt, oh, those boys who arrived at my door that day, they said they were from Easton and they wanted to write a book about artists, and they thought of me first, and to think now the leader of them is gone. Gone in bed, the lucky boy, swept away really, is the way to put it. Which is why my brother, not a fool, as you say, never a fool, assuredly, has got it wrong. Death makes no distinction, madam. Death is blind and life is inscrutable. I love your lemons"—Raphaelle's eyes grew wide and then his face dark, it was no longer evident he could control his chatter—"it gives me pleasure to stand here and look at them with the sun coming from behind and your face in the shadow. I rather thought my brother might have chosen me to pose as the form of intemperance. I might have added the sense of reality to the composition. My father, should you have occasion to view the picture, is the unmistakable figure of ripe old age."

Chapter XXII

Charles Willson Peale, alone at Belfield,
January 17, 1821

A had sent Mrs. Peale into the city under the pretense of purchasing on my behalf some fresh pigments for my palette. This was not normally my procedure, but I could not very well have her in the house upon the arrival of Raphaelle, for whom she is known to reserve her gentleness and patience. The time for that is passed, I am afraid. Nay, I am a fool for having myself extended such good humor and encouragement to the boy. Has it once been reciprocated? Ah, he was spoiled from the get-go and I have only myself to blame.

I went into the greenhouse. It is winter and yet the pea vines are insistent. In my hand was a short roll of twine in case any of the spindles needed tying to the trellis. For a moment I was arrested by the beauty of the flowers, glistening white in the early sun, a touch of purple, a heat about them that can only be compared to that otherworldly sensation produced during fornication, and I almost forgot about the imminent arrival of my eldest son. Dare I say it? Betrayer of the family, and worse, of the family name.

A silence, like that of chiaroscuro, filled my painting room; the boy stood before me, gaunt, feeble, not to be pitied, I am afraid. To be mourned, to be excised. Though his face had some of the same qualities of the *Jesus* of Rembrandt van Rijn—a calm, a dispassion. I assumed he knew exactly why I had called for him and so I wasted no time with formalities; I would not deceive him, he who had deceived us all (and in a worse offense, himself). And, to my surprise, he was sober. This was a good sign. "Don't you wish to know how I learned of this folly?" I asked after revealing my knowledge of the passage in the aborted book by the Russian.

"My brother, I'm sure," he said. "But what does it matter? You will do what you will."

"Why did you even desire to work with this man? He had already made a laughingstock of himself and forced your brother to leave his own city."

"Rembrandt left because no one could countenance his French tastes. You, yourself, lamented his interest in nudity. The whole thing was a battle of bores, neither won."

What I cannot countenance is the plodding tone of Raphaelle's voice, the deliberate slowness of thought. "But the Russian is despised," I said, trying to control my anger. "Now he is a fugitive. Bonaparte has a claim against the Russian crown."

"And they, surely, against him. *Qui se resemble s'assemble.* But you forget I knew the lad who died."

"He was mine!" I said, my voice rising unexpectedly, my lips, wet with reproach, quivering slightly. And then just as quickly I changed the subject. "And you have your convenient alliance with Krimmel. Have you no shame?"

"Now you sound like an old fool. The fire was probably meant for him."

"That's not what I mean. You deceive yourself most of all. You are your own victim, dear boy. That is what's worst of all."

It's impossible to speak to a silent face.

"I know that painting is yours," I went on. "One hardly needs proof, but the boy Cloud confirmed it."

"You're a liar. The difference between us, my dear father, is that I have no interest in interfering in the public discourse. Talk cannot be controlled."

"Yet you are happy to speak through the actions of this

Society of American Artists. Nay, your pamphlet has done quite a good deal of talking—and written by my own shameless child, witness to the invention of the Academy—I am only comforted to realize you spit on yourself as easily as you drool all over me."

The wastrel raised his hand as if—.

"You don't get it. What was art on this continent before me? What was painting? Mere copying of the masters, nay, not even the masters of Europe, and the learning and teaching art, copies of the copies still. I felt it was my calling to cull, to take, siphon, perhaps, as much of the tradition of art from our mother continent, but merely as a place to start, and always with the notion that art in America would be more useful, more accessible, more inspiring to the mere citizen of this republic to make him a better citizen, art that began as food for the power and prestige of kings would serve and dignify the people. My boy, before me, there was no American history, natural or political. No pantheon, no character, and there were no heroes. I invented all of that. I see your look of pity, it is just as well, criticize me for not being myself a master painter—though I dare you to put my mastodon painting or my staircase painting up against any work of any American-born painter but West, who counts not because he has lived an entire life in London, where it is possible to absorb the work of every master—but don't dare denigrate my life's work, which is not only to invent, build, establish this thing called the art and beauty of America, but also to ensure it would extend to yet another generation. This is what was necessary, what is always necessary, that what we do might endure. Not in imitation of the Europeans, but because we as Americans were starting from scratch. And what do you inscribe on the tabula rasa, my dear boy? You use the symbols and letters you have been granted by heredity, and you start writing. Soon enough you fill the slate with words and sentences that not only betray this heredity but also the new perspectives of your new civilization. And you choose to judge me? You choose to make me a fool? Your brother may be pompous and insecure in spirit, but you, eldest, are filled with hatred and bile. To grant a stranger such power over us, and one as demonstrably foolish as this, betrays your own lack of judgment. I must be somehow to blame and therefore it is I who is going to act, once and for all. This sour economy, which finally is showing signs of life, and the recalcitrance of this city's councils, have forced me to become yet more decisive. I will not be taken down." Raphaelle turned away for a moment and I began to fear that when he turned back he would strike me. But then I remembered he is weak; the boy can barely stand.

He smiled sourly. "So why make me come all this distance? A letter would have sufficed."

"If the city councils choose yet again this year to ignore my proposal for a public charter for the museum, I will reincorporate it as a private concern, with a board of trustees and shareholders. Your brother has made a case for this approach. Listen to your father. Listen now!" As soon as I raised my voice I regretted losing control. I paused and then, just above a whisper, I said, "You will not be made a member of the board of trustees, not so long as I am alive. Nor will you be granted shares in the corporation."

"'When the gust hath blown his fill,'" he replied, as usual, deflecting all his hurt and anger toward some unknown realm. "'Ending on the russling Leaves, / With minute drops from off the Eaves.'" He is a genius mimic, the sad, sorry creature. I left him there and went out to ready my plow. The elk, I noticed, was stomping around with an aggressive gait and fire in his eyes.

Edward Hicks, at his desk in the earliest light of morning, Newtown, February 1, 1821

The room was filled with the most unbearable pretension. Had I taken a moment to think about it I would have realized. But I did realize, I knew precisely, in fact, what such a meeting would be like.

I inscribed my name in the registry. The man sitting at the

registration table, thank God, paid me no attention. I looked up from the book. The din frightened me. "You don't belong here," I said to myself. The voice, which is sometimes murky, was clear enough. No one came to shake my hand. I pursed my lips. I sat in the back of the room.

What had compelled me to join this inaugural session of the Society of American Artists? I had gone to Meeting in Philadelphia. At least I know why I was compelled to do that: despite the rift between myself, my uncle Elias, and the "country" Quakers and the heathen Orthodox of the city, one must attend yearly Meeting, one must take measure. The Society of Artists was meeting across the street. This wasn't an accident — or rather, I didn't just happen to notice the Society's meeting and walk in on a whim. Before I entered, I had nestled the idea of it in my head. I could have left and gone home. I could have walked into the din and taking notice of the sensation of repugnance, turned around. I wouldn't have been missed.

But what are you? I asked myself during Meeting. A cabinet maker, a farmer, a sign maker, a minister, a coach painter? All those things may be true. A failure of a farmer, but nonetheless. But where do I hide with my hand trembling? In the back of the work room, where the ceiling is low. I am buried there.

I am alive there. In Meeting, I heard these very words, and trying to force them away from my heart, I failed. I could not. I wilted upon the interrogation. I didn't know what to do. Like a fool I took leave of Meeting.

Walking across the street, I told myself I would learn of special deals on pigments and canvas. I believed this was to be one of the advantages of the Society, one of the practical benefits that would apply to my sign and coach painting business. You are a terrible liar, I said to myself, or a very good one.

When I am working on one of my *Peaceable Kingdom*s I am removed from the world completely. This body disappears. Yes, at first my arm tires, it becomes heavy and dull, my hand shakes, my eyes tear slightly. My thumb inside the palette aches, it tingles, and past that? Nothing. The body disappears yet the brush still moves, more forcibly and gracefully than ever. This doesn't happen in the midst of sign painting. I cannot achieve this when gilding a coach or a frame. This I should call art? And thus I am an artist?

Never before in my life had I to endure so much chatter; each motion made at the front of the room was followed by a wave — yes, a wave is the most fitting way to describe it, one can imagine being pummeled by a wave, or at the very least soaked — of crying, of paragraphs of discontent, of points labored over and then torn apart, of haughty laughter. I felt the notion to flee. "Look west," the man sitting next to me whispered, "there we will find the future of American art." I had no idea what he meant. This man removed his spectacles and leaned forward in his chair and I thought he was going to stand and make his pronouncement aloud to the entire room. But he never did. I had traveled west past Buffalo and the falls at Niagara and I had seen the apparently endless forest and drunken faces and Indian children walking along the road.

There were three items of pressing business before this "Society." The direction of art instruction was the most loudly contended. Beyond that, the members would have to decide to pool their money for the securing of a permanent hall for instruction and exhibition, and they would have to choose a leader. I couldn't be sure I understood the tenor of the debate happening near the front of the room, but it was apparent enough that this was a rebellion from the Pennsylvania Academy. It was an angry rebellion, to be clear — and it was easy for me to draw the parallels between it and the correcting actions my uncle Elias and I had taken against the Orthodox of the Friendly tribe.

Besides, I told myself, you have your own gripes with the pretenders of the Academy. Hadn't they rejected you at just the fragile moment you had stupidly dared to proclaim yourself an artist? No reply ever came, did it, to your request to submit a *Peaceable Kingdom* to the annual show?

I would deliver and install it myself, I had written in the letter.

At the front of the room, a motion came on the course of study. Resolution the first: life drawing should proceed from life and therefore living people, undressed and exposed to the students, would be secured for proper instruction. "It is not even an afterthought in the academies of Europe," I heard said, "and yet is somehow immoral in the Pennsylvania Academy."

"The place is run by prudes and bores!"

I heard words of lechery too and I twisted my hat in my hand.

Resolution the second: The Society of American Artists hereby rejects the prevailing notion that the making of art must be equated with the writing of moral, religious, or political dogma. No artist will be rejected or discouraged who wishes to explore the full range of the human experience or the boundless power of the landscape, for its beauty or for its latent danger.

These fools are more dangerous and more pretentious than the devils who run the Academy, I though, and gazed out from the sea of risen hands.

Resolution the third: That given the ambitions outlined above, a visionary leader is needed, and nominated, in the form of John Lewis Krimmel, the artist.

Who was this maudlin fellow?

A bashful lion, apparently.

I stood to leave.

Mr. Krimmel, said my neighbor, had been charged by Academicians with blasphemy.

"A lion doesn't give much thought to others," I said.

I received no response.

"He listens only to himself."

"His painting made a fool of Peale," my neighbor continued.

The world is full of hearts of darkness.

"That is why he will be voted in on the first ballot."

"Humans are the only animals so predictable," I said and walked out of the hall before the votes were even counted.

*John Lewis Krimmel, in the rented office of the Society of
American Artists, Fourth Street near Sassafras, February 15, 1821*

The last person I expect to see standing before me in the
worn down little room we've secured to house the Society of
American Artists is Mr. Charles Willson Peale.

He stands before me as if it were I who has called upon him
for the meeting.

His eyes are like stars flashing in the tiny room, but it is his
hands I find myself attracted to, hands I hadn't ever taken notice
of before, hands that must have penciled out a thousand lives.
They are rough, the fingers thickly calloused at the joints, the
tips bent slightly with age, the fingernails risen yellow and half
removed, and for one mere second they transport me to large
wooden table beside the ovens of my family's bakery, and I am
certain I hear the sound of my grandfather's quiet and humble
voice. He is humming a psalm and pounding the dough.

There is but one window in this tiny room and I have closed
it to keep it from rattling in the wind.

I beg of the old master to sit and I apologize for not being
able to offer him a cup of tea. It is evident he is perspiring from
the warmth of this day in early spring. He wipes his brow and
sits. He doesn't cross his legs, I notice, but straddles the chair
and leans in, as if he means somehow to take charge.

Outside, a carriage wheel is caught in the mud.

"You are an influential man, Mr. Krimmel," he says. His nos-
trils sniff out the feeble air of the room. "I suppose you know
why I am here."

"Not exactly, sir." I find Americans too often think it somehow makes them appear sophisticated if they beat around the
bush. "But I am pleased to listen."

"I haven't seen you recently at my museum." His tone is
accusatory.

"My hands have been full."

"Recently, I have been forced to return to the management
of that venerable institution."

"I'm sorry, I hadn't realized. Rubens is no longer there?"

"Rembrandt's exhibition of the *Court of Death* is so success-ful that he has asked for his brother's assistance. They are trav-eling up and down the country. The people yearn for moral in-struction."

My boredom surprises me. "You haven't come, sir, to de-liver the family news, I assume." I say this without a hint of contention.

"I am not surprised by the success of your Society," he said. "I am reminded of the early days of the Academy. Nay, I must admit it is healthy for our system."

"What system is that, sir?"

"The system of our fragile republic."

"I must admit I am surprised to hear you say that." Had he come to seek my acceptance of an apology?

"It has always been my greatest concern, Mr. Krimmel. And my museum my beloved weapon in the fight."

Or is it my apology he seeks? He is dying, is that it—

"You have your reasons for what you do, it's your right, it's to be expected," he says. "I don't come to contest them."

The monkey is not yet out of the bag, I think.

"It is no fabrication to say the Peale Museum, Mr. Krimmel, is as much responsible for the advancement of art and learning in your adopted nation as any other institution. I put it ahead of the Academy on that front," he says.

"But it will be out of business in weeks for lack of cash. This murderous economy—"

His eyes are like busy spiders.

"I have petitioned the City of Philadelphia for assistance, not only in reducing my burdensome rent but in investing in the Museum as a keystone of our civilization. I have placed this before them and they know the consequences of inaction." He pauses; outside, the carriage wheel is finally unstuck. "It's a matter of priority, of a question we've long been asking"—long before my time, he means to say—"about the direction of the country."

"You carry a bully pulpit," he says, "and a unique perspec-tive of someone drawn to this city"—his voice rises, he smiles pleasantly, his eyes calm—"because of its history in the arts. You can make this case more convincingly than others can, if I am to properly interpret your recent success."

"Hah! Beware of making faulty assumptions," I say, now standing.

He stands too. For an old man, Peale moves gracefully. "The voyage of an immigrant, I've always admired it," he says. "At sea, I have imagined, nay, I have dreamed of the emptiness, without any distractions, when the moment of moral decision becomes clear."

"I take it you have never crossed the sea."

"Tell the city councils you support my museum, tell them about the cities of Europe."

Bring me the hand of Harriet Miller. The thought slips into my mind, and I leave it there to linger like the sweet tingle that remains on one's lips after the bite of an apple. Let her linger with me, let her taste me. "Ensure that I am the recipient of the recent commission to paint William Penn arriving in Philadelphia."

"An unlikely choice for a painter of genre scenes."

"You doubt my capacity?"

"My eldest son has a generous heart."

"If you wish my heartfelt advocacy—"

"Who is to say I have any control over that commission?"

"I have seen you exercise your power."

"And I have seen yours, Mr. Krimmel."

Charles Willson Peale, at his desk in the Peale Museum above the State House, February 15, 1821

"Ensure that I am the recipient of the recent commission to paint William Penn arriving in Philadelphia," he said, and his eyes dared me to laugh. He is an unprepossessing fool.

To tell the truth, I was surprised to hear this response. I had assumed he would ask me to have him reinstated in the Academy. But then I assumed it was unlikely he would agree to help me at all. But a grand-scale history painting? What did he know of the great Quaker's vision for the New World?

Then I thought: If he receives the commission he will expose himself a fraud.

And then: But he will surely enlist my crazy son in the adventure. The boy will do it and receive no credit as usual.

The truth will one day emerge, I counseled myself, let the German have his commission. Besides, if I can arrange to have him receive it, it will be a small price to pay for his support. It is not, after all, that Rembrandt will desire it.

And what if he does? My mind in that instant was rabid, like that of a silly child. It should be awarded to Rembrandt, for he is the most qualified.

And my museum will be doomed.

"Tell me, Mr. Krimmel, why you should be considered for the Penn commission."

He smiled sweetly, like a sick child whose fever has touched him to God. His face had blossomed red.

Was he truly sick? If so, I would hold my ground. "Tell me why and I'll push forward your recommendation," I said blandly.

"What about Mr. Bonaparte?" he asked in an offhand way. "A committed patron of the arts."

"What Mr. Bonaparte does is no concern of mine," I said. It was apparent he was trying to distract me. "You haven't answered my question."

"You don't think I deserve it?"

"Indeed, you have proven you deserve it."

"You are afraid I won't show my support for your museum."

I saw we had come to an impasse and couldn't stand to go any further. "The day is drawing short," I said.

"So it is," he said.

"What I mean is my influence is waning, but I will not go away easily, Mr. Krimmel."

He smiled again.

"But a man doesn't persist as I have without making

compromises." I paused. Without thinking, I walked to the window. "You wish to shroud the great William Penn in darkness and uncertainty, is that it?"

"I am certain the members of the Society will be firm advocates of your museum, sir, if you were to grant them space for exhibition."

Like that, he had shrewdly placed a second requirement on our agreement. But this one, it occurred to me, would strengthen my position in the long run and I quickly agreed. I left his minuscule office almost immediately, for I felt an overwhelming desire to enter the doors of my museum, to walk its halls, to illuminate my showcases.

Chapter XXIII

Harriet Miller, in her room at the Miller house, February 20, 1821

ow can a man who is so observant be such a poor listener? Or is it that all men have thick heads, and this one is merely a man like any other? His head is indeed thick, and topped with golden locks of hair, his eyes inset so as to appear lost in the world he is sketching. He spends all day with the sketchbook, seeing inside of things, he says, but I'm not sure I believe him.

Never mind the silly rumors that we are affianced, rumors that seem to have a mind of their own, that have no end and no beginning—there have even been rumors that he and my sister have become engaged, it was told to me with the utmost sincerity by an old friend of my poor mother who I happened to see as I came off the stage at the market square—from the beginning in his classroom, I've told him no. I still do, and now he smiles, and I still notice the same sensation—it is as if this were just a game to him. Do you know who I am, I say, do you care to know what my hopes are for the world? Is it not obvious that marriage is of no concern to me?

Can one commit oneself to the pursuit of justice and to a husband, a home, and a family?

"What is marriage?" he asks me. "Does it come with a single definition?"

"I'm afraid for you it does," I answer. "That's what I'm afraid of. You don't realize it, or, worse, you won't recognize it, but marriage does mean something very specific to you."

"Then you don't know me," he says, eyes downcast, because men have thick heads and they revert to childhood with terrifying ease. I tell myself I am not his mother, whoever she was. Whatever ideas about the world she had, they can't be mine. "If you knew me, you would know that my life hasn't followed any pattern. I am always becoming."

Likely not true, in fact.

"So you will see, we will learn together."

He is nothing if not persistent.

He already feels like he is part of the family.

My sister Caroline says, "He is a success now, Harriet. His name is going to be famous." She didn't always think this way. She was afraid I would marry him and be forced into a life of poverty. "How will an artist support you?" she said. "You have to think of your needs."

My needs? But what about the thousands of slaves no one bothers to consider, men and women no different from us. They're not even allowed to have needs. This is what I wish to say in response, but I refrain because it would do no good. She would merely scoff and say, "If you could only hear yourself, Harriet!"

Does she think me ridiculous?

She tells me his painting, which was rejected by the Academy, has received the highest reviews. I know, I say, our sister has shown me the newspaper clippings. The Count of Survilliers has purchased it, she says, you know who that is, don't you?

I don't answer. Caroline isn't pregnant yet. Two years of marriage. I stare at her belly.

Now he is the president of the Society of Artists — not just of this city, but all America.

"Ten years in America," said Mr. Krimmel.

You are still becoming?

He was elected by all the artists who joined him in walking

out of the Academy in protest, she informs me. Ten years ago he spoke no English.

The immigrants from Africa aren't allowed to become, I want to say.

And he loves *you*, Harriet. You were afraid but also excited, I remember. He put you and Henrietta in that picture.

"I don't want to have to trust him," I say.

"But Harriet, has he faltered yet?"

John Lewis Krimmel, in the quiet of the Phoenix Tavern, February 23, 1821

She says she has no time for marriage.

We are sitting in the parlor of her father's house. Only one candle is lit. Darkness seeps through the doorways. I say marriage can be any way we wish it to be, but she is stuck in her notions. Her face drifts in and out of the gray, stibbling light. I long to touch it. I offer visions of a life together.

You're part of the family, she observes.

It's her lips I want to touch.

Henrietta is in the next room. Her footsteps press heavily on the wood floor. What would it be like to marry Henrietta I think and in that very moment Harriet leans toward me—she leaves her glass casing, it seems—and whispers, "my sister is the one to marry."

The footsteps stop. I am conscious of it: the footsteps and the air, which is thistle gray and heavy and dull, sucks across the room as if it were entering a glass chamber of its own and only Henrietta, in the other room, and I are in the glass chamber, only she and I. But then, I break out of it. "No," I say, loud enough for a person in the next room to hear, "you have me wrong."

Harriet Miller, in the kitchen of the Miller house, April 8, 1821

I am concerned about my sister. It is well into April and she hasn't begun preparing her garden. The potting room is dark; last year's growth, heavy and dark, black with spring's rain, collapses to the ground. Mice and birds hunt the carcass. Henrietta is still inside.

Joseph Bonaparte, at his hunting lodge, Saratoga, New York, April 10, 1821

There is no greater trait among the Americans than the recourse to always look ahead. Never reflect on misfortune, never dwell upon misery, but, and I have seen this time after time, turn to what is called scripture in search of a heartening passage, one that helps steel oneself to the conditions, and move on. I see this very philosophy, minus the scripture, *bien sûr*, in the letters of Girard. In the face of misfortune he will inevitably caution one to be philosophic — Girard habitually grits his teeth — eat one's losses, and move on. This works for him. The moment I hear of some business catastrophe, he is already making money hand over foot yet again.

The great Mr. Peale is no different. Though I find the man almost preternaturally unrefined — like so many Americans he is the son of a fugitive — I have come to find a charm in his perseverance. After the fire that destroyed my manor, he was among the first to offer his condolences. His son Rembrandt had similarly experienced the errant heart of the Russian in a famous incident involving the portrait of my brother. The Russian, at least, knew the picture wasn't painted from life, and this Rembrandt took as a direct attack on his character. One accused the other of this or that, causing a great upheaval among the artists, and Rembrandt to doubt his every skill (perhaps with some reason), ultimately leading to his abandoning of Philadelphia. Thus, wrote Mr. Peale so kindly, I understand what it means to be the victim of this man's alacrity with fire. This reference I didn't understand completely, unless what Peale meant is that the Russian set fire to the community of artists here, which I understand was at the height of its splendor and activity (though I struggle to find a masterwork among all the pictures). Anyway, continued Peale, was there anything like an art critic about him, or a diplomat? The Russian was a fool as much as he was evil, he concluded, which Peale thought had something to do with the chronic malnutrition found in Russia. Of course it was charming for him to feel this way and to express these ideas in camaraderie with me. Though I am sure he is aware of the differing implications of our collisions with this man. The czar disavows his actions, according to my sources in Moscow. They say he was acting alone, or from an imagined sense of self-importance, as deranged and idiotic and pitiful as a Quixote.

Peale mentioned in his letter that he had known the young gentleman who died, Mr. Victor Blanc. He wished me to know, as if the background of a guest in my house would have escaped me, that he had come from the village of Easton to the northeast of Philadelphia, hungry to be part of the cultural flowering of the city. And, in fact, he was a first-rate engineer and draftsman. Then he wrote something unmistakably strange, perhaps too intimate for a letter between strangers. He said it was well known the success of his two eldest sons, whose work he hoped had come to my attention, but that these two boys had never ceased to provide him with apprehension and anxiety. "At times," he wrote, "I feel like I don't understand either of them, and as I must know the parent-child relationship is anyway fragile, one is never sure if one is being a little too severe in judgment or not severe enough." This was a most unusual letter! "But," he wrote—the page was filled with mistakes in spelling, apparent even to my eye untrained in the English language—his fourth son, who died at a young age, was a boy he had named for Titian. Of all the masters it was Titian's coloring Peale had admired the most. This Titian was the favorite of Peale. He was easygoing and yet spirited, devilish in a manner that bespoke genius, and loving to all the rest of the family. Well, and I must guard against my own melancholy in recalling this, the young gentleman from Easton who perished in the fire that destroyed my house had reminded Peale of his Titian. He offered to show me the painting he had done of Raphaelle and Titian—not the actual ones, the copies!—climbing a staircase, a painting made to trick the eye. "Even in this inadequate reproduction," he wrote, "you will see why I came to see my son in the person of Mr. Victor Blanc."

"I do not wish to dwell on this source of pain," I wrote back to him in reply, declining the invitation, "but rather to dream all the more intensely of the future," and I thanked him all the same for sharing with me these most intimate reflections. Soon after, I received a reply, and thus began a series of correspondences that have lasted until now, enduring much of the year 1820. In the second letter of his, Peale included a plan of a house, should I be interested in his ideas on the construction of large houses. "The most important thing," he wrote, "is that the house be conducive to healthy air." He learned this, apparently, having lived through several episodes of the yellow fever, which struck Philadelphia in the 1790s. "Without the proper ventilation of his townhouse," he wrote, "it is likely he wouldn't have survived. The plan he sent was therefore meant to draw the healthy breezes from the river through the house from side to side, while leaving the stagnant and pestilent air that sometimes collects at water's edge as far from the structure as possible. Thus he encouraged me to erect my new manor on a hillock, if there was one, above the river. His letters continued on like this, offering advice and ideas for my estate and, supposing it would impress me, even sharing excerpts of an exchange of his with Thomas Jefferson on the design of a garden.

To tell the truth, I began to look forward to these letters. Mr. Peale is genuine in his solicitation of ideas, and he isn't without wisdom in his judgments. But recently, a letter came with a proposal that seemed based on improper assumptions he'd made about my plans. Would I consider, he wondered, incorporating his museum, "the famed Peale Museum," into my plan for a *maison de la culture*? He explicitly envisioned a joining of forces, a museum, he dreamed, to rival the very greatest of Europe.

I wished him well, but I had to explain that I had withdrawn plans for a palace in Philadelphia. I wouldn't reveal this to him, but the price offered for the ground by M. Girard was too high, and in the meantime I had lost interest.

But then, he wished to know in his prompt reply, considering that my change in plans would free me to pursue other things, would I consider taking a stake as an investor in the Peale Museum? He went on to explain why the museum was so important to the city and to the nation and why therefore it would be to my benefit as one so invested in my adopted country to make such an investment. Reading these words made an impression on my heart and I felt a surge of pity for the man. Declining his offer, I invited him for a walk at Point Breeze. Perhaps in that lovely place high above the river, where the sound of the tide like the whispers of a lover floats so gently, and yet not without a certain intensity, we might walk arm in arm, discussing schemes of planting and the proper pitch of one's garden path.

PART FIVE

Chapter XXIV

I don't know what I'm doing here," said Dixcy. I tried to tell him that I didn't either, and how could we?

"It's as if we've lost our head," I said.

"I don't think you really understand," he said. "I'm not going back with Rembrandt. I refuse to be a charity case and he needs someone who he can rely on. This spring, he wants to take the exhibit beyond the cities, to every little town from here to Buffalo. I'll go home to die. I'm not going to be your charity case, either. Don't pretend."

I insisted I go with him, and anyway, I said, I would want to visit the watchmaker and Victor's mother. "We should let them know."

"Let them know what?"

"Exactly who their son was, the kind of person — we followed him, Dixcy." Krimmel had made a sketch of Victor — it was done in the room at Mrs. Chamberlaine's — and I thought to give it to his parents.

"He followed us as much as we followed him. But, make him a god, if you wish. A mortal god."

"We will take a stage this time, Dixcy."

I told Mary Bench I would return in a few days and I took

Dixcy home. "Maybe it's worked out for you," he said, while we were traveling.

My mother had a boarder who acted as if he were her husband. When I confronted her, she shrugged her shoulders. "What do you want from me?" she said. "I went to the watchmaker, just like you asked me to in your letter, Caleb, because you and his son were friends, and you were there when his son died, and I told him I was sorry, and he said his son never knew any bounds, and whoever isn't careful of the fire might get burned. I thought this was a terrible thing to say, after all he did burn up, and it couldn't have been his fault. I doubt he'll want to talk with you."

I gave her some money and figuring that Dixcy hadn't any desire to visit Victor's parents, I went there myself. Victor's father—slender and as compact as Victor was infinite—was in his workshop. The space was well lit by two lamps and it was sparse and carefully organized. In comparison to Hicks's shop, this was a place neither of desire nor relief from the rest of the world, or even desperation, but of absolute control and authority. This was the world entire and dying unnecessarily in a fire was an affront to it, an act of sloppiness, I gathered, a transgression. Still, I went on. Victor's father didn't look up. I explained who I was and quietly I held out Krimmel's sketch.

The man, who was handsome and boyish like his son, didn't raise his head. For a moment, I became unsure of myself. Was this really Victor's father? Or an uncle, perhaps, or an older brother Victor had failed to mention? The silence lasted some time. I thought of my mother, her shallow features, the bend of her nose. It was a girl's face, not that of an old woman—it wouldn't ever be—with some wrinkles painted on, her voice full of nervousness and chatter. She had come here out of loyalty to me, no other reason.

I begged the man's pardon.

"I know who you are."

"I was there."

"I didn't see you at the funeral. The Frenchman came, Maillard. He came the day before. His mother wept at the man's feet. He didn't stay. The sallow one with the dirty eyes didn't come either."

"Dixcy is sick," I said. But Victor's father didn't hear.

I started talking about La Mettrie and how we three had gone in search of a world that, I tried to explain, was every bit as serious and moral as the world he — the father — was inhabiting, but which would allow us participate in the "flowering of America."

"Maybe each generation has different ideas," I went on, aware that my little speech was full of assumptions and beside the point and that, probably, Mr. Blanc had no idea what I was saying. Nevertheless, I felt it necessary to assure him. "But he spoke of you with reverence, you gave him the certainty, the confidence."

"He behaved foolishly."

"Take the picture. It was drawn by a friend of ours, a German named Krimmel."

"And what do I need this for?"

"He talked of you frequently, he said there was no watchmaker like you." I tried to breathe and at the same time sound normal. I wanted to talk about his designs for the mill. I wanted to mention Peale. "It was an accident, Mr. Blanc, we did all that we could."

"You got yourself out."

"Dixcy and I both, we would have kicked in the door."

"I am happy for you. Now you can go."

"I felt I had to come here, that's all."

"Now you have taken up my time."

"He took his good looks from you, sir."

"Why did he die? You were there. The Frenchman who came to see us wouldn't say. His English was terrible. What were you doing at the house of a man like that? I don't understand."

"It was a party. The painter Krimmel, our friend, got us invited. We were writing a book about artists." I realized I sounded plaintive. "He wasn't going to stay here," I said, attempting to regain my composure.

"Why say that? Insider knowledge? You read minds?"

"You have to give a man his due, sir, otherwise I'm not sure he is a man. Please take this picture. Our friend gave it to me to give to you."

"He was asleep? I don't understand. A man wakes up. A man wakes up if he has any sense, if he wants to live." Finally, he took the picture. "He is the spitting image of his mother. It's her soul inside him. But I can't give this to her. She hears his voice in her dreams still; every night this seems to happen, every night for just a moment he is alive. Try to imagine that."

I looked at him intensely. I remembered Victor's two-headed Indian doll that he had stolen from Greenpoint and I thought of the Victor that was and the Victor that might have been. My mind wandered further still, the lion on the one side, the leopard on the other.

"What made you think you should write a book about artists? This is what you do?"

I said I do, at times. "I write about art."

"Every time she hears his voice she forgets. He keeps dying over and over."

I left Dixcy in Easton. "You'll forget about me," he said.

"When you're better you will return—we'll go on to New York, we still have Washington Irving to visit."

"He lives in England. Besides that, he preys on the unenlightened. Don't be a fool, Caleb."

Despite the cold I walked back to Philadelphia. I slept one night in a room in a house with eleven children. I don't know where it was. That morning, as I set out, I began to fear the directions the family had given me were wrong and that I was headed west instead of south and east. It was a miserable day, gray from top to bottom, and gray inside me; there was no wind, but this seemed to make it worse. It corroborated the thinness and silence of the world. Mary Bench, at least, awaited me in Philadelphia. Or did she? Or did I care?

I am your maiden, she would say, but her point was the

opposite, wasn't it? She was free, and I wasn't about to marry her, anyway. "Life is pretend," she whispered one time, and then, after that, she would repeat it any time we were together, it didn't matter the mood. Maybe it was all the same to her.

Libby didn't say a word when I returned to Mrs. Chamberlaine's. There were potatoes and a stew and I ate by myself. The pots were rattling and I knew she was avoiding me. There was another boarder in the house, a student in medicine from South Carolina, but he had already eaten. I thought to yell into the kitchen, Clean your pots later, sit with me as I eat, I'll tell you about Dixcy, he is stronger than you think and doesn't look half-bad, there is something inside him that subverts everything, perhaps death included, Libby, he makes you forget him, but he is always there, he endures — no it isn't that, endurance implies effort and Dixcy just is, and is always willing to tell you to fuck off.

The front door of house on Spruce Street where Krimmel boarded was open, so I entered without knocking. I came to his room door, which was also unlatched — "What's the point?" was his set answer when asked why he never locked his door — and once inside the little apartment, I looked around. The place was spare and noiseless, like a plowed field just before dawn. For some reason I didn't see Krimmel. He was right there, at his drawing table, but he moved only slightly, and didn't seem to breathe.

He was working on secondary sketches for a large painting that would depict a parade of cattlemen and butchers coming up Chestnut Street. He made it clear it was the kind of commercial work he'd rather not be doing.

"I have to use a project like this to advance my ideas."

I shrugged. He didn't seem unhappy.

"So far, I've just gone out with the camera obscura to capture the dimensions of the space, the mass and proportions of the buildings, the depth of the sidewalk, which will be my picture plane, that sort of thing. But I will fill it — with hundreds of people, all in motion. You should write about it in *Poulson's*."

"Hundreds?"

"Four or five hundred. Each one with his own personality. We're all always moving — "

"But for you, apparently. When I walked in here, you were so still I didn't see you."

"Maybe motion is our greatest challenge. I am recording a moment, but at any given moment, some people are still, some people are moving. Same of course with horses or dogs, or even the leaves and branches of a tree. Now, let me ask you. What do you see? Watch me. I am getting up, turning my head, my hair is undoubtedly swaying across my face. Do you see the motion or do you see the object at each particular moment of the motion, as if stopped, or isolated?"

"I think I see the motion," I replied.

"But what if I was to make a painting of a group of people and all you see is the motion? It would be illegible. So I have to find the middle ground. I have to present the essence of the motion, the horse stomping, the dust kicking up, the child tugging at its mother's sleeve. But if I show you this stopped — we might say frozen — merely for the sake of clarity, then my figures will look awkward, like puppets." There was desperation in his face, the same torment in his family portrait, as if he couldn't free himself from a dream of being swallowed by a wave. "Human beings aren't puppets."

"No, we must not imagine it that way," I said. "Though a parade is like a puppet show."

"The finest puppets are more real than — "

"You mean you want the painting to feel more real than life?"

"Yes, and in real life you can't freeze motion."

"You're after the Penn commission."

"It goes back to waiting and watching for the moment of anticipation, do you see, he has in his mind all these ideas, all these plans, but he doesn't know anything, not really, and he doesn't know what we know, about how it turns out."

"What do we know?" I asked, but Krimmel ignored me.

I asked if he had a chance to win the commission.

He smiled calmly, perfectly still, the walls of the room—a painter's room—bare, mustard-colored, and Krimmel's face pink. "Which is the very moment that matters? Can you tell me? It isn't as easy as it sounds," he said. "Harriet Miller finally said no."

I told him I would go, so he could focus on his work.

Later that week I received a note from Titian Peale. His father's elk was about to lose its antlers. "It's a sight to see, a wonder of nature," he wrote. He hoped to sketch it. Did I want to come see?

I found Titian sitting on top of a ladder that had been specially fashioned with a seat. One antler had already fallen. "The elk retreats afterwards," said Titian, "as if he is ashamed. And more so, I think, because he is lopsided. His shame is perhaps the incomplete birth."

"And that's what you are sketching? The shame?"

"Not exactly. I am trying to sketch the elk and the one horn, which is still on the ground next to him, as if it were a still life. I see the antler just as my oldest brother would see a stalk of celery, or a bunch of asparagus, like fingers, reaching out to the elk and at the same time into infinite, solitary space, as if it's in its own relationship with God." He offered for me to climb the ladder and take his seat so I could see for myself.

"What would happen if you went in the cage?" I asked.

"My father went in this morning. Naturally, the elk knows him best. He was still shedding and nothing happened, but still, until it loses the other horn, I prefer this bird's eye view."

I asked how long it would take before that might happen.

"Usually it's one and then the other in quick succession. Within hours. But there isn't any sign the other horn is about to fall. It's hard to stop watching when nature goes awry."

I looked up at the ladder propped against the cage.

"When is the next one going to fall, Mr. Cloud? And will he ever get up again? I see it this way: the elk is dying a little at a time."

"But Mr. Peale isn't glued to the scene."

"He prefers not to dwell on the imperfections in nature. It rubs him wrong. Anyway, he's probably gone to measure for his raceway. Or the fall of the dam. He's been out there since four in the morning."

"He's going to build the mill himself? In March, with all the mud? Are the Peales really going to spin cotton? Are you planning to help?"

"He owes me a position in the museum."

Titian came down from the perch so that I could watch the elk. In the wild, I presume, an elk walks away from the shed antlers, but here indeed it was forced to confront the fact of it, like a still birth. It didn't want to look at the antler, but at the same time, the elk seemed aware of nothing else.

A week later, I returned to Belfield. A layer of snow had fallen overnight. Now the sun was out and there was a warm breeze. Peale, to my surprise, was in his painting room and with Titian and Franklin, he was building a scaffold. The windows were open.

"Noah's Ark," said Titian.

I wasn't sure if he was referring to the scaffold or the subject of a painting, for which, presumably, the scaffold was being erected. "A magical quality about Peale I hadn't really noticed before," I wrote in my notebook, "a calm, a sense of harmony, despite Titian's quiet doubt." The old man was whistling. It smelled of wet pine and sugar. The hearth fire was low. Peale, who was directing, wasn't aware of my presence. Titian was sitting atop the scaffold, taking the planks from Franklin, who was sawing. From time to time Peale would climb up to test the sturdiness of the structure. When he noticed me, the old man came down immediately. He wondered how I was. He asked if

Dixcy was well. I admitted I didn't know. And how are you, sir? "Work is a singular grace, isn't it?" he said, his eyes unflinching. He took me by the shoulders in a warm and fatherly way. "I know you agree. You ought to write that book, my boy, maybe you are already back at it. It is always best to turn one's grief into something tangible." He paused, and only then did I realize this was an offering of forgiveness for my article. "You see what my boys and I are erecting? So that I can join the ranks of the exhibition painters. One is never too old to learn."

"You're speaking with Noah," said Titian.

"Is this the ark?" I asked, referring to the scaffold, "or is the ark on the canvas?"

"The ark is on the canvas. Titian, naturally, is going to sketch my animals."

"Together, we shall sketch them."

"Of course, two by two," said Franklin.

"In the dominion of Charles," said Titian, meaning that in this version of the story it is Noah and not God who represents the patriarch.

"And anyway," said Peale, "nature is our great museum, isn't it? And we, aren't we the caretakers? Thus it is in our hands to enforce the order of the natural world. God grants that power originally to Noah, who has grown old and righteous. That's how I see it. A young man needs to earn such power, he needs to earn and he needs to learn. I see a ray of light bathing the old man. The flood hasn't happened, the animals aren't two by two, Franklin, because that's not how they exist in nature. The order of the beasts is there, but only Noah, given the light, can see it."

"Noah in the Garden of Eden, then," I said.

"In a way, yes. Because God is about to test Noah, isn't he? But being wise he will pass the test, the beasts look to him as king and he is gentle and kind. Also stern and farsighted."

"Well, he wants control, doesn't he?" said Titian.

"He has been given control and he has taught himself how to exercise it."

Peale, who must have been nearly eighty years old, looked more fit than when I had last seen him. He was hale. He was a lion and yet at the same time he was a hawk. Later, I learned he was sleeping only four or five hours a night and drank only water. He had been restricting himself to a vegetable diet, which means he was neither lion nor hawk.

Nor lamb nor spider climbing the wall of his painting room.

"You plan to start this painting at the same time you're building a cotton mill?" I asked.

"It's too muddy," said Titian.

"I had thought," said Peale, "this would be the time. The ground is soft enough for digging. Victor had argued —"

"I should think a mill's raceway should be dug in late summer," I said, "when the flow has slowed and the bank has drained naturally."

"Then we won't be spinning cotton this autumn."

"I am afraid," said Franklin, who had looked up from his sawing.

Titian explained the second antler took five more days to fall. That hadn't ever happened before? No, said Peale. He is listless, said Titian. The great beast has been of little use, noted Peale. A protest against confinement, suggested Titian, but his father had begun swinging a hammer, and it was very hard to hear.

Later, I explained that I was going to submit an article to Poulson on the commissioning of a painting of William Penn landing in Pennsylvania. Peale said it wasn't surprising, eventually someone would come back to Penn. "I wish I had done it myself. Somehow the man has been forgotten." His back was humped slightly as he climbed the scaffold — a man withdrawn into habit.

For a while no one spoke. A heavy silence invaded the room.

"Who will receive the commission?" asked Titian.

Peale's faced turned dour. "It should go to Krimmel," he said.

"What?"

"Let the German prove his mastery," said Peale.

Chapter XXV

One day in early April I returned to Belfield. It was a perfect early spring day, yellow flowers blossoming along every creek bank and marsh, the sky indigo, the trees ripe and heavy, their tips desirous, the leaves at the forest floor rising, the earth itself rising, though it was a silly thought, and underneath my coat, I was sweating. The door was open, but the house was silent. I hadn't seen anyone in the garden; I had tried to look through the lath to have a peek at the elk, but I couldn't get a clear view and so I gave up. The house was cold, certainly colder than it had been a few weeks before, and Peale wasn't in the painting room. I sat down there anyway and for a while wrote in my notebook observations on the hesitancy and also the forcefulness of nature, what seems to us as gradual change really is aggressive action and vice versa. The heat of July always takes everyone by surprise even though it has been building for weeks, months, day by day, but a bud on the end of a branch is only the nub end of the branch, which swells so quietly you don't even realize, until one day it is angry red and insistent and capable of glowing because the light is still low and long. Since Victor's death I had stopped reading La Mettrie, and in a way I had forgotten, the state of one's soul is connected directly to the state of his body, of the location and activity of the body, the soul is blind, it is merely a receptor, but once it receives, does it have a mind of its own? No, no, in thinking that I am only falling into the same trap as the religionists, who give the soul its own being. La Mettrie wrote all this so clearly, thinking as he was writing, speaking aloud without care of consequences, confident in his own observations, capable of taking the opposite tack without convoluting the argument, giving it light, stretching it out, and examining it as if it were a patient whose illness wasn't completely apparent. Yet despite his care and carefulness, he was brutally persecuted as an enemy of God, as a threat to the people, he who dared to replace doctrine with instinct, God with nature, blindness with reason. He was forced into exile, and yet now it is cold inside and warm outside; the king, Louis XV, decided that a philosopher ought to be given protection, even if he is insistent on courting his own ruin, perhaps anyway I believe every word he is saying, secretly of course. Officially, I myself am still a direct descendant of God, caretaker of the wretched souls of France. That was 1748 and now, exactly seventy-three years later, we are all free to do and think as we like without worry of infernal punishment, and half this country thinks, secretly, that the mysteries of life can only be endured through prayer and belief in omnipresent God. La Mettrie went to Berlin. He was placed in the Royal Academy of Science. He produced two major treatises on medicine, one on dysentery, the other asthma; he wrote more philosophy only to have the works stolen and their authorship misappropriated (he sued, I think, to reclaim them). And then he died. It might have been syphilis that did it.

Peale marched into the room, climbed the scaffold, set to work on the assemblage of animals—elephant, horse, zebra, tiger, lamb, ram, dog, peacock, turkey, and still more, I couldn't see from across the room—which had an appearance similar to those of Hicks, in a word, muted. Yet did they still have will? In Peale's picture all the animals are turned to look at Noah, bathed in a direct ray of light from heaven. The animals appear to be awaiting word on their fate, and the sea in the background appears calm. The calm before the storm, I suppose. Peale hadn't seen me, and when I said something about Hicks's pictures, comparing only the faces of the leopard, which seemed similar for their watchfulness, I startled him. "I thought I'd leave you to your writing," he said, covering up, and then, "I thought at first I would be able to draw each animal in exact proportion to the other, but Titian told me that would be impossible, and he said that was the wrong way to approach it in the first place because we don't perceive the world that way. A dog of course is not as great as a leopard, but a dog looms large to us, doesn't he? The opposite may be true of certain birds that flutter around us without making much impression, and so I have made them small, almost invisible, while the peacock of course, a magical bird, is, in our minds, much larger than its actual dimension." High up on the scaffold, Peale had continued painting—he was working on the fronds of a palm tree—and gazing back at me, and he went on: "It only reinforces the message of the picture, don't you agree? That man, should he see himself that way, has been graced with the central position, and Noah is an under-rated figure, you agree with that, don't you? Of all the major figures in the Bible..." He stopped and surveyed his painting. "Of all the major figures in the Bible, Noah is the least compli-cated and most deserving. The older I get, the clearer it seems." He stepped across the scaffold to show me, I think, the eyes of each of the beasts. He reached and pointed to the elephant, the horse, the zebra, the rhinoceros, the tiger, the dog, the turkey, the rat, and he started to say, "The eyes, all the same, they tell us..." He reached for the rat, at the very corner of the painting. "They tell us we're part of the same family. In all these eyes, I find a most profound intelligence, and awareness, and a sense of expectation." Then he reached a little further, for there was a fox gazing toward the rat, a tiny fox positioned between the hind legs of a tiger. I don't know what he wanted to say about the fox. Peale must have thought of something because he lost concentration and stepped where there was no board. He slipped off the scaffold, hit his head on the cross bar midway, and landed on the floor face down.

I pulled him away from the scaffold. He was breathing. Peale's eyes flickered open and closed and then for a moment he stared at me intently, as if he were studying the behavior of insects or the particular veins of a leaf. He must have thought I was one of his sons and was trying to figure out which. I pulled him into the center of the room and wrapped his head. There was a gash above the right eye and a bruise on the cheek—he must have hit his head twice. I didn't notice a deep cut on his left forearm. I searched the house, and finding no one, walked up the narrow road to the Tharp mill, where the waterwheels and rollers were going and the men were absorbed in their assigned tasks. I found Tharp's wife Caroline in the house. Henrietta was with her. For some reason I had a sense they were planning a garden, but I can't remember what made me think so. They quickly gathered a few things. Henrietta had a book, and Caroline scolded her and whispered to me, "Keats has died, the news came yesterday." For a moment, I didn't know what she was talking about, and then I remembered the English poet, one of Henrietta's obsessions. Caroline seemed stern. But she moved with some grace and the ease of knowing what would be needed. It turned out I had found the right person, for Caroline was competent and moved quickly. Within an hour we had properly bandaged Peale's head and his arm. The skin of the forearm was deeply torn. We washed it carefully and wrapped it with dressings and a clean bandage. "Injuries in the mill are not infrequent," she said. Henrietta held Peale's hand. It was her face he saw when he regained consciousness. By this time we had managed to get him into his bed. He gritted his teeth and she rubbed his hands and kept warm compresses on the wound. Caroline suggested a doctor might be called, but Peale emphatically disagreed. Then he slept. Later, I was told it was for three days, and when he woke he wasn't even hungry.

For Peale had no intention of dying, or sitting still. Eleven days after the accident, Victor's schematic drawing open on his writing table, he began to dig the raceway for the mill. It was only mid-April. He hired a few hands to assist in the labor and Linnaeus was somehow convinced to help. Titian and Franklin hadn't been seen for days.

But how, in order to build the dam, do you drain a section of the stream below the surface when the water just seeps into any crevice or hole? How can the structure of the dam, a frame of wood weighed down by stone, attain a footing on the loose ground? Linnaeus, the mercenary, was fool enough to help his father.

Poulson promised me space in the paper to report on the commission for the painting of William Penn. The Frenchman Du Ponceau, whose large house faced the State House, was in charge of the project. The location of his house was no accident: Du Ponceau had become an unapologetic American. When I came to see him there, he kept referring to the State House as if it was a sacred site. "It ought to be a monument. This country was born there, was it not? Some people talk of tearing it down. I won't let that happen." He said this with a kind of frozen calm. His skin was oily and his fingers slightly plump. According to him, this was the very point of the William Penn painting: to preserve sacred memory. "This man brought the first laws here, he laid out the streets, he established the freedom of religion, yet you would think he never existed. Remember, without Mr. Penn, there is no State House. That's what I tell people every day." He smiled knowingly and had sandwiches brought in.

Bonaparte, he said, was also a loyal American. How can that be, I wondered, if unlike you, he had never taken American citizenship? "It's the America of the mind," he said, "the America of the heart. In any case, the count is a citizen of the world."

"That seems to me a contradiction," I said.

"Everyone wants this commission, Mr. Cloud. Every artist in this city. This is gratifying. In fact, I received a letter from Baltimore, from Rembrandt Peale. He wishes to know if I will meet with him to discuss his ideas for the painting."

"But on the whole, you prefer Mr. Krimmel?"

"One seeks answers, the other asks questions. We are in the age of inquiry, don't you agree? The country is a fact. It exists. My God, it has proven that. But we make our monuments, not for the past generation, but for the future."

Du Ponceau went on a bit more. He was more perceptive than I had thought. Here is a man who glides through the world, he greets every passerby with a smile, a tip of the cap, a story. It is all like a dream. If it were a dream, it was more like the kind in which the world is collapsing all around and you march on, you step through fire, you stand on the edge of a tree limb, you walk on endlessly through the half-ruined forest. And yet looking at him, I had the feeling, not of respect or admiration, but of immeasurable sadness. Did it matter who would win the commission, the truth seeker or the questioner?

Peale's mill dam flooded three times before he could dig the wheelpit. Once, the tumbling log came loose and jammed the gate in the forebay. Another time, in June, the wall of the dam breeched and destroyed the head race, and the wheelpit, which had by now been dug, got clogged with dirt and stone. So much for the drawings! Had the mill been already operating, it would have destroyed the wheel. Titian said his father planned to build the looms himself rather than have it done by a manufacturer. He rises in the middle of the night to check on the level of the dam, he said, fearful of it flooding, worried that it will back up into the tailrace of Tharp's mill. At the same time, he said, he frets when the Tharp mill isn't running. When this is so, and Tharp's dam is filling, the stream slows to a trickle leaving nothing to fill Peale's dam. Can't they agree to a schedule?

"It comes down to this," said Titian. "Tharp doesn't trust my father—not as a miller, anyway. He keeps sending his men down to help with our mill. My father built it himself. He doesn't know what he's doing. He only just keeps digging and mounding stone and dirt, and boasting of how little the whole thing cost."

I was walking along the Ridge Road, not too near Bush Hill, but not far either, still much closer to the Schuylkill River than the Delaware, and in a daze, and also actively thinking about Mary Bench's body, aware of it as a landscape, with places of ease and comfort and places of terror and danger. Not the obvious places, however, and some of them with characteristics of both. When I came to Ninth Street, I turned, and passing Chapman's bookshop I looked in the window, and thinking I saw Krimmel, I stepped inside. But it wasn't Krimmel. For a moment I thought it must be his brother, who was depicted in Krimmel's family portrait. That didn't make sense because Krimmel's brother wasn't interested in art and wouldn't be wasting his time in a bookstore in the middle of the work day. I saw Chapman coming to the front of the shop and for some reason found his presence, or the idea of it, anyway, unbearable. So I left the store, turned down Arch Street, and kept going into the heart of the city. It felt as though I were walking downhill, as if the street was a whirlpool. I wasn't being sucked, for there is something in the notion of that word that implies resistance, but rather hurled, and before I knew it the ships of the Arch Street wharf were on top of me, and there was Edward Hicks pacing around. His face was red, not as if he had been doing strenuous work or drinking, but as if he had been in the sun all day and failed to wear a hat. His hands kept going in and out of his pockets and his lips were pursed. Even so, he looked very much like a squirrel eating a nut.

To my surprise, he remembered me. Then, after we briefly reminded ourselves about that day in his workshop, he fell silent, and I became solicitous. Are you still working on your lions and leopards? Have they changed, do you adjust the theme, style, setting, figures? Does it make you calm, still, to work in secret between cabinet and sign and coach painting jobs?

"Calm?"

"Like God is inside you."

"What business is it of yours?"

Silence again, though a group of riggers at the edge of the wharf were singing. It was a lewd song and I smiled. Did Hicks hear the song? Could he hear the song?

"You haven't asked if I've sold a painting or not."

"Should I ask?"

"Isn't that what people like you wish to know?"

"I will ask what brings you into the city. I had thought this wasn't your favorite place."

"There were whores and lepers all over Babylon."

"I guess that's my point."

"And there are men in masks."

We walked across the street and into the market, which was empty and which hadn't yet been cleaned. We stepped over the rotting fruit and the entrails, the puddles of blood and feathers, as if it were a battlefield and we had lost the rest of our battalion. Hicks, I noticed, didn't look down. "Why am I here?" he went on, "I suspect you know already."

"The Penn commission?" I guessed.

"Actually, I came to participate in a meeting of the Society of American Artists."

We came out at Fourth Street. I said something about it being a relief, about Babylon, about the poor carters whose job it is to take away the refuse. I mentioned that I used to come to the market when I was a child, but in those days it was rarely cleaned and my mother used to cover her mouth with a kerchief. "Now everything gets whitewashed," I said, "and the market manager will fine you if you violate the rules of sanitation."

"I went to this meeting with one purpose," said Hicks. "It was to offer a resolution. Really it was to pose a choice to the members in light of the corruption of the leader." Hicks paused, but I didn't interrupt. "Corruption is suffocating, you understand? If I put my hands around your throat right now and squeezed so tightly so as to constrict your breath, that would be like corruption. I told this once to a friend, actually it was to the late Mr. Greenpoint, and he said I was wrong to think it, that what I called corruption is really, and quite simply, normal human behavior. People form alliances for their own benefit, and even these alliances have no real meaning, they form them, they disband them, the only considerations are convenience and advantage. So, of course they do things that tilt the scales in their favor. Half the time it goes on, said Greenpoint, you don't even realize it. Then he admitted that he will befriend someone merely to gain his business. He will stop him on the street, compliment him on his carriage or his wife and ask him to tea. It's a slow, quiet process sometimes, he said, that which you call corruption. It's our animal instinct, the way we use each other to survive."

"I suppose it is a matter of proportion, then," I said.

"You are just as much a fool as Greenpoint," said Hicks. "You rig the system to gain something you don't deserve. You're corrupt, my friend."

"And that's what has happened at the Society?"

"If there is to be a commission for a painting of William Penn, who do you imagine should win that commission?"

"You mean, who deserves it?"

"And who will win it? I will tell you, the man in a mask, who doesn't know a thing."

"The man in the mask is Krimmel?"

"He has to be stopped."

"What do you mean, 'stopped'?"

"This is a dangerous man. He doesn't understand the sacred."

"So you think he should either resign from the presidency or withdraw from consideration for the commission."

"I think a corrupt man must pay," he said. He leaned far forward like a man peering into a casket at the dead. "I don't want to win anything," he said, "do you understand?"

According to Peale, by July the mill would be operating. But heavy rain returned in early June. Water was tumbling over the dam but also seeping through it, and once Peale had to open the gates to keep it from dislodging completely, washing away the stone and dirt and wood and flooding the wheelpit. He hadn't dug a spillway to relieve the dam during such emergencies. Nor had he constructed a trash rack at the front of the wheel pit to protect the water wheel from stones and errant logs. Another time, a week later, the wall of the spillway gave; Peale knew the construction was shoddy. Titian said the old man barely slept during this period, and if it started to rain in the middle of the night, he would awaken, go to the dam and try to repair the rupture.

To run the mill properly, Peale needed to keep his dam filled with a certain amount of water. Thus, he needed to coordinate the operation of his mill with Tharp's schedule. If Tharp wasn't running his mill then Peale's dam wouldn't fill. But after the tumbling dam gave, Peale rebuilt it too high. The water stopped tumbling over it and backed up all the way to Tharp's mill. "He can't seem to gain control," said Titian, "a single heavy rain and both mills could be destroyed."

Around this time, Tom Sully was visiting Rembrandt in Baltimore, and the two were working in Rembrandt's painting room. Rembrandt was making some changes to the *Court of Death* and Sully was finishing his large painting of Washington crossing the Delaware. During the visit, which was by all accounts productive, Rembrandt asked Sully about the Penn commission. Did he agree Rembrandt was the best suited for it?

Having grown up in Philadelphia, he understood the gravity of Penn, and moreover, it would make a suitable bookend to his father's pantheon of American heroes. Apparently, Rembrandt had been reading history, because he kept insisting to Sully that Penn was the father of American law. Sully had no idea, but he promised, upon his return, to speak to Du Ponceau about the commission on Rembrandt's behalf.

But Sully couldn't really understand Rembrandt's interest in the commission. It seemed to him the painting might travel on exhibition, but it would never attract the audience Rembrandt had grown accustomed to. After all, *Court of Death* was breaking records for attendance in every city on its tour. Sully surmised the motivation had something to do with a disdain for Krimmel. Nevertheless, he made no secret of his feeling that the commission ought to go to a less established artist. Back in Philadelphia the first week of July, Sully proposed to Du Ponceau that the commission be awarded to Krimmel. He has enough stature now, Sully said, and his role in the Society will help bring more attention to the finished product.

As it turned out, Du Ponceau had already decided to choose Krimmel. He didn't think Rembrandt would have the time or the focus for Penn. But Krimmel still had much to prove. At that meeting, he told Sully he had received a visit from Hicks, who he said was a "strange, unhappy man, and yet apparently enlightened." Du Ponceau hadn't ever heard of him. Hicks told him that he had painted dozens of pictures of Penn, but when he asked to see one, Hicks ignored him and, said Du Ponceau, "He began talking about Penn as if he were something like a pope and that we were wrong to want a secular picture." Krimmel, Du Ponceau said, will be "open to our ideas."

"Krimmel is absolutely not burdened by dogma," said Sully.

"Then the air is really clearing," said Du Ponceau, who explained that it was the right time to raise up Penn. He had lingered forgotten too long. All the more because of the rumors of Napoleon's death. "A great man rises and a despot falls," he said, begging the pardon of his friend Joseph Bonaparte. "It's his brother, but I think even Joseph will feel a great relief."

Chapter XXVI

eale continued to fight with his dam. The issue was restricting the flow of the creek without stopping it all together. When he set the dam too high, the water backed up to Tharp's, sometimes causing damage to the indigo mill. When he set it too low, it didn't retain enough water to fuel his own mill. Tharp had originally offered assistance to Peale. But the walls of the dam and the headrace kept giving way. "It just keeps gushing," said Titian, "and my father keeps muttering about your friend Victor, his plan wasn't right, or it was right, but the conditions had changed, if only he was here to make adjustments, and all the while mounding stones and mud as if that will hold it." Tharp had become so frustrated that he decided for the time being to carefully retain as much water as his dam would hold, thereby cutting off Peale's flow. This would give Peale a chance to set the dam right. But no water until then.

The standoff lasted until Sunday, July 15. Rembrandt, Titian, and Peale were sitting in Peale's summer house. According to Titian, the floor was wet.

"Why is the floor here wet when—"

"I told you to forget the dam. Sell the place if you have to. You're burying yourself."

"I can't figure out this floor," said Peale.

"You ought to run the museum. The country experiment is over."

"I am. There is a plan before the city councils," said Peale, but his mind seemed as though it was on the floor, the dam — and then as an afterthought he said. "I paid for that."

"What?"

"I paid for the support, that's the way things work. I have already given over the space at the end of the long room in the museum to them."

"To whom?"

"To the Society of American Artists. They had nowhere to exhibit. Attendance is up."

"Krimmel's group?"

"Fifty-seven members."

"But you made a deal with the German. You old fool. It won't turn out any better than the dam."

"He gets the Penn commission." Peale looked up at his son; never before, according to Titian, had their roles so soundly, so utterly been reversed.

"Son of a bitch. Sully said — "

"It doesn't matter what Sully said. My word still matters and I gave it to him."

Rembrandt gave his father a look of terrible pity. But then he stood and looked out across the fields of Peale's farm as if he had just remembered something he had left somewhere. "You're wrong," he said.

"I thought it was a fair deal."

"It isn't possible — ." Rembrandt's voice trailed off.

"What's it to you?" asked Titian.

"You're cut off here, do you see? Tharp is stealing from you." And then, strangely, Rembrandt sat. "First things first, get your water back. Then we'll deal with Krimmel." And then to Titian: "If you hadn't abandoned the mill this wouldn't have happened. You left it to an old man."

Titian shook his fist at his brother and the two nearly came to blows. Their father pushed himself between them. "Let's resolve this with the Tharps," he said. "It's Krimmel we have to resolve," said Rembrandt.

So with the sun setting, like a sheepherder the son drove the father up the path to Tharp's mill. The pink that seeped across the sky darkened the lines of the clouds so that it appeared a giant semi-translucent wing of a dragonfly, with its intricate map of veins, was covering the world.

Just then, after a long dinner at Miller's house to which Mary Bench and I had been invited, and during which Isaac Miller lauded Krimmel for winning the commission for the painting of William Penn — with Krimmel looking a bit shy and Harriet calmer than ever — the whole band of us descended on the Tharp house for an evening swim.

The mill pond was heavy with black water and the mourning doves drew heavily on the night air, the torches flaming against the kidney sky. Tharp's flask skipped from hand to hand and wings and needles and whistles and air that had no forbearance, no viscosity. Only it was filled with flies. Into this field of shadows coiled over shadows, tree hung, smoke-whisp, starlings drinking of the enormous pot, came Peale and his second son Rembrandt, dressed like classical scholars from another age.

Rembrandt's voice lifted off, spooked by derision. "What's the sycophant doing here?" he cried, not full but hollow, thin as the air itself was abundant. His father grabbed Rembrandt's forearm and said something like, "be careful," or "choose your words carefully." Peale found Tharp's brother, who was standing beneath a tree untangling some rope. They exchanged words. There was something Peale wouldn't let alone. Then Tharp disappeared. Peale must have convinced him to release the dam because he disappeared. In the next moments there were shouts — it must have been Tharp warning us about the lowering dam. The water must have been moving, but we didn't understand it. Rembrandt was coming for Krimmel. And there was Henrietta, laughing. She couldn't stop laughing. She came up behind Krimmel standing at the edge of the dam. He hadn't yet stripped. Rembrandt's voice hung in the air. "You don't," he said. Krimmel didn't respond. There was an inward kind of grin on Henrietta's face, a look of selfish abandon, as if she was playing out a dream. Her eyes seemed to be closed

Tharp's brother had been shouting "don't swim." Only no one heard or understood. Then: "You can't swim!" He was closer now. But it was too late. Where was Harriet now? I can't seem to ascertain in my memory. Henrietta pushed, she laughed and laughed: a child's laugh. She hadn't heard, I am certain she hadn't heard. "We can't swim!" Krimmel stuttered a little—she was strong but hadn't pushed that hard—but then he slipped on a rock. Immediately, the current took him, and for an instant he disappeared in its embrace. Even clothed, the black water must have felt cool on the sultry night. A thousand mosquitoes were buzzing in our ears and at our feet. Then Krimmel emerged free, but as a lover who takes a long gaze before plunging in. His eyes, though, were fixed on the exceptional sky. For a while, Krimmel seemed to float; it's possible he even laughed at Henrietta's foolishness. Tharp went to the edge of the pond and reached out to him—Krimmel must have hit a rock or gotten pulled by the swirling current. No longer in an embrace, he fought the water by pushing off from rock to rock. On his face now was a look of calm and concentration, as if he were sketching a wall of bricks or the feathers of a turkey, each one with its own intricate system, as brilliant and reflective as the water. When finally we grabbed him from the water—in only an instant—he was face down, his head bruised. Was he breathing? Tharp thought so, and tried to revive him. Henrietta took his hand, her dress steeped in the puddle that had formed around him. I had hold of his feet, and I knew well before Tharp had given up that he was gone.

LAST WORDS

Raphaelle Peale, in his painting room,
Fifth Street near Sansom, August 14, 1821

One can tell these things, I tried to tell him, when you've lived long enough, or as long as I have. Krimmel was in this room, maybe this is the court of death, or the painting he made here is anyway, all of the faces in the painting, the faces of ghosts, I tried to tell him this too, the boy from Easton. He sat here and I said take another sip of the rum, and I took one as if to demonstrate, and I took another for him, the one he declined. He sat here in the painting room and he refused to talk about Johann Krimmel, he said what interested him was the painting I was working on, and I told him it was a secret and he would have to wait. I took another swig from the bottle and I watched him, I didn't take my eyes off him, I watched him as Johann might have, so that I could memorize the expression on his face, the turn of his ankle, the movement of his hands, one into the other like a pendulum swinging, and the way he leaned forward from the chair, but quietly, pensively. He was the most thoughtful of those boys from Easton, thoughtful but also solid, nothing like his name, which is Cloud, of all things, nothing like it at all.

What did my father say? Cloud wanted to know, he was curious, he said, did he write about the tragedy of Krimmel? He asked quite a few questions like this. I should oblige him, and make him laugh—we will laugh because laughter is the same as weeping, when you are doing one you are also doing the other, put a hand to the stomach, the sensation is the same, no matter. I assured him my father didn't say a word, the next letter that came from him didn't arrive until August 23. Caleb didn't believe this, or so he said, how could it be, after what had happened, did he even mention his name, or present his death as an item of news, oh, by the way Mr. Krimmel the young artist died, they say he slipped on a rock, he was going to have a swim in the mill pond at the township line. He didn't say any of that? I passed the bottle and this time he gratified himself with a long swig, and I said that's more like it, keep going. And he said, nothing? And I said, nothing, careful to draw it out, because I knew, one knows, how to draw these sort of things out for effect. Only he did mention one thing, perhaps you might like to know, I said, as calmly as possible, as if I were telling him the state of the weather, I loved those boys from Easton, they gave me something I hadn't had before, in long enough anyway, and Johann Krimmel too, they restored me long enough, they held me above the water long enough, I said, Caleb, he did tell me one thing, my father, the elk has died. As I uttered those words, I extended the bottle to him, and he tilted it and laughed, which is the same thing as crying, and we both laughed. Did he butcher it, he wanted to know, so as not to waste the life of the poor beast, and I said, no, you don't know my father very well, he's already preserved it, a monument to the triumph of American nature, above all, he said, taking another swig, you can't fence it in.

He was laughing so hard tears were running down his face and I was laughing so hard tears were running down my face and so I stood up despite my burning legs, and walked to the corner of the room, and pulled out the canvas, which up until then had been my secret, a copy of the portrait done of me by my father, and I said, this is only the beginning, a painting ought to have layers, and in this one I am baring my soul, baring it then burying it you might say, my father isn't going to have the last word. As what? he said. What do you mean, as what? I responded, as my soul? What am I baring it as? As a naked woman, I said, and I really did weep then, and Caleb couldn't stop laughing, he found it so damn funny.

Charles Willson Peale, Belfield, October 23, 1821

Morning taunted me and I rose immediately, as is my custom. There is little reason to sleep anymore. Two nights ago we buried Mrs. Peale. She had nursed me after I contracted the yellow fever, but upon catching it herself, she wasn't able to will it away. She succumbed so quickly and quietly. Nay, without even a word of complaint.

I dressed in my most comfortable, loose-fitting garments. And then I descended the stairs. Though my mind was scattered, I was conscious enough of each footstep. I had already written out the instructions for Rubens on the sale of the farm, a list of its attributes and measurements, and of the millseat, the latent value, yet unrealized by me. Never, I decided, to be realized by me. I drank two glasses of water.

If I am to live, I had decided, I would have to be reborn. If I am to live, I would have to prove my worth. And if I faltered, so be it. The decision was liberating, and all the world seemed to spread before me. I wanted to paint it as proof of the sensation of God, and then it occurred to me I would have to leave such thoughts behind. What you think is all the world is only darkness. Are you man enough to step into the void?

The velocipede was propped up against the wall of the house. I had oiled the wheels and tightened the handlebar. In a small case I placed a loaf of bread, some money, and two keys: one to our city house, the other to the museum. Would I need the keys? I wasn't certain. It didn't matter. Whether I am found dead or alive, on this two-wheeled machine I shall go fast enough to reverse time.

ACKNOWLEDGMENTS

First and foremost I have to thank John Lewis Krimmel for speaking to me from the streets of the fledgling nation (out of Gary Nash's magisterial *First City*) and Charles Willson Peale for leading me along an uncertain trail.

My thanks to Jim Savoie and John Eliason for giving me the time for research as the writer-in-residence at Philadelphia University and to the university's president Stephen Spinelli for his enduring interest and support.

My sincere appreciation goes to Roy Goodman of the American Philosophical Society for leading me to Peale's journal, to Carol Soltis of the Philadelphia Museum of Art for taking the time to help me understand early American art, fashion, and Rembrandt Peale, and to Adam Levine for helping me figure out the location of Krimmel's drowning.

Grateful thanks go to James A. Butler of LaSalle University, who has kept Peale alive at Belfield, Andrew Cosentino, who took me to Point Breeze, and Point Breeze archaeologist Richard Veit, who was so generous with time and materials.

In addition, I read carefully and consulted heavily the scholarly books on Krimmel, his peers, and the Peales, including *John Lewis Krimmel* by Anneliese Harding and the earlier *John Lewis Krimmel* by Milo Naeve, Gordon Howard's article "Death of an Artist" in the *Germantown Crier, Charles Willson Peale: Art and Selfhood in the Early Republic* by David C. Ward, *New Perspectives on Charles Willson Peale*, edited by Lillian B. Miller & David C. Ward, *The Peale Family: Creation of a Legacy 1770-1870*, also edited by Lillian B. Miller, and Miller's *In Pursuit of Fame: Rembrandt Peale 1778-1860*, Alexander Nemerov's *The Body of Raphaelle Peale: Still Life and Selfhood 1812-1824*, Phoebe Lloyd's controversial "Philadelphia Story" in *Art in America*, the critically important "Unveiling Raphaelle Peale's *Venus Rising from the Sea – a Deception*" by Lauren Lessing and Mary Schafer in the *Winterthur Portfolio*, and *The Kingdoms of Edward Hicks* by Carolyn J. Weekley.

Thank you to the book's earliest readers, Marsha Wittink and Lizanne Haimes, for setting me on the right course and to Deepam Wadds, Christine Stewart, Emanuel Ardeleanu, of my Author Salon peer group, and to Bruce Baldwin for his belief in this book and his critical insight into the characters and the plot. Thanks also to Michael Neff for his time, support, and high expectations.

To Jeff McMahon, who shared his insight into the artistic lives of my characters and taught me to understand color and paint.

To Sam Katz, Cristina Vezzaro, Michael Prell and Pam Prell, and Meredith Broussard for critical moments of support.

To Paul Dry, for many fruitful lunches.

To Anders Uhl, who got it right from the start and to Peter Woodall, for the last two astonishing years.

A lifetime of gratitude is owed to Peter Siskind, without whom there would be no *Lion and Leopard*.

Thank you to Nic Esposito for taking this on and to Linda Gallant, for such a nimble editorial hand. I am so grateful to the entire team at The Head & The Hand Press: Amanda Gallant, Kerry Boland, Claire Margheim, Jeannette Bordeau, Michael Baccam, and Chloe Westman.

Finally, to Joan and David Popkin and Carol Buchalter and to Rona, Lena, and Isaak, for unwavering patience and love.

ABOUT THE AUTHOR

Nathaniel Popkin is an author, editor, film writer, architecture and literary critic, journalist, and historian. Since the 2002 publication of his first book *Song of the City: An Intimate History of the American Urban Landscape* (Four Walls, Eight Windows-Basic Books), and continuing into his role as co-editor of the *Hidden City Daily* and writer of the film series "Philadelphia: The Great Experiment," he has been a distinctive voice in the conversation about cities: past, present and future. *Lion and Leopard* is his third book and first novel.